CRYSTAL HEALER

A StarDoc Novel

D1009167

S. L. Viehl

A ROC BOOK

ROC
Published by New American Library, a division of
Penguin Group (USA) Inc., 375 Hudson Street,
New York, New York 10014, USA
Penguin Group (Canada), 90 Eglinton Avenue East, Suite 700, Toronto,
Ontario M4P 2Y3, Canada (a division of Pearson Penguin Canada Inc.)
Penguin Books Ltd., 80 Strand, London WC2R 0RL, England
Penguin Ireland, 25 St. Stephen's Green, Dublin 2,
Ireland (a division of Penguin Books Ltd.)
Penguin Group (Australia), 250 Camberwell Road, Camberwell, Victoria 3124,
Australia (a division of Pearson Australia Group Pty. Ltd.)
Penguin Books India Pvt. Ltd., 11 Community Centre, Panchsheel Park,
New Delhi - 110 017, India
Penguin Group (NZ), 67 Apollo Drive, Rosedale, North Shore 0632,
New Zealand (a division of Pearson New Zealand Ltd.)
Penguin Books (South Africa) (Pty.) Ltd., 24 Sturdee Avenue,
Rosebank, Johannesburg 2196, South Africa

Penguin Books Ltd., Registered Offices:
80 Strand, London WC2R 0RL, England

First published by Roc, an imprint of New American Library,
a division of Penguin Group (USA) Inc.

First Printing, August 2009
10 9 8 7 6 5 4 3 2 1

Copyright © S. L. Viehl, 2009
All rights reserved

 REGISTERED TRADEMARK—MARCA REGISTRADA

Printed in the United States of America

Without limiting the rights under copyright reserved above, no part of this pub-
lication may be reproduced, stored in or introduced into a retrieval system, or
transmitted, in any form, or by any means (electronic, mechanical, photocopying,
recording, or otherwise), without the prior written permission of both the copyright owner and the above publisher of this book.

PUBLISHER'S NOTE
This is a work of fiction. Names, characters, places, and incidents either are the
product of the author's imagination or are used fictitiously, and any resemblance
to actual persons, living or dead, business establishments, events, or locales is
entirely coincidental.
    The publisher does not have any control over and does not assume any re-
sponsibility for author or third-party Web sites or their content.

If you purchased this book without a cover you should be aware that this book is
stolen property. It was reported as "unsold and destroyed" to the publisher and
neither the author nor the publisher has received any payment for this "stripped
book."

The scanning, uploading, and distribution of this book via the Internet or via any
other means without the permission of the publisher is illegal and punishable by
law. Please purchase only authorized electronic editions, and do not participate
in or encourage electronic piracy of copyrighted materials. Your support of the
author's rights is appreciated.

"To live as a doctor is to live so that one's life is bound up in others' and in science and in the messy, complicated connection between the two."

—Dr. Atul Gawande

CRYSTAL HEALER

One

The Iisleg, the people of my homeworld of Akkabarr, never believed in peace. The word itself has no meaning in their language. They name the time between conflicts as either *malatkinin*, an opportunity to recover from the last battle, or *kininharkal*, the chance to prepare for the next.

Until this moment, I thought I had left that sort of idiocy behind on my homeworld.

"You can't do this."

The dark blue faces of the three males watching me remained impassive as I rose from the conference table and moved around the room. Someone clever had worked hundreds of *t'vessna* flowers into various arrangements, doubtless to honor my return. I plucked one small purple flower from a hanging silver basket and held it to my nose. The sweet fragrance calmed me a little.

I had been brought here after my husband and I returned to Joren, the homeworld of my adopted people, and landed our scout vessel *Moonfire* at HouseClan Torin's main transport. I had been told the meeting was some sort of official welcome. Instead, I had been treated to an intense round of questioning, and informed of what amounted to a declaration of war on another world.

"Healer Torin."

They didn't like my moving around; they wanted me where they could see my face. I returned to the table. "You can't do this," I repeated. "Over two thousand beings live on that colony."

"Your pardon, Healer Torin, but we must." Malaoan Adan, the Jorenian Ruling Council's chief legal adviser, was the oldest of the three, judging by the number of purple streaks running through his braided black hair. He spoke slowly and carefully, both to project the gravity of the situation and so that the vocollar translation device I wore around my neck converted his words correctly into Iisleg, an obscure form of Terran, the only language I understood. "This matter has now become a legal issue."

"How so?" I knew almost nothing about Jorenian law, but as I remained one of Joren's chosen rulers, I saw no reason to confess that. "I have related to you everything that happened to me and my husband."

"I must respectfully question your account of the events, Healer." Volea, HouseClan Torin's chief of security, wore his solid black hair in a warrior's knot, and had several healed scars on his face from blades, pulse burns, and impact injuries.

If they doubted me, they had some reason to do so. "On what basis?"

Volea consulted the datapad in his hand. "According to the information retrieved from the *Moonfire*'s database, your ship did not make an emergency landing; it was fired upon and crashed. Audio records indicate that you and your bondmate were forcibly removed by drones not under your command."

"You have interpreted the data incorrectly." I was glad my husband had survived our ordeal on Trellus, because as soon as I saw him, I was going to kill him. "While we were journeying through space, my husband and I ran some simulations of those scenarios. The database and the audio records must have been damaged during the emergency landing, or they would indicate that."

Volea shifted in his seat. "Healer, biodecon scans performed on the *Sunlace* revealed new tissue that would indicate you and your bondmate sustained multiple recently healed injuries."

"Reever and I both acquired some minor flesh wounds while running the simulations." I smiled. "Our bruises and scratches were no more serious than what one would sustain during a practice sparring match with a drone opponent."

"You did not fight a drone," said Xonea, my adopted ClanBrother and captain of the *Sunlace*. The largest of the three males, he commanded attention, although I hadn't given him much. Xonea troubled me for a number of reasons, not the least of which was the ominous suppressed emotion glittering in his white-within-white eyes. "We detected Sovant's DNA embedded in your garments. What say you tell us how you simulated that?"

I thought of the alien predator I had helped to capture and exterminate on the quarantined colony of Trellus. It had been a voracious, horrific thing that had possessed the bodies of sentient beings, destroying their minds and then masquerading as their prey while devouring them from the inside out. I could not tell them that Reever and I had been forced down on the planet to serve as bait for it.

"That was likely from some form of accidental contact." I clamped down on my rising temper. "We could have brushed up against something already contaminated with the DNA."

"Indeed." Xonea flattened his six-fingered hands on the table and leaned forward. "You and Reever unintentionally collided with something doused with at least two liters of Sovant blood, bone, and brain tissue?"

I couldn't tell him about the final battle we had fought with the colonists against the Sovant, so I folded my hands in my lap. "Garments become contaminated with all manner of foreign DNA, particularly when one visits a multispecies colony. It may have happened over a period of weeks—"

"Healer, there is no need to deceive us any longer," Malaoan said gently. "You are under no obligation to protect the Trellusans. It is clear to us that they committed or were involved in these acts. We have only to declare ClanKill before a witness of your House."

Now I understood their unwavering determination to pursue complete extermination. On Joren, if one makes a threat against one of the people in the presence of his blood kin, he would be publicly declared ClanKill, treated as prey, and hunted down by the entire House-Clan. The Jorenians would not stop until he was caught, and whoever did so first would eviscerate him with their bare hands.

Such was always done, even if the offender had made only a verbal threat. What had happened to me and my husband on Trellus had been much worse, and they had evidence of it. Naturally, they were outraged.

This was why these three calm, pleasant men were proposing to send Jorenian ships to Trellus to destroy the entire colony from orbit.

I needed to stall them until I could find Reever. "There is no reason to declare ClanKill on the Trellusans," I said as firmly as I could. "My husband and I have returned safely to Joren."

Volea smiled at me. "For this we thank the Mother of all Houses each day."

With his hands—Jorenians used gestures as well as words to speak—Malaoan made a beautiful motion that I recognized as agreement. "We understand your inherent need to preserve life, Healer Torin, but in this case it is not applicable under the law."

"Really." I needed to change some laws.

He nodded quickly. "Multiple offenses have been committed. The colony is small and has few defenses. We need send but two or three vessels to eradicate the population. We would not have troubled you with this matter, but we wished to reassure you that justice will be served."

The pressure increasing at my temples made me imagine for a moment my skull flying apart. "You are not listening to me. *I* was stranded on the colony with my husband. *I* know what happened and who was involved. The colonists are not guilty of any crime. I made a full report. It is over. I wish to see my daughter now."

"So you will, once this matter is decided." Xonea smiled at me, and not in a particularly friendly fashion. "As first ClanSon of the Torin, I say it is far from finished."

I heard a sound that made me think of the jaws of an ice snare snapping around my ankle. Fortunately, it was the access panel behind me, opening to admit a tall, lean male dressed in black garments, his golden hair loose around his handsome if somewhat impassive features.

"Duncan." I rose and almost knocked over a stand of *t'vessna* worked into the Jorenian symbol for the path, and went to my husband, taking his hands in mine. I needed to touch him in order to establish a telepathic link between our minds. *They are going to send a fleet of ships to destroy Trellus. They found evidence of what happened and they're blaming the colonists. They even found the wretched Sovant's DNA on our garments when we were scanned.*

Worry not, beloved. He pressed his mouth briefly to my brow before his clear blue eyes moved to study the faces of the other males. "I was not made aware that this welcoming committee intended to separate me from my wife in order to intimidate and interrogate her."

Malaoan and Volea shifted in their chairs, clearly uncomfortable.

Xonea, in contrast, didn't twitch a muscle. "Much as we were not made aware of your true reason for leaving Joren. Sit down, Duncan."

When I began to tell him that he had no right to order

either of us to do anything, Reever put one of his hands over mine. One newly healed wound slashed across the lattice of old white scars covering the flesh from his knuckles to his wrist.

"As you say, Captain." He led me back to the table and sat down with me, his eyes never leaving Xonea's. "Before anything more is said or decided, Jarn and I shield the colonists of Trellus."

"As bondmate of a naturalized Jorenian, you have limited rights under our laws, Linguist Reever," Volea said, his tone decidedly cool. "They do not include making decisions for a Ruling Council member, or shielding those responsible for threatening her life."

"Then I will say the words," I told him. "I shield the colonists of Trellus."

Malaoan's expression turned sympathetic. "Under ordinary circumstances, that would be acceptable, Healer, but in this case special considerations for your current mental state must be made."

I tried not to grit my teeth. "What has my mental state to do with anything?"

"Your medical records indicate that you suffered extensive brain damage and severe emotional trauma while being held captive on Akkabarr," the legal adviser said. "You persist in referring to yourself as another persona named Jarn. Add to this the ordeal you must have endured on Trellus, and it is apparent that your ability to make rational decisions has been compromised. In such cases, under Jorenian law, the affected individual's HouseClan is required to intervene and provide consent."

It took my vocollar a few moments to relate all that

to me in the language I could understand. Not that I understood it. "Do you mean to say that I am too *crazy* to shield the Trellusans?"

"No," Reever said, his eyes never leaving Xonea's face. "He is saying you need a member of HouseClan Torin to approve your decision."

"The Healer's closest blood kin, to be precise," Malaoan clarified.

Reever spared him a glance. "My wife is not Jorenian by blood or birth. Her only blood relative is deceased. Under Terran law, as her husband, I am her closest relative."

"Once my ClanBrother Kao Chose her, Cherijo became Torin," Xonea said. "After he embraced the stars, my House assured that she would remain our kin by granting her citizenship and formally adopting her."

I felt bewildered, as I often did when being confronted by actions I had never taken. All of these things had happened to Cherijo Grey Veil, the woman who had inhabited my body before dying on Akkabarr.

"I do not consider myself Terran or Jorenian," I reminded them. "I was born on Akkabarr, among the skela of the Iisleg. According to their laws, I am the property of my husband and subject to his will alone."

"You may consider yourself whatever you wish, Healer," Malaoan said kindly, "but your citizenship has never been revoked by you or your HouseClan. As such, it takes precedence over this claim of Akkabarran citizenship."

"Very well." It seemed obvious that they weren't going to allow me to escape this special consideration. "So who do you define as my closest blood kin?"

"That"—Xonea kept his gaze locked with Reever's—"would be me."

If I was not crazy now, I soon would be driven to that unhappy state. "Then, Captain, would you please give me your approval?"

At last he turned toward me. "First you will provide more information so that I may know you are making a wise choice."

My limited experience in dealing with my adopted Jorenian brother had not been terribly successful. On a previous occasion, when he had tried to prevent me from attending to the victims of a plague that was destroying the Hsktskt homeworld of Vtaga, I had been forced to threaten to take away his command in order to stop his interference.

Now, it seemed, he had the upper hand. My former self had referred to this sort of situation in her journals. She had called it *payback time*.

I resigned myself to dodging more questions. "What do you wish to know, Captain?"

The big male sat back in his chair, seemingly at ease now. "I want the name of the offworlder who harmed the female patient you operated on just before you and Duncan departed Joren. I want to know why you concealed the fact that the explosive device implanted in her body was mounted with a trigger specifically designed to detonate upon contact with your DNA. I want to know who is trying to assassinate you."

Xonea didn't care for my request for time to verify the medical facts behind his last barrage of demands, but I felt sure he wouldn't accuse me of stalling in front of the other Jorenians. He didn't. Nor did he protest when I suggested we reconvene the meeting at HouseClan Torin's medical facility in the morning. I think he knew he had me right where he wanted me. I think my husband's cold, unwavering stare also may have played a part.

Volea and Malaoan, who also sensed the rising tension between Xonea and Reever, quickly agreed to an adjournment, and after making polite farewell gestures, departed. As my ClanBrother left the conference room, he paused for a moment to loom over me.

"If the true reason for this fact-finding delay is to provide time for you and Duncan to leave Joren," he said, a muscle twitching under his eye, "you will find that you must also obtain my permission for travel offworld."

"Why would I want to do that?" I made my expression bland. "According to you, I am a mental deficient, and you have seen to it that I will be treated like one. My freedom has been taken away and my decisions will be made for me. Life could not be easier unless I were brain-dead."

"I will have the name of the one responsible for this, Cherijo," Xonea promised, glancing once more at Reever before he strode out.

After the door panel had closed and we were alone, my husband put an arm around me, and I allowed myself to lean against his shoulder.

I felt as weary as if I had spent three days fighting in a bloodsports simulator, until I formed a new link with my husband and his strength came flooding through it. *How much do you think he knows about what really happened to us on Trellus?*

Enough to justify an attack on the colony. Out loud,

Reever said, "Marel is waiting for us with Salo, Darea, and Fasala at the pavilion. They arranged for us to have a private meal with them."

I hated that we could not speak openly and freely, but Reever and I both suspected that the Jorenians were keeping us under constant drone surveillance—on Xonea's orders, no doubt. "Then why are we standing here?"

After spending all my life on the frozen, wind-torn surface of Akkabarr, then weeks in the crowded, utilitarian envirodomes of an airless rock like Trellus, I could better appreciate the vivid charms of Joren. Above our glidecar, the sky, streaked with a multitude of colors, looked down at its beautiful reflection in the wide, gleaming fields of silvery *yiborra* grass. Flowering plants, the main staple of the Jorenian diet, grew everywhere, and in more colors than I could name. Nor did I mind the warmth and mild climate, although I suspected I would never feel at home anywhere but on the ice fields.

"It is lovely here," I said to Reever. "Did Cherijo like it?"

"She did, although we never had the chance to spend very much time on Joren." Reever maneuvered the vehicle around a slower-moving transport conveying cargo containers and some strange-looking equipment. "Do you remember anything of Terra?"

"I have your memories of North America and France." I did not wish to insult his natal world, but both regions had seemed sterile, boring, and overpopulated. "We will never return there, will we?"

"No." He sounded grim. "It would be too dangerous.

We . . . Cherijo and I barely escaped with our lives the last time we were on Terra."

The only blood family my former self could claim, aside from Marel, were the other products of Joseph Grey Veil's illegal experiments in genetically engineering humans. I knew from her journals that Cherijo believed she had several "brothers" who, like her, had been made in Grey Veil's laboratory, although something had gone wrong with each of them. One in particular, a disturbed young male named Rico, had captured and tried to kill both her and Reever as vengeance for how cruelly he was treated by their "father."

I had no desire to visit Terra, and I could not think of returning to Akkabarr, not after experiencing the freedom of living among the ensleg. Offworld species like the Jorenians respected and valued their females; they were considered equal to males. The rebellion had changed how females were regarded on Akkabarr—we had gained much status while caring for the wounded on and off the battlefield—but if I ever returned to live among the Iisleg, I could still be beaten to death for something as minor as questioning an order issued to me by any male. So, for that matter, could Marel.

It struck me then how dangerous this situation with Xonea was. If I did not make peace with him, he might repudiate me, Reever, and Marel from HouseClan Torin. I did not know the laws governing those who had been thus expelled, but I doubted I would remain a member of the Ruling Council or be permitted to make a home among the Jorenians here unless I also remained a ClanDaughter of the Torin.

If I did not settle this and secure our place among the Jorenians, we might have no homeworld.

Like the Iisleg tribes on Akkabarr, the Torin resided together, only in much larger numbers than the people of the iiskar I had known. Each HouseClan occupied a native pavilion, a massive complex of adjoining structures in which every member of the HouseClan dwelled under one roof. The Torin pavilion, built of glowing white stone, was so large that it resembled a small range of ice cliffs.

The only time Torins left their pavilions was when they selected mates, joined the crew of a HouseClan vessel on a sojourn, or traveled to visit friends or blood kin who resided elsewhere. Females were obliged to Choose a husband from an outside HouseClan, and leave their natal HouseClan to reside with their bondmate and his blood kin after their joining ritual; this likely to prevent inbreeding.

When Reever and I had departed Joren the last time, we had asked Salo and Darea Torin to keep Marel and watch over her. The parents of Marel's favorite playmate, Fasala Torin, Salo and Darea had taken our daughter with them on an extended journey to visit other House-Clans. Reever and I never wished to be separated from our child, but after Marel had been abducted with me and Reever on Vtaga, we were determined to take stronger measures to protect her from harm—even if that meant leaving her behind to be protected by our friends.

Reever and I were greeted by every Torin we passed at the pavilion, so it took some time and many promises to meet again before we could go to the private room where our child and friends were waiting. But Marel found us before we reached the dining chamber; she rushed around a corner and threw herself into her father's arms, pressing noisy kisses against his cheeks.

"ClanFather! You're back. I've missed you so much."

"As I have you, *avasa*." Over her head Reever exchanged a glance with me. The activation and translation from my vocollar indicated that Marel had spoken to him in flawless Jorenian.

I did not mind if she preferred to use the language of Cherijo's adopted people over her cradle tongue. From what Reever had told me, Terrans had not done a great deal to distinguish themselves among the sentient species of the galaxy—other than becoming hostile isolationists and xenophobes who liked to start wars.

"Was I not missed as well?" I asked the wall panel.

Bubbly blond curls bounced as wide, clear blue eyes fixed on me. "ClanMother." She wriggled until Reever set her down on her feet, and then gazed up at me solemnly. "Your pardon, Mama," she said in Terran. "I know you don't speak Jorenian."

"I have no doubt they will force me to learn it someday soon." I crouched down in front of her and performed a quick visual assessment. My small, delicate daughter didn't weigh much, but she practically glowed with good health. "You have behaved well for Salo and Darea while we have been gone?" I watched her nod. "You have studied your lessons and attended your teacher's directions faithfully?" Another nod. "Did you kill anything interesting during your journey?"

"Mama, I told you before, we don't use animals

for . . ." Dimples appeared in her soft, round cheeks. "You *know* I didn't kill anything."

"I thought I should check, just in case." I touched my brow to hers in Jorenian fashion. "Daddy and I missed you every day." As her arms encircled my neck, my love for this small, beautiful creature clawed beneath my breastbone, tearing at my heart. I had never known such sweet pain as this, and I would do anything to keep feeling it forever.

It was not possible, I knew. While Reever and I had been physically altered to be virtually immortal, Marel had not. Our child would keep growing and aging until she reached the end of a normal Terran life span, when she would die—unless I did as Reever had asked me to and altered Marel's body with chameleon cells, which, as they had for her father, would repair any cellular damage she acquired from age, disease, or injury.

I had refused to do it. Immortality had been a curse on my former self; because Cherijo had been created with an immune system that didn't allow her to become ill or age, she had been experimented on, hunted, imprisoned, tortured, and otherwise abused. As much as I wanted Marel as a part of our lives, I would not deliberately inflict the same fate on my child.

My husband rested one of his scarred hands atop our daughter's head. It seemed strange that two such unlikely parents had created such a glorious being. I had no memory of her, and before meeting my daughter I had existed in a strange, frozen state that did not allow me to care for anyone. Reever's childhood, spent on one alien world after another, had deprived him of feeling or showing true human emotion.

Marel and the love she had brought into our lives were slowly righting the terrible wrongs done to us.

"Come," I said, standing and holding out my hand. "We should not keep Salo and Darea waiting."

Unfamiliar with the pavilion's interior, I expected to walk into our friends' quarters, but instead Marel led me into an enormous area well able to entertain a thousand. It had been decorated with cascading showers of purple, gold, and green flowers; baskets of fruit; and several small trees.

In the center of a web of woven *yiborra* grass, a single table draped with a densely embroidered cloth stood packed with enough food to keep an Iisleg hunter and his family fed for an entire season. Salo and Darea were at a prep unit, filling servers with hot, fragrant tea, and their daughter had just set down yet another platter of golden, intricately shaped breads.

"Is the rest of the HouseClan joining us?" I asked Marel as I admired the bounty.

She grinned up at me. "They wanted to. Everyone is happy that you're home, Mama."

The three Torins greeted us with smiles and fond embraces. Like all Jorenian children, Fasala had grown quickly, and now stood almost as tall as her regal-looking warrior ClanMother. From her ClanFather she had inherited a calm, thoughtful demeanor that often made her seem older than she was. Only when she grinned and chatted with our daughter during the meal did I remember that she was barely halfway through adolescence.

"Fasala was Marel's size when we first met Cherijo," Darea said as she, too, watched the girls. "Soon she will be a woman, walking her own path. During our journey she told us that she wishes to go to Omorr to study planetary engineering. She wants to someday help build new worlds for those who have lost theirs."

World building had become a critical industry since the war between the Hsktskt and the Allied League of Worlds. Both sides had decimated and destroyed hundreds of planets during their battles; thousands of species had been displaced as homeless refugees.

"That is a noble and useful ambition," I said. "Just before we left Trellus, the colonists gave us an Aksellan planetary mining map. It is handmade and very old. Perhaps Fasala would like to see a scan of it? I can transmit a copy to your quarters."

"That would be of great interest to her. She spends most of her time studying maps and star charts." Darea's mouth tightened before she took a sip from her server of tea.

I knew that look. I saw it on my own face whenever Marel did something to worry me. "You are not entirely happy with Fasala's plans."

"In truth, I cannot bear to think of her so far away from us," the Jorenian woman admitted. "If something were to happen to her while she is studying on Omorr, it would take weeks for us to reach her."

I would have pointed out that the Omorr were an honorable species, and especially protective of children, but I knew she didn't distrust them. "When Reever and I left Marel with you, I could not relax. Even as I know you and Salo regard her as if she were Fasala's sibling, the little one is *my* child. My head knows that she was safe with you, but my heart still believes that no one can protect her as well as I."

"Yes. That is exactly what I feel." Darea set down her server with a small thump. "We create these children in honor, and bring them into our world so that we may fulfill our Choice. Then but a few, paltry revolutions later, we must allow them to leave us and walk their own path." Her jaw set. "How did our ClanMothers manage to do it?"

"I cannot say." I did not have to remind her that neither I nor my former self had been born to a living woman, for she immediately remembered and made an apologetic gesture. "No, Darea, I am not offended. I was never a child except in my mind. Our headwoman, Daneeb, would tell the new skela who were cast out of the iiskar and came to us to live in the now rather than memory or hope. That to dwell on what was, or what may be, diminishes our appreciation for what is."

The tight lines around Darea's mouth eased, and her expression turned thoughtful. "She was right. All we truly ever have is what is."

Neither Reever nor I were particularly hungry, not after the troubling reception we'd been given at Main Transport. Still, I tried to eat as much as possible. On my homeworld, to waste food was unthinkable. I was gratified to see that the Torins, with their enormous Jorenian appetites, made short work of the feast.

Darea spoke only of their journey until the two girls excused themselves to attend to feeding the small cats, Jenner, Juliet, and their new litter of kittens. When we were alone, she nodded to Salo, who secured the outer door panel before setting two devices on the table and switching on the smallest of the pair. It projected a semitransparent field of pale green light that enclosed the table and the four of us.

"We may speak freely now," Darea said, and nodded toward the device. "Salo brought this signal jammer after he noticed several recording drones had been planted in this room. You know, of course, who arranged for us to meet here."

Reever's expression darkened. "Xonea."

Salo made an uneasy gesture. "Duncan, neither Darea nor I condone what our ClanBrother is doing. Spying on you and Jarn is an unpardonable intrusion. I will challenge Xonea to explain himself before the House-Clan . . . if that is your wish."

"No," I said, before my husband could respond. "That is what Xonea wants: to provoke us into a confrontation, during which he can force us to disclose what happened to us on Trellus."

It seemed ironic that Xonea was doing all this—monitoring us, having me declared incompetent, threatening to destroy the colony—in order to get what he wanted. Aleksei Davidov had been equally inventive and ruthless when he used similar tactics to force us to help him draw out and kill the Sovant.

"Can you tell us what this is about?" Salo asked. "It would help to know, and we will not speak of it outside these walls."

I glanced at my husband, who nodded, and began relating what had happened, from the surgery I had performed on the Jorenian female who had been made into a living bomb to our last day on Trellus.

I related our battle to find and destroy the Sovant, as

well our discovery of a surface crater filled with black crystal, the indestructible, poisonous mineral life-form that Cherijo's alien surrogate mother, Maggie, warned would eventually wipe out all life in our galaxy. I also told them of Tya, one of the Odnallak, the last survivors of the species that had created the black crystal. I did not mention Swap, the larval rogur who with Tya's help had saved all of us, and whose existence Reever and I had sworn to keep secret.

"The name of the Terran who instigated this," Salo said. "That is what Xonea wants."

During the interrogation, I had not named Alek, Reever's former friend, or mentioned that he had lured us from Joren and forced us to crash on Trellus in order to use us as bait for the Sovant. "He will be disappointed, then."

"Not if I tell him," my husband said.

"We can't." I knew Reever was still angry over his friend's deception and the terrible danger he had exposed us to. But after the Sovant died, Alek had told us why he had gone to such lengths, and although I didn't condone what he had done, I understood his motivation. "We agreed to let him go."

His voice chilled. "Perhaps that should not have been our decision to make."

Reever still felt betrayed, but there was more to it than that. I think he understood only too well the emotions that had driven Alek to do such things. "Do you remember how you felt when you were searching for Cherijo? How desperate you were? How close to the brink of madness you came?"

Reever didn't like to be reminded of that time. "It is not the same."

"No, it is not. You had hope, and a wife to find," I reminded him. "Your friend did not. He had only a dead wife and her killer. Tell me you would not have done the same, had the Sovant taken me from you."

"It nearly did, thanks to him."

Reever didn't show many emotions, but he radiated fury now. I didn't like confronting my husband, but I couldn't back down. Not from this. "That is something for which he has been harshly punished."

"So he can never return to Trellus unless he wishes to die instantly." Reever made a contemptuous sound. "You know as well as I do that he never will. How is that a punishment?"

"He lost his beloved. He destroyed your trust. Now, I think, he will remain alone for the rest of his days. No love. No friends. No connections. No hope of happiness." I had seen the emptiness in Alek's eyes; I knew what he had become. I had been the same, a mere shell of a creature, before Reever had found me. "That is why he wanted them to kill him—why he dared them to. For him, *life* is the real punishment."

Reever's expression did not change, but his eyes lightened, and he took my hand in his.

"There is something more you should know. We intercepted this transmission just before you returned to Joren." Salo opened the second device, which turned out to be a small data viewer, and activated the screen.

The image that appeared was that of a lumpy, chinless, light-skinned being wearing a utilitarian male pilot's jumpsuit hemmed by wide straps and belts holding a great many odd-shaped weapons and spare ammunition. He wore a helmet filled with an iridescent gas, which moved in lazy swirls as parts of his face swelled, flapped, and deflated.

After a moment I realized the odd sounds that accompanied the image were speech; he was burbling in his native language. My vocollar did not translate the sounds into speech, but Reever paid close attention. The being displayed a handful of glowing gems, repeated some of the bubbling sounds he had made, and then the image abruptly shut down.

"Who is he? Do you understand what he said?" I asked Reever.

My husband pressed a button on the viewer, causing the transmission to replay. "He's a Thekka raider, offering a thousand verdant Rabbat pearls for information about us, our whereabouts, and security arrangements." He stopped the video and studied the screen carefully.

My heart sank as I recalled Alek's final warning. "He must be the bounty hunter looking for us."

"The Thekka are thieves and murderers, not bounty hunters," Reever said. "They attack cargo ships by launching small drones that attach themselves to the hull and pump poison into the environmental systems. When everyone inside the ship is dead, they dock with it, board, and retrieve the cargo."

Outrage darkened Darea's face. "That is horrible."

"It is their only real advantage over other species," my husband said calmly. "The poisons they use create a synthetic version of their homeworld atmosphere, which is highly toxic to most offworlders. In any event, this Thekka is not hunting us."

Salo frowned. "Why then would he offer so much for information?"

"He was forced to make this transmission." Reever adjusted the image so that it focused on and magnified a portion of the Thekka's helmet, and a dark shape reflected on it. "There. Someone is standing just out of range of the viewer." He enlarged the image again and traced the outlines with his fingertip.

Whoever had been with the Thekka had been holding a pulse rifle aimed at the mercenary's head.

Two

The Torins assigned large, lavish personal quarters for us at the pavilion and provided every comfort we could wish for. After our meal with Salo and Darea, we retreated to our rooms and spent the remainder of the evening there with Marel. I took a moment to send a scan of the old Aksellan mining map I had promised for Fasala to Darea, and then gave our daughter my full attention. It took her some time to tell us all that she had seen and done during her journey with our friends.

"ClanUncle Salo took us to HouseClan Kalea, and their ClanLeaders look like us, Mama," my daughter said as she brought her image viewer to me. "Kol and Jory are part Terran, see?"

I examined the picture of Marel standing between a male and female at a gathering in a beautiful formal garden. The pair was tall and wore Jorenian garments, but the female's black hair was short and curly, and the male had only five fingers. Both had tanned but definitely Terran skin.

"They are a handsome couple." I noted the other

Jorenians around them also appeared to be crossbreeds with a variety of interesting body types. "Did they speak to you in Terran as well?"

"Jory did because she's from Terra, and she lived there almost her whole life. ClanLeader Kol tried, too, but he's always lived here on Joren, so he couldn't say some of the sounds. Then Jory laughed and he chased her around the table and pulled her behind a trellis. They stayed back there a long time." Marel wrinkled her nose. "I think they were kissing. Why do grown-ups always have to kiss each other so much after they bond? It's silly."

"Is it?" Reever leaned over and brushed my mouth with his. "Hmmmm. Do you feel silly, *Waenara*?"

I smiled up at him. "Not as often as I wish, *Osepeke*."

"Daddy, stop." Our daughter gave us a disgruntled look. "You're both too old to be kissing all the time."

Despite the happiness I felt in being with my family, I did not sleep well that night. As I lay in my husband's arms and listened to his slow, quiet breathing, thoughts of Xonea, the Trellusans, and the Thekka mercenary snarled in my mind, tightening into knots of doubt and fear.

Near dawn I gave up and rose, dressing silently so as not to disturb Duncan or Marel. One of our small felines, the silver-furred male called Jenner, perched on the end of the bed to watch me. As I armed myself with several blades, his blue eyes narrowed, probably out of jealousy that he could not do the same. My husband and child insisted the cats were warm and affectionate pets, but in their eyes I saw the same, cool deliberation of any clever predator.

"You will guard them while I am gone," I told the little beast. "Or I will make you into a head wrap for the cold season."

Jenner yawned and jumped down to join his mate, the black-furred Juliet, where she lay curled up with three of their new younglings.

I slipped out and made my way silently through the empty corridors until I found a door that led to the open central courtyard, which the Torins had decorated with more of the flowering plants they loved and white marble sculptures of male and female Jorenian warriors. The Iisleg sometimes carved pillars of ice into pleasing shapes for certain tribal celebrations, but I had never seen stone made into people. For a time I sat on a bench by the largest of the female warrior statues, one that held a primitive, wicked-looking spear as if she might impale ten enemies with it. I looked up at her, wishing I could borrow some of her fierceness for what lay ahead.

"Who sits at the feet of Shanea Torin?" a deep voice said. A tall, older male with a full head of purple hair stopped before my bench. He wore the colors of the Torin with a length of woven silver cloth draped from his right shoulder to his left hip, an indication of his rank. Attached to his belt was a cylinder I recognized as a scroll case, in which important handwritten documents were carried.

He smiled down at me with genuine pleasure. "Ah, it is my favorite healer. Welcome home, ClanDaughter."

"I thank you, ClanLeader Torin." I rose and tried to make a formal gesture of respectful greeting, but found myself in his affectionate embrace. I returned it, gingerly, before stepping back. "I was just preparing to leave for the medical facility."

"Please an old man and speak with me first." He gestured toward the bench.

I sat, feeling uneasy. As well as being the Torin Clan-Leader, Xonal Torin was Xonea's sire. I had met him only a few times, but I knew from Reever's memories that Xonal and Cherijo had been very close. Talking with him might be as hazardous as crossing a dripping snow bridge.

"We have not had the chance to speak privately since you were returned to us," he said, studying my face. "Darea explained to me about what happened to Cherijo on Akkabarr. I understand that you are a different person, one named Jarn. May I use that name for you?"

"Of course." It pained me to hear him ask permission for such a thing. On my homeworld, Xonal Torin would be a rasakt, the leader of the tribe. An Iisleg rasakt would not lower himself to acknowledge my existence, except to issue an order to kill me or drive me from his iiskar. "I do remember you, ClanLeader. My husband was able to transfer his memories of Cherijo's life to me."

"Then you will remember when the League attacked Joren," he said. "Cherijo surrendered to them in order to prevent an invasion of our world."

They always made her sound so noble. "That was part of her bargain with OverLord TssVar, to give the Hsktskt access to the League ships so that they could take them over and turn their crews into slaves. In truth, she surrendered herself and eight hundred other unsuspecting beings."

The side of his mouth curled. "Darea mentioned to me that you do not much care for the woman you were."

"I never knew her. I was born the day she died on the ice." I met his white-within-white gaze. "My people, the Iisleg, believe in speaking plainly. The truth is that Cherijo did many things that I cannot condone, and I do not always care to be associated with decisions I would never have made. But if what I have said about her offends you, I ask your pardon. I know how much your people honored her."

"Do not trouble yourself, Jarn." He touched my arm in a reassuring manner. "I speak of Cherijo now only so that I might explain why my ClanSon, Xonea, is so determined to keep and exercise authority over you."

I lifted my eyebrows. "He thinks I will invite the Hsktskt here again?"

"He blames himself for not protecting Cherijo when the League attacked. He swore to his ClanBrother, Kao, that he would never allow her to be captured or taken from us." Xonal released a heavy sigh as his hands moved like snow drifting down from a still night sky. "Your bondmate was not the only one who suffered when you—when Cherijo disappeared. Xonea greatly honored her. If not for her bond with Duncan, I think he would have Chosen her a second time."

"Cherijo wrote in her journals that Xonea Chose her only to protect her when she was suspected of murder," I said. "Later she mentioned protecting him for the same reasons, but she was angry, and a great deal of what she wrote didn't make sense."

"My ClanSon has great pride. He could never repay

Cherijo for what she did for him," he said, "nor, do I think, could he forgive her for deliberately breaking his Choice of her."

"I thought the only thing that breaks Choice is . . ." I fell silent as Reever's memories told me exactly what she had done. "Cherijo had Squilyp induce cardiac arrest. She killed herself." And my husband had watched her do it.

"For three minutes—the required amount of time under Jorenian law to be pronounced dead," Xonal said. "The Omorr was able to revive her, but only just. The shock of it put Cherijo in a coma. When she awoke at last, she Chose Reever."

No wonder the two men sometimes looked as if they wanted to tear each other apart.

"When the story was first told to me, I believed she did so only to prevent my ClanSon from Choosing her again. Now I think not. Cherijo and Reever were . . ." The ClanLeader made a complicated gesture.

I nodded. What my former self and my husband had been to each other often defied explanation. More of Reever's memories poured into my mind. "Xonea didn't take the news very well."

"At the time, my ClanSon was under the influence of a psychotropic drug being administered to him without his knowledge or consent." Sadness drew down the corners of his mouth. "But even afterward, when he had regained his self-control, he was never the same. Nor has he ever spoken of that time to me or anyone among the HouseClan."

"I think she must have wounded his pride as much as his heart," I said softly.

"I must agree. And when Cherijo disappeared during the Jado Massacre, Xonea's path changed again," Xonal said. "Upon his return to Joren, my ClanSon distanced himself from us. He rarely ate or slept, and he spent many weeks in solitude." He glanced at me. "That is not our way, Jarn. We Jorenians share everything with our kin, even the worst of our sorrows. But Xonea lost all interest in family and work and life. If Reever had not convinced him that Cherijo yet lived, I think my Clan-Son would have abandoned his path altogether and embraced the stars. Now that you are found, well, perhaps you understand why he behaves as he does."

I nodded. "Xonea will make sure that I never leave Joren again."

"Just so. But do not imagine that his ClanMother and I support his actions against you and Duncan. We believe that our ClanSon is wrong in what he does." The ClanLeader touched the petals of a pale yellow flower blooming on a vine curled around the statue's base. "Were I to pluck this lovely thing from its place and keep it cradled in my hands, it would be safe. I would ensure that nothing would ever harm it. Yet in time it would still wither and die. It was not meant to be mine." He gazed at me. "As Cherijo—as *you*—were never meant to be Xonea's."

I felt some of the weight of worry ease inside me. "What can I do, ClanLeader?"

"My ClanSon knows well our modern laws, but has somewhat neglected studying our most ancient." He took the scroll case from his hip and handed it to me. "This ruling, in particular, may be of some value to you."

"I will not know what it says," I advised him. "I cannot read Jorenian."

"The scroll contains the full text of a ruling from the days before the HouseClans united," he said, smiling at me. "It concerns the rights of an injured Torin warrior who was saved by a Varena healer."

After leaving Marel at the Jorenian day school she now attended with Fasala and the other Torin children, Reever and I went to the HouseClan's main medical facility. I looked back several times, wondering how quickly I might resolve the conflict with Xonea and return.

"Stop worrying about her," my husband said as he drove away. "Marel has many friends at school, and she enjoys her lessons. All of the instructors are Torin, so if anyone threatens her—"

"Her teacher will eviscerate them with her bare hands, I know." I gave him an exasperated look. "My concern is not about her safety."

"Then what is?"

I couldn't say that every time I looked upon our child, I wondered if it might be the last. "Do you think this bounty being offered for us is another trick by your friend to lure us away from Joren?"

"No. While you were gone this morning, I signaled some contacts I have." Reever's tone grew grim. "It would seem that my *friend* has taken his tricks and left the quadrant."

"Then what he told us is true. There is someone else hunting us."

My husband nodded. "So it would seem. Whoever is offering the bounty has taken extraordinary measures to protect their identity; the Thekka used to send that transmission was found dead shortly afterward."

"Dead?" I was astonished. "Murdered?"

"No, he was found to have died of natural causes," Reever said. "That is all my contacts have been able to discover."

The lack of information frustrated me. Also, the death of the Thekka sounded suspicious; as a doctor I knew of a hundred different ways to kill someone and conceal the fact that they were murdered. *A doctor.* "Could it be Cherijo's creator who searches for us?"

"No. Cherijo and I both saw Joseph Grey Veil die on Terra." He hesitated, then added, "Jarn, if we remain on Joren, mercenaries will come for us. It is possible that they will even join forces and attempt an invasion."

The thought of Joren being attacked—and the House-Clans' inevitable response—made me feel sick. "How can you know that?"

He glanced at me. "It is what I did to take Cherijo from the League."

All of his memories of that time came rushing back into my head, making it ache slightly. "Then perhaps we had better make some travel arrangements, before you are forced to do the same for me."

Reever stopped the glidecar outside the main entrance to the medical facility. When I moved to climb out, he stopped me. "If we do not give Xonea what he wants, he *will* find a lawful reason to attack Trellus. I know you're sympathetic, but we cannot sacrifice all those innocent people merely to protect the one responsible from your ClanBrother's vengeance."

"If it becomes a choice between him and the colonists, I will tell Xonea everything he wants to know," I promised him. "But I think I can put a stop to all of this today."

Just inside the entrance, the Torin's Senior Healer, a tall, dark-eyed Omorr male in a modified white and blue doctor's tunic, hopped back and forth on his one leg. The white prehensile gildrells covering the lower half of his dark pink face were writhing, indicating he was agitated. As soon as he saw us, his living beard twisted into bunched knots.

Xonea must be already here, I thought. "Good morning, Senior Healer."

"Would that I could say the same, Jarn." He used one of his three upper limbs to gesture toward the administrative area on the north side of the facility. "Captain Torin has commandeered my offices and is even now searching through our database records. He also plans to interrogate me and the staff of the post-op ward. Apparently, he believes that you knew that the explosive planted in the belly of your last surgical patient was put there to kill you, not her."

Xonea had been busy. "He said as much to me yesterday." At least my ClanBrother had not taken a different approach, or what I had planned might not work. "Come. Reever will go and keep him from making a mess of things while you and I make rounds."

"Rounds?" Squilyp echoed at the same time Duncan said, "I will what?"

I regarded both of them. "Duncan, you would do better away from the patients in recovery; the smell of blood always makes you feel nauseated. Watch Xonea, but allow him to find whatever he can. It will make him feel better to know he was right." I turned to my friend the Omorr. "You have some objection to my performing rounds with you?"

"While we allow your ClanBrother to collect enough evidence to lawfully declare ClanKill on someone's world or species?" he snapped. "Why no, not at all. What are the lives of a few million helpless beings in comparison to the twenty I have up on the ward?"

"Squilyp," I said, hanging on to my patience, "Xonea will do nothing, I promise. Now, I have been marooned for weeks on a dome colony with no hospital and no doctors. When someone wasn't trying to kill me, they were making me operate with amalgam blades on patients in airlocks. Not to mention what the giant slime-covered worm did to me and Reever."

Squilyp's dark eyes widened. "Giant? *Slime*-covered? What—"

"So now that we have returned to civilization," I said, ruthlessly interrupting him, "I would like to put these unhappy experiences behind me and do the work that I was trained for in the proper environment. That is, if you have no objections, or believe, as Xonea does, that I am too mentally unbalanced to make decisions without assistance."

"Why would he think . . . ?" The Omorr pressed one appendage end over his eyes, rubbing at them with the webbed membranes that served in place of more humanoid fingers. "No. Don't tell me. I do not wish to know. We will make rounds." He eyed my husband. "And you— you will not get in Xonea's way or send anyone to the trauma center, is that clear?"

Reever said something in Omorr that my vocollar would not translate, and walked away.

On the surgical ward, I reviewed each chart of the post-op patients while Squilyp checked their vitals, performed routine scans, and otherwise behaved himself. We spent the most time with one patient, an older Jorenian male who had sustained multiple internal injuries when the loading platform where he been working had collapsed, dumping nearly a ton of cargo containers on top of him.

"The organ repairs and bone grafts you performed appear to be healing, but his lung capacity remains diminished, and he sustains a fever despite the antibiotic treatments." I paged through the chart until I found the latest respiratory scan and blood work. Even given his age and the severity of his injuries, the results were not as they should have been. "You have him scheduled for an exploratory tomorrow?"

Squilyp nodded absently as he adjusted the patient's monitor leads. "I may have missed something during surgery."

I had operated alongside the Omorr often enough to know that he never missed anything. His meticulous methods and habits were perfection; he also had a peculiar, natural aptitude for sensing and finding potential troubles during procedures that weren't readily apparent. The cause of the patient's poor condition had to be from another source.

I regarded the Jorenian male, who was awake, although his eyes seemed unfocused. "Good morning, Palalo Torin. My name is Healer Jarn, and I must talk to you about your accident. I know your throat has not healed enough yet for you to speak, so I will ask questions that require only a gesture of yes or no as an answer. Can you do this for me?"

With his left hand he made a modified affirmative gesture.

"I thank you." I paged through his chart to the initial intake report. "You were unloading containers of agricultural equipment when the platform failed, is this correct?"

He repeated the affirmative.

"Did the containers break open after they fell?" Palalo made a negative gesture. "Did they leak fuel or liquids?" Another no, but this time not as definite. "Did anything come out of the containers that fell on you?" He hesitated, and then turned his hand over and spread his fingers in a gesture I did not recognize.

"He is not certain," Squilyp said. "He lost consciousness during the platform failure, and short-term memory loss associated with head trauma is not uncommon among Jorenians."

I took the Omorr's scanner and modified the settings before I passed it over the patient's chest. The resulting readings indicated elevated levels of nitrogen. I had to increase the depth of the scan twice more before the device would identify the source: trace amounts of fungi, now lodged deep inside small ruptures in the patient's lung tissue, which had become inflamed and closed over.

"You need not operate," I said to Squilyp, and handed him the scanner. "Fungus has infected his lungs, but we can clear them with a change in his medication."

"He aspirated mold?" The Omorr consulted the chart. "There was no trace of this in his blood work."

"There wouldn't be," I said as I wrote up orders for the new meds and a deep-tissue breathing treatment.

"This is a hybrid fungus, created specifically to prepare soil for cultivation. It breaks down old plant matter and other solids while releasing nitrogen into the soil as a by-product."

Palalo's eyes widened, and he made a strong affirmative gesture.

"We should have detected trace amounts in his blood work," Squilyp said.

I shook my head. "Irrigation or immersion in liquid neutralizes and disperses the fungus; exposure to Palalo's bloodstream would have rendered it untraceable."

The Omorr gave me an odd look. "How did it get so deep into his lung tissue?"

"It was also designed to plant itself." I called over a charge nurse to review the changes in the patient's treatment before I moved to the next bed. Squilyp, however, kept watching me in an intent manner that made me feel somewhat uncomfortable.

"Don't you agree with my previous assessment?" I finally asked. "Or has my face become a new diagnostic tool?"

He seemed to choose his words carefully before he replied. "You used mold like the one infecting Palalo's lungs to treat the soil on Akkabarr?"

"There is no surface soil on my homeworld, only ice. The Iisleg do not farm; they hunt." I skimmed through the next patient's chart and noted that the back injury the patient had sustained had responded well to corrective spinal therapy.

"How did you know what the mold was without checking the medical database?" Squilyp persisted.

"I treated several cases of the same type of infection

on K-2. It's a common complaint among agri workers. They call it planting lung." I turned to the patient, who was sitting up with an expectant look on her pretty face. "Good morning, Tabrea Torin. You appear to be ready for discharge."

The big female smiled. "That I am, Healer."

"Tabrea, your pardon," the Senior Healer said unexpectedly. "I must consult for a moment in private with Healer Torin." Squilyp took hold of my arm and guided me away from the berth until we were out of hearing range. "Jarn, are you certain that you treated patients for the same type of mold infection that Palalo has?"

"Of course I am." His apparent disbelief puzzled me. "The mold is a universal soil treatment used on hundreds of worlds. I've seen the same type of infection in the ER dozens of times."

"Tell me the names of these patients."

"Their names?" Impatient now, I planted my hands on my hips. "Squilyp, why are you making such a big deal about this? If you don't agree with my diagnosis—"

The Omorr interrupted me with a curt gesture. "You can't remember their names, can you?"

I thought for a moment. "No. I can't. Should I declare myself unfit now, before someone files a grievance against me?"

"You can't remember their names because you've never treated any patients with this mold infection," the Omorr said. "You've never been to K-2, Jarn."

I opened my mouth, closed it, and then exhaled slowly. "Of course, you are correct. I misspoke. *Cherijo* saw this type of mold-aspiration infection while she worked on K-2. Does that satisfy you, or must I contact the colony and have someone pull the charts out of the archives to verify the facts?"

"Did Cherijo write about these patients in her journals?" he asked. When I shook my head, he added, "Then Reever must have shared with you his memories of her treating patients with this condition."

"No, Reever never . . ." I trailed off as what he was saying sank in. "No. My husband did not witness the treatments. He would not have memories of them." I stared at the Omorr. "I'm right about the source of the infection. Squilyp, I *know* I am."

"I have no doubt that you are," Squilyp said. "That is not what troubles me. Making a correct diagnosis is based on a combination of a physician's education and personal experience. You have no education, and your practical medical experience is limited to treating the rebels on Akkabarr, the Hsktskt on Vtaga, and some of the colonists on Trellus. Yet somehow you are able to retrieve very specific information about these cases on K-2. Only Cherijo had knowledge of them."

Anger swelled inside me. This was my body and my life. I was not surrendering them to anyone, even the woman who had owned them first. "Cherijo and her knowledge died on Akkabarr."

"The brain damage from her head wounds in effect wiped her mind clean," Squilyp said, as if correcting me. "Her body survived, and the tissue destroyed in the hippocampus as well as the entorhinal, perirhinal, and parahippocampal nodes fully regenerated. You are the ego and personality that developed after the body's original mind was destroyed. If you can remember Cherijo's experiences, her patients . . ."

I made a rolling motion with my hand. "What?"

He glanced down and then back up at my face. "We must discover how you are able to access these memories."

"Senior Healer, Healer Jarn." A distressed-looking nurse from one of the lower wards rushed toward us. "Captain Xonea Torin and a detachment of militia are on the recovery ward. They wish to question one of our patients." She glanced at me. "Your bondmate is there, too, Healer. He says they may not."

Squilyp and I accompanied the nurse to the rehabilitation ward, which was occupied by patients who needed extensive physical or mental therapeutic treatment. I saw Xonea's men gathered outside one of the private rooms. They did not have their weapons drawn, but their expressions indicated that might soon change. The only sound I heard were two male voices coming from the room: Reever and Xonea, arguing in Jorenian.

"He never listens to me," I muttered as I stalked toward the room. Squilyp followed, and Xonea's men wisely moved out of our way.

Inside the patient room were my husband and my ClanBrother, standing on opposite sides of the berth occupied by the Jorenian female from whom I had removed the arutanium grenade.

"You *will* step aside, Linguist," Xonea was saying to my husband, "or I will have you detained."

"You may try," Reever replied.

I glanced at the patient, who had her berth linens pulled up around her neck and her eyes tightly closed. She appeared utterly petrified of both men—not that I blamed her. I doubt I would have enjoyed waking up to find a Jorenian warrior and a grim-faced Terran hurling words at each other over me.

"I don't recall giving either of you permission to speak to my patient," I said as I went to the end of the berth and picked up her chart. "Good morning, lady," I said to her, smiling as she opened her eyes. "I apologize for this intrusion. Generally we do not consider terrorizing patients as an acceptable form of therapeutic postoperative treatment."

"Healer," she said, her voice laced with panic. "I do not remember what I have done, but I would ask pardon for it."

"Up until this moment, you have been recovering from major gastrointestinal reconstructive surgery," I informed her. "For that, you need never apologize." I turned to Xonea. "Captain Torin. Unless you acquired a medical degree with a specialty in gastrointestinal surgery while Reever and I were on Trellus, you have no business being in this room."

Xonea scowled. "Cherijo, as your ClanBrother I have the right—"

"Forgive me, was I not specific enough? This is a patient's private room. You are not a physician or a therapist." I pointed toward the entry panel. "Get. Out."

He glared down at me, his shoulders rigid with indignation, and then he strode out of the room.

I regarded my husband. "I suppose you did not signal me about this before confronting Xonea because your wristcom is malfunctioning."

"Something like that," Reever agreed.

Squilyp hopped over to the patient's berth. "Would you

excuse us, lady?" When she made a small, tight, affirmative gesture, the Senior Healer led us into the adjoining treatment room and closed the door panel. "There is something I have to tell you before this goes any further."

"You are not allowing Xonea to question my patient," I told him.

"Of course I wouldn't," he snapped. "It wouldn't do any good if he did."

I closed my eyes briefly. "What is it?"

"In light of the patient's amnesia, I ordered a full neurological workup," Squilyp said. "Whoever planted the grenade in her body also injected her with a drug we have still not identified. Here are her latest brain scans and the neurologist's prognosis." He handed me a datapad.

Reever also looked at the data and read the report summary before he looked at Squilyp. "Have you told her?"

"Yes, after I consulted with several other neurologists," the Omorr said, and saw my scowl. "Jarn, she deserved to know the truth."

"The truth might have waited until her body healed." I had not had time to perform a proper visual assessment, or I would have checked her neck for her Clan Symbol, a small black birthmark that in normal Jorenians indicated genetic lineage. "Her Clan Symbol remains indistinct?"

"Yes. We have sent out signals to all of the House-Clans, along with a detailed physical description and images of her features, but none have claimed her." Squilyp hesitated before adding, "Her DNA does not match any known HouseClan profile."

"Run the tests again," I said, "because that isn't possible."

"Were she born on Joren, I would agree with you." The Omorr's gildrells undulated with agitation. "She has the physical appearance of an adult Jorenian female, but there are some cellular anomalies in her tissues and fluids that are not inherent to the species."

"She may have been alterformed specifically to infiltrate Joren," Reever suggested.

The Omorr shook his head. "There are always signs on the cellular level of genetic tampering: strand splicing, chromosome deformation, and the like. I did not detect any of them. Once I could not match her DNA profile to any HouseClan, I thought she might be the product of forced breeding by a slaver."

"No freeborn Jorenian would reproduce in captivity," Reever said. "They do not tolerate enslavement. Like the Hsktskt, they commit suicide at the first opportunity."

I recalled Marel's pictures of Kol and Jory. "Not all. The members of HouseClan Kalea are the children of enslaved Jorenian females who were force-bred by their owners. Perhaps something like that happened to her Jorenian parent."

"Whatever her origins, this female is in many ways like a newborn infant—much like you were, Jarn, when you first came to consciousness on Akkabarr," Squilyp tagged on. "Xonea can question her all he likes, but she will be unable to provide him answers. We believe the drug administered to her effectively destroyed her memory center."

"Are all forms of amnesia considered mental defects on this world?" I asked.

The Omorr shook his head. "Not unless it is accompanied by delusions or psychosis."

"It's nice to know that I'm either delusional or psychotic." The time had come for me to put an end to Xonea's scheming. "Here." I took the scroll case out of my tunic and offered it to my husband. "It's written in old Jorenian script. If need be, can you read it?"

"Yes." Reever removed the scroll and unrolled it, his eyes skimming over it. "An interesting document." He replaced it in the case and met my gaze. "I will not ask where you obtained this."

I nodded. "That would be best."

The three of us returned to the patient's room. The female's eyes darted toward the open panel leading out to the corridor before she moved to sit up. The motion made her grimace.

"The exercises are helping, but sometimes my stomach yet pains me," she said almost apologetically. "The nurse says it will be some days before I may rise from the berth."

I saw Xonea watching us. "Shut the door panel, Squilyp." I made my voice loud enough for him to overhear. "The lady deserves privacy for her exam."

"I do not think I am well enough to walk." The patient made a gesture toward the corridor. "But Captain Torin said he would provide me with a glidechair when he transports me to security headquarters."

"Captain Torin is not taking you anywhere," I informed her. "My name is Jarn, and I am the surgeon who removed the grenade from your abdomen. I would have first obtained your consent, but your delirium made that impossible. Also, aside from the obvious risk of explosion, the device was leaking trace amounts of arutanium, which would have quickly poisoned you. I had no choice but to immediately operate."

"So I have been told." She gave me a tentative smile. "The Senior Healer has said that I would be embracing the stars now, if not for you."

"I regret that we cannot do more about your memory loss." No, I didn't, as she might be the only thing to stop Xonea from wreaking havoc in my name. "Perhaps someday a new treatment will be found for your condition."

"It frightens me to think about it," the patient admitted. "I cannot fathom why someone would do such a thing to me."

"We believe that you were used in order to get to me," I said. "The explosive planted in your body was designed to kill any Terran who touched it. But the one who did this to you knew that I would recognize the device, and that I had the skill to remove it safely."

She frowned. "Then why was this done, Healer?"

"The goal was not to kill me, but to force me to leave Joren." I saw her confused expression. "The circumstances are difficult to explain. It was a complicated situation that has now been resolved."

"I am happy to hear it." She reached out and touched my forearm briefly. "I am also grateful for my life, Healer. Anything I have is yours."

"I must ask you to do something for me," I told her. "When Captain Torin and his men return to this room, I want you to shield someone."

"I may only do that if someone has threatened to harm me or one of my kin in my presence." She seemed bewildered now. "No one has done so, and the Senior Healer is unable to determine who my kin are. Whom shall I shield?"

"The male who implanted the grenade in your body." I sat down on the edge of her berth and gazed into her shocked eyes. "I know what he did to you was a terrible thing, lady, but I assure you, he has been made to pay for his crimes." When she didn't respond, I added, "I would not ask this of you, but more than what was done to you is at stake. Many innocent lives are in danger. Your forgiveness may be the only thing that can protect them."

"The one who did this might have easily killed us both." She hesitated and placed a hand over her abdomen. "You saved my life, Healer. If it is your wish to have his life in return, then I make it yours."

"I thank you, lady." I nodded to Squilyp, who called Xonea and his men back into the room. "Captain, by operating on this female, I saved her life. DNA tests indicate that she does not belong to the Torin. Do you dispute either of these facts?"

He peered down at me. "Why should I?"

"If you do not understand the question," I advised him, "I will request another representative from House-Clan Torin to attend me."

His normally elegant hands made choppy motions as he spoke, betraying the anger underlying his impatience. "I do not dispute that you saved her life or that she belongs to another House. That does not prevent me from questioning her."

"No, it doesn't. But first the lady has something she wishes to say before witnesses." I turned to the patient. "Madam?"

She glanced at Xonea before she said, "I shield the one responsible for implanting the grenade in my body."

"How know you to ... ?" Xonea's face darkened as he realized the implications of her statement, and swung around to glare at me. "This female may shield whomever she wishes, Cherijo, but it changes nothing."

"Actually, it does," I said, stepping between him and the berth. "By shielding her attacker, my patient has forgiven the harm done to her and, by extension, the indirect threat made to me."

"There was nothing indirect about that grenade," he grated. "It was designed to explode the moment a Terran touched it. *You* were the only Terran surgeon on Joren. Do not bother to deny it."

"I have no intention of doing so," I assured him. "But I recognized the device and took care not to touch it while I was operating. Thus the grenade was a threat only to her life, not mine."

"There were other patients present," he said. "Nurses."

"The grenade had a contact trigger," I reminded him. "By the time I took the lady into surgery, which is the time when the device presented the threat, the facility had been evacuated. I used only a drone assistant." I smiled at him. "Try again."

"She was sent here to assassinate you," Xonea shouted.

I shrugged. "Whoever made her into a bomb has been shielded. Everything related to that act is irrelevant now."

"The lady brought a bomb into this facility," my Clan-

Brother sneered. "Willingly or not, that was a direct threat. You are not permitted to shield her without my consent. So I can just as easily declare her my ClanKill."

The Omorr hopped over to stand beside me. "You will first have to claw your way through me."

"No, Senior Healer, that won't be necessary," I said softly. "By law, any injured warrior treated by the healer of another HouseClan is shielded for the duration of their treatment and recovery. No word, intent, or act on their part may be declared as a threat to the House."

Xonea looked ready to declare everyone in the room his ClanKill, starting with me. "You invoke the law of mercy?"

"I do. I even brought a copy of it for consultation purposes." I gestured toward my husband. "Duncan will read it out loud to you, if you like."

"I know the law, and it grants only a temporary reprieve." Xonea spat the words as he would a curse. "I can wait until she recovers."

"Then you will spend a lifetime waiting, Captain," I said. "The lady will never recover completely from all of her injuries."

"Drug-induced brain damage has caused her permanent memory loss." Squilyp handed him the datapad with the neurologist's report. "Read for yourself."

Silence fell over the room, growing thick and uncomfortable as Xonea skimmed through the data. The datapad went flying across the patient's room, smashing into the wall and dropping in pieces on the floor. The patient's eyes widened, and she yanked her linens up over her head. Squilyp went to the wall panel and signaled security.

Reever, his face blank and his eyes so dark they looked black, took a step toward Xonea.

I put a hand on my husband's arm. "No." I watched my ClanBrother's face. "Wait."

Xonea regarded me as he spoke to his men. "We are finished here. Return to your stations."

I felt a twinge of sympathy for him. "Xonea, I know you were only trying to do what you thought was best. But your efforts on my behalf are not necessary."

"*Your behalf?*" His tone may have been soft, but a lethal rage filled his eyes. "I have done nothing for you."

I gestured from the patient to the shattered datapad. "Then why all this?"

"Your neurologist is wrong, Omorr. Nothing lost is gone forever." Xonea looked down his nose at me. "You think because I do not use your name that I do not know who you are? I know. You are not Cherijo. You may have her skills, her voice, even her bondmate and child, but you can never be Cherijo."

"No." My spine turned to ice. "I can't."

He leaned down, his voice going soft. "Do not become too comfortable in that skin, Akkabarran. Someday my ClanSister *will* return to us, and when she does"—he looked from my head to my footgear and back again—"she will take back all that you have stolen from her."

Three

Xonea's prediction sat like tainted food in my belly for some time after we left the medical facility. I had long wished him to acknowledge that I was not Cherijo, but now that he had, I could take no pleasure in it.

He had been angry; I knew that. His reason for saying such things to me may have been only to strike back at me for depriving him of revenge. Still, the blow was a heavy one. To be called an Akkabarran, as if I didn't deserve my name, was surely the worst. Since leaving my homeworld, I had struggled daily to prove my worth. I did the work and adjusted as best I could to ensleg ways. I believed that I had helped those in need.

In Xonea's eyes, however, it meant nothing. Just like me.

Despite my own curdled feelings, at least now I grasped the cause of all of his maneuverings. He was not simply angry at us for leaving Joren. He saw me as an intruder, a thief who had stolen what did not belong to me. He wanted me gone and Cherijo returned. Which was the same as wishing me dead.

Reever said nothing about Xonea or his ugly behavior as we went to the HouseClan pavilion to return the scroll to Xonal, but I sensed his concern hovering between us, silent and watchful.

I stopped in the courtyard and turned to him. "Stop it."

His eyebrows rose. "Stop what?"

"You are watching me out of the corner of your eye, waiting for me to have some sort of hysterical female reaction," I told him. "I was an Iisleg woman. A *skela*. I have been despised for simply breathing. I have been shot, beaten, starved, and left for dead. I have walked the ice fields and dragged the dying from them as Toskald ordnance exploded all around me. Believe me when I say that some harsh words thrown at me by one angry man will *not* make me collapse."

"I would, but I have this one problem." He tucked the scroll case under the belt of his tunic and then framed my face with his scarred hands. "I love you."

"Well." I rested my hands against his chest. Once I believed that he had loved only my body, as it was all he had left of his dead wife. Now I knew better. "I suppose I could tolerate it a little longer," I said gruffly.

"Xonea does not know you," Reever continued, stroking the curves of my cheeks with his thumbs before taking his hands away. "He looks at you, but he sees Cherijo."

I recalled the set of the Jorenian's face, and the savageness in his voice as he lashed out at me. *You can never be Cherijo.* "Evidently, he did not see her today."

"Jarn, Duncan." Darea entered the courtyard and crossed it to join us. She also carried a cylindrical case, but this one had been fashioned of clear plas and held other, marked rolls of plas inside. "Do you have a moment? My ClanDaughter discovered something quite interesting about the scan you sent us."

We went to a table and sat down together. Darea removed several rolled sheets of marked plas from her case and spread out one of them onto the surface of the table.

"Fasala studied the copy of the original map, but she was not able to decipher some of the Aksellan symbols," Darea said. "Over the centuries, Joren has collected an extensive star chart library, with records from all known space-traveling species. I scanned the map's symbols and input them for comparison, but they are not recorded in our database."

"The Trellusan who gave us the map claimed it was very old," I told her. "Perhaps they predate your records."

"We believe the same—and there is more. As Fasala could not use the symbols, she filtered the scanned image to show only the star systems and the Aksellan's marked travel routes. Here is what the map looks like without the symbols." Darea pointed to circles and lines on the transparency. "Salo has traveled through some of this region, so he was the first to notice the mistakes in the route patterns."

I knew little of star charts, but Reever had extensive pilot training and had traveled a great deal on his own. "What is wrong with them?"

Reever frowned as he leaned over to inspect the plas. "The lanes are too long and convoluted."

Darea smiled at him. "My bondmate was not so diplomatic; he called them utterly ridiculous. He said no ship's captain would waste the time or resources by following such courses over more direct routes. But to be certain, we checked each course on the map against the trade routes presently being used in those systems. The lanes the Aksellans marked on this map are three to five times longer."

"Perhaps it was for trade purposes," I suggested. "They may have diverted their ships to worlds in need of the ore they mined."

"These routes took the ships away from the most populated planetary systems," my husband murmured as he studied the transparency. "The Aksellans were diverting their ships away from these worlds. It may have been to protect from raiders the ore they were transporting."

Darea nodded. "I, too, thought they may have taken the routes as a security tactic, until Salo began checking the symbols I had removed." Darea unrolled another sheet of plas and placed it over the transparency of the planets and shipping routes. "The systems they avoided had two things in common: inhabited worlds, and a dark triangle marking all of them. But we do not know what that symbol means."

"We do." Troubled now, I met my husband's gaze over the map. "The miners were avoiding worlds with deposits of black crystal."

My former self had encountered the black crystal several times in her past. She had found it to be the cause of diseases on Catopsa, Taercal, and Oenrall. I, too, had witnessed its effects on Trellus, when it mesmerized Reever. But we knew that nearly all of the worlds presently infected with the mineral were not even aware of its existence, or how it might be affecting their population. "How could they have known it was there so long ago?"

"The Aksellans have always been a highly intelligent species, but I do not believe these map makers knew of the crystal," Xonal said, startling me as he appeared at my side and leaned over to inspect the transparency. "According to legend, they were far more reserved than their modern descendents. They avoided other sentient species, and mined only unclaimed comets, asteroids, and meteor fields." When we all looked at him, he moved his hands in an easy gesture. "As a youth I was as interested in geology as well as exploring space. I spent two years serving as chief navigator on an Aksellan ore hauler."

Reever straightened. "You think that they avoided these worlds because they were inhabited, not because they have deposits of black crystal."

"This symbol here." Xonal traced one of the dark triangles. "It is a greatly simplified form of two modern Aksellan glyphs. One represents the number three, the other means 'outsider.' Used together, they translate to *threat*."

That made more sense, until I considered another interpretation. The black crystal affected only living, sentient beings. If it was as lethal as my surrogate mother had promised, it might infect worlds only where it could find some prey. "Are there any inhabited worlds on the map that are not marked with the dark triangle?"

Reever consulted the transparency. "Yes. Joren, Akkabarr, and oKia, in the Saraced system." He pointed to each planet.

Joren was on one end of the map, Akkabarr in the

center, and oKia on the opposite. "Is it possible that at the time this map was made, the black crystal had not yet reached these three worlds?"

"The mother's cloak has always protected our planet," Xonal said. At my surprised look, he added, "Her cloak is a thick layer of volatile gases in the upper atmosphere. Free-falling minerals cause them to ignite, so that nothing smaller than a large asteroid could pass unprotected through the layer successfully."

"Akkabarr's *kvinka*—the storm currents enveloping the planet—do the same for the Iisleg," I said. "What of oKia?"

"I cannot say if they have escaped the black crystal, but it seems unlikely," the ClanLeader told me. "It is an ordinary, cold-climate world with no unusual atmospheric conditions. The dominant species, the oKiaf, are sentient tribal hunters, much like our ancestors were."

"Are they primitive?" If they were, that would present different problems.

"Not since the turn of the century," Reever said. "The League recruited oKia to join them by offering advanced technology in exchange for the service of their trackers in the military. oKiaf were said to be the best troop marshals in the quadrant."

I used my datapad to access Joren's planetary database, but it listed only a scant amount of statistics on its solar system and planetary surface conditions. "There is hardly any information recorded about this world."

"Few sojourn to oKia or any of the planets within the Saraced system," Darea admitted. "That region of space is too remote and sparsely populated to tempt many traders, and too ordinary to lure our explorers. After

Skart was destroyed during the war, many have avoided it."

"oKia recently resigned from the League, canceled the contracts of all their people serving in the military, and recalled them to the homeworld," Reever said. "They also banned all contact with offworlders."

"They follow Joren's path." Darea exchanged a wry look with Xonal before she added, "They are not the first to break with the League since the war, Duncan. After Raktar Teulon revealed the truth about the Jado Massacre, and how the League's finest officers were responsible for causing it, many worlds have chosen to do the same."

"I would agree with your theory," my husband said, "but they have banned contact with all other beings, not merely the League. No member of any species is permitted to travel through their space."

"During the war, the Hsktskt destroyed Skart, one of the neighboring worlds in oKia's solar system," Darea said. "That may have decided everything for the oKiaf."

"If their planet still remains free of the black crystal, we must find the reason for it." A sojourn to the Saraced system might also keep the mercenaries hunting us from invading Joren, and give Reever time to discover who was offering the bounty for us and why. "We should go to oKia and survey it, even if we must do so from orbit."

"The oKiaf will have something to say about that, I think," Xonal said. "As will Xonea."

My ClanBrother's desire to keep me on Joren was going to be a problem. "We can't fly a scout to the opposite side of the galaxy. We will need a vessel capable of interstellar flight." I regarded the ClanLeader. "Perhaps you could persuade Captain Torin to permit us to use the *Sunlace* as transport for the expedition."

"I believe that can be easily arranged." He smiled, made an affectionate gesture and left us.

Darea gave me a shrewd look. "I think you are not so interested in traveling to oKia as you are in leaving Joren."

"I do wish to know if the oKiaf have something that has prevented the black crystal from infecting their world," I said. "Whatever has spared them could prove invaluable to removing the crystal from other worlds it has already infected."

"But after all that Xonea has done to spy on you and Reever, why would you wish him to transport the expedition?" Darea asked, perplexed.

"My ClanBrother has done all these things so that he can keep me here on Joren," I said. "What better justice is there than choosing him to be the one who must transport me off the planet?"

After our experience with Alek Davidov forcing us to crash-land on Trellus, and now this new bounty being offered for our capture, I knew we would once more have to leave our daughter behind on Joren. The League still did not know of her existence, and for her sake, we intended to keep it that way. Yet the thought of being separated from Marel again, so soon after our reunion, made slow, sharp daggers of guilt stab into me.

"A proper mother does not abandon her child," I muttered as Reever and I cleared the servers from our evening meal interval. I glanced over at the cleansing unit, where our daughter was merrily playing in her bath. "Especially a girl child she barely knows. Yet no matter how I try, this is all I seem to do to the girl."

"Would you rather stay behind with her?" my husband asked as he rinsed the plates. "I can sojourn to oKia alone."

"The last time we were separated, I died, and you nearly cracked up," I reminded him. "I think you and I had better stick to one another . . . like . . ." I stopped as I realized what I had been saying. "Glue."

"Jarn?"

I grabbed a handful of his tunic and twisted my hand in it as I fought back the anger and fear. "What is that word?" I said through clenched teeth. "What is *glue*?"

"An adhesive form of plas, used to hold separate things together, or repair them when they split or break apart." He covered the fist I had wound in his tunic with a gentle hand. "Think, Wife. You must have had something like glue on Akkabarr."

I backed away from him and went to the cleanser, breathing in deeply. As I picked up a server, I scrabbled through the words whirling in my head.

He came up behind me. "Jarn, you need not—"

"Yes," I said, almost shouting. Quickly, I lowered my voice. "Yes, we did have something. Joining paste. Boil ptar claws for three days and let the liquid cool. We use it to fix our sleds. We did."

"It's growing worse, isn't it?" he asked quietly.

"No. I am well." The server in my hand cracked, and the sonic jet turned pink. "Ignore that."

Reever took hold of my wrist and turned it to see the gash across my palm. The bleeding stopped a moment later and the wound seemed to shrivel in on itself.

His eyes gazed into mine. "You are healing much faster than Cherijo could."

"Candy is dandy, but liquor is quicker," I muttered under my breath. I watched the stream from the cleansing unit turn clear again. "I don't know what those words mean, either, Duncan."

"It is only a joke I told once," he assured me.

"You lie." I knew his memories, and those words were not his. "You never tell jokes."

The words—the joke—had come from Cherijo. I knew it as well as he did. But she had never spoken them to him. These were words they had never once shared.

Reever's hands cradled mine. "We will go and see Squilyp in the morning."

"No. He will say the same thing as before. Amnesia victims routinely have anxiety attacks. I must have absorbed the words from another source of which I was not aware, or that I no longer recall." I curled my fingers over the laceration that was no longer there. I wanted to weep. I wanted to strike the man I loved in the face.

"Mama?" Marel called from the tub cleanser. "Why did you shout at Daddy?"

"I am telling him a joke." I carefully picked up the pieces of the broken server and put them into the disposal unit. Without looking at Reever, I went over to help our daughter out of the tub. "Duncan, how quickly can you teach me StanTerran?"

"I don't know," he said. "The Terran you speak is very old and corrupted by Toskald. A purer form may confuse you. Jarn, what happened just now—"

I rubbed a drying linen over Marel's damp curls. "It was nothing," I lied. "As Squilyp says, a momentary thought disorder. But I would know the meaning of *all* the words that come out of my mouth."

"I can teach you Terran, Mama," my daughter said as she pulled on her night garments. "I have all the language files on my datapad. We can read together every night and in the mornings before I go to school."

"It will have to wait for now." This was the perfect time to tell her about the expedition, but instead I crouched down and took her into my arms. "Daddy must tell us a sleeping-time story."

We did not hurry through our evening rituals, and by the time Reever finished telling a strange but stirring tale about a young shepherd who had used his wits to slay an armored giant, Marel had fallen asleep in my arms. I breathed in the soft, sweet scent of her as I covered her with her bed linens. I wanted to lie on the floor and sleep beside her, but I made myself turn down the emitters before I walked out of her room.

Long fingers laced through mine, tugging me back against my husband's chest. *Candy is a sweet-tasting treat favored by Terran children. There is no word in Iisleg for it because your people do not have the means to make treats or sugars. Liquor is a liquid once made of fermented botanicals. The alcohol produced by the fermentation made it an effective intoxicant. It is synthesized now. I did spend four years in a boarding school on Terra. I must have heard the words during that time.*

My shoulders stiffened. *Your lies are not going to make this any better. They were her words, not yours, and I remembered them.*

Very well. We will talk about something else. Or do

something else. He kissed the tip of my nose. "Do you have any suggestions?"

I could not dismiss it so easily; I felt as if I couldn't breathe.

"I need air," I told him, pulling away and crossing the room to the courtyard access panel. "I'm going for a walk." When he began to follow me, I turned and held up one hand. "By myself. Please."

He studied my face. "As you like."

The nights on Joren were cool and dry, causing the indigenous flora to close their blossoms during the darkness. That cleared some of their perfume from the air and made it seem less alien to my nose. As I walked the pathways through the courtyard, I still felt trapped.

I did not belong here, on this world, in this pavilion, inside this body. *She* had been born to do all of these things, not me. Xonea was right in that sense. I had not meant to, but I had stolen everything from Cherijo: my body, my husband, my child, my *life.* None of them belonged to me.

Was Cherijo still somewhere inside my mind? Had her personality somehow survived the crash and the brain damage? Was she returning to this body, to take back what was hers?

I walked blindly for a time, until I found myself standing in a field of waist-high, silvery *yiborra* grass. Above my head the stars glittered, a hundred thousand tiny, hostile eyes.

I did not mind being alone. I had spent years in silent solitude on Akkabarr, living in my head as I came to know who and what I was. My sister skelas' superstitions made them believe my survival meant I was touched by the goddess, and so they had cared for me while I ignored them. They had loved me in their way, but I had never truly cared for them. I remembered the time when I had considered walking out on the ice in the night, when it was too dangerous and cold to cross, simply so I could escape their noise, their smell, and the shadows in their eyes.

Among the ensleg, I had done little better. Reever loved me, but who was I for him to love? Who was I to be a mother to the child Cherijo had made with him? A presence, a thing that had filled a void.

I could not even be properly called a person. I had not been born. I had no parents, no family, no one to call my true kin. If I had not awoken in Cherijo's body, no one would have cared what happened to me. If not for the work she had begun, and that I was obliged to carry on, I would be useless, pointless.

Wasted.

"When Kao Torin died, a part of Cherijo died with him," Reever said as he came to stand beside me. "That did not happen to me when she died."

I glanced back at the pavilion. We were too far from the child out here. "Marel is alone. We should go back."

"Fasala was happy to come and stay with our daughter for a few hours." He put his arm around me. "You dislike it when I speak of Cherijo's first love."

No, I didn't. Sometimes hearing his name made my chest hurt. "He is dead. We do not speak of the dead on Akkabarr."

"Indulge me this once." His hand stroked the crown of my head. "Do you know why Cherijo's death did not affect me as Kao's passing did her?"

"You didn't learn of it until several years after it happened." I shifted my shoulders. "When you did, you had me to take her place immediately."

"Is that what you think?" Reever turned me to face him. "I became Cherijo's lover, and eventually her husband, so that I might take Kao's place in her heart, as I had promised him that I would. But I could not."

"She was an idiot to refuse your love," I assured him.

"It had nothing to do with her. I have told you that I loved her, but the truth is that I did not. I could not." He reached out and caressed the tips of the *yiborra* with his palm. "When Cherijo and I became lovers, I still had no human emotions. I did not know what it was to love."

"Now you will tell me that you know how I feel and that this is why we love and are meant to be together," I predicted, scowling up at the stars. "You don't have to say it, Duncan. You're wrong. You do have emotions. I have felt them. I know you love me."

"I did not have these emotions for her," he said slowly, as if speaking the words were painful. "I knew I had to be with her—I sensed that she might in some fashion be the most important person that I would ever meet—but she was not my first love here." He tapped his chest. "You are."

"What did you feel for her, if not love?" I demanded, unwilling to believe him.

The corner of his mouth curled. "Curiosity. Desire, certainly. All I wanted was her, but I didn't understand why. I used my promise to Kao Torin as an excuse to keep her with me so I could fathom it. Near the end, I thought it was to prepare me to be a father to Marel. That I was never meant to love Cherijo, but simply learn from her how to be a parent to our daughter. I was wrong about that, as well."

I swallowed against the tightness in my throat. "Do you know now?" He nodded. "Then why? Why stay with her if you knew you didn't love her? Why did you spend all that time searching for her?"

"Jarn." He put his hand to my cheek. "It was you. All this time with her, I was waiting for you."

I saw the truth in his eyes, and relief and shame took turns choking me until I began to weep. I buried my face against his tunic, but the garment didn't muffle the sound of my sobs very well. Reever put his arms around me as my knees buckled, and knelt with me in the soft, cool grass.

For me, the safest place in the universe was in my husband's arms, and this night I reveled in it. I flung away my fear and held on to what was mine. *My* husband, *my* beloved. He belonged to me and only me now.

Flickers of light danced against my closed eyes, and I looked through the blur of my tears to see long ribbons of luminous color weaving all around us.

"Wind dancers," Duncan murmured against my hair. "They're attracted to our body heat."

I lifted my hand, and a length of iridescent blue landed on my palm, curling around it briefly before its glow intensified and it fluttered away, leaving a cool sensation on my skin. Nothing on my homeworld compared to it, but something as delicate and beautiful as this would have been ripped to pieces by Akkabarr's lethal winds. "It steals warmth from other creatures."

"Only a little." His hands brushed the hair back from my face, and his mouth touched the curve of my cheek. "Are you cold?"

That startled a laugh out of me. I had survived for years on a world that never knew a single moment as warm as this night. "I think not." I put my mouth to his, tasting him slowly before I pulled him down into the grass.

A rainbow of light settled around us, reflecting off the shining blades of the *yiborra* as we tugged off the garments separating our skins. I had never coupled with Duncan in such an open place, and feeling the air and the cool flutter of the dancers touching my body aroused me almost as much as his hands.

It was my habit to let Duncan do as he pleased with my body, as everything he did gave me great pleasure. Tonight I felt something shift deep inside me, something that wanted to be more than a woman of the Iisleg.

I pushed my husband onto his back and straddled him, pressing his shoulders into the grass as I bent and used my mouth on his neck, shoulders, and chest. When I seized a handful of his hair and brought his face to mine, he lifted my hips and guided me over him. I sank down, taking him as he had so often taken me, with all the passion I felt. I could not feel empty or alone, not with our bodies like this. Not in this.

Wind dancers twined their sinuous bodies in my hair as I moved, caressing the thickness of him with my softness. He pushed deeper, groaning as he filled me, and I clamped down on him, squeezing him in a tight, ceaseless rhythm.

"I love this," I whispered, pressing my fingers to his lips when he would have spoken. "No. Only feel it, Duncan. Feel what we are together."

I kept him a prisoner of my body, and rode him that

way until his fingers dug into my hips and his eyes became as intent and blue as a jlorra's.

"Jarn." His muscles shook, so eager to spill himself inside me, yet somehow he held back. "I will not go over. Not without you."

The thing inside me shattered as I rolled, and the single thrust of his body into mine brought us both to the very brink. Duncan kept his eyes open as he lowered his mouth to mine in a kiss so soft and tender that I lost myself to it. Then the pleasure brought me back, into his heat and his eyes and the blessed release we found together.

We lay in the grass as the wind cooled our skins and the glowing dancers rose all around us and drifted away. I listened to the frantic pounding of Duncan's heart gradually slow to a smooth, comforting pulse against my cheek.

"Do you think she would hate us?" I heard myself ask. "For what we have together?"

The hand stroking my back paused, then resumed its soothing motion. "Cherijo hated many things. Ignorance, incompetence. Bigotry, slavery, and war. She hated them with all of her heart." He pulled me closer. "But not love. Never love."

Four

We went back to our quarters and I slept in Duncan's arms, better than I had in weeks. The next morning I sent my husband off to take Marel to school, and went to meet Squilyp at his private lab. We'd arranged it the day before, officially to discuss the results of the tests he had performed on Reever's most recent tissue and blood samples.

Unofficially, we needed to talk about a lot of things.

"Wait, there is something on you." Squilyp stopped me just outside the lab and used a gildrell to pluck something from my hair. He showed me a fragment of *yiborra* grass. "Have you been rolling in the grass, Doctor?"

"Only once or twice. Reever and I were too busy doing other things." I took the bit of grass and tucked it into my tunic pocket. "Speaking of mates, have you signaled Garphawayn lately?"

"I signal my mate each night, thank you. If I did not, she promised to separate my head from my shoulders when she and our sons return to Joren." He keyed in the access code to the lab, which he had built and designed for his personal use, and led me inside.

"They're coming back from Omorr to visit you?" This was news to me.

"They will come back to live here with me. I have been offered a position as Chief Medical Adviser to the Ruling Council, and I intend to accept." Squilyp went to his central control panel and turned on several emitters, illuminating the interior. "We have already been granted permanent residential status. All my mate needs to do is decide among which HouseClan she wishes to live. It would be more convenient to reside with the Adan, but she has become very attached to the Torin."

I had been planning to ask Squilyp to join the expedition to oKia, but now I hesitated. As much as I wanted the Omorr in Medical, this position sounded far more important. Squilyp also had a rather demanding wife, to whom he was utterly devoted, as well as two young sons he adored. It would be selfish to expect him to drop everything to jaunt to oKia with us.

"What about your families on the homeworld?" I knew the Omorr lived almost as closely as the Jorenians did. "Do they approve?"

"My family acknowledges the honor of the position. Her family"—he rolled his dark eyes—"is displeased by our decision to raise the twins away from Omorr, but I think they will come to accept it. Thus far they have made only the token arguments."

I went to examine an interesting-looking experiment in progress. "They're more afraid of her than you."

"Everyone is," he agreed. "Don't open that."

I studied the contents of the culture dishes. "What is it?"

"My latest batch of epithelial scaffolding cells." Squilyp hopped over and peered into the culture incubator I was inspecting. "As I suspected. They're not bonding with Reever's tissue samples. I'm afraid that so far, nothing has."

"If the chameleons don't bond with host cells, then how can they repair and replace damaged organs?"

"When I discern that," the Omorr said, "I will be the wealthiest surgeon in the galaxy." He saw my expression and sniffed. "Cherijo was never so gullible as you. The reason I commissioned this lab was to protect my research. No one can know about Duncan's condition, Jarn. If I can discover how to implant chameleon cells in another host body, they could be used by less virtuous researchers to create virtually indestructible armies."

We went over the test results, which had yielded little new information. Squilyp·had performed a comprehensive series of scans on the chameleon cells I had harvested from Reever's kidneys and liver, but they did not respond or behave like any other form of human cell.

"My best guess is that in an environment outside the body, the cells become dormant," Squilyp said. "They may have been engineered to do so to prevent unnecessary growth or accidental transfer. They are not fooled by implantation into simulated bodies, either."

"You can't experiment with them on living beings." I gnawed at my bottom lip. "Have you tried organic stimulants?"

He nodded. "Organic, recombinant, and synthesized. The results are the same. No reaction; no growth. Scans show the cells are alive, but inert."

That reminded me. "I have some other samples to give you for testing." I put my medical case on one of the worktables and opened it, removing several vials of blood and cellular samples I had prepared. "These are from my body. While we are gone on this expedition, I would like you to perform some specific tests on them, as well as my husband's."

"Of course." He transferred the samples to a refrigerated case. "What do you want me to check?"

"I want to know how to reverse the bioengineering that Joseph Grey Veil performed on us," I said. "In my case, I need a treatment to repair the tampering performed on my DNA in utero, and in Duncan's, a process that will safely remove all of the chameleon cells from his body."

"What?" Squilyp stopped fiddling with the incubator's controls and stared at me. "Why?"

"If we can somehow undo Joseph's genetic tampering, Reever and I would be able to live normal life spans," I explained. "We could have more children, grow older, and die a natural death."

For a long moment, the Omorr said nothing. Then he turned his back on me. "No. I won't do it."

I had not counted on his resistance to the idea. "Give me back the samples, then, and I will do the research myself when I have time."

He swiveled around. "Do you even know what you're asking me? Essentially, you want me to find a way to kill you and Duncan."

"Not immediately. Barring disease or injury, the average life span of a Terran in good health is ninety to one hundred twenty years." On Iisleg, we would have been fortunate to live half so long. "That should be sufficient for us. It is for every other Terran in existence."

"I cannot believe you." Squilyp began hopping around the lab. "You and Duncan are immortal. Every being in the known universe would wipe out entire star systems to have what you've been given. Now you tell me that you wish to throw away this tremendous advantage?"

"We want to be like every other being and live a normal life span." I gestured toward the incubator. "Whatever you discover in this lab, I can tell you now, immortality is not an advantage. It is death. The greed for it causes madness and war and destruction. If Duncan and I were like every other Terran, no one would fight over us. No one would care."

"If you were like other Terrans," Squilyp spat out the words, "Reever would be dead, and so would Cherijo. They would never have met. You wouldn't even exist. Neither would Marel."

That hurt, almost as much as Xonea's hatred. "Do you know what Duncan asked me to do while we were stranded on Trellus?" I countered. "He told me that I should implant chameleon cells in Marel's body. Do you know why?"

"She has no need . . ." The Omorr stopped and his eyes rounded. "Of course. As you are, you will both outlive her."

"Undoubtedly." I folded my arms. "I told him I wouldn't do it. I would rather give her away to be raised by the Jorenians—by anyone—than force her to endure what we have."

"Marel is only a child," Squilyp argued. "This is not a decision you need make now. You have many years before she reaches adulthood."

I held on to my patience with grim determination.

"You built this lab to protect your research because you're afraid of it being misused. Bounty hunters are out there, right now, looking for us. How much longer do you think it will be before the research is stolen, or we are found and taken and dissected?"

The Omorr's hide turned a darker shade of pink. "The Jorenians will protect you."

"If I were a bounty hunter and I knew two immortals lived on this, do you know what I would do?" I pointed toward the ceiling panels. "I would gather an armada of ships and launch an attack from orbit. I would wipe out every sign of life on this planet. Then I would go down and find the only two people left alive. That would be me and Reever."

Squilyp's shoulders sagged. "No one would attack Joren to capture you. No one would dare."

"They already have," I reminded him. "Twice. Three times, if you count the patient that was made into a bomb."

He sat down behind his desk and rested his head against his membranes. "We could arrange an accident—fly a scout into a star and make it look as if you were killed. We could create new identities for you. Hide you on a world where you would not be found."

"Would you wish to live like that?" I asked softly. "Always running, hiding, afraid of being discovered? Would you wish Marel to do the same, and grow old while her parents remain young? Do you think you could watch your children grow old and die, all the while knowing that you could never journey to the next life with them?"

"Omorr do not believe in a next life." He rubbed his

eyes, and then saw my face. "No, Jarn. I could not bear the burden of it."

"Then please, old friend, help us." I sat down in front of the desk. "Find a way to reverse what was done to us." I reached across and took one of his membranes in my hand. "Give us a chance at life. Ordinary life. One we can live in peace."

"I will try." Squilyp gripped my fingers for a moment, and then rose. "Come. I want you to meet one of my new residents."

I had a great many tasks to attend to in order to prepare for the expedition, including telling my daughter about it. "Perhaps another time. I have much to do."

"You'll want to meet Jylyj," the Omorr assured me. "Xonal told me about this expedition you're planning, and I think this resident could be very useful. Aside from the fact that Jylyj is a gifted surgeon, he is also Skartesh."

I frowned. "I was told that world had been destroyed during the war."

Squilyp hopped out into the corridor. "It was, but many of the Skartesh escaped before the end." He waited until I came through, and then secured the access panel. "The survivors have recently established a new colony on one of K-2's moons."

I recalled what Reever had said about the Skartesh being isolationists. "Why is this Jylyj not in residency there?"

"According to his transfer papers, he left K-2 soon after the Skartesh were tricked into attempting a mass suicide. He does not speak of his people at all, so I imagine it had something to do with that." Squilyp shrugged.

"Whatever Jylyj's origins, he's the finest resident I've ever trained. Brilliant in and out of the surgical suite. I've been assigning him the most challenging cases on the ward, and he's yet to lose a patient. As it happens, he has a reputation of having a magic touch. All the patients he treats have healed quickly, and with no complications."

I accompanied Squilyp to the surgical ward, where the nurses were preparing for rounds. I had no difficulty spotting the Skartesh, as he was the only non-Jorenian on the floor.

While Squilyp conferred briefly with the charge nurse, I watched Jylyj assessing a post-op case. He wore a green resident's tunic, fitting for a four-limbed humanoid male. I had not yet grown accustomed to seeing furred species, so at first glance the dark brown pelt covering his body and face made him seem more like an animal than a person.

After my initial, unfavorable reaction, I saw reassuring signs that my first impression was in error. The dense black ruff of fur surrounding Jylyj's features had been trimmed short, as had the five curved black claws on his paws. His eye, as solid black as the Jorenians were white, made me wonder for a moment if he were a crossbreed. ClanLeader Sajora Kalea, a crossbreed Jorenian, had possessed solid green eyes. The resident's ear flaps stood straight up on either side of his head, and small circles of some amber alloy hung from the right flap.

Animals, I knew, did not adorn themselves.

The black coloration of Jylyj's slanted eyelids, pointed nose, and lining of his long, narrowed-jawed mouth gave him a menacing look, as did the heavy musculature of his frame under the fur. At the same time, he moved carefully, and the low tone of his voice as he spoke to the Jorenian patient sounded warm and pleasant. I noted how gently and efficiently he used the long, clawed digits of his paws to check the surgical dressing and adjust the berth to a more comfortable alignment. He might look like a killer, but he had the air and focus of a natural healer.

Jylyj looked up and met my gaze.

I could not put a name to what I saw on Jylyj's face and in his eyes. For the most part, ensleg emotions still mystified me. It was what I felt that made me take a step back. I had never seen him, had never encountered his kind here or anywhere, and yet . . . I knew him.

As he knows you, something whispered soundlessly behind my eyes.

"Senior Healer." After what had happened last night, I did not want to listen to any more voices in my head. "May I speak to you?"

"Forgive me. Two new patients were admitted and I had to schedule their procedures," the Omorr said as he joined me. "Why the Torin must beat each other senseless in the warrior's quad to prove their manhood, I will never understand." He followed the direction of my gaze and stepped in front of me, blocking Jylyj from my sight. "You look terrible. What is it?"

I shook off the unnerving sense of recognition. "Nothing," I lied. "A minor headache. Please introduce me to your resident."

For the first time since coming to Joren, I did not impress a fellow colleague. Once Squilyp had introduced me with the usual amount of unnecessary detail, the Skartesh resident made a brief, modified version of the Jorenian gesture of welcome, and immediately returned to attending to his patient.

"No," I murmured when the Senior Healer began to call him back. Unlike the Omorr, I understood the resident's behavior, and it had nothing to do with the look we had exchanged earlier. Now that I knew what— and who—I was dealing with, I could act accordingly. "You will perform rounds this morning with him. I will observe."

"That," the Omorr told me flatly, "is ridiculous. You are a surgeon, not a student."

"Indulge me." I smiled a little at the bizarre sense of satisfaction I felt. At least with this ensleg, I knew exactly what to do.

We made rounds of the ward, and I took care to remain silent and observant, and spoke only when asked a direct question. At first Jylyj treated me with polite suspicion, but when I did not intrude on his conversations with the Senior Healer or offer any unrequested opinions, most of his animosity dissipated.

By the time we had finished assessing the patients, Jylyj was speaking freely. Squilyp's evaluation of his abilities had been on the conservative side; the Skartesh had a sharp eye for details as well as a phenomenal memory. Not once did I see him consult the diagnostic database to confirm his opinions, all of which were completely accurate.

Squilyp and I left Jylyj calibrating a patient's bonesetter, and only when we were out of earshot did I abandon my ruse. "I will need to speak to your resident alone."

"You will first explain this farce to me," the Omorr countered.

"The Skartesh does not work well with your female nurses, does he?" I guessed. "He likely performs their tasks as well as his own, and refuses to ask for assistance."

Squilyp seemed taken aback. "I have heard some minor complaints, but who told you about it?"

"He did. Or, rather, his eyes, the way he holds himself, the brevity with which he spoke to me. They told me that my presence on the ward is deeply offensive to him." I saw the Omorr still didn't understand. "Squilyp, his kind subjugate their females. Just as the Iisleg did."

"Not on this planet," the Omorr snapped, and then made a disgusted sound. "I should have known. Well, if he is to serve as a healer on Joren, he must accept that we value ability and dedication, not one gender over the other."

I saw Jylyj watching us from across the ward. "Accepting and liking are not the same. He may not even be aware of what he is doing." I scanned the ward and spotted a small, unoccupied office. "I will wait in there. When he is finished with that patient, send him to me. Alone, please."

A few minutes later, the Skartesh entered the office. "You wished to speak to me."

"Yes." I gestured toward a chair. When Jylyj made no move to take it, I said, "What I did during rounds was a courtesy to you and your kind. Now you will show me the same."

His blunt claws curled over against the pads of his paws, the only physical reaction he showed to the abrupt shift in my demeanor. He sat down but remained poised on the edge of the chair, as if he intended to rise and walk out at any moment.

"I understand your discomfort with me." But I had no intention of indulging it, so I remained on my feet. Jylyj had to look up at me; something an Iisleg male would have found intolerable. "On my homeworld, females within the tribes were forbidden most freedoms. Before the rebellion, all a woman could do was prepare food, care for children, sort salvage, and provide physical relief. Until the Raktar came, all of our healers were male. Since I left my homeworld, I, too, have struggled to adjust to these ensleg ways."

The tight lines bracketing his eyes softened a few degrees. "How may I help you, Healer Cherijo?"

"You may begin by calling me Jarn," I told him.

He gazed at a spot on the wall just to the right of my head. "How may I be of service, Healer Jarn?"

It was almost, but not quite, an insult. One I would have to overlook, too, if I was to convince him to join us. "My husband and I are leading a scientific expedition to the Saraced system. The Senior Healer tells me that you are a native of that region."

"I was. Skart no longer exists."

I could offer him sympathy, which he obviously didn't want, or get to the heart of the matter. "Our expedition will be traveling to survey a planet called oKia. Have you ever sojourned to that world?"

He sniffed, and at first I thought my question had offended him. Then he did it again, and I realized he was smelling the air itself, perhaps in much the same way the Hsktskt tasted it with their tongues.

He stopped sniffing and reluctantly inclined his head. "I know oKia."

Doubtless he would be more open with Squilyp or even Reever, but I refused to admit defeat. As healers, Jylyj and I would have to work together on the *Sunlace*. We could not do that if he would not lower himself to converse with me. "What can you tell me about this world?"

The black fur around the base of his ears bristled. "It is cold. There are mountains and tundra. The natives are tribal primitives. Your kind call them lupine, like the wolves of Terra."

How could he know that, and when had he interacted with Terrans? More questions to be answered.

"We are in need of a guide for the expedition." I took a seat behind the console panel. "Someone who is familiar with the worlds in that region of space, especially oKia." On Iisleg, females were not permitted to make requests of males unless invited to do so, but there were ways around that. "There is no one else on Joren with your personal experience."

"I am a surgical resident," Jylyj said, almost snapping out the words, "not a pathfinder. My duties are here."

"This mission is very important to us." I kept my tone level but soft, hoping not to goad him into a rage. "You have knowledge of this world that we do not. You would be a great asset."

His jaw worked, and I could almost hear his back teeth grinding together. "Healer Jarn, no ship will be permitted to travel through oKiaf space. oKia resigned from the League. They refuse to have any contact with offworlders. Save yourself the trouble and have your husband call off your expedition now."

"My husband is a talented linguist, and hopes to persuade the oKiaf to make an exception for us." I sensed something more than anger coming from him now. He was afraid, but of what? "You could still join the expedition as a healer and an adviser—"

"No." He stood. "I cannot accept. I will not."

There was one more thing I had to know. "Do you know me?" When he glared, I added, "When I first saw you, I had the sense that you recognized me."

"I have never met you before today, Healer Jarn, so I could not recognize you. Your pardon, but I have patients waiting for me to attend to them." Before I could reply, he turned and strode out to the ward.

I stayed in the office and thought about the Skartesh's words and behavior until Squilyp came in.

"Jylyj told me that he refused your request, and then suddenly developed a headache that prevented him from finishing out his shift," the Omorr said. "Either your headache is contagious, or both of you are lying to me."

"If I explain all this, *you* will have the headache," I warned him. "What do you know about Jylyj?"

"Why should I answer your questions when you will not answer mine?" Squilyp countered.

"Something about him feels . . . wrong."

"It cannot be his skills as a healer," the Omorr assured me. "He's the finest resident I've ever supervised. His work is faultless."

"I am not questioning his abilities." I did, however, want to know more about his past, and who had been a part of it. "Can you acquire copies of Jylyj's personnel and transfer data, and send them to my quarters?"

"I can." Squilyp made an impatient gesture. "I will still need a reason why."

"I think Jylyj may have known Cherijo." And I did not want to talk more about that possibility until I reviewed his records. "I must go now."

"I want to know whatever you find out," the Omorr called after me.

I left the medical facility to return to the Torin pavilion and face my next task: telling Marel that her father and I were once more leaving her behind on Joren. So engrossed was I in sorting out how I would explain the necessity of the separation to our daughter that I did not see the resident waiting outside for me until I nearly walked into him.

"Oh. Your pardon." I stepped back, dropped my gaze, and made to go around him.

Jylyj stepped into my path. This close, he towered over me. "I must ask forgiveness for my discourtesy to you earlier, Healer Jarn."

"Why?" Puzzled now, I regarded him. When he did not reply, I said, "Resident, I may appear Terran, but I was born on a world where males subjugate females. They do not offer apologies to them. Why should you?"

"Wherever your homeworld, you are not a Skartesh female." He forced himself to meet my gaze. "It was rude to treat you as such. I am sorry."

I felt as uncomfortable as he did now. "Apology accepted."

He wasn't finished. "My beliefs require me to make amends. If you are still willing to have me serve on the crew, I will join your expedition."

Astonishment left me mute until I realized he was

waiting for a response. "That seems a great deal of trouble to go to when you have already apologized."

"We Skartesh have very specific codes of behavior," he explained. "The only alternative to granting your request would be to prostrate myself in ritual contrition. It involves providing a period of personal servitude, fasting for several days, and shaving off all of my mane."

The mental image his confession provoked made me press my lips together. "That doesn't sound very comfortable."

"Proper contrition rarely is."

I looked at him, trying to discern a real motive. His features gave nothing away. "Very well, I accept your offer, and will inform the Senior Healer and make the arrangements. I thank you, Doctor."

"I prefer to be called Jylyj," he said, rather stiffly. "Do you still wish to be addressed as Jarn?" When I nodded, he inclined his head. "Until we meet again, Jarn." He strode away.

Five

Male laughter greeted me as I entered my quarters at the pavilion. Inside I saw our friends Qonja and Hawk sitting on the floor with Marel and playing a game of chase the string with the cats.

Reever met me at the door panel and took my hands in his. "You are late." Through the link his touch established, he added, *I have warned them that Xonea is monitoring us.*

"Forgive me, but I had to speak with Squilyp's resident." I kissed him. *How did you manage to do that?*

"You might have signaled." He took Marel's school datapad from his tunic pocket and, using his body to shield it from the drone monitors, typed *carefully* on it before he cleared the screen.

Hawk, the crossbreed avatar-Terran who had helped rescue Cherijo after Joseph Grey Veil had abducted her and taken her back to Terra, appeared very tanned and healthy, as if he had been spending a great deal of time working outdoors. The wide, brown-feathered wings he had once concealed by pretending to be a hunchback now lay folded beneath his broad shoulders.

"Jarn." Hawk came to envelop me in his arms and wings for a fond embrace. "It is good to see you."

I hugged him back before exchanging a warm gesture of greeting with Qonja, Hawk's bondmate. The Jorenian male also looked quite fit and happy.

"I'm glad to see you, but surprised, too," I told Qonja, and turned to touch my brow to his in the Jorenian manner of greeting. "I thought Reever said that you were dwelling with the Kalea now."

"We were. As soon as we received word of your return, we thought it a prudent time to pay a visit." Qonja indicated some beautifully woven Jorenian baskets on our dining table. "We brought some of Galena Kalea's morning breads, which are finer than any I have ever tasted, including those of my former ClanMother." A flicker of sadness crossed his handsome face before he added, "Hawk has a new dish he wishes you to try, as well. What say we share a meal?"

I glanced at Reever, who nodded. "I think we would all enjoy that very much."

Over an enormous meal of breads and a tasty stew Hawk prepared from spicy native roots and blossoms, we spoke of mutual friends and recent events on Joren. Qonja and Hawk did not ask about Trellus, and Reever and I did not speak of the colony or our upcoming expedition. For the most part, we listened to our daughter chatter on about her friends and schoolwork, and some of the sights she had seen while traveling with Salo and Darea. Then Fasala arrived to take Marel to an evening gathering for the HouseClan's children, leaving the four of us alone. I prepared tea for everyone and then sat down with the men.

"That was a fine dish, Hawk," I said, "and if you will program it in our prep unit, I will be most grateful. But did you really come all this way to prepare a new dish for us?"

"Not exactly." Hawk looked at his bondmate.

Qonja took his hand as his expression turned solemn. "We have news, unhappy as it is. While you were away, Hawk and I petitioned the Ruling Council to recognize our bond and overturn the repudiation from my House-Clan. They have refused."

Hawk and Qonja were both male, and under the present law were prohibited from Choosing each other as bondmates. The fact that they had done so, and had gone so far as to openly declare their bond in front of Jorenian witnesses, had caused Qonja to be repudiated by his natal kin, HouseClan Adan.

"So the council is siding with the Adan," Reever said. "You must have expected that."

Qonja nodded. "We had hoped, of course, that they would break with tradition and rule in our favor, but we were not startled when they did not. Our oldest customs and laws govern matters of Choice. It will take more than one petition to effect changes."

"Can you petition them again?" I was a member of the council; surely I could do something about this.

"It would not be advisable. As it is, our presence on Joren is only tolerated out of respect for my former ClanFather," Qonja admitted. "A second petition might provoke the council into taking more aggressive action, such as rescinding my citizenship and residential status. If that happens, Hawk and I will both be deported."

"I have tried to convince him to revoke our bond,"

Hawk said, his unhappiness plain. "It would placate the council and the Adan, and we can still be together, if we are discreet."

Qonja kissed the back of Hawk's hand. "I will never hide my honor for you, *evlanar*." With his free hand he made a careless gesture. "It matters not. Even now, word of our bond is spreading throughout the HouseClans. The customs and laws regulating Choice has been questioned for some time by younger Jorenians. Despite the beliefs of my people, it would seem that not everyone who Chooses wishes to procreate."

"Such changes often take a very long time to happen, especially among sexually repressed species," Reever said. "What do the Kalea say about this?"

"Like me, they are crossbreeds," Hawk said, "and the ClanLeaders, Jakol and Sajora Kalea, have openly accepted our bond. They even accompanied us before the council to show their support for our petition. But if the council decides to take further action against us, such support could also result in serious repercussions for the Kalea. Some of the more conservative Adan have spoken of having HouseClan Kalea declared lawless and officially disbanded for offering us shelter."

"Which we cannot allow to happen to our friends, not after all they have done for us," Qonja added. "Until the law changes, Hawk and I feel we should make our home away from Joren."

"Terra will not grant you asylum or residential status," Reever said. "Where will you go?"

"We would prefer to find an open and tolerant multi-species colony, like the one established on Kevarzangia Two," Qonja said. "But I think it would be best if we left

Joren as soon as possible. Xonal Torin mentioned to us that you are heading an expedition into the Saraced system. Would you consider allowing Hawk and I to serve as members of the crew?"

"Of course," I said at once. "We would be glad to have you with us." I thought for a moment. "How would you wish to serve on the crew?"

"My people on Terra lived under primitive tribal conditions," Hawk put in. "I may be able to help you interpret some of the customs and practices of the oKiaf. I also have first-aid training, so I can assist you in the medical bay when necessary."

"I can serve as the expedition's psychologist," Qonja said. "Or your personal bodyguard, as before."

The door panel chimed, preventing my answer, and I went to answer it. One glance at the external display made me frown.

"Xonea." I opened the panel.

"I would speak to you and your bondmate." The captain of the *Sunlace* walked in past me and stopped as he saw our guests. "Forgive me, I do not mean to interrupt."

"Then you should have waited rather than come here at this hour," Reever replied.

I saw that my husband was still spoiling for a fight with my ClanBrother. "Whatever the hour or circumstance, we are all still friends. Come and join us, Captain."

Xonea greeted Qonja and Hawk in a polite but reserved fashion, refused my offer of tea, and remained on his feet. "My ClanFather has spoken to me of this expedition you intend to take to Saraced. Given the current political situation there, I advise against it."

"He must have also told you that oKia is one of three worlds on the Aksellan map that was not marked as harboring the black crystal," I said. "It is important that we discover if that is still the case, and if so, why."

"You acquired this mining map from the Trellusans," Xonea said. "What if it is not authentic? What if they counterfeited it in order to lure you and Duncan to this world?"

"Why resort to such an elaborate ruse?" I spread out my hands. "They had the means to keep us imprisoned on Trellus. If they wished to collect a bounty for us, why would they give us a map and let us go? How could they know we would choose to sojourn to oKia, for that matter?"

His mouth tightened. "I do not like this. We can protect you better on Joren than in open space."

"That is why I asked Xonal to have you transport the expedition on the *Sunlace*," I pointed out. "There is no one we trust more to keep us safe."

My ClanBrother turned his head and eyed Reever, who nodded his agreement. "Very well. If you are to go, it will be on my ship." He then regarded Qonja and Hawk. "I suppose you two intend to accompany us."

"Jarn has consented to our joining the crew, but it is your ship," Qonja said, his tone cool. "If our presence is as unwelcome there as it has been almost everywhere else, we should be told now."

Xonea had been the one to expose Qonja and Hawk's relationship to the Adan, I recalled.

"There has been much debate among the Houses over your bond," Xonea said. "I am like most of our people in that I value our traditions and wish to see them preserved. I also believe the primary responsibility of those who Choose is to have children. Still, even one such as I can see the bond that exists between you and Hawk. It appears as real and enduring as"—he glanced at me—"any other I have witnessed."

Qonja put his hand on Hawk's shoulder. "It is."

"Then this time, I will save you some trouble and assign you both to the same quarters on the *Sunlace*." Xonea turned to Reever. "The ship has been undergoing some refitting at the Zamlon docks. I am traveling there tomorrow to inspect the work. If you and Jarn wish to accompany me, I will call for you in the morning."

Like Xonea's, my husband's expression gave away none of his feelings. "We would, thank you."

"Be ready to leave by midrise." With a nod to the rest of us, my ClanBrother left.

"Am I hallucinating?" Hawk asked softly, "Or did I just hear Captain Xonea Torin acknowledge our bond?"

Qonja grinned. "If you did not, it was a shared hallucination."

I heard a low, distressed sound, and looked past Qonja to see our daughter standing on the other side of the room with Fasala just inside the entrance to the courtyard.

"Your pardon, Healer Jarn." Fasala looked miserable. "I did not wish to interrupt your visit, so I brought Marel back through the courtyard."

"It's all right, Fasala." The stricken look on Marel's small face told me how much of our discussion she had overheard. "I am sorry we did not have the chance to talk to you about the sojourn first."

"You told ClanUncle and Hawk and even Fasala." Marel knuckled away the tears in her eyes and gave me a defiant look. "You told everyone about it. Everyone but me. Now what will my friends say?" She ran off to her room, and Reever followed her.

"I think we should go," Hawk said, and gave me a brief farewell embrace. Against my ear, he murmured, "The young are very forgiving."

After I saw out Qonja and Hawk, I returned to hear the sounds of my daughter sobbing and Reever speaking in a low, soothing voice.

"Since your return from Trellus, Marel has been telling our friends that you would be staying and making your home here with us," Fasala explained. "She even spoke to our ClanLeader about planting a garden of Terran vegetables, to see if they would grow here. I think this is the cause of her distress."

"I knew she was becoming attached to this world, but . . ." I stopped and rubbed my eyes with my fingers. "We cannot take her with us on this expedition; it is too dangerous. Perhaps she will feel better when she knows that."

"I think not, Healer," Fasala said. "Each time you leave her, Marel fears you will not return. Her true happiness is walking within beauty with you and Linguist Reever." With a sympathetic gesture, the Jorenian girl also departed.

When Marel was upset, Reever always managed her better than I could, so I busied myself with tidying up. An hour passed before he emerged and joined me in the food prep area.

"She is sleeping now." He put his arm around my

waist. "Don't blame yourself, beloved. We knew this news would be difficult for her to accept."

I knew, and still it did not make a difference. "I know it must be this way, and still I cannot bear to hear her weeping like that." I took a deep breath and faced him. "Fasala mentioned something. It seems our daughter has been telling the other children that we were to make a home here. A permanent home."

Reever frowned. "I have not said any such thing to her. Have you?"

I shook my head. "Who would make her believe something like that?"

"Perhaps something was said by someone who wishes us to remain on Joren." His gaze shifted to the drone concealed in a nearby wall.

Xonea, of course. Another of his controlling tactics, and this time he used it on my daughter.

This time, he had made my daughter cry.

I couldn't bear another moment of this farce, so I reached into the storage container and removed the largest, sharpest blade from it. "Look over there, Husband." I made my voice as loud as I could without disturbing the child. "I think someone has planted a spying device in our quarters."

"Jarn." Duncan shook his head.

He was right; what I meant to do was a foolish thing. And I didn't care. I went over to the wall and drove the knife into the embedded drone. The plasteel shattered the monitoring device, causing a short spray of sparks to shoot out of the wall.

"I wonder if there are others. Let me look." I went to the next. "Oh, dear, here is another one." I used the blade to pry this one out of the wall panel, and peered into its tiny lens. "Are you getting *this* picture, spy?" I dropped the drone to the floor and stomped on it until it lay in small pieces.

Reever did not stop me as I went from drone to drone and systematically destroyed all but one of them. With the last, I carefully removed it from its hiding place and brought it over to the disposal unit.

"Hello," I said to the drone. "Please be advised of the following: If I find another monitoring device within a hundred meters of me, Reever, or Marel, I will have the person responsible explain why to the Ruling Council." I paused. "After I beat him senseless for intruding on our privacy and deceiving our child."

I crushed the drone in my hand before I dropped the remains into the disposal.

Reever came to stand next to me. "Regarding the beating, you will have to wait your turn."

"Good." I turned and went to the room terminal, and prepared a formal text signal before I asked my husband to translate it into Jorenian for me. As he read the message, I said, "I will send it now, unless you have any objections."

He gave me one of his rare half smiles. "None at all."

Marel woke up early, but said little to us as she had her morning meal and prepared for her day at school.

I did not like this silence, not when I had grown accustomed to the child's bright, endless chatter. But Reever had suggested I let her have some time to adjust to the news of the expedition before I discussed it with her.

Saying nothing made me feel as unhappy as the child, but I knew he was right.

We did not talk at all during the brief walk from our quarters to the school, but just before she entered her class Marel looked up at me.

The storm-dark color of her eyes told me she had not yet forgiven us for disappointing her. "Will I stay again with ClanUncle Salo and ClanAunt Darea while you are gone, Mama?"

"That is our wish." I knelt down in front of her. "Marel, we love you, and we are very sorry that we hurt you. We should have told you first about the expedition. You are the most important person in our lives."

"I want to be like the other kids here," she told me. "They never have to be away from their families. Everyone stays together. That's what kin does. If you and Daddy can't be on Joren with me, then you should take me with you on the expedition."

"We could," I agreed. "But we will have much work to do, and this time there will be no other children on board the ship. I fear it would be very boring for you."

"Then don't go, Mama." Tears sparkled in her eyes. "Stay here with me."

I took her hands in mine. "An Iisleg woman cannot break a promise she makes, you know that." When she nodded, I said, "When we return from this sojourn, I vow that Daddy and I will take you on a special trip. We won't work or have meetings or be away from you. We will go only where you want to go, and only be where you want us to be."

"I miss my friends at HouseClan Kalea. ClanLeader

Jory said the next time I visited that she would teach me how to ride a t'lerue." Clearly tempted, Marel bit her lower lip. "You promise, Mama?"

I pressed her hand to my heart. "I swear it."

Marel flung her arms around my neck and hugged me tightly. I held her until her teacher came to the entrance, and only then did I release her to join the class.

Reever stood waiting for me outside the pavilion. "Xonea signaled while you were out. He has gone ahead to check some of the engine work."

"Perhaps he can have the Zamlon fix his monitoring drones, as well." I went with Reever to the glidecar waiting at the end of the walking path. "I promised Marel that we would spend some time with her after the expedition. It is not enough, though. Soon we must decide how and where we are to live as a family."

"We can discuss it during the sojourn." Reever opened the passenger side of the vehicle for me. "For now, stop it."

I glanced at him. "Stop what?"

"Worrying about our daughter, the expedition, the new bounty being offered, Xonea, and everything else in your head." He buckled me into my harness. "We are together. Marel is safe. That is enough for now."

I envied Reever that unwavering assurance, especially when I saw the glint from a tiny lens wink at me from a corner of the interior floor covering. As my husband went around to the other side of the vehicle, I bent down and swiftly yanked the monitoring drone out of the textured material.

"This should not take too long," Reever said as he climbed in behind the control console. "Xonea has much to do to prepare for the sojourn."

"Good." I pocketed the drone. "So do I."

On the trip to the Zamlon dock yards, Reever kept me distracted from my thoughts by reviewing the crew manifest for the expedition. Many of the most experienced flight officers among the Torin had been slated to accompany us, along with a full complement of skilled nurses to serve in medical, and combat-trained militia for security. I was a little surprised to discover my husband, not Xonea, had consulted with Xonal to handpick the crew.

"Are we going on a sojourn, or declaring war on the oKia?" I tried to joke.

"I prefer to be prepared." Reever slowed outside a restricted area and presented our identifications to a Zamlon security officer.

Beyond the gated entry stood open framework enclosures built around a dozen massive star vessels in various stages of construction and repair. Surrounding them were smaller, sleeker scouts and launches perched on lifts or suspended from cranes. Zamlon shipbuilders swarmed around, over, and under the vessels as they worked on them. Drone transports glided back and forth from enormous storage structures as they hauled heavy loads of cargo and construction materials.

I knew the Jorenians drew on forms from nature to design their star vessels; the *Sunlace* resembled the spiraling shell of a sea creature. Now I saw other, strangely compelling vessel designs that ranged from a cluster of falling stars to the closed petals of an enormous flower.

One ship in particular stood out from the others; a twin-hulled vessel only partially completed but already a magnet for the eye. Made of some dark golden alloy, the ship had an unusual amount of large viewer panels and double launch bays large enough to hold twenty or thirty smaller scout vessels. I had seen the remains of thousands of vessels during my years on Akkabarr, yet none of them even remotely resembled the design of this ship.

"Is that golden runner some sort of troop transport?" I asked my husband as we left the glidecar and walked to the *Sunlace*.

Reever paused to study it. "It's not carrying enough weapons." He saw the two launch bays. "It's designed primarily to transport smaller vessels, but far more than the crew and passengers would ever need." He tilted his head. "Those containment sections appear to be made to hold a separate type of atmosphere."

"They hold water," a low, pleasant voice said as a Jorenian in heavy welding gear joined us. "The crew are mostly 'Zangian aquatics. The ship itself will serve as an orbital base ship for planetary biorescue missions."

The Jorenian removed his headgear, revealing a bald, dark green head and friendly white-within-white eyes.

"You must be the Kalean shipbuilder," I guessed.

"Nalek Kalea," he said, grinning to show strong, white Jorenian teeth as he made a warm gesture of greeting. "You two are the little comet's parents, Jarn and Duncan."

"We are." I raised my brow. "Little comet?"

"Our pet name for your ClanDaughter," Nalek said. "Never have I met a child as small, fast, shining, or determined as Marel."

Nalek exchanged more formal greetings with Reever before escorting us to the *Sunlace*'s dock.

"Preparations for launch are nearly complete," the Kalean told us after introducing his project manager. "The ship should ready to return to orbit before the end of the week."

"I understood you to be a ship designer," I said, eyeing some unfamiliar exterior changes on the vessel. "Why are you involved with the work on the *Sunlace*?"

"Captain Torin requested modifications be made to the weapons systems. Here, I will show you." Nalek brought us to the starboard weapons array, and indicated some unfamiliar fittings and emitters. "Here the defense cannons have been modified. They can now deliver both pulse bursts and displacer ordnance."

"Jorenians don't use displacer technology," I said, more confused now. "Only the Hsktskt do."

"Pulse weapons are more precise, but displacer charges do more damage," Nalek explained. "Captain Torin was quite specific about fitting the ship to deliver both."

I spotted the Jorenian in question walking toward us. "Was he?"

Xonea offered a brief greeting before speaking to Nalek about an engine modification. At last he looked at me. "You will wish to go on board and inspect the medical bay."

"I intend to," I said. "But first I would like to know why you've had the ship's weapons array refitted to deliver displacer ordnance."

"We have received reports of recent attacks on ships traveling throughout the quadrant," Xonea said, "carried out by a small band of mercenaries. Their success is due to a new technology that shielded their ships against standard League pulse weaponry."

"Surely we can outrun some raiders," I said.

"Several vessels that were attacked by these mercenaries have been brought to the docks for repairs," Nalek said. "From what the captains tell us, the attackers come out of nowhere to disable their engines, perform intensive remote scans, and vanish again."

"What sort of intensive scans?" Reever asked.

The shipbuilder made an uncertain gesture. "Nothing our equipment can identify, but they're powerful. They scan the entire ship, access all the databases, and then leave."

"Slavers used the same tactic on captured vessels," my husband said. "They board them and use the readings from remote scans to locate what they want."

I glanced at Reever, and my heart tightened. "Or who."

He nodded, and then told the Jorenians, "The mercenaries are most likely bounty hunters scanning the ships for Terran life signs. They're looking for me and Jarn."

Nalek thought about it. "If they're only interested in finding two Terrans, it will not be difficult on a ship crewed mainly by Jorenians."

"I have had Nalek increase the sensitivity of our ship-to-ship proximity alarms," Xonea said. "As soon as they transition anywhere within one hundred thousand kim of the *Sunlace*, we will know and take action."

"It would be better to make them think there are no Terrans on board," my husband said, and turned to Nalek. "When I piloted a slave runner, we adjusted the external reflectors to shield the crew by constantly projecting Rilken life signs. All it required was a portable simulator and some creative circuit bypasses."

Nalek grimaced. "A clever ploy. No slaver would attack a Rilken ship, not even if they were desperate."

Reever nodded. "Perhaps the same can be done by adjusting the *Sunlace*'s buffer grid to use the dimensional simulators to alter my and Jarn's life signs to read as Jorenian as the rest of the crew."

Nalek slowly smiled. "With some very improper rigging, yes, I think it possible." He glanced at me and Xonea. "May I borrow your bondmate for a few minutes?"

I agreed, and waited until the men boarded the ship before I spoke to my ClanBrother. "Did you get my message last night?"

He stiffened. "I received no signal from you."

"It wasn't a signal. At least, not after I destroyed all the drones you planted in our quarters. But you needn't worry. I saved one that I found this morning." I took from my pocket the monitoring drone I had found in the vehicle. "Here, let me repeat the message." I dropped the drone on the ground between us and crushed it under my footgear.

My ClanBrother looked away from the ruined device, but said nothing.

"I don't care that you dislike me, Xonea," I advised him, "and out of my regard for our mutual kin I've tolerated your pathetic attempts to spy on me and Reever. But lying to my child? That seems excessive, even for you."

Now he glared at me. "Jorenians do not lie."

"I know you were the one who told Marel that we would be making a home here on Joren," I snapped. "Neither Reever nor I have ever agreed to do so. No one else would be so cruel."

"You are a member of the Ruling Council. A ClanDaughter of the Torin," he reminded me. "Joren is your home."

"Last night I resigned from the council," I told him, and enjoyed the jolt of shock that crossed his stern face.

"You cannot resign without my approval," Xonea finally said. "I will petition the council to have you reinstated."

"On what grounds will you file the petition on my behalf? Mental instability due to the effects of the amnesia?" I made my smile icy and sweet. "That *was* the reason I gave for my resignation."

Xonea stepped closer. "You think you have prevailed over me? I am still your closest blood kin. As such, I can call off the expedition. I can revoke your privileges as a citizen. I can even have you committed to a psychiatric facility for as long as I think appropriate."

"*If* I remain a member of HouseClan Torin. I can think of several ways to provoke an act of repudiation. Threatening to kill a ClanBrother before our kin, for example, would serve quite well." The words hung between us for a time. Then I said, "If that is what it will take to put an end to your harassment of me and my family, Xonea, I will do it."

"You would destroy the honor of my ClanBrother Kao, of my kin, simply to thwart me?" Horror filled his eyes. "You are mad."

"No more than someone who would rather see me imprisoned than allow me my freedom," I shot back. "You are no better than the bounty hunters or the League. Or Cherijo's father."

Xonea turned his back on me with a jerky motion and stared out at the horizon. After a long silence, he said, "So now the path changes."

I recalled what I had learned of Jorenian philosophy, and made the correct response. "So, too, must the traveler."

"You will not withdraw your resignation from the council?" He watched me shake my head. "Neither would she. Cherijo did not believe in half measures or surrender. She fought unto the end."

"So will I," I promised him.

I saw Reever and Nalek emerge from the ship and start toward us. "How will it be, then, Captain?"

Xonea picked up the pieces of the drone and put them in his tunic pocket. "You have your freedom, Healer."

Six

Reever and I left the rest of the preparations for the expedition in the capable hands of the crew, and spent the remaining time we had on Joren with Marel. I knew we had not banished all her worries over the coming separation, but neither of us wished to distress her further by referring to it or trying to explain all the important reasons we had to go.

Instead we did what we had had precious little time to do: enjoyed each day together as a family, taking her on outings, playing all of her favorite games, and accompanying her to the Torin's evening gatherings. After several days of having our undivided affection and attention, Marel regained most of her natural, sunny happiness, and seemed to forget that we were soon to leave her again.

A reminder came when Nalek Kalea signaled Duncan early one morning to request his presence at the docks to inspect some interior modification on the *Sunlace*.

"I would send someone else, but no one understands the specifications as well as I do," he told me. "I will return in a few hours."

We had been late returning from last night's gathering, and the child was still sleeping, so I saw no harm in it. "If Marel wakes before you come back, I will take her down to the shore." I kissed him. "But don't be too long."

Soon after that our daughter did wake, and grew petulant as soon as she realized her father had left. "You and Daddy said we would go to see the new baby t'lerue today. ClanAunt Darea says they are just starting to lope."

"We will," I told her. "But first I would like to walk down to the water. You said that you would show me where to find the prettiest shells."

She pouted. "You don't like shells, Mama. The first time you saw my collection, you asked me why I was keeping jars of skeletons in my room."

I suppressed a wince. I had been vaguely horrified to find Marel collecting the remains of deceased crustaceans, until Duncan had explained that they were considered by many species as ornamental objects.

"There are no seas or sea creatures on Akkabarr, so I did not know the proper term for them." That much was true. "I like them well enough." That wasn't.

Marel saw right through me. "You're just saying that so I won't be mad about Daddy being gone."

"I am a healer, and I may be called upon to treat patients with exoskeletons," I said, keeping my tone firm. "Learning more about them could help me with my work." If I ever went to a sea world and had to rescue mollusks.

That seemed to placate her. "All right. But I want to take some string so I can make a necklace for Daddy."

"Of course." I squashed the unappealing image of Reever wearing a loop of tiny skeletons around his neck. At least she hadn't wanted to make one for me. "I know he will love it."

HouseClan Torin's territory was known as Marine province, and for good reason. The distance from the pavilion to the shoreline was less than a mile, an easy walk from our quarters. Yet by the time we reached the dark, golden sands of the beach, Marel's enthusiasm had dimmed again.

"Here we are." I ignored her unhappy expression and took her hand, leading her up to the top of a dune to look across the seemingly endless stretch of amber sand forming a pretty fringe on the purple waters. "Where should we start searching?" I pointed to a promising-looking cluster of small dead bodies. "There?"

"No, those are too old. They're all bleached out from the sun." She sat down at my feet and rested her chin against her knees. "I don't want any shells."

I sat down beside her. "We could build dwellings of sand. You could sculpt a Terran castle for me, and I could make . . . a jlorra enclosure."

Her face turned up. "Mama, let Daddy go alone on the sojourn. Nothing bad will happen if you stay here with me."

If Xonea had made Marel think that I was in danger by going on the expedition, this time I'd smash more than a couple of recording drones. "Why do you think something bad will happen?"

"My dreams." She ducked her head. "I have them almost every night now, and they're really awful. In the dreams I see you go away, and you never come back."

"You are not dreaming; you are remembering what happened after we visited Oenrall." I put my arm around her. "That was when I was taken from you and Daddy, and I didn't come back. Daddy had to find me."

"No, it's not about the time when I was a baby. It's different," she insisted. "In my dreams you're wearing your blades under your tunic, and there is a little purple flower in your hair. You hug me and kiss me good-bye, and then I never see you again."

"Well, I know what to do about that," I said. "I promise you, I will never hug you again."

"Mama."

"Or kiss you. As for this little purple flower"—I rolled my eyes up toward my hairline—"I will slice open the first person who tries to put it on my head."

A giggle escaped her. "What if it's me or Daddy?"

"I can't gut either of you. Hmmm." I pretended to think about it. "I know. I will yell 'No' very loud, and then I will run away." I touched my forehead to hers in Jorenian fashion. "I promise you."

"Mama, you're so silly." Sighing, Marel pulled me to my feet. "Come on, I'll show you the tide pools. That's where the best shells are."

We half ran, half skidded our way down the side of the dune, and then walked toward a cluster of flat stones that held shallow pools of dark water.

Something caught Marel's eye, and she stopped and pointed. "Who's that, Mama?"

I shaded my eyes with my hand and saw in the distance a tall, lean figure rising from the water and removing a breather. Black swimming trunks covered the man's hips, but the rest of his body remained bare. At first I thought him a crossbreed like Nalek Kalea, until he shook himself all over to shed the water from his dark brown pelt.

"I think that is Jylyj, a Skartesh resident who works at the medical facility." I cupped my hands over my mouth and called out his name, and then waved.

The Skartesh halted and turned toward the sound of my voice, but instead of returning my call or waving back, he waded out of the water, picked up some gear, and disappeared behind a dune.

"Why did he go away?" Marel asked, clearly disappointed.

"I don't know." I watched for a moment longer, but Jylyj did not reappear. "Perhaps he had to report for duty. It matters not." I held out my hand. "Come."

We hunted shells for the rest of the morning, collecting a large variety from the tide pools. Although they still looked like skeletons to me, I admired each one and helped Marel string the smallest and most colorful to make a necklace.

On our walk back to the pavilion, Reever met us halfway, and gravely ducked his head so Marel could loop the necklace of shells around his neck.

"Do you like it, Daddy?"

"I have never had such a gift. Thank you, *avasa*." He picked her up in his arms and gave me a pointed look. "Next time you must make one for your mother."

"Mama says healers can't wear ornaments because of the scanners they use," Marel confided to him. "The shells would make the readings wrong."

"I could speak to the Senior Healer," Reever suggested. "Perhaps he could adjust the scanners."

"No need." I showed my husband some teeth. "I will take pleasure in seeing you wear yours."

On the way back to our quarters, Marel told her father about the tiny water creatures we had discovered in the tide pools, and how they tickled our fingers as we searched for shells.

"There are more bigger ones that live out on the sandbar, but Mama doesn't swim, so she said we couldn't go there without you." Marel glanced at me. "Mama, you should ask the wolf man to teach you to swim."

"The wolf man?"

"We saw Jylyj at the other end of the shore," I explained. "He was swimming."

Reever gave me an odd look. "You must be mistaken."

"No, I'm almost sure it was him." Something occurred to me. "Unless there are other Skartesh on Joren—that might explain why he left as soon as I called out to him."

Later that evening, after Marel had gone to sleep, Reever asked me again about seeing the Skartesh down at the shoreline. "Tell me everything you remember."

I described how Marel had spotted Jylyj coming out of the water, how the Skartesh had removed his breather, and how quickly he had left after I had called to him.

"It could not have been Jylyj," Reever said after I had finished. "His species cannot tolerate water."

I shook my head. "Every living thing needs some form of water to survive."

"Come here, I will show you." Reever took me to the room terminal and accessed the database for information on the Skartesh.

I read the section displayed about species environmental hazards. "They are hydrophobic?"

"To such an extreme degree that no Skartesh would voluntarily go near the water," Reever told me. "Exposure to any amount makes them ill. Immersion causes shock and unconsciousness."

"The male I saw was tall, dark, and covered in fur," I said, "and he moved like Jylyj. I am convinced it was him. But if no Skartesh can endure water exposure, then . . ."

"He cannot be Skartesh," Reever said, finishing my thought.

My husband and I had already encountered one alterformed being on Vtaga. PyrsVar, a renegade Hsktskt male whose body had been altered to appear Jorenian, had been one such being. SrrokVar, one of Cherijo's old enemies, had alterformed the renegade as part of his plan to infect League worlds with the Vtagan plague.

I didn't want to believe that I had invited an alterform to join our expedition. "He would have had to submit a DNA sample in order to obtain a transfer from K-2 to Joren."

Reever nodded. "But as a doctor living among the Skartesh, he could have easily obtained a genuine DNA sample from one of their males and submitted it as his own."

I felt a little sick. "I should ask him if that is what he did."

"If Jylyj has been alterformed, it could not have been for any innocent reason," Reever said. "Confronting him is too dangerous."

"I agree, but as he is a member of the expedition, I would rather find out now than while we are in space." I picked up one of my medical scanners and turned it over in my hands. "If only I could perform a physical on him. I could say it is a requirement for everyone going on the expedition."

"That is not standard crew procedure, and he has worked on Joren for some time now. He will know you are lying." Reever took the scanner from me and set it aside. "We'll think of something else."

"Jylyj was off duty this morning, so he will be working the night shift at the medical facility," I said. "There are some patients I would like to see before we leave. I think I will go over there now."

Reever didn't like that. "What are you planning to do?"

"If I can obtain a sample of his DNA, that should confirm what he is." I glanced down as Jenner rubbed his head against my calf, and then leapt up onto my lap and butted his head against my chest.

"Whether he is Skartesh or not, you will have to have his cooperation to obtain a sample," my husband warned. "He will first want to know why you want it."

"True." I put the cat down on the floor, and looked at the stray silver hairs left on my trousers. "Unless I can collect the DNA from somewhere other than his person."

"Be careful." Reever handed me my blade harness. "For if you do not return in two hours, I will go to collect the Skartesh's DNA. With a blade."

Driving to the medical facility took only a few moments, and after signing in with the duty nurse at reception, I went up to the surgical floor. I didn't bother to announce myself, but made my way around the quiet, dimly lit ward, stopping here and there to read charts.

As I expected, Jylyj left the ward station as soon as he saw me and came to the berth where I stood.

"I was not aware you were on call, Jarn," he said, his voice low so as not to disturb the patient.

"I'm not. I couldn't sleep, and I know Squilyp is in the capital, so I thought I would stop in and check on the ward." I handed him the chart. "This female's bone scans look very good." I pulled up the linens covering the bonesetters clamped to her fractured legs, exposing her to the waist, but did not pull them back in place. "If her progress remains stable, she should be scheduled to begin physical therapy by the end of the week."

"I stated the same on the consult I sent to the physical therapist earlier this evening." He hung the chart on the end of the berth before re-draping the patient's limbs. "Is there anything else?"

"I saw you today down at Adalan Point as you came out of the water." I came around the berth and looked up at him. "Why did you ignore me when I called to you?"

"I don't know what you mean. I was not in any water." He didn't look guilty or angry, only bewildered. "My species cannot tolerate immersion of any kind."

"I saw a Skartesh male walking out of the water," I said. "To my knowledge, you are the only Skartesh, male or female, presently on Joren."

"I'm sorry, but it was not me," he replied. "I had a duty shift scheduled for tonight, so I spent most of the morning asleep in my bed."

I mimed a doubtful expression. "Then who did I see down there?"

"Perhaps no one," he said very tentatively. "Stress

combined with exhaustion sometimes causes visual hallucinations. Have you spoken to the Senior Healer about your insomnia? He'll be returning tomorrow, and he might prescribe a tranquilizer to help you rest."

His concern seemed so genuine that it nearly convinced me of his innocence. I did not have hallucinations, however. I also knew that an alterform would be trained to put on a superb performance, including how to justify any mistakes he made.

I would have to rely on what his DNA told me.

"Thank you for the advice. I will speak to Squilyp about it before we leave." I lifted my medical case. "While I am here, I would like to recharge my personal syrinpresses and requisition some additional equipment. Would you ask one of the nurses to meet me in the drug storage room?"

He nodded and went off to the nurses' station. I quickly pulled on a glove and retrieved the three long, dark brown hairs adhering to the strip of spray adhesive I had surreptitiously applied to the edge of the berth linens, and placed them in a small specimen container. By the time a nurse reported to me I had stowed the hairs in the bottom of my case.

Once I had recharged my syrinpresses with the standard medications a traveling physician carried, I asked the nurse to requisition a DNA scanner for me, and added that to my case.

My request did perplex the nurse, who asked, "Do you expect to do a great deal of genetic testing during your sojourn, Healer?"

"I doubt it, but I would rather be prepared than not." I glanced out at the nurses' station, where Jylyj was writ-

ing up patient orders. "The path is not the only thing
that changes."

I returned to our quarters and immediately removed
from my case the hairs I had collected from Jylyj to scan
them. Reever brought me a server of tea and watched
silently as the results appeared on the display.

"The DNA from his hair follicles is that of an adult
Skartesh male," I said, disappointed. "Either he really is
Skartesh, or a shape-shifter like Tya, who can manipulate his own DNA. Either way, he is not an alterform."
One unusual reading caught my eye—an elevated PH
level—and I scanned the hairs again, but this time for
minerals. "There are trace amounts of sodium chloride
on the outside of the follicle and the hair shaft."

"It could be salt residue from his sweat," Reever
suggested.

"Or from seawater." I went to the terminal and accessed the database. Like most furred beings, the
Skartesh did not sweat through their pores. "It is not
from sweat. Jylyj perspires only through his respiratory
tract."

Reever leaned over my shoulder and tapped the console, bringing up another section. "Skartesh also cleanse
themselves by applying dry sand to their pelts."

That confused me. "What has sand bathing to do with
salt residue?"

"In antiquity, this region was covered by seawater,"
he said. "I doubt you will find any soil on Torin land that
does not contain some trace of salt."

I hated it when my husband destroyed one of my theories. "So there is no valid reason to suspect that Jylyj
is anything but what he appears to be." I thought about

what the resident had suggested. "What if this has something to do with me instead of him? Could it have been some errant memory that made me imagine that I saw him in the water?"

"Neither I nor Cherijo had any contact with the Skartesh," Reever said. "The species were still living on their homeworld when she was serving on K-2. By the time they fled their planet, you were already on Akkabarr."

"Where I never saw a single Skartesh, either." I pressed the heels of my hands against my eyes. "Perhaps I did make a mistake, and saw someone else who resembled Jylyj. That would explain why the male did not respond to my call." But I had been so sure, and that still bothered me.

"Let it go for now." My husband reached over, switched off the terminal, and drew me to my feet. "Come to bed."

Thinking about the Skartesh kept me from sleeping well that night, but near dawn I finally drifted off from exhaustion. I woke alone, and found a message from Reever stating that he and Marel had gone on an outing to see the famous tiered gardens of HouseClan Varena, and would return later that day.

I suspected my husband had been aware of my restlessness and had taken our daughter out to allow me additional time to sleep. But I had no desire to return to bed or spend the day in idleness. Fortunately, Squilyp signaled soon after that to ask if I would work a few hours at the medical facility.

"The Adan have invited me to stay for another day,"

the Omorr explained, "and I won't return in time to make surgical rounds. Jylyj mentioned that you stopped in last night to look in on some of the patients, so I thought you wouldn't mind paying them another visit today."

I wondered exactly what the resident had said to the Senior Healer. "I have no objection, but your resident might."

Squilyp looked surprised. "Not at all. In fact, I assumed you and Duncan were off with Marel, so I wouldn't have signaled, if not for Jylyj's suggestion. He would rather have you than one of the on-call Jorenian healers." Humor glinted in his dark eyes. "I think you have made another conquest, Doctor."

I thought the exact opposite, but I wouldn't find out what Jylyj's motives were by hiding in my quarters. "I'll be there shortly."

This time I put a pistol belt as well as my blade harness under my tunic, and strapped my forearms with the twin sheaths I had worn on the battlefields on Akkabarr. Whatever Jylyj wanted from me, I intended to be prepared for the worst.

The Skartesh stood waiting outside the entrance to the surgical ward, as if watching for me, but greeted me in his usual reserved fashion and thanked me for replacing Squilyp. His voice sounded as tired as I felt, and the weight of the weapons concealed under my tunic dragged at me, as if to condemn me for my assumptions.

"We have two post-op patients just transferred from recovery," the resident said as we walked down the line of berths. "One male had a moderate reaction to the anesthesia and is not yet lucid. With your consent, we should start with his case."

Jorenians rarely had reactions to sedation, but when they did, they could become combative. "Have you put him in restraints?"

Jylyj nodded. "We had trouble shifting him to the berth. I had to use all the nurses to hold him in place while I strapped him down."

The patient in question, an enormous male with serious internal injuries from a transport mishap, was semiconscious and trying to move despite the restraints. As soon as he saw us, he began babbling nonsense and straining to lift himself away from the berth.

Much more of this and he would tear open his sutures. "Why didn't recovery administer neuroparalyzer?"

"They did," Jylyj said. "Three separate doses. It had no effect."

The only reason for that would be the presence of a counteragent. "Run a tox scan." I went over to the side of the berth and put my hand on the patient's brow. "ClanSon, you must be still now. You are only making your wounds worse by fighting."

The male stopped moving and stared up at me. "Who are you?"

"I am Healer Torin. This is Healer Jylyj."

The white eyes shifted from my face to the resident's and back again. "Where am I? What are you?"

I realized too late that my Terran features and Jylyj's Skartesh countenance would seem strange, even frightening, to a patient in his condition. "You are in House-Clan Torin's medical facility. We are the healers who are caring for you."

The male looked down at the scanner Jylyj was passing over his chest and fought wildly against the straps.

"ClanSon, you must be still," I began to tell him, but then one of his arms ripped free of the straps. I saw a huge blue fist coming at my face, turned quickly and took the blow on my shoulder. The force of the impact still sent me flying across the next berth and into a storage unit, which collapsed under me.

I winced, sitting up and reaching for whatever was stabbing into the back of my shoulder. I couldn't reach it, and my hand came away red with blood.

I looked over and saw that three nurses now surrounded the berth, holding down the patient while Jylyj reinforced the restraints and administered an infusion. By the time I staggered to my feet, the patient was unconscious.

Jylyj came to me and saw the blood on my tunic. "You are injured."

"Something's stuck in my back." Wet warm inched down my spine, and I felt the familiar dizziness that accompanied rapid blood loss. "I'll get a nurse to see to it. Check our patient for internal hemorrhaging. What knocked him out?"

"I don't know, but he's not bleeding inside. Jarn." Jylyj caught me as I sagged, and lifted me into his arms. He began issuing orders as he carried me into a procedure room.

I found myself facedown on a treatment table. "You don't have to do this," I told the resident. "A nurse can clean out the wound. Go take care of the patient."

"Must I put *you* in restraints?" He slit my tunic from hem to neck and pulled it aside. He didn't do or say anything for a moment, and then I felt blunt claws trace a strap of my blade harness. "Why are you armed?"

"I'm always armed." I lifted my head and tried to look over my shoulder. "What's making me bleed?"

"A piece of alloy. Hold still." Jylyj brought a suture tray over to the table and cut away more of my tunic, exposing my right shoulder.

"Don't give me a local; they have no effect on me." I felt impatient as he scanned the wound. "Whatever it is, just pull it out and repair the bleeders. It won't kill me."

"No, but it could paralyze you. One end has lodged close to your spine." Soft fur touched the back of my neck as he covered my face with a surgical drape. "You must not move when I am removing it."

"I won't." I gripped the edge of the table with both hands. "Do it."

He enabled a suture laser, then his fur brushed my skin. The thing in my back slid sideways, and I took in a sharp breath as pain slashed across my shoulders.

The extraction took only a few seconds, but it felt as if it took forever. My vision blurred, and I heard metal hitting a tray. The rawness of my wound turned scalding hot as Jylyj went to work with the suture laser.

"I've found three bleeders," he told me as he worked. "None of them are serious."

"Right." I gritted my teeth as the smell of my own flesh being cauterized filled my nose.

To Jylyj's credit, he worked very fast, pausing only to scan the wound for debris before he irrigated it, closed it, and began to apply a light dressing.

"I don't need that," I told him, lifting my head under the shroud. "Take this thing off my face."

"Something's wrong." Blunted claws curled over the back of my neck. "Stay where you are."

"It's no cause for alarm." I could feel the edges of the wound shrinking, and knew he was watching it happen. "I heal very fast."

"That would explain why one of the shallow bleeders repaired itself." The clamping hold he had on my neck eased, became almost gentle. At the same time, a deliciously warm sensation spread out over my back. "You're not Terran or Akkabarran. They don't heal like this."

"It's a long story." I didn't like the way my body was going limp. "What are you . . ." The rest was lost along with my consciousness.

When I opened my eyes some time later, I saw the ceiling of the procedure room. Jylyj had turned me over, removed the remains of my tunic, and draped me with a modesty shroud. I saw him hovering, and glanced down at the sponge he was using to clean the blood from my neck.

"How long was I out?"

Dark eyes met mine. "Only a few minutes. Reaction to the blood loss, I think." He used a folded square of linen to dry my throat. "How are you feeling?"

I moved my injured shoulder, which felt vaguely sore but otherwise normal. "Much better. Tell me you did not signal my husband."

"I did not signal your husband." He lifted me into a sitting position, and I slapped a hand against the drape to keep it from falling away from my breasts. That was when I realized what else he had removed.

I looked around the table. "Where are my blades?"

"I put them and the harness in the sanitizer." He brought me a scrub tunic. "They were covered in blood.

So were your pulse pistols, but I cannot clean those with this equipment."

"I will hand clean them later." I held the drape in place as I awkwardly worked the scrub top over my head. "What about the patient?"

The Skartesh removed the stained linens from the table. "He is resting comfortably."

I eyed him. "How did you manage that?"

"I infused him with karokain to neutralize the existing chemicals in his bloodstream." Jylyj helped me work my arms into the sleeves. "It seems prior to his accident, he was taking neuromuscular stimulants."

"He has Satala Varena Syndrome." Jorenians suffered from few diseases, but very active males in midlife sometimes developed a dysfunction of the nervous system that caused progressive deterioration of the muscles. "One of the drugs used to treat it is made from the primary counteragent for neuroparalyzer. Have you—"

"I have him on an oxygen feed and will keep him under close monitor," Jylyj said, answering my question before I could finish asking it. He rested one of his paws on my shoulder to steady me. "If his lungs begin to fail, we will intubate."

Being alone with the resident and the way he kept touching me made me feel uncomfortable, and I swung my legs over the side of the table. "He will need to resume his medication for the Satala as soon as possible."

"I have scheduled the appropriate dosage to be administered as soon as he stabilizes. Let me help you." He put his arm around my waist as I moved off the table, and frowned down at me. "I see some blood in your hair."

He used his claws to move aside some tangles. "Did you hit your head?"

"I don't think so." This close to the resident, I could smell his scent, which was as warm and soft as his fur. There was something about it that reminded me of the pungent herbs Reever sometimes used when he prepared food. I reached up to touch my scalp and feel for a wound.

"No." Jylyj caught my fingers and held them. "There is nothing there." He bent his head, bringing it closer to mine, and his breath touched my cheek. "The blood must have come from the shoulder wound."

I went still as I felt him stroking his claws through my hair. "Jylyj, I will brush out my hair after I cleanse."

He made a vague affirmative sound as he brought a length of my hair to his nose and breathed in. The paw he held against my abdomen spread and pressed against me.

"Doctor." I made my tone sharp and clear. "I'm fine now. I think we should go and complete rounds."

Jylyj raised his head to look into my eyes, and his teeth flashed. For a moment I thought he might try to bite me, until he removed his paws and stepped back.

"Yes. Of course." He turned away, his back muscles rigid. "I will join you after I finish cleaning up in here."

I left the procedure room and went to the post-op patient who had hit me. The nurse taking his vitals gave me a concerned look.

"Healer Jarn, are you well? We were worried—"

"I'm fine." I scanned the patient, but the readings only confirmed everything Jylyj had told me. If anything, the patient's condition had improved dramatically.

I didn't know what to think about what had happened between me and the resident in the procedure room. It reminded me too much of the time I had been abducted by PyrsVar on Vtaga. After taking me to his desert hideout, the alterformed Jorenian had made plain his intention to force me to become his mate.

What Jylyj had done was far more disturbing. He had behaved almost as if he didn't realize what he had been doing—or couldn't stop himself. Even more bewildering were my feelings of confusion and guilt. Had I done something to make him believe I would welcome such attentions from him?

PyrsVar had frightened me, but I had fought back and freed myself before he could force himself on me. I didn't know what to do about the resident. Reever and I shared the same passion for each other, so I welcomed his touch. Aside from dealing with PyrsVar's lust, I had no other experience with aroused males.

An Iisleg male could make use of almost any woman. The only reason I had not been used was because I had been taken in by the skela. Forbidden by tribal law to touch the living, the dead handlers were never used by the men of the tribes.

To my knowledge, hardly any ensleg males were permitted to freely make use of their females. According to Reever, Terran females had to give their consent before a male could couple with them, and some required marriage first. Jorenian customs were even stricter than that; they were obliged to pledge their lifelong loyalty and fidelity to one female before they were permitted to couple for the first time in their lives.

Jylyj had not behaved like any other ensleg male I

had met since living on Akkabarr. Still, after serving on Joren for so long, he had to know that he could not help himself to any female he desired. From what Darea had told me, rape was one of the rarest and most despised crimes on Joren. Males found forcing a woman to couple were not even given a hearing—they were immediately disemboweled.

I felt a sudden, compelling desire to get as far away from Jylyj as I could. "Who is the on-call healer for this shift?" I asked the nurse.

She checked her datapad. "It is Healer Atovea."

"Signal him and have him report to finish rounds with Resident Jylyj." I handed her the chart and walked quickly off the ward.

Once I returned to my quarters, I secured the door panel and stripped out of my garments. Reever could read my thoughts as easily as a display screen, and if I kept dwelling on the incident he would eventually discover what had happened. Whatever the resident had or had not meant to do to me, I had to stop thinking about it.

I spent the next hour in the cleanser, washing the blood out of my hair and Jylyj out of my thoughts.

Seven

The day of our departure from Joren arrived, and at dawn Reever and I reported to Torin Main Transport. We had kept Marel up late the night before, saving our farewells for when she went to sleep, and did not wake her to accompany us to the ship. After I told him about the nightmares she had been having, Reever thought it better that she not be there to see the ship launch.

"I know we have to do this, but I still feel as if I'm betraying her by leaving," I confessed as we walked to the lift to board the *Sunlace*. "Her dreams have convinced her that I won't return this time."

"This is not the first time she has had such dreams," Reever said. "For years after the Jado Massacre, she would wake in the night, crying and calling out your name. The nightmares didn't stop until I found you on Akkabarr."

We handed over our cases to the cargo master and entered the boarding lift. Reever held the gate open for a porter carrying a tall stack of slat-sided containers. The Jorenian thanked my husband, grimacing because he could not use his hands to make the usual polite gestures, and braced himself against the back of the lift.

I eyed the stack, which wobbled as the lift jerked into motion. I saw some *t'vessna* petals sticking through the slats, and Marel's voice rang in my ears.

In my dreams you're wearing your blades under your tunic, and there is a little purple flower in your hair. You hug me and kiss me good-bye, and then I never see you again.

I swallowed against my dry throat. "Duncan, why are they loading plants onto the ship?"

"The Jorenians prefer their native foods over synthetics, so the Torin bring a select amount of edibles on board the ship," Reever said. "On long sojourns, they even grow them."

I pointed. "They don't eat those."

"The *t'vessna* are kept in pots in the crew's quarters and common areas to improve the quality of the air. They are also the symbolic flower of HouseClan Torin." Reever looked up and moved quickly to catch the top container as it tipped over and fell from the stack. Some of the contents spilled out and were blown off the lift by the strong morning breeze.

"No," the porter groaned. "That was all the *t'vessna*. There is no time to collect more." He made an archaic gesture. "This is an ill omen for your journey."

I glanced over the side to see the cascading shower of purple blossoms drift down on the head of the bewildered cargo master. "I'm afraid I cannot agree."

At the entrance to the lower docking bay, a smiling duty officer gave us official permission to board the *Sun-*

lace. Reever helped the porter with his burden, and then turned to say something to me.

When he only gave me an odd look, I asked, "What is it? Did you forget something important?"

"Yes." He pulled me into his arms and tilted my head up, burying his hands in my hair as he kissed me soundly.

"Oh." I grinned. "That was quite important."

He slipped one hand into his tunic pocket. "I am meeting Qonja at the survey lab to recheck the storage units. Why don't you come with me?"

"I should look in on medical first." I saw the concern in his eyes and lowered my voice. "I know you're worried, and the first hours apart from her are always the most difficult for me. But I won't change my mind or jump off the ship. I promise."

"Good." He bent to kiss me again, this time on my brow. "Signal if you need me."

Squilyp had personally supervised preparing the medical bay for the sojourn, and left it in such a state of pristine perfection that I had nothing to do until the rest of the medical staff arrived. I went next to the quarters assigned to me and Reever and unpacked our cases, but that didn't take very long, as neither of us carried much in the way of possessions.

I did set a framed image of our daughter on the table beside our sleeping platform, and spent a moment examining her sweet face.

"As soon as we come back," I told the picture, "we are going to make a home for the three of us. You, me, and Daddy."

Reever and I had left the pavilion without bothering with a meal. I still had no appetite, but to stay busy I prepared a light meal for the men, packed it up in some food containers, and carried it down to the survey lab.

I entered the lab's open door panel and looked around. Nalek had installed a massive amount of equipment, most of which I didn't recognize. I saw my husband and Qonja standing inside a large, seven-sided plas chamber built in one corner; Reever appeared to be mounting a very large specimen container on a console of some sort.

"Duncan? I've brought you two some food." Then I saw the glittering dark column inside the specimen container, and quickly put down the containers. "Why do you have that black crystal in there?"

"It's the specimen we collected from the impact crater on Trellus. We need to study it, and use it for comparison with any new deposits we might find." Reever came out of the chamber through a narrow gap between the plas panels, and after Qonja did the same, a shimmering wall of energy filled the aperture. "We have already discovered some of its properties. The crystal may look solid, but according to our scans it is actually part solid, part plasmoid, and part liquid. There is also a fourth, as yet unclassified, form of matter in the crystal's core."

"How can it be all those things and still look like a shiny rock?" I asked.

"For some matter, existence in a variety of states is possible," he told me. "Water becomes a gas at temperatures above one hundred degrees Celsius, a liquid between zero and one hundred degrees Celsius, and a solid below zero degrees Celsius. If you drop ice into a server of steaming-hot water, you can observe it in all three states."

I eyed the lethal mineral. "*That* is not made of water."

"No. While gases, liquids, and solids are the three most common states, there are several others that we have classified, and another hundred or so that have been proven theoretically possible. Matter in dimensional shift, for example, is temporarily converted into a trimorphous solid by the phased energy that moves it from one reality to another." He nodded toward the chamber. "I believe a similar factor is affecting the crystal's physical state."

I didn't care what it was doing; I wanted it off the ship. "What if it gets out of there?"

My husband shook his head. "Drefan provided the container. It's made of etched crystal, and once sealed it cannot be reopened."

I realized I was staring at the crystal and quickly averted my gaze. "You are putting a great deal of faith in a container, Duncan. That crystal is lethal. Even looking at the light it reflects can be dangerous. You can't keep it out in the open."

"The container's shielding prevents any light refraction," Qonja told me, "and if it should fail, the drone response system Nalek Kalea installed will immediately engage. The dimensional grating responds to any spatial distribution of matter."

I turned to my husband. "Explain this in words I can understand."

"The chamber is under constant monitor by a failsafe program. If the crystal's container breaks or is opened, the failsafe takes immediate action to remove it from the ship." He gestured to various parts of the chamber as he spoke. "A probe programmed to fly into the nearest star will enclose the crystal and its container as soon as the breach is detected. The probe will then be ejected from the ship through the chamber's airlock."

"We hardly know anything about the crystal or its properties, except that it controls, maims, and kills any living being that comes in contact with it," I reminded him. "What if something goes wrong with your failsafe and the crystal contaminates the ship? How can we protect the crew?"

"Nalek designed this chamber with a buffer modified to remain in perpetual energy shift," Reever told me. "It will remain engaged for the entire sojourn. Even if the failsafe measures don't work, the crystal cannot escape the chamber."

I still didn't like having it on board. "As soon as we're finished with the survey, I want that specimen dropped into the nearest star."

"I have no desire to begin a collection," my husband assured me as he removed a disk from his tunic pocket and turned away from me. At the same time, something fluttered to the floor, and I bent down to retrieve it.

As I straightened, I closed my hand over it and said, "I have to report to medical. Excuse me."

Only when I was outside in the corridor did I open my hand and stare at what had fallen out of Reever's pocket. It had been crushed by a strong hand, but I recognized it. Several containers of the same had fallen from the lift that morning, just before my husband had taken me in his arms and kissed me.

I remembered the odd look, the feel of his hands in

my hair as he kissed me, and went to the nearest disposal unit.

In my dreams you're wearing your blades under your tunic, and there is a little purple flower in your hair.

I dropped the mashed thing in the intake receptacle and switched it on.

You hug me and kiss me good-bye, and then I never see you again.

Once the disposal had reduced the remains of the *t'vessna* flower to an organic mush, I vented the unit's contents into space.

An hour later, when the entire crew had reported for duty, I held a brief meeting in medical to introduce myself and become acquainted with my new staff. Squilyp had given me a full complement of experienced nurses, three interns, and an orthopedic resident in her second year. Jylyj, however, was the most experienced physician on staff, and with some misgivings I designated him as the Supervising Healer, which gave him the right to act as Senior Healer whenever I was off duty or not on board the ship.

"Unless the sojourn requires us to do otherwise, we will work standard three-shift rotations," I told my staff. "As we have no patients at present, your first assignment is to run diagnostic checks on all of the equipment. I know Senior Healer Squilyp likely had you do that before we left Joren"—I noted the wry smiles all around—"but the stress of launching and transitioning has been known to cause random equipment malfunctions. We don't want to assume everything is working; we want to be certain of it. Do you have any questions?"

One nurse lifted her hand in a polite gesture. When

I nodded to her, she said, "Very little information on the oKiaf is available from our database, Healer Jarn. Is there a comparable species we can study in order to better prepare for the jaunt down to the planet?"

"The Skartesh and the oKiaf possess nearly identical physiologies," Jylyj said, startling me. "You may access my medical records, or request data from Kevarzangia Two. The physicians at the colony's free clinic have treated thousands of Skartesh refugees."

I didn't know whether to admire or suspect the Skartesh for recommending the medical staff contact K-2 for more information on his species while making his own records available to them. He either had nothing to hide or had hidden the truth so well he presumed they would never discover it.

Before I could comment on his generosity, a voice from the bay com panel announced that the ship would be transitioning in five minutes.

Like my former self, I had trouble staying conscious during the interdimensional jumps the Jorenians used to shorten the length of their sojourns. I ended the meeting and asked a nurse to accompany me to one of the isolation rooms, where I occupied a berth and had her restrain me.

Jylyj appeared and looked down at me. "What are you doing?"

"Sparing myself some bruises." At his blank look, I added, "I often lose consciousness during ship transitions. This spares the crew much of the trouble involved with reviving me."

"Have you ever determined why you faint during transition?" he asked, taking out a scanner.

"Squilyp and I have both tried, to no avail. The Omorr

thinks it has something to do with my brain chemistry." I frowned as he initiated a cerebral scan. "We have not yet transitioned, so that is useless."

"The technology the Jorenians use for transitioning first releases a modified phase-energy pulse to create a dimensional aperture." He switched on a pen light and checked my pupils. "You may be sensitive to the effects of the pulse."

I blinked. "No one else faints or sees the ship turn into a swirl of color."

"No being undergoing a dimensional transformation preserves its sense of spatial relation." He spoke absently as he scrolled through the scan.

"I read no signs of injury or infection, and yet your white-cell count is elevated." He scanned me a second time. "It is still increasing."

"My immune system has been enhanced to respond more aggressively than the average Terran's." I felt the vibration of the *Sunlace*'s engines growing stronger, and closed my eyes as I braced myself. "Whatever happens, don't code me."

I felt Jylyj bending over me a moment before the sickening slam of the ship's transition took over my senses and sent them into overload. My stomach dropped as the unpleasant sensations of reality bending and twisting around me grew unbearable. I felt something else—a touch on my face—before the stress and nausea rendered me unconscious.

When I next awoke, I still felt the vibrations of the engines, although now they were subsiding. The Skartesh no longer stood beside the berth, but had been replaced by one of the senior nurses.

She flinched with surprise when I asked her to release the restraints. "Your pardon, Healer Jarn. We were told you would likely remain unconscious for several hours."

My brow felt very warm, and my stomach clenched slightly with a remnant nausea that vanished as soon as the nurse released me and I sat up. "How long has it been?"

She glanced at her wristcom. "Three minutes, forty seconds since the ship completed transition."

I had been healing faster than my former self; perhaps I was adjusting to transition better. I got up, walking slowly until I felt sure I had regained my equilibrium, and then washed the sweat from my face at the scrub unit. As I used a linen to dry myself, I remembered Jylyj's comment about my white-cell count and performed a quick blood scan. All of my counts read at normal levels.

White cells did not vanish in a few minutes; once created by the body they remained present and active in the bloodstream for days. Either the Skartesh had made a mistake or he had lied to me.

I glanced around the room and asked the nurse, "Where is the scanner that Healer Jylyj used on me?" She handed it to me, and I checked it for the last set of readings.

The display showed nothing. The unit's memory core had been erased.

The *Sunlace*'s interdimensional jump had moved the ship from Joren to a region just outside the Saraced system located on the opposite side of the quadrant. It would take another three days' travel to reach oKiaf space, where we would hopefully make contact with the local authorities and obtain permission to conduct a survey on-planet.

I used the time to work with the staff in medical and prepare the supplies needed for the jaunt to the planet.

Hawk proved invaluable to me as he spoke of tribal medical practices and made suggestions on how the survey team should dress and conduct themselves around the oKiaf. I conducted several meetings with the rest of the staff, during which I had him relate what he knew of tribal medicine.

"In most primitive societies, healing the sick and injured among the tribe is performed by a single male or female who serves as the group's shaman," Hawk explained during one such meeting. "The oKiaf have been exposed to advanced technology, so it is unlikely their healers have remained dependent on native treatments and religious rituals. Yet these will still be important to the people, and may be incorporated with what technology they continue to use."

Herea, the second-year intern, grimaced. "Without detailed knowledge of their rituals and homeopathic medicines, anything we do is likely to offend them."

"Their exposure to offworld practices has probably resulted in a degree of tolerance that other primitives with no outside contact would not offer," Hawk assured her. "The important thing to remember is to go slowly and carefully with them, and always be respectful of non-harmful practices. Casting fragments of bone next to patients or painting their bodies with native pigments may seem pointless to you, but such healing rituals are often tightly bound to the tribe's belief systems and sense of identity. As such, they give reassurance, and can even have a positive effect on the patient's recovery time."

I discovered the Skartesh had very stringent restrictions on the circumstances under which their healers—like the Iisleg before the rebellion, always male—could treat female patients. They required certain preparations to preserve the female's modesty, and never completed their work without the female's mate or a male family member present.

Jylyj also provided some helpful information by relating the observations he had made during his visits to oKia.

"It is the practice of each member of the tribe to care for their own minor injuries or illnesses," he said. "They expect privacy for this and will not allow you to treat them."

"So, in essence, every oKiaf is a healer." I thought about this. "What if they are too ill or badly injured to care for themselves?"

"If their condition is more serious or they are rendered incapacitated by it, the chieftain will summon an alleviator," the resident said. "He treats the incapacitated tribesman until they have recovered enough to take over from him."

"Is this alleviator a trained physician?" I asked.

"Not exactly," the Skartesh said. He spoke slowly now, as if choosing his words more carefully. "He has some skill with healing, but his primary purpose is to provide practical care until such time as the patient improves enough to care for himself."

"Does every tribe have an alleviator?" Hawk asked.

Jylyj shook his head. "The alleviator who treated the tribe I visited also served ten other tribes."

Although the resident sounded as if he knew what he was talking about, I had the sense that he wasn't being entirely truthful. "How are such males chosen?"

"I cannot say." He avoided my gaze.

I had not confronted Jylyj about what had happened during transition or the readings he had deleted from the scanner, but I had been keeping him under close watch.

The Skartesh preferred to work with the male staff, that much was obvious, but to the female staff he remained courteous and cooperative. Off duty he stayed in his quarters and rarely ventured out. I never saw him making use of the recreational areas or sharing a meal with others in the crew galley where most of the Jorenians congregated.

In fact, the only times I saw Jylyj voluntarily interact with others were at the medical staff meetings or in the bay during shift change. He proved to be an effective supervisor who ran medical as efficiently as Squilyp, and made a point to personally ensure that all of the daily tasks assigned to his subordinates were completed properly and on time.

To keep the staff from growing bored, and to give myself something to do, I conducted several trauma and surgical simulations in the environomes. The preset programs, which had been designed by Squilyp and based on actual emergencies that had occurred in the past, simulated everything from single operations to full-scale disasters.

One morning, after Herea and I were finishing a complicated spine injury case, one of the nurses signaled to indicate a real patient had reported to medical with compound fractures of the radius due to an accidental fall.

"This one is yours, so go and perform the initial assessment," I told Herea. "I will join you as soon as I clear and reset the program."

Pleased to be placed in charge of the case, the intern started for the nearest lift, but then she stopped and turned to me. "Healers at my level are required to be supervised at all times by a licensed practitioner."

"You just restored function to all six of this training torso's limbs," I pointed out. "You know what you are doing. Unless you want me to hover over you while you examine the patient?" She made a swift negative gesture. "Then what are you waiting for? Go. Be a doctor."

She grinned and hurried off.

Squilyp would have been scandalized by such an obvious violation of the rules, but I thought ensleg medical practice too often focused on protocols and not enough on the needs of the patient. Herea was the most sensible and coolheaded of the healers I had been assigned; she had repeatedly demonstrated a natural gift for diagnosing and treating all manner of skeletal disorders and injuries.

"The Senior Healer rarely uses the Tingalean torso for training purposes," a male voice said from behind me. "Their spine cases are among the most difficult of the reptilian species to treat and repair."

"I cannot see the sense of practice if it is not difficult." I looked over my shoulder at Jylyj. "You finished your shift only an hour ago. You should be sleeping."

"I was interested to see how the intern performed during the simulation," he admitted. "I watched you both from the observation alcove." He came to the training torso and examined the repairs Herea and I had made. "Interesting choices. Somewhat risky, as well. I would have started at the fourth lumbar and removed the bone fragment lodged in the wall of the left lung."

"Relieving the compression injury at the primary vertebrae restored circulation to the rest of the spine, and preserved the greatest degree of limb function." I gestured toward the monitors. "Had the patient shown any signs of respiratory distress, I would have attended to repairing the lung."

"That is not standard procedure," he said. "Being able to walk is not as important as being able to breathe."

"You should check the database for cases of Tingalean paralysis," I advised him. "You will find that the post-op infection rate triples, and most die within the first year from complications related to immobility. Being able to walk, at least for Tingaleans, is what keeps them breathing."

His expression became skeptical. "How often do you think a Jorenian healer like Herea will operate on a Tingalean patient?"

"Now that the war is over and travel restrictions have been lifted, Herea may choose to join the crew of a House-Clan exploration vessel. Tingaleans and several other reptilian species often serve on Jorenian ships." Belatedly, I recalled that a reptilian species—the Hsktskt—had destroyed his homeworld during the war. "If you have some personal objection to treating coldbloods, you should make it known to the Senior Healer when we return."

"I was called to healing from birth. I knew what it would be when I answered." He came to stand behind me. "You were born to it. You know what it is to look upon a wounded enemy and only see their pain and suffering. You operated on that female with the grenade in her belly, knowing that she was sent to kill you."

Was my ClanBrother trying to use the resident to gain my confidence? "Who told you such a thing?"

"I read the case file and did some research on the ordnance." He shifted closer. "Given the facts, it was the logical conclusion."

"You are mistaken." He stood too close to me now; I could feel his breath on the back on my neck. "Am I blocking your view?" Before he could answer, I stepped aside and went around the training torso, putting the surgical table between us.

Jylyj braced his paws on the edge of the projectors, causing part of the holographic torso to disappear. "You do not care for me."

Did he expect me to confirm or deny it? "I don't know you."

"They talk about you, the Jorenians. Some think you are cold because you were stranded on that ice world too long." His dark eyes remained locked on my face. "I should tell them how foolish they are not to see beyond the mask you wear. But that would require me to discard my own."

I didn't like knowing the staff discussed me in my absence, any more than his tale carrying. "Be careful, Skartesh. You do not know me at all."

"I think I do, better than most. And you have sensed it from the day we met." He straightened. "When you tire of this charade, *sadelenne*, come to me. I will show you everything you deny yourself."

In that moment, I at last understood. This was not about female subjugation or prejudice. Jylyj desired me. I knew nothing of Skartesh mating practices, but to pretend I did not know what he was about might be in his eyes a kind of encouragement. Although I would probably offend him deeply, I had to make my feelings plain, right now.

"I will never come to you. I love my husband, and there is no other for me." I switched off the simulation projectors. "Excuse me."

I did not look back as I left the environome, but by the time I reached medical I felt as if I had run all the way there.

The encounter with Jylyj left me feeling uncomfortable and somewhat at odds with myself. I said nothing about it to Reever, and kept the Skartesh out of my thoughts whenever we were together. I had never tried to actively hide anything from Reever—to attempt to do so when he could read my thoughts whenever he liked was pure idiocy—but I worried that he would misconstrue what had happened.

Nothing had happened. Nothing would.

Knowing that Jylyj desired me also heightened my awareness of him, and I sometimes caught myself watching him or looking for him. That was the reason I discovered the strange fascination the Lok-Teel had with the Skartesh.

Like the rest of the staff, Jylyj made regular use of the Lok-Teel to clean the decks and equipment in medical. The sentient mold, first discovered on Catopsa by my former self, lived on any sort of unwanted organic waste and excreted an astringent antiseptic substance that cleaned whatever surface it touched, making it an almost perfect housekeeper. The specimen Cherijo had brought from the slave depot had reproduced prolifically, creating enough offspring to provide dozens of little helpers for every Jorenian medical facility and star vessel that desired them.

The mold was cooperative, even friendly in its own way, so everyone liked it. The Lok-Teel, however, had never shown a preference for any of us—or so I assumed until the evening I saw five of them scurrying along the corridor to join another ten waiting outside Jylyj's quarters.

Instinctively, I held back and watched, as I knew from the hour that the Skartesh would soon be exiting his quarters to report for his shift. After a few minutes the panel opened and he emerged, stopping as he saw the Lok-Teel waiting for him.

Jylyj did not kick them aside or step on them, but looked down until they seemed to sense they were blocking his path and drew back out of his way. He then walked down the corridor toward medical, and the fifteen Lok-Teel followed him.

I did the same, taking care to hang back so that I could observe this oddity without giving away my presence. At the entrance to medical, Jylyj gave the secured entrance his voice print to gain access, but stood to one side as the panel opened. Only after all fifteen of the Lok-Teel following him passed over the threshold did he go inside.

"That is a very enigmatic expression you wear," Qonja said as he joined me. "What do you out here?"

"Have you ever noticed the Lok-Teel following anyone?" I asked him.

He shook his head. "To be truthful, I rarely notice the Lok-Teel, much less what they do. Whom have you seen them following?"

"The Skartesh, Jylyj," I said. "He seems to attract them."

"Naturally. They love eating his fur." Qonja grinned at the surprised glance I gave him. "Have you never noticed how much he sheds? He is like your cats that way."

"Those small beasts are not mine." I had not seen a single dark hair in medical or anywhere Jylyj went, however, so what Qonja said explained their behavior. "How goes the work in the survey lab?"

"Your bondmate is a relentless taskmaster, especially with himself. I think he means to discover everything about the black crystal before we reach oKia." He paused, and then asked, "How does Hawk in medical?"

"When I am not working him relentlessly, he's been teaching all of us a great deal of what to expect with the oKiaf." I noted the relief that passed over Qonja's face. "No one has treated your Chosen with anything but friendship and respect."

"That is because there are no Adan on the *Sunlace*." His mouth took on a bitter twist. "Would that I had been born to the House of Torin."

"Reever is meeting me for the evening meal interval," I told him. "Would you walk with me there?"

As we made our way to the galley, I told Qonja a little of what it had been like leaving Akkabarr behind.

"I disliked the ways of the Iisleg, especially in how they treated females, so I felt eager to leave them behind. Then I found myself surrounded by you Jorenians, and your smiles and laughter and friendliness. And the touching." I grimaced. "All you people do is touch. It is as if you cannot keep your twelve fingers to yourselves."

That startled a laugh out of him. "I suppose we do."

"In my eyes, all of you were too loud, too boisterous, and far too familiar. You did nothing properly. By the end of my first week on the *Sunlace*, I became convinced that I had made a terrible mistake, casting my fortunes in with what had to be the most annoying, insufferable ensleg species in existence." I waited for his laughter to end, and added, "You terrified me."

His mirth subsided. "We are nothing like the Iisleg, but why would we frighten you?"

"I disliked my people, but I knew their ways. Even while I was made to live as an outcast among them, the skela followed the customs and practices they had brought with them from their iiskar. With your people, I was welcomed and made free, but I never knew what next to expect." I halted outside the galley. "You and Hawk can return to Joren and find a way to live among your people. Your bond may forever make you an outcast among them, but you know what to expect from them. Out here, among those who are your ensleg, it will be different. Perhaps you will find them annoying and even aggravating. But among them, you will be free."

He sighed. "That is the truth of it."

"I will tell you a secret." I leaned close and lowered my voice. "Every time I think of returning to Akkabarr, and everything known to me, I imagine Marel growing to womanhood there, and the desire dies at once. For they would do to her what was done to me. When you miss Joren, when you think of the Adan, imagine what they could do to Hawk."

He nodded slowly, and made an elaborate gesture of gratitude before he glanced into the galley. "Reever is not here yet. That is strange. He told me before I left the lab that he was meeting you in a few minutes."

I used my wristcom to signal my husband, but there was no response. I went to the wall panel and requested Reever's location.

"He's still in the lab." I frowned. "He never forgets to meet me."

The first time my husband had seen the black crystal on Trellus, the dangerous refractive qualities had mesmerized him and nearly caused him to walk into a crater. Despite the assurances both Reever and Qonja had made about how well the crystal was guarded, I didn't like my husband being left alone with it.

I used the wall panel to signal the terminal in the lab. "Duncan? Please respond."

"Jarn," his voice said at last, although some sort of static crackled over the sound of it. "Would you signal Qonja and ask him to come back to the lab? I'm having trouble with the com units."

A deep, resonant vibration accompanying the static interference made my ears ache, but Qonja didn't seem to react.

"What trouble?" I waited for a reply, but the resonant static increased, blocking out the sound of Reever's voice before the relay terminated. "Did you hear that, beneath the static? That thrumming sound?"

"I cannot say that I did." Qonja touched my forearm. "I will go. I am sure it is only an equipment malfunction."

Just as I had the feeling it wasn't. "I'll come with you."

I didn't hear the resonant sound again until Qonja and I entered the survey lab. There we found Reever on his back under the main control panel. I rushed over, only to stop as my husband's hand appeared and groped for a tool from the repair kit sitting beside the console.

I knelt down. "What do you need?"

"The smallest impact wrench." When I placed it in his hand, he took it and said, "Thank you. What are you doing here? I thought you were working an extra shift."

"No, I left at shift change and went with Qonja to the galley to meet you." I frowned. "Why did you think that I was working late?"

"That is what I was told when I signaled medical to tell you I would be delayed." He hammered on something, and then eased out from under the console and stood.

"I will check with the staff to see who wishes to overwork me." The thrumming sound made my ears itch. "What is making that noise?"

Reever stood up and turned to me. "What noise?"

"Never mind. Qonja couldn't hear it, either." I glanced at the plas-sided chamber, and the black crystal in its shielded specimen container. Although the opaque housing muted its dark glitter, its presence still made me feel uneasy. It looked larger, too, which alarmed me. "Is that thing growing?"

"It cannot," Qonja assured me. "The interior of the chamber is a vacuum that is kept at absolute zero."

"It looks bigger to me." I turned to my husband. "Have you the means to measure the size of it?"

"I can run a comparison scan, but it is as Qonja says. There is nothing it can use to add to its matrix and expand its dimensions." He switched on the console and tapped a few controls.

I walked closer to the chamber and studied the crystal from all angles. Although the men didn't hear the resonant sound, and the crystal hung motionless in its vacuum, I felt convinced that it was responsible for the sonic interference.

"You are correct, Wife." Reever said, his voice tight. "The crystal's matrix has increased in size. It is growing."

Eight

"This cannot be." Qonja went to the console to examine the readings. "There must be an error in the original readings."

"The atoms in the crystal matrix are active," Reever said. "They are vibrating about their equilibrium positions with amplitudes comparable to low-temperature plasma phasing."

The Jorenian muttered something under his breath. "That sort of thermal agitation is not possible, not at absolute zero."

"It is bigger than it was," I put in, "so it has to be doing something."

"It may be displacive restructuring," Qonja said. "Stable silica has a rhombohedral structure in low-temperature form. Heat it above five hundred seventy-three degrees Celsius, and the atoms interconvert into hexagonal symmetry." He saw my blank look, and explained, "That would mean it is changing shape because of the temperature, not growing."

"I would agree, but we still haven't identified the interatomic forces responsible for the black crystal's cohesion and stability," my husband said. "Until we do, we cannot assume it is restructuring."

"We can if we look at the cause instead of the effect," Qonja insisted. "Shifts in temperature and pressure are the most common factors involved in an enantiotropic polymorphic transformation. We have placed the black crystal in a zero vacuum. It is not unreasonable or unusual to observe a structural response to the change in environment."

Reever shook his head. "Its atoms are neither ionic nor covalent. They're not intercompositional, and don't resemble any known matrix. It may look like a crystal, but I assure you, it is something else entirely."

I left them to debate their theories and drew closer to the plas chamber. The impact crater we discovered on Trellus had been solidly paved with black crystal, I recalled. Trellus was a dead, frozen, airless rock of a planet; nothing could live on its surface without protection. I had assumed that the crystal in the crater had been deposited there, carried by some ancient meteor that had slammed into the surface.

What if it had not landed, but instead had *grown* there?

I turned around to face the men. "How fast is it growing?"

Qonja consulted the console. "According to the scans, its matrix increases one millimeter every thirty hours."

I did some calculations. "If it continues to grow at this rate, it will breach the specimen container in ten days. Do you agree?" He nodded reluctantly. "Duncan, can you enable this failsafe of yours manually?"

"We have an override," he said. "Before you tell me

to eject it from the ship, I want you to think about something. We have never observed the crystal in a state of change. This may be the only opportunity we have to do so under controlled conditions, and what we learn could help us combat the threat it poses to all life."

"Your controlled conditions will be useless in a few days." I knew he was right, but I didn't have to like it. "It will have to be closely watched, Duncan, in the event this restructuring or growth or whatever it is becomes more rapid. You and Qonja cannot do that by yourselves."

"I'll ask the captain to assign a security officer to the lab during our off-duty hours." He came to stand with me and held my hand. "Thank you."

"You are welcome." I tugged him toward the console. "Now show me how to engage the manual override. I want to know exactly how to feed this wretched thing to the stars."

We arrived on the edge of oKia's solar system and assumed a stationary position, from which Xonea planned to send a remote signal requesting permission to enter oKiaf space. Reever and I joined him in communications in the event the authorities needed more information about the nature of the expedition.

My ClanBrother never had the chance to send the signal, for an alert came from the command center indicating that the *Sunlace* had been intercepted by two well-armed patrol vessels.

"This does not bode well," Xonea said as we relocated to command. "Duncan, were you able to locate one of your allies in the area?"

My husband nodded. "Last night. Uorwlan should be arriving shortly to meet us."

Xonea took the helm and studied the scans of the patrol vessels. "Both of these ships are scout-class vessels, but they're outfitted like attack strafers. They're also carrying drop mines and have large cryotanks attached to both sides of the fuselage."

"Drop mines are only used for short-range air-to-surface bombardment," I said. "Why would they use them out here?"

"To blow large holes in a vessel," Reever said. "Once they breached the hull, they'd drop the cryotanks inside and trigger them to flood the ship."

I knew of only one species whose troop carriers would be susceptible to such a bizarre attack. "They're armed to fight League and Hsktskt invasion forces. But why? Peace has been declared."

"Declared by the Hsktskt and the League," Reever amended. "The oKiaf obviously think otherwise." He turned to Xonea. "If they have stopped using League technology, they may no longer use signal translators. Without direct contact with the oKiaf, my ability to interpret will be limited."

"We already have a native interpreter," Xonea said, nodding toward Jylyj, who at some point had come into command and now stood to one side.

Xonea sent a standard greeting to the patrol ships, adding a phrase in universal at the end they could easily understand. One of them responded almost immediately, but thankfully used a translation-enabled signal.

"This is Sentinel Wilnas of oKia," the patrol commander said. "You have entered restricted flight space. State your reasons for doing so."

The image of a pilot appeared on the console display. For a moment the face seemed so familiar I thought it Jylyj, until I noticed the lighter fur color and longer, narrower features. The eyes, too, appeared different; with light-colored irises containing a central oblong pupil. Colorful polished beads and small pieces of carved wood hung from the pilot's intricately woven mane, through which many streaks of white hair were scattered.

The pilot wore a flight suit, but this, too, had been altered in unique ways. What appeared to be a length of spotted skin had been sewn to the shoulders; gleaming dark green and brown stone beads had been arranged on the stiff collar in what I guessed was his rank insignia.

"I am Captain Xonea Torin from Joren. My crew and I are conducting geological surveys of inhabited planets in this region. We collect data only and intend no harm or intrusion."

As Xonea gave the oKiaf official a carefully worded version of the truth, I noted that he didn't mention me or Reever, which I thought a prudent decision. The oKiaf might have been able to keep offworlder ships out of their space, but offworld signals had to be detected before they could be jammed. If they didn't care to have contact with outsiders, they probably wouldn't hesitate to hand two of them over to a bounty hunter.

After Xonea had finished explaining our mission, Sentinel Wilnas did not respond. Xonea didn't seem troubled by this.

"A patrol officer has only a limited amount of authority under specific conditions," he said. "We are not

League, and we are not here to conduct trade or deliver passengers. Our mission does not require us to come in direct contact with the oKiaf. He is likely signaling his command to request new orders."

"If we detect black crystal on their planet," I said, "I will need to examine some of the natives."

"We will do as much as they will permit, Jarn." Xonea turned back to the console as a new signal came over the channel.

"Captain Torin, you will take your vessel to these coordinates," Wilnas said, and relayed the data. "When you reach the security station there, dock at the off-loading bay. There your ship will be boarded, and you will be questioned."

"Why do they want that?" Xonea murmured, and then signaled back with, "Sentinel, I am happy to answer any questions you have now."

No reply came over the channel, and a moment later the patrol ship terminated the relay.

Xonea eyed the display. "This could be a ploy to capture us."

"They will not fire on you unless you ignore an order or attack them," Jylyj said. "They prefer to avoid violence with offworlders."

"Then why have they enabled their weapons?" Xonea countered.

Jylyj glanced at the display. "The oKiaf avoid violence, Captain, but from outsiders they have come to expect it. They are preparing for the worst."

"If reporting to this security station is standard procedure," my husband said, "Uorwlan will confirm it."

My ClanBrother nodded. "Send a signal to the trader.

Do not encrypt it; they will be monitoring everything we do, and we do not want to appear secretive."

Reever went to the com officer's console and sent the signal. The trader responded soon after that.

"The oKiaf maintain security stations at four points along their system grid," Uorwlan said. "All ships entering the system are required to first dock at the nearest station for inspection. You needn't be concerned about it, old friend. They will ask a lot of questions and inspect every part of the ship, but they wish only to see for themselves if you are telling the truth."

The signal was audio only, so I couldn't see the trader's face, but the voice sounded soft and beguiling, as if they were discussing something far more personal and intimate.

"How long before you reach us?" Reever asked the trader.

"We've had some engine problems, so we won't be there until tomorrow." Uorwlan said something else in a language that the ship's translator did not recognize, and then terminated the relay.

"What did that last part mean?" Xonea wanted to know.

Reever gave him a bland look. "Nothing but a farewell."

Xonea was almost convinced by Uorwlan's reassurances, but still performed a remote scan of the security station. The results showed it to be an artificial satellite, three times the size of the *Sunlace*, with an array of powerful defensive weaponry, ten docking bays, and a small fleet of patrol vessels.

"It seems an excessive amount of security to guard

a planet of primitives," Xonea said as he contemplated the scans.

"In the past both the League and the Faction have occupied this system," Reever said, "and Skart was destroyed by the Hsktskt. If that happened in your solar system, how open would you keep your borders?"

My ClanBrother's expression darkened. "I wouldn't bother to board or question unexpected arrivals." He looked at my husband. "This trader's information, you are sure it is reliable?"

Reever nodded. "I freed Uorwlan and a dozen other Takgiba from slavery. She is bound to me by a life debt. She would not lie or lead us into a trap."

She. So this Uorwlan was female, knew my husband well, and owed him her life. Already I didn't like her. Still, what Reever had done in the past was of little concern to me, and the life debt practically guaranteed the Takgiba's loyalty.

"I agree with Duncan," I told Xonea. "We should go to the station."

The two patrol ships escorted the *Sunlace* to the oKiaf station, where Xonea performed another remote scan before maneuvering alongside the dock. Only when our engines were powered down did the patrol ships depart.

Reever and I accompanied Xonea to meet the boarding party. The oKiaf sent a group of ten armed security officers along with four station supervisors to inspect the ship. At the boarding platform airlock, Jylyj pulled me aside.

"oKiaf females are not permitted to serve in the defense forces or leave the homeworld," he said. "Males are not accustomed to dealing with women in official capacities, and your presence here may cause discomfort."

I shrugged. "I rarely make anyone feel comfortable."

"Know that the males will not address you directly, and they will be offended if you speak to them," he warned. "They may even ask that you be removed. If that happens, do not object. It is not personal."

"An Iisleg female who does not obey a male is usually beaten, often until she dies," I told him. "I think I will tolerate being sent from the room."

After arranging crew escorts for the oKiaf security detachment to take them around the ship, Xonea invited the station supervisors into a nearby conference room.

Reever sat on my right, and Jylyj on my left. The resident drew almost as much attention as my husband and I did, and was the first person the oKiaf in charge of the boarding party spoke to.

"I had not expected to meet one of those lost to us," Colonel Pegreas said to Jylyj. He ducked his nose down and twisted his head to the right and left before raising his eyes. "You are very welcome here, brother."

The resident bowed his head in a similar fashion. "This son of Rushan is grateful to have made the journey, Colonel."

"We have heard your people have endured much living among the outsiders." Pegreas spared Reever a dark glance. "It is hoped that you are being treated fairly by these outsiders."

"I am." Jylyj touched the front of his tunic. "They have provided work, shelter, and kinship. I have no complaints, but much praise for their kindness to me."

Pegreas seemed to relax a little. "What of your people, Brother?"

"The faithful were briefly deceived by false prophets, but were saved by allies on K-2," Jylyj told him. "The sons of Rushan could not remain on the colony there, but the aquatics offered sanctuary on one of their moons."

"So it is true. We had heard rumors, of course, but given the nature of that world ..." Pegreas shook his shaggy head, causing some of the beads woven in his silver mane to clink together. "Is that why you have come to dwell with these strangers? To escape that wet horror?"

"I have answered my calling," Jylyj said flatly. "That is all you need know."

The colonel seemed a little taken aback by the resident's tone, and for a moment I thought Jylyj had offended him. But Pegreas recovered quickly and inclined his head.

"As you speak, Brother, so I hear." He turned to give Xonea a far less friendly look. "We have had some limited but favorable contact with Jorenians in the past. Your people also broke with the League before the war. Those are the only reasons I permitted you to come here."

"We are grateful for your consideration, Colonel," Xonea said. "Our mission is an important one, and the data we collect here may save many lives on other worlds."

Pegreas didn't seem impressed. "You mission means nothing to the oKiaf. We no longer concern ourselves with what happens outside our borders."

"If this black crystal has infected any of the worlds

in your system, it will poison your species and possibly cause mass extinction in the future," Xonea said. "I would think that to be of great concern to the oKiaf."

"How do we know you are not attempting to mine the crystal for use by the Allied League as a weapon?" Salanas, one of the other supervisors, demanded. A smaller, darker male, he had sharp teeth and eyes so light and cold they seemed made of alloy.

Xonea kept his tone calm and reasonable. "Our ship is not equipped as an ore hauler, and we have no treaty with the League."

"Your people have served on their ships." Salanas gestured toward me and Reever. "You even brought two of them with you."

"You are mistaken," Xonea said. "Jarn and Duncan are citizens of Joren, not the League." He turned to Pegreas. "You have had contact with our people. You must know that we have never been warmongers or invaders. One of our ClanLeaders, Teulon Jado, negotiated the terms of peace that ended the war between the League and the Hsktskt."

"After the League massacred his kin and sold him to slavers," Pegreas replied, evidently unmoved. "While Joren is famous for its neutrality, we know that the Jorenians have never been a particularly forgiving people. How do you explain the Jado's actions?"

Salanas sniffed. "They smell to me of cowardice."

Xonea's eyes narrowed, but it was Jylyj who said, "Perhaps you have had your nose buried too long in your own affairs."

Salanas's expression turned to one of astonishment, and again Pegreas gave the resident a startled look.

"I am Jarn of Akkabarr, and I served the Iisleg as a battlefield surgeon during the rebellion," I said before the oKiaf could respond or anyone could stop me. "Raktar Teulon was my general."

"There," Salanas said, making a rude gesture toward me. "He favors females. Is that not indicative of his own character?"

"When our rebels prevailed over the Toskald, Teulon had the means to wipe out their civilization and send thousands of ships against the League and the Hsktskt armies," I told the supervisor. "He set aside the revenge he wanted—and surely deserved—and sought instead to bring peace to all the worlds involved in the conflict." I regarded Salanas. "*That*, Supervisor, took more courage than you could possibly understand."

"You see?" Salanas turned to Pegreas. "They use females to speak for them. She even questions my intelligence. Is this not proof enough of their perversions?"

"I don't care if females have no voice among your people, Colonel," I told Pegreas. "I will not hear my general being slandered by your officer and remain silent. His ignorance needs correction."

As Jylyj had predicted, the oKiaf colonel didn't care for me addressing him any more than Salanas had; the pelt around his skinny muzzle drew into a faint snarl. But as he looked into my eyes, his expression eased.

"The honor and actions of Teulon Jado will not be questioned by the oKiaf." He said the words while looking at Xonea, but they were meant for me. "Supervisor Salanas will keep his opinions to himself."

Salanas opened his mouth as if to argue, saw Pegreas's cold eyes, and fell silent.

"What has happened to oKia?" Jylyj asked, sounding impatient now. "The war is over. You have no valid reason to close the borders and repel outsiders now."

"We lost more than Skart and your people to the war," Pegreas said. "When the Hsktskt invaded, they raided our cities and killed thousands. We drove them out, but not before they leveled Hafila, Matuk, and Asani."

Jylyj went rigid. "They attacked the Elphi?"

"Indeed. They murdered the Highest One and every member of his tribe before the eyes of the people, hoping to instill fear and submission to their will."

The Skartesh sighed. "Fools." He glanced at the rest of us. "The Elphi is the elected leader of the oKiaf people. If he is harmed or killed by anyone, his chieftains swear blood vengeance. It is a death vow, and cannot be revoked until vengeance is taken."

"Our chieftains summoned the tribes from the valleys and the mountains, from the ice lands and the forests. We surrounded the beasts and we slaughtered them until they ran to their ships and fled oKia." Pegreas paused as if to savor the memory. "After our world was free of the invaders, the chieftains did not elect a new Elphi. They led the people back into the wilderness, where we could fight on our terms. But the beasts, cowards that they are, never returned, and so it was decided that the people should remain one with the land."

"You abandoned all of your cities to live in hiding?" Xonea sounded perplexed.

"We were not hiding, Jorenian." Salanas bared his teeth. "We did that in the cities, in the structures built by the League, smothered by their cursed technology. When we returned to the land, we rediscovered the freedom we had sacrificed. We took back what we had lost."

"You must not have abandoned everything," Reever said. "Or you would not be manning these security stations or flying patrols around your system."

"My men and I volunteered to live on the stations and maintain constant patrols in order to protect the tribes," the colonel said. "So we have, since the end of the war."

Jylyj gave Pegreas an odd look. "None of you have ever returned to the homeworld? Why?"

Pegreas pulled up his sleeve and showed a clean-shaven place on his forearm with burn scar tissue that formed a three-sided symbol. To the rest of us, he said, "We are the last of the Elphian guard. As we once dedicated our lives to guarding the Elphi, so we now live here in space to watch over oKia."

Xonea glanced at the viewport. "I would think you could do that just as well on the planet."

The colonel replaced his sleeve. "When we left the League, they sent spies to our world to infiltrate the people. When we caught them, they claimed they meant to stop our 'cultural regression' by persuading our chieftains to return to the cities and take up their ways. But what they truly wished was to convince our young men to again serve in their militia."

"It's said that the oKiaf were some of the best intelligence officers in the League," Reever said.

"We were, and our resignation from the League did not sit well with them. They infiltrated our homeworld and made a nuisance of themselves again and again, until it became apparent stronger measures had to be taken," Pegreas continued. "We Elphian took charge. We had the League spies send for supply vessels with the materials we needed to build the security stations. They gladly gave us all the patrol ships we requested, thinking that we would in turn hand over our men. They were quite surprised when we finished the preparations and sent them to Quadrant command with orders to stay out of our space."

"We burned our words into their cringing back hides, so there could be no further misunderstanding." Salanas uttered a rough sound of sour amusement. "Even so, they still sent more."

"They kept coming until we destroyed the three of their ships." Pegreas didn't sound especially happy or remorseful, only matter-of-fact. "In the end, that was the only message they understood."

"We have no desire to meddle with your people or your politics," Xonea said. "Our mission is to perform orbital and surface scans to detect the presence or absence of black crystal. Given the tasks at hand, we have no reason to engage in contact with the oKiaf, although my medical staff would appreciate the chance to scan the natives for crystal contamination."

"You can scan me if you must," Salanas snapped.

"Supervisor, your offer is appreciated," Reever said, "but by your own admission you have not resided on the planet for some years, and there are no signs of the crystal on board this station."

Pegreas seemed to be thinking it over. "How many do you wish to send to the surface?"

"We can keep the survey team small in number."

Xonea watched the older male's face. "Colonel, I give you my word, we will respect any restrictions you impose on my ship and crew."

"I will allow five to go down to the planet by the end of this day," the colonel said at last. "You must dress in native garments and take only a small amount of equipment, which will be first inspected by my security officers. You may remain there for three or four days. At the end of that time, you will return to your ship and leave our space."

That was not nearly enough time, and I was about to say so when I felt Jylyj touch the back of my hand. I glanced at him, and he shook his head slightly.

A security officer came in and briefly conferred with Pegreas in a low voice before leaving again.

"My men have finished inspecting the ship," the colonel said. "You appear to be everything you say that you are. Nevertheless, the ship will remain here, at the station. You will permit a security detachment to stay on board and monitor your crew's activities as long as your survey team is on the planet."

Xonea stood and made a formal gesture of acceptance. "We thank you, Colonel."

I managed to wait until the supervisors left the conference room before I confronted my ClanBrother. "How are we to conduct a thorough planetary survey in just three days, with one team on the planet and the *Sunlace* kept under guard here?"

"I would suggest you do it quickly," Xonea said, his mouth hitching.

"What they said does not make sense." I rubbed the back of my neck. "Why prohibit all offworlders from visiting oKia if their dispute is with only members of the League?"

"The League frequently uses alterforms to infiltrate hostile or dangerous species," Jylyj said, startling me. "Doubtless they have encountered them in the past."

"Pegreas will not let us near oKia unless we accept his conditions," Reever said. "I suggest we do so. Xonea, scan as much of the surface as you can from here. I'll take a remote transceiver down to the planet and contact Uorwlan from there. The oKiaf trust her and her crew; perhaps she can help us negotiate for better terms and more time."

"Captain, with your permission, I will go and speak alone with Colonel Pegreas," Jylyj said. "He is sympathetic to my people, and I may be able to ease some of his fears."

Xonea nodded. "Do what you can, but do it swiftly. If I have judged the length of their days correctly, the survey team must leave for oKia in four hours."

Nine

I went with Reever to the survey lab to retrieve the equipment we would need on the planet and to check the black crystal. Qonja was waiting for us, and for once had a little good news—or so I thought at first.

"The growth rate of the matrix has decreased dramatically over the last hour," the Jorenian told us. "The amount of fluid in the center inclusion has tripled, and the surfaces are showing distinct flaws. It's almost as if entering oKiaf space has in some way damaged it."

I went over to the plas chamber with Reever. The crystal no longer glittered, but looked old and cracked. The hollow space in the center of the shaft had bubbled outward toward the crystal's surfaces, and the cloudy liquid inside seemed to be moving in a sluggish swirl.

Reever scanned the container. "The atomic structure is losing cohesion."

"Hydrated silicates contain water in channel intersections," Qonja said. "The fluid is only minimally bound in the crystal matrix and can be leeched from it through interstices. Perhaps it is the same with the black crystal."

"Such water inclusions don't destroy the structure of the crystal when they are expelled or replaced," Reever said. "The black crystal is not acting like a zeolite molecular sieve." He gave it a thoughtful look. "It may be cannibalizing itself."

"What would make it do that?" As far as I knew, nothing had changed except the position of the ship. "Are we being exposed to some form of radiation unique to this part of space?"

"None that registered on our sensor arrays," Qonja answered. "If the deterioration continues, in a few days all that will be in that container is a puddle of black sludge."

I saw Reever frown, and asked Qonja if he would go and help Jylyj and Hawk prepare for the jaunt down to the planet. When we were alone, I touched my husband's arm. "What is it?"

"I don't think it's degenerating," he said slowly. "This change has all the signs of a thermal disturbance, but there is no heat source; no vibration to cause the rotational motion of the liquid."

I thought of the resonant sound I had heard that no one else could detect. "What if the disturbance is a high-frequency signal or sound wave of some sort?"

"Even if we couldn't hear it, it would still register on our equipment. I did check when you said you heard that sound, but it was not detected at all by the monitors." He set aside the scanner and brought me over to the console, where he pulled up a set of scans showing the crystal as it had been. "I made these scans yesterday, when the crystal was still increasing in size. The readings indicated the inclusion fluid was composed of a plasmoid substance that contained no known elements."

"A liquid made of nothing?" It didn't seem possible.

"Here are the readings from the scan I just made now." He downloaded the data from the portable scanner and put them up on the display beside the old readings. "The liquid now shows a growing concentration of the black crystal's atoms. But they are not binding to each other. They're floating in a suspended state. That's why the liquid appears clouded."

I studied the two images. "So it is as Qonja says, and the crystal is deteriorating from the inside."

"We know the crystals can survive extreme pressures, temperatures, and radiation exposures, or they wouldn't be able to travel through space. What if the crystals are more like the seed pods or spores of a botanical lifeform? They may be able to remain dormant for long periods of time—millennia, perhaps—until the conditions are right for them to awaken and germinate. Then the crystal breaks itself down into individual atoms. Atoms that can grow like seeds."

"But why now?" I glanced out the viewport at the blackness of space. "Nothing has changed on the ship. You haven't warmed the container or tried to stimulate the crystal, have you?"

"No, but we've just entered a solar system with an inhabited world." Reever met my astonished gaze. "Jarn, I don't think traveling into oKiaf space has damaged the crystal. I think proximity to oKia has caused it to germinate."

I shook my head. "If that were true, then bringing the

crystal to Joren would have done the same thing. It did not change while you kept it on the *Moonfire*."

"Not if the awakening process takes a significant amount of time. Bringing it to Joren may have only started the process." He came and looked out at the brown-green planet the ship was approaching. "Or there is something on oKia that is stimulating it that was not present on Joren."

That could be a hundred thousand different things, from the gravitational field around the planet to the radiant energy emanating from its sun. "If it is . . . germinating, as you say, and all of those atoms will grow and become new crystals, how long can we hope to keep it contained?"

He returned to the console and checked the readings. "The process will be completed in seven days."

"We should destroy it now." I thought of how suspicious the oKiaf had been. "The oKiaf will be monitoring everything we do, won't they?"

My husband nodded. "If we attempt to destroy it here, they may misconstrue our actions, especially if they retrieve the probe before it can fly into their sun."

If Pegreas retrieved the probe, he would surely open it. "We should never have brought it on the ship."

"I promise you," Reever said, "as soon as we leave the system, I will destroy it."

"If you don't, I will." I couldn't stand to look at the deadly thing another moment. "I'll meet you down in launch bay."

On my way to medical, I encountered Herea, whose cheerful face wore an uncharacteristic scowl.

"Healer Jarn," she said, making a quick gesture of

greeting. "Is it true that the captain is not permitting any females to go to the surface?"

"No, for I am going," I said. "The oKiaf have only allowed us to send a team of five. Were there room for more, I would have you with us."

"It still does not seem fair that the Skartesh and that crossbreed are permitted to go." She gave me a guilty look. "Your pardon, Healer. I mean no disrespect. It is just that . . . this is my first sojourn away from the homeworld. I am very disappointed."

"Jylyj is the only member of the crew who has already visited this world," I told her. "I would take you and leave Hawk behind, but I need an experienced healer to run things here while we are gone." I put my hand on her shoulder. "Should anything go wrong and the oKiaf patrols attack the *Sunlace*, I am depending on you to keep the crew alive. You have reviewed your trauma protocols, have you not?"

"Five times." She hesitated, and then asked, "Think you they would attack us?"

"They are very suspicious, heavily armed males who already don't like us being here, and they have attacked other vessels in the past." I gave her a grim smile. "Should they try anything, I have no doubt the captain will respond in kind. Such battles often result in many casualties among the crew. You may have your hands full."

"We will see to their needs." She stood a little straighter. "I am honored by your trust in me, Healer."

I accompanied Herea back to medical, and took a few minutes with her to brief the nursing staff. Rather than issue orders, I instructed the nurses to follow Herea's instructions, and turned the briefing over to her.

Before I left, I leaned close to the intern and murmured, "You may do as you wish, but I would advise you have them run trauma drills while we are gone. It will keep them alert and well prepared for any real casualties. That, and it allows you to shout at them now and then, something I've always found helpful in stressful situations."

Herea nodded, her eyes glowing with amusement, and then turned back to continue the briefing.

I went to find Jylyj and Hawk, who were in the supply room. They had packed as many field supplies as could fit in the small cases we were being permitted to carry down to oKia; Qonja was just finishing rigging each case with shoulder straps.

As Qonja and Jylyj left to load the rest of our supplies on the glidecart, I went through one pack, squeezed in a few small hazardous-specimen containers, and then tested the weight of it by slinging it onto my back. "Good. We should be able to carry these without difficulty." I glanced at Hawk's wings. "With the exception of those of us who can fly."

Hawk grinned and showed me the waist and arm straps affixed to his pack. "I told Qonja to use a front sling, but he thinks I will not be able to take off from the ground with it hanging from my neck."

"You didn't have a problem snatching me off the shockball field, and I weigh more than that pack." I reached under my tunic to adjust my blade harness, and then saw Hawk's face. "Forgive me, I'll do this in private."

"No, it's not that." He gave me a searching look. "You remembered."

"Remembered what?"

"The day I took you from the field."

"It was the first time I ever saw you fly." My belly tightened, and then I understood his reaction. "No. Forgive me, I misspoke. It was the first time Cherijo saw you fly. You and I did not meet until some years later."

Hawk didn't let it go. "Jarn, can you see that day in your memory?"

I could, although I didn't want to admit it. Then I seemed to slip into a trance. "It was very bright. There were people, so many people, screaming at me. I stood on strange grass and held a silver sphere, the shockball, between my hands. It had been rigged to kill Duncan." I looked up at him. "By my brother."

He nodded slowly.

"You jumped from the top of the place, and your wings ripped your garment apart, and you flew down to me." I pressed a hand against my head, which now felt as if I were whirling around in a fast circle. "I think I'm going to be sick."

Hawk grabbed me to keep me from falling, and helped me over to the disposal unit. He supported me with one arm and held my hair back as I vomited. When I had emptied my belly, he wiped my face clean. "I will call for Herea."

"No." I took the cloth from him and wiped the tears from my eyes before I blew my nose. "Duncan saw it from the field. He gave me the memory of it. That is how I know." I took a deep breath and forced a smile. "Sometimes it is difficult to think of myself as two people. Forgive me, Hawk."

"Don't apologize." He seemed afraid of me now.

"Jarn, are you sure you should go on this jaunt? No one would object if you chose to stay behind and rest."

"Do you know what Cherijo would say to that?" My smile twisted. "I do. She wrote it in her journals: 'I can rest when I'm dead.' This, when she knew she was made so that she might live forever."

"I think she knew she would not. Perhaps that was why she fought so hard to save the lives of others." Hawk touched my cheek. "As you do. None of us know how much time we have left. Does Duncan know about these shared memories?"

"No." I felt stricken. "Hawk, please don't tell Duncan about this. Not now."

"I won't, if you will agree to tell him when the expedition is over." I nodded quickly. "One more thing." Hawk removed one of his bead necklaces and hung it around my neck. "Wear this for me."

"It is beautiful." I looked at the small, gray-blue stones, and saw streaks of other colors glimmering in them.

"The beads are made of Terran moonstone," Hawk said. "My grandfather believed the gods cast them down to earth whenever it rained, to remind us that we cannot have rainbows without a storm." He picked up our packs. "Now come. The others are waiting for us."

I tucked the beads under the collar of my tunic, where the cool weight of them lay against my aching heart.

The Elphian did not allow us to take one of the *Sunlace*'s launches to the planet, but flew us there on a station shuttle. The vessel had been built to transport more cargo than passengers, but our seats allowed us to see a little through one small viewport beside the loading platform panel.

"I was able to persuade Colonel Pegreas to take us to one of the more populated lands in the eastern mountain region," Jylyj said. "We may interact with the natives, as long as we do not interfere with them."

"I would like a definition of *interference*," Reever said.

"With the exception of medical scanners, we are not to use any of our devices or equipment in their presence. We are not to talk about politics, other species, worlds, or cultures. And while we are on the planet, we are subject to and must obey tribal law."

"We don't know what tribal law is," I pointed out.

"I have some knowledge of it," the Skartesh said. "The most restrictions will be placed on you, Healer Jarn. As a female, you must not directly address any male unless he has first spoken to you. Nor can you examine any male without me attending. It should also be made clear immediately that you belong to Linguist Reever."

I rolled my eyes. "So it will be like Akkabarr, without the beatings and the ice."

"Oh, there are plenty of snow and ice in the mountain regions," Jylyj assured me. "This is their summer season, however, so the daylight temperatures should remain tolerable."

"It seems pointless for Pegreas to have given these instructions," Qonja said, "for he has no way to know what we do on the planet."

"I believe he will," the Skartesh replied. "Not all of the surviving Elphian left the planet. They live among the tribes, and no doubt will be keeping close watch on our activities."

"There it is," I said, seeing the rim of the planet appear in the viewport.

oKia's surface was a swirling mottle of dark red, green, and brown, liberally salted with white patches indicating snow-covered areas. As we grew closer, I noted the rough, uneven ranges of mountains, some of which extended the length of the planet.

"No oceans," Qonja murmured. "Is there any water on the surface?"

"oKia has many lakes, primarily in the valley regions," Jylyj said. "They are forbidden areas and the people do not dwell near them."

"Are the oKiaf as hydrophobic as the Skartesh?" I asked.

"They share a similar aversion, but for different reasons. The ancient tribes believed they came from water, and used to sink the bodies of their dead in the lakes to return them to their birthplace. The oKiaf now bury their dead, but the lakes are still considered sacred." His gaze became shuttered. "The oKiaf do not swim, so when a member of the tribe chooses to end his life, he often jumps from a cliff into a lake and drowns himself."

The station shuttle easily traversed the upper atmosphere, and when the distorting streaks of heat outside dissipated, I saw a conglomeration of linear shapes and roads that comprised one of their cities. The lower we descended, the bigger and more detailed the city grew. The total absence of people, lights, and movement within the structures made it seem ugly and empty; little more than a neat pile of containers discarded by an uncaring hand. I thought the roads and passages between the buildings were made of white stone, until we dropped enough for me to see that they were blocked by snowdrifts, some as tall as the building rooftops.

As soon as we entered the lower atmosphere, the shuttle pilot flew away from the city and up into the mountain range beyond it. There he chased a line of peaks, weaving in and out of the tallest before he slowed and used the com to tell us to prepare for landing.

"My orders are to leave your team near the Parrak erchepel," the pilot said. "Theirs is one of the oldest settlements in the region, and their chieftain, Dnoc, once served as a city administrator. He will deal fairly with you."

I glanced at Jylyj. Such generosity seemed odd, especially after Pegreas and his men had shown such hostility and resistance toward us. What had the Skartesh done to convince the Elphian supervisor to make so many concessions?

The station shuttle landed on a wide, flat plateau that sloped down an incline to a series of terraced stone shelves that reminded me of the steps leading up to the main hall at HouseClan Torin's pavilion. The shuttle pilot engaged the cabin's biodecon controls, effectively decontaminating all of us before he opened the hull doors.

Dry, cold air immediately swept in to fill the cabin. My cheeks and nose chilled, my eyes teared, and still I could have groaned with pleasure. As lovely as the warm, perfumed air of Joren was, I had missed the cold.

Jylyj stopped each of us to check the native garments and footgear we had changed into before boarding the shuttle. He adjusted the belt of twisted strips of hide that cinched in the waist of my long shirt, moving the knotted ends to rest on my hip.

"You should take down your hair," he suggested. "It will make you look more like the women of the tribe."

"The wind out there will knot it more tightly that this belt." I sighed and removed the clip, and then remembered how I had once woven the heavy length into cables. That would keep it from becoming tangled. "Are oKiaf females permitted to braid their hair?"

"They are, although you should wear it in a single braid." He tugged on one strand in a teasing fashion. "Wearing two means that you seek a mate."

I looked into his dark eyes and saw nothing playful there. He stood too close now, and when I glanced down I saw him winding a piece of my hair around his claws.

This had to stop. "I have a mate," I told him, and tugged my hair free.

"I will braid it for you," my husband said, stepping between us. "Jylyj, Hawk needs assistance with his leggings."

I watched the Skartesh reluctantly move away, and saw Reever's eyes had turned dark. "What is it?"

He leaned close as if he meant to kiss my cheek, and said in a low voice, "I don't like the way he looks at you, or touches you."

An ensleg female would have likely taken offense, but I only felt relief. "Neither do I. I am trying to discourage his interest. Perhaps you can assist me with that."

Reever nodded and glanced over at the other members of the team before moving around me and lifting my hair with his hands. Deftly, he divided it into three parts. "I would rather be alone with you to do this."

Duncan's fascination with my hair and his love of grooming me had become an integral part of our intimate times, and I smiled to myself. "Someone will have to unbraid it later."

My husband wove a loose braid before tying it off at the end. As he adjusted the back of my collar, his fingers touched the necklace of beads Hawk had given to me to wear. "This is one of Hawk's prayer necklaces."

"He gave it to me to wear for good luck," I said, uneasy now. "I could not refuse such a gift from a friend."

"No, you cannot." Reever took my arm. "Stay close to me, Jarn. I don't want you out of my reach while we are on this world."

I had no intention of straying far from his side, but the harsh note in his voice made me look up at him. "Don't worry, *Osepeke*. Everything will go well."

It was only after we left the shuttle that I wondered what sort of prayer went along with Hawk's necklace.

Following the directions relayed to us by the shuttle pilot, we left the plateau and walked down the stepped incline until we reached a crude path winding out of sight among a thicket of trees. I had seen trees before, both on Joren and in the images from some of the stories Reever downloaded to Marel's reading pad, but these did not resemble any of those.

Each tree had exposed root systems that rose from the dark red soil and formed precise right angles to the trunks, of which there were a minimum of three for each tree. The trunks themselves soared high above our heads, where they divided and spread out in formed branches covered with bunches of thick, dark purple leaves and long, oval seed pods.

"These are heartwood," Jylyj said, touching one of

the trunks. "The tribes use them for kiafta supports and to sustain the cooking fires. They burn very slowly."

On Akkabarr we burned methane in our heatarcs, so the thought of setting a tree on fire seemed bizarre to me. "What are kiafta?"

"Temporary shelters the oKiaf dwell in on the land." Jylyj sniffed the air and pointed toward the path. "The erchepel lies in that direction, on the other side of the thicket. I will go ahead and present myself to the men on watch." He trotted along the path until he disappeared into the trees.

We followed the path at a more sedate pace, keeping alert as we made our way through the thicket. In addition to the heartwood trees, I saw many other types of plant life, from orange and green pools of frilled spikes to dense thatches of pale green shoots, the ends of which were adorned with cup-shaped blooms filled like servers with green liquid.

Reever tried to name some of them for me, but even he stopped and stared at one plant, a single wide pad of blue from which sprouted hundreds of tiny white berries. He scanned the berries before picking one and sniffing it.

"What does this remind you of?" he asked, holding it to my nose.

I breathed in. The scent of the berry was unexpectedly dark and rich, and reminded me of my favorite Terran beverage. "Coffee."

"According to my readings, they're safe for us to consume. If they taste as good as they smell, we should be able to steep them." He gathered several handfuls and placed them in the pouch he wore on his belt.

The heartwood trees thinned, and then we passed through the last of them and into an open clearing. I stopped as soon as I saw Jylyj on his knees in front of two native males. He held his paws behind his back and his head bowed, which alarmed me until one of the males spotted us and said something.

Jylyj rose, turned, and walked back to us. "They have sent for the chieftain, who is out hunting," he said as soon as he had rejoined us. "Until he arrives, we will be taken to a place of safety."

"We are not in any danger, are we?" Qonja asked, reaching unconsciously for Hawk's hand.

"They are concerned with the tribe's safety, not ours," Jylyj explained. "We will not be badly treated, but no one will speak to us until the chieftain gives his consent."

I didn't like the idea of being herded off somewhere and held prisoner, but Pegreas had made it clear we were to follow tribal laws. This might even be some form of test, to see if we would.

"Leave your packs here," Jylyj said as we started toward the men. "We can carry nothing into the erchepel yet."

"Some of the instruments in my pack can kill if used in ignorance," I said. "Will they be searching through them?"

"No. They won't be touched." He gave me a sharp look. "Remember to keep your eyes down, and do not try to talk to any of the men."

If Jylyj meant to intimidate me, he failed. I was not afraid of this place. For the first time since the end of the rebellion—no, since coming to consciousness on the blood-stained ice—I did not feel strange, clumsy, or wrong. Everything made sense, from the scent of the air to the shifting of the soil under my feet. I drank in the colors of the sky, the sound of the wind. When Reever brewed the white berries he had found, I knew they would be more delicious than any coffee on Terra. For here on this world that I had never seen, among people who were not my kind, everything around me put me at ease.

I felt as if I had finally come home.

Ten

The two men on watch split apart to flank us on both sides. Both carried hunting and skinning blades hanging tucked into series of loops sewn along the upper sleeves of their garments, which, like those the Elphian had given us, were made of soft, cured animal hide. Each also held a spearlike weapon with a pronged end carved of wood. Embedded in the twin shafts of the prong end were dozens of blackened, sharp-looking thorns.

Although the design of it was unfamiliar to me, the sturdy fashioning of the weapon and the wide space between the prongs made sense. Its primary use was likely to pin down something and hold it in place while the tribesmen used their long, sharp claws for the kill. If thrust like a blade into a body, the prongs would inflict two deep, penetrating wounds, while the barbed thorns would inflict even more damage as the weapon was jerked free.

The tribe came out of their shelters and many light eyes watched us as we were marched over to one side of the settlement. I found it difficult to keep my head down and avoid eye contact, especially with all the attention we were drawing, so I tried instead to look at the objects in the camp. The tribe's kiafta, made of enormous purple-and-gray-striped hides stretched over a framework of poles, numbered in the hundreds. The tall, oblong shelters did not stand alone, but had been built in groups of three with covered, open-sided lattices leading to and from each shelter. Airy-looking twists of pink and gold vines grew on the lattices, but instead of flowers sprouted large, dark red globes with smooth hulls.

Intricate native symbols had been somehow carved into the darker strips of the shelter hides in long columns; as I passed close to one such hide I saw the symbols were actually carefully denuded spaces in the short, dense hair of the hide.

"What do the symbols mean?" I murmured to Jylyj.

"I don't know," he whispered back. "I cannot read their language."

In the center of the encampment stones had been stacked in a sprawling spiral, in the center of which a well-tended fire blazed. Embers lined each of the spirals curving away from the center, and stone pots hung from simple frames steepled over the coals. Thin, pale pink smoke rose from the burning heartwood, and colored the cold air with the faintly sharp but not unpleasant scent of hot resin.

I couldn't see what the tribeswomen tending the pots were cooking, but I saw one of them toss a handful of dried stalks into a pot and stir them into the contents.

Our guards stopped at an area marked off from the rest of the encampment by rows of dark stones, and enclosed by a three-sided lattice covered with the pink and green vines. A plain hide with the center cut away covered the area. I saw the reason for the hole when I spied the small fire that had been built beneath it. Around the fire were large, hide-covered, flat stones that appeared to be seats of some sort.

"This is where we are to wait for the chieftain," Jylyj said. "Remain here. As your scout, I have to first inspect it to ensure that it is suitable."

I watched the Skartesh as he walked inside the structure and made a circle around the fire. He knelt and sniffed at the ground several times, and then straightened and looked above at the interior of the hide. Only then did he gesture for us to join him.

I didn't have to look at the tribesmen to see their approval. Obviously, these rituals were important to them, and by observing them Jylyj showed both knowledge and respect.

The fire kept the interior space quite warm despite the open-sided lattices. Acting on instinct, I waited for the men to sit down around the fire before I joined my husband.

"Put your hand on the top of her head," Jylyj said to Reever. "It shows approval and possession."

Duncan stroked the crown of my hair. "I could become used to this."

"So could I." I resisted the urge to cuddle up against him, and glanced at the Skartesh. "How long do you think we'll be kept here?"

"The men on watch sent runners for the chieftain. Hunting parties never go farther than a two-hour run." He glanced up through the smoke hole to study the sky. "They should return by midday."

I noticed Hawk kept looking back at the encampment through the entrance to the enclosure, his expression intensely curious. "Are the people here like the Native American tribes on Terra?" I asked him.

"As some of them were in ancient times, yes," he said. "The tribe lives literally off the land, in harmony with nature. The animals they hunt feed the people, while their hides make shelters and clothing." He turned to Jylyj. "They do not cut down the trees for firewood, do they?"

The Skartesh shook his head. "It is against custom to harm living trees, so the firemakers take only fallen or dead trees, and cure them in seasoning racks. The custom is practical, too, as fresh heartwood doesn't burn very well."

Hawk nodded thoughtfully. "Tribal customs usually come about as a response to some aspect of the environment. The ancient Hebrews on Terra had very strict laws forbidding the consumption of certain meats. Centuries later, scientists discovered that parasites dangerous to humans commonly infected the prohibited animals."

The sound of a polite cough distracted me, and I watched a tribeswoman enter the enclosure. She moved in a curious hunched fashion, holding her head down and cradling a basket of food against her belly. She tentatively approached us, set down the basket, and drew back. Her light green eyes met mine for a moment before she turned and left as quietly as she came.

Jylyj picked up the basket and examined the contents.

"Journey food," he said, picking through the oddly shaped items. "It's commonly the first meal offered to those who have crossed great distances. They know we have come a long way to be here."

"How can they assume that? From our appearance?" Qonja asked.

"Likely they have an Elphian watcher in the erche-pel." He offered the basket to Reever. "It's safe to eat," he added when my husband hesitated.

"Until our scanners are returned, Jarn and I will use our rations." Reever passed the basket to Hawk without taking anything from it.

Hawk and Qonja both sampled some of the oKiaf journey food, and seemed to enjoy it, although the Jore-nian pronounced it very rich and filling.

"It must be very high in calories and nutrients," the Jorenian said, examining one of the blue globes from the basket. "I thought the oKiaf were mainly hunters. Do they grow this?"

"There are some tribes who travel to planting grounds in the warm season and cultivate quick-growing crops, but most of the people rely on hunting. The women are skilled gatherers, however, and have many ways to preserve foods. They often keep the tribe from growing hungry during the long winters when game is scarce and hunting parties return with nothing to show for their efforts."

One of the men on watch came to the enclosure and pointed first at Jylyj and then at Reever while uttering some terse words.

"The chieftain has returned and will receive us," the Skartesh said.

"Why me?" my husband asked.

"I told them that you are our leader," Jylyj said. "I

am being allowed to accompany you to serve only as an interpreter."

I touched my husband's hand. "Be careful."

He nodded and left with Jylyj and the oKiaf tribesman.

A short time later, the female who had brought the basket of food slipped inside, and with her eyes cast down came to sit beside me. I couldn't fathom why until Hawk leaned close.

"Jylyj said females are never left alone with males they are not mated to," he said. "I think she is here to act as your chaperone."

I suppressed a chuckle. "If only I could explain to her how safe I am in your company."

Qonja laughed out loud at that, startling the tribeswoman, who glanced at him before covering her mouth with her hand. That was something I recognized; Iisleg females did the same when they were amused by something a male did or said.

The Skartesh had said I could not speak directly to the men of the tribe, but I saw no harm in trying to communicate with this female.

I caught her gaze, gestured toward myself and said, "Jarn."

"Trewa," she responded, pointing to her breast. She darted a glance at the men.

"Qonja," I said, indicating the Jorenian, and then pointed to the crossbreed. "Hawk."

"Jarn, Qonja, Hawk," Trewa repeated slowly. She seemed pleased to know our names. "*Antea hsfar,* Jarn." She made a sweeping gesture toward the sky, and then brought her hand down to the ground. "*Dyalmatak.*"

"I wish Jylyj was here," I said, smiling helplessly at the other female and shaking my head slightly to indicate that I didn't understand her words.

Trewa picked up a twig, moved back, and began scratching marks in the red soil. She drew five figures, an oval shape, and a triangle before she looked at me expectantly.

Hawk studied the drawing. "Our survey team, what might be a ship, and one of their dwellings, I think."

"The triad seems to be a very important symbol to them," Qonja observed. "If you noticed when we were brought in, everything in the encampment is grouped in threes." Another tribesman, one we had not seen before, came inside the enclosure and spoke to Trewa. She nodded, ducking her head as she rose. The male gestured for us to do the same.

Trewa stayed with us and walked beside me until we stopped before the three largest kiafta in the encampment. With another shy look she unwrapped from her arm a coil of square green beads interspersed with short slivers of pale, smooth wood and pressed them into my hand before hurrying off.

The tribesman made a motion indicating we should wait, unfastened part of the kiafta's hide covering, and stepped inside. A moment later, Jylyj appeared.

"This is the chieftain's place, which he shares only with his mate and his children," he said in a low voice. "It is a great compliment to be invited here. It seems we have impressed the tribe with our manners."

"Should I wait outside?" I asked.

He shook his head. "The chieftain is particularly interested in you, Healer. Just stay by your husband."

We followed him into the dark interior of the shelter.

Given the oKiaf's nomadic culture, I did not expect to see any sort of furnishings. While the inside of the ki-afta was not crowded, there were large stones arranged to serve as a table, seats, and what I thought were sleeping platforms.

I wondered why the oKiaf would bother to use such heavy objects for furnishings when I saw the bases of the stones, which were weathered by time and use and stood deeply embedded in the soil. From the way it looked, I imagined that the stones had been used by many generations of oKiaf and left in place. Each chieftain must have come to this same place and erected his shelter over the stones.

Reever stood at the back of the kiafta, partly shadowed by a draped piece of hide. Next to him the chieftain, a tall and proud-looking oKiaf, stood in silence. They didn't look at us.

"Sit here." Jylyj indicated a row of seating stones, and stopped Hawk from sitting beside me. "That is Reever's place."

Hawk nodded and moved down the row. I sat and looked at the ornament Trewa had given me so I wouldn't be tempted to stare at the chieftain.

"That is a *renatak*," Jylyj said. "Did one of the women give it to you?"

I nodded. "The female who brought the food. Should I wear it?"

"Yes. I will show you." Jylyj uncoiled the length of beads and wound it around my wrist, turning it one way and then another until the coils hugged my arm.

"Why did she give it to me?" I asked as I admired it.

"It is a fertility object," Jylyj said. "She wishes you to become pregnant." At my wide-eyed look, he added, "Being with child gives the female higher status among the tribe. In a sense, it is her way of saying that she wishes you well."

My immune system made it almost impossible for me to have any more children, so the explanation left me feeling a little depressed. Still, I intended to thank Trewa the next time I saw her. "What are the words a woman uses to thank another for a gift?"

As Jylyj told me, Reever came out of the shadows and sat down beside me, taking my hand in his. He glanced at the bracelet but said nothing, and I realized why when the chieftain came out and began speaking in oKiaf. At the same time, Jylyj translated his words for us in a low voice.

"I am Dnoc, made leader of the Parrak erchepel. It is through our lands that you walk and on our bounty that you feast."

Reever turned to Jylyj. "Tell him we are here to look for a crystal that can cause the people to fall ill. Ask him if we may have his permission to survey the land here."

Jylyj spoke rapidly to Dnoc, who nodded and walked around our group to look at each one of us. He then spoke to the Skartesh at length.

When Dnoc had finished, Jylyj said to Reever, "The chieftain has been in contact with the Elphian. He will allow us to stay in their erchepel for the night, and in the morning he will give us a guide."

Reever shook his head. "We don't need a guide. We can use our equipment."

"It is not an option," Jylyj said. "There are several

places where outsiders are not permitted to go. The guide is not to show us around as much as to keep us from trespassing on prohibited grounds."

"Why are these places off-limits?" Qonja asked.

"I cannot say." The Skartesh glanced at the chieftain. "The oKiaf do not discuss such matters with outsiders."

While the men were talking, Dnoc came and crouched in front of me. He turned his head and muttered something to Jylyj.

"The chieftain wishes to speak to you, Healer Jarn." The Skartesh moved beside us. "You may look at him."

The chieftain had piercing blue eyes, one of which was surrounded by six parallel scars that formed deep grooves in his black fur. So many beads and small wood carvings had been added to the dozens of braids in his mane that his entire head seemed to sparkle with light.

He spoke at length, and only when he finished did Jylyj translate the words.

"Dnoc has been having vision dreams of an off-worlder female marked by ice and fire," the Skartesh said. "So have some of the other men of the tribe. The oKiaf believe their dreams are portents, so they were not surprised to see you. He is gratified to know that you are a healer. He believes that is also a sign."

Dnoc reached out and hooked a sharp claw under the moonstone beads I had tucked under the front of my long shirt. He gently tugged them out and examined them, and repeated a handful of words.

"He says the necklace you wear is proof of the portent," the Skartesh translated. "He believes it is made of fire and ice, trapped in stone. He says it marks you as belonging to the great healer."

"We won't tell him that Hawk gave it to me as a gift of friendship." The chieftain's story intrigued me, however. "Who is this great healer?"

"It is only a figure from an old myth." Jylyj didn't seem very interested in it, either. "You should express your gratitude to the chieftain. He pays you a great compliment."

I nodded and said, "Your words honor me. I thank you."

Once Jylyj had translated that into oKiaf for the chieftain, Dnoc grunted and gave my face a fond pat before standing. He called out, and a moment later three tribesmen appeared.

As Dnoc spoke to his men, Jylyj said, "They are taking us to the kiafta reserved for special guests. We are to eat and rest until the night fires."

When we emerged from the chieftain's personal kiafta, the crowd of oKiaf waiting outside surprised me. I had thought the tribe would continue to keep their distance until word that we had been made welcome by their leader had been passed around the encampment.

Then there was their unnerving interest. Hawk and Qonja should have received the most attention, as they were the most exotic-looking members of the team, but everyone seemed to be staring at me.

I held on to Reever's hand. "Why are they looking at me like that?" I murmured to him.

"I don't know," he admitted. "But whatever happens, stay close to me."

One young male stepped boldly in front of us, stopping us in our tracks. He moved past Jylyj, Qonja, and

Hawk and approached me. I studied his pale gray pelt and the many scarification marks he had on his arms before I realized I was staring. I quickly ducked my head and bit my lip, hoping he hadn't noticed.

The male went down on his hands and knees as he sniffed at my footgear and leggings. He did the same to the front of my long shirt, rising slowly until he loomed over me. He bent to sniff my hair, his breath blowing some of it over my eyes.

Reever pushed me behind him and uttered a few words in oKiaf. At the same time, Jylyj moved in and bumped his shoulder into the young male's as he said something in a challenging tone.

The young male stepped back, looked me over one more time, and then rejoined a group of males. They cuffed him on the arms and chest and talked very fast.

"It's all right," Jylyj said. "Some of the younger men of the tribe like to test certain boundaries. It's usually tolerated unless it gets out of hand." He turned to my husband. "How did you know what to say?"

"I absorbed some of their language during my contact with Dnoc." Reever scanned the faces watching us before giving the Skartesh a flat, unfriendly look. "I hope I made my meaning clear."

"You have," Jylyj said.

I had the feeling they weren't talking about the young tribesman anymore.

"I'm getting a little hungry," I said to my husband. "Jylyj, will they bring our packs to the guest shelter? We need our rations."

The Skartesh nodded and turned to speak to one of our escorts.

Reever gripped my hand a little more firmly. "Nicely done," he murmured.

"I think enough challenges and meanings have been dealt with for one day," I said. "And, as it happens, I *am* hungry."

I slowed my steps as we walked past the large central cooking pit to look in some of the pots and see what the tribeswomen were preparing. Thick, rich-looking stews filled about half of the pots, but others were covered with leaves. I saw one female uncovering a pot, and watched as she used two short-handled, hand-sized versions of the pronged weapon the men carried to lift a browned haunch of meat from the pot.

Jylyj told us to wait there, and he went with Reever and one of our escorts to retrieve our packs.

An older female tending the pots noticed my interest and gestured for me to come closer. When I crouched down beside her, I saw she was preparing a piece of meat, as well. She used a chipped piece of stone to fish one of the embers out of the pit, and skillfully wrapped it with a white substance in a piece of tough-looking hide before wedging it in the last space between the meat and the inside of the pot. The scent of salty smoke grew stronger and teased my nose before the woman covered the meat and the bundles with layer after layer of the leaves.

I had smoke-cured enough meat on Akkabarr to grasp the process if not the ingredients used, and when she gave me a questioning look, I nodded. She turned her head and spoke to the woman who had finished cooking her meat, and the other female used her claws to carve a piece from it and came to offer it to me.

I knew I shouldn't have accepted it, not without properly scanning the meat first to make sure it wouldn't disagree with my stomach. But it had been so long since I had tasted real meat. The Jorenians ate only flowers and plants, and Reever told me that he and most of the other ensleg no longer used game for food. Since hunting was not possible on a ship, and not permitted on Joren, all I had eaten since leaving the homeworld had been synthetic protein.

In the end, I couldn't help myself. I tested it with a small nibble, and then groaned with pleasure as the dark, aromatic flavor of it spread over my tongue. Before I could think twice about it, I had eaten the rest and licked my fingers like a youngling.

The women dropped their gazes abruptly as a shadow stretched over me.

I looked up at the Skartesh. "Where is Duncan?"

"He is trying to signal that trader friend of his." He seemed amused. "Did you like the taste of the *namas*?"

"It was delicious," I told him. "How do I tell them that, and thank them?"

He told me the words in oKiaf, and I repeated them carefully to the women. They seemed pleased, although the older woman gave Jylyj an odd look.

The three kiafta reserved for guests of the tribe had not been marked with any symbols, and seemed plain-looking compared to the others in the encampment.

Jylyj gestured to the largest of the three. "That is for you and Reever. I will take the small one on the left, and Qonja and Hawk can sleep in the right."

I appreciated the chance for privacy, but Qonja seemed concerned.

"Should we sleep apart?" he asked the Skartesh. "Would it not be safer for us to occupy one together?"

"If we do, the tribe will think we are *mataerel*," Jylyj said. "It is what they call a mated group." He noticed Hawk's discomfort. "Be at ease, crossbreed. As long as those who are involved are agreeable to it, the oKiaf do not forbid mating with more than one partner, or with someone of the same gender, which is known as *litaerel*. Children who are orphaned at a young age are usually adopted by *litaerel*, as they cannot have children of their own."

"Would that I could bring my former ClanFather here," Qonja muttered as he ducked inside the kiafta Jylyj had suggested he and Hawk use.

The crossbreed didn't follow him, but remained with us. "I am surprised that the oKiaf have such progressive views about mating, and yet subjugate their females as they do."

"What you call subjugation is in truth a biological imperative," Jylyj said. "oKiaf females produce a large amount of hormones that cause them to be naturally timid. It often suppresses their survival instincts, and they will not defend themselves, no matter what opposition or danger they face. The males of the species also make a generous supply of a similar hormone, only the effect it has on them drives them to be very aggressive and dominating, particularly toward females. The oKiaf culture evolved as a result."

"Is the same true of the Skartesh?" I asked. When the resident gave me a surprised look, I added, "You have to admit, you have displayed some of the same male characteristics."

"Our glandular systems are slightly different, but it's believed that the oKiaf and the Skartesh are the decedents of one species. I will try not to be too aggressive or dominating." He sounded stiff now, as if I had offended him. "The fire gathering will begin as soon as the sky is dark. You should rest while you have the chance." He disappeared into the smallest kiafta.

"May I accompany you inside your shelter?" Hawk asked.

Still bewildered by Jylyj's reaction to my observation, I nodded, and led him into the kiafta.

Some of the same stone furnishings we had seen in the chieftain's shelter occupied the interior, but these did not appear as old or worn. A long hide mat stuffed with what sounded like dried plant material lined the stone sleeping platform, as well as a coverlet of very soft golden fur. I ran my fingers over the beautifully worked pelt and felt some small bumps, and parted the hairs to find more of the carved wood slivers. Each one had been carefully sewn to the underlying hide and then concealed under the fur.

"Those are likely talismans," Hawk said, examining my find. "All people are vulnerable when they sleep, so they're probably protective charms."

"Or fertility symbols, to help a female conceive." I drew back the coverlet and sat down on the mat, which was comfortable without being too soft. "The longer I am here, the more I like this world."

"So do I, but there is something that troubles me." Hawk went to close the hide over the entry before he came to sit beside me. "Jarn, Jylyj knows a great deal about the oKiaf."

I nodded. "He has been very helpful. We probably wouldn't have done as well with Dnoc without his advice."

"That is what I thought, until he spoke of their mating practices, and how accepting they are of those like me and Qonja." Hawk stroked his hand over the pelt coverlet in an absent fashion. "Such matters are part of the private lives of the tribe. On Joren, you never hear the people speak of how Choosing is forbidden to those of the same gender—especially with offworlders."

I had to agree with him; if Reever had not told me I would have never known about the taboo. "Do you think what he told us is wrong?"

"It is not what he said, exactly. We have heard him speak to the oKiaf, and they understand him completely. He gave us their words for the different relationships within the tribe—very personal, private words. He also knew that *litaerel* couples adopt orphaned children because they cannot reproduce naturally. For an offworlder who has only visited this world a few times, he knows so very much." Hawk made an uneasy gesture. "Too much, I think."

I considered what he had said. "We don't know how long he stayed here during his visits. Obviously, he learned their language, so his visits had to be of some duration. When you consider how much importance the oKiaf give to ritual matters, it may be that he studied their culture extensively before he even came here."

"It worries me, Jarn," Hawk persisted. "Jylyj is not merely knowledgeable about the oKiaf. He is practically an expert. You know how carefully the League prepares their intelligence operatives."

"I had my own suspicions, and went so far as to perform a DNA test on him," I admitted. "Jylyj's genes are pure Skartesh."

"Then he cannot be a League spy sent to sabotage the mission." The crossbreed Terran gave me a rueful look. "Qonja says my imagination does run away with itself sometimes."

"We should ask him about how he learned so much," I said. "I'm sure he can explain everything."

"Yes." Jylyj stepped through a slit in the hide opposite the entry. "I think I will start with how easy it is to hear what is being said in a nearby kiafta."

Hawk moved quickly to his feet and his wings spread out, one curling over my head. "I apologize for any offense my words have caused," he said, "but they were not meant for your ears."

"Such words are generally the most offensive." Jylyj gazed down at me. "You might have asked me to take the DNA test voluntarily, Healer Jarn. I would not have refused you."

I felt miserable. "Hawk, would you allow me to speak with Jylyj alone?"

The crossbreed didn't seem happy, but he nodded and left the shelter.

"Is this wise?" Jylyj asked. "If I am a League spy, I might take this opportunity to sabotage the mission."

I didn't like the way he was snarling at me. "You must not have been listening too closely, or you would have heard me defending you to Hawk."

"You trust me only because I have the proper genes. Forgive me if I am not overwhelmed by your confidence." He moved as if to leave, and then turned back to me. "I do know much about oKia. For many years I have done nothing but dream about someday returning again to live among the tribes. But I am not one of the people, and my calling has assured that I never will be. Is there anything more you want to know? Ask me."

"There is one thing." I stood. "Can you stop shouting at me before Qonja comes in here and declares you his ClanKill?"

"In truth, I have no HouseClan," Qonja said as he stepped in through the other side entrance. His dark blue claws gleamed. "That simply means I can gut anyone I wish, whenever I like."

"So it would seem." Jylyj gave the Jorenian a measuring look. "Your pardon, Healer Jarn. I should not have spoken in anger to you."

"I think you had some cause, but I accept." I glanced at Qonja. "I shield Jylyj."

"Yes, of course you do." The Jorenian sighed his disappointment and retracted his claws. "Three females are waiting outside with food. They are becoming terrified. I suggest we invite them in before we frighten them off for good."

Eleven

By the time I had neatly arranged on the table the baskets of food the tribeswomen had brought, Reever returned with our packs. I scanned the food and found most of it to be edible, although two types of fruit contained an alkaloid that would have made me, Reever, and possibly Hawk very ill. I set those aside and asked Jylyj if he would mention to the tribeswomen that we could not eat them.

The Skartesh remained in a silent, sullen mood, but nodded and gathered a portion of the food before retreating to his kiafta. Qonja and Hawk did the same, leaving me alone with Reever.

He gave me a wary look. "Something happened while I was gone."

"These hide shelters make it easy to eavesdrop on one's neighbors," I said. "Jylyj heard me speaking with Hawk about him. He became angry. Qonja threatened to gut him. I protected him. It's over and done with."

Reever's mouth twisted and he put his arms around me. "I can't leave you alone for five minutes."

"Of course you can. I have my case now, and the next time something like this happens, I'll sedate everyone." I went to the table. "Come, sit down and eat. Were you able to contact your friend?"

"It took some time, but I finally established a secure relay with Uorwlan's ship," he told me, walking over to inspect the native foods. "She passed along some new information about the mercenary offering the bounty on us."

I retrieved some pouches of water from our packs. "How would she know that?"

"All of the traders in this region have been receiving regular signals from mercenaries and bounty hunters re-questing information about us," my husband said as he sat down and sorted through a basket of nuts. "Uorwlan convinced one she has crewed with to tell her what he knows. It seems the bounty is being offered by a wealthy Terran with friends among the League. The Terran has been using some of their transports as lookouts."

As we ate, I thought of the League general responsi-ble for the Jado Massacre and Cherijo's abduction from Oenrall. "You don't think Colonel Shropana is the one hunting us?"

Reever shook his head. "Shropana isn't Terran, and he's too afraid of what Teulon Jado might do if he crosses us again." He gazed down at the pieces of meat I offered him. "We have synpro rations in the packs."

"We did not kill these animals," I informed him. "The tribe did. It's very good. At least try it."

His expression turned cold. "You've already eaten some of it."

"One of the women offered me a taste. I saw no harm

in it." I felt exasperated with him. "Duncan, using animals for food is no different than eating plants. Both are alive. Both must die to sustain the life of another."

"Plants do not have minds," he pointed out. "Animals do."

"I wouldn't say that to a Psyoran." I saw that he wasn't going to change his mind. "I suppose you don't want me to eat it, either." He gave me a pointed look, and I set aside the meat. "Oh, very well. I will eat only mindless plants and the synpro from the rations—and I will be very cranky about it, too."

He covered my hand with his. "Thank you."

We finished our meal while discussing the information Uorwlan had offered. We once more considered and discarded the idea that the bounty was being offered by Alek Davidov. Even if he had returned to the quadrant, he had known we were on Joren; he wouldn't have wasted credits sending mercenaries out to hunt for us.

"You are certain that the information your friend received is accurate?" I asked.

"No," Reever conceded. "But Cherijo was created on Terra, and her father must have kept some records about his experiments on her. If they were discovered after his death, they might have motivated another researcher to offer the bounty."

"You said what was done to make Cherijo was illegal," I pointed out. "That her creator even had laws written so that no one else would be permitted to experiment on humans, while he did so in secret."

"Times and laws change," Reever said. "Especially when the secrets of immortality are involved."

Something occurred to me. "What if they are not looking for Cherijo? What if they are looking for you?"

His eyebrows rose. "I am useful to them only as a tool to manipulate you."

"Joseph Grey Veil had time only to experiment on you before he died," I said. "If what he injected in you was all he had, then the chameleon cells in your body are the only ones in existence. They might have discovered that fact among his records."

"Squilyp said the cells remain dormant until some damage or illness occurs." Reever rubbed the spot on his chest where a drone on Vtaga had stabbed him. "In that state, they can't be distinguished from my body's natural cells. They wouldn't be able to find them to extract them."

My arm twinged, reminding me of what had happened to Cherijo when the Hsktskt had tried to brand her with a slave identification. "They could if they first tortured you."

Both of us had little appetite after that, so I packed away the food and performed a quick survey of our packs to ensure that none of our equipment or supplies had been removed. As I was separating what I would need for the next day's trek, Reever inspected the inside of the kiafta, and retrieved a piece of hide that had been left under the sleeping platform. He brought it to the table and began studying the many symbols embedded in the fur.

"The oKiaf use a modified form of pictographs as their written language," he told me. "Each symbol is representative of a concept rather than literal translation of a spoken word."

I noticed the three-sided symbol repeated over and over on the hide. "Qonja said the triangle symbol must be important to them. He called it a triad, and noticed that they also group many things in the encampment in threes."

"Trinities or triads are common in many primitive belief systems," my husband said. "They are usually represented by a central deity, a representative of the common people, and an intermediary figure. On Terra, the cult of Christianity worshipped a paternal God, his half-human son, and a Holy Spirit. The Jorenians hold sacred the Mother of All Houses, Tarek Varena, and the path they forged together." He glanced at me. "You rarely speak of Iisleg beliefs."

"Dævena is the goddess of women, and Kette is the god of men," I told him. "The people do not worship them together, and there are other, minor gods, but Dævena and Kette are the two central deities. I suppose the vral represent an intermediary. They were believed to be sent by both gods to reward courage by restoring the brave to life."

Reever eyed me. "I have no faith, Jarn, but I would not deny you your beliefs."

"The skela, miserable as they were, insisted that Dævena watched over them. I saw no evidence of that, but it was simpler to go along with what they believed." I shrugged. "Faith demands a great deal of the believer. I have paid my respects to the goddess through prayer, but I could not bring myself to sacrifice an animal to her. I could not see how giving her my food would make my life better, especially when I was hungry."

My husband took one of the recording units we had

brought to take images and measurements, and took several images of the symbols on the hide. He then isolated the images of the symbols themselves and wired a wristcom to the device.

"Do you think the translator will read them for you?" I asked, amused.

"No, but it will download into the unit's memory every corresponding pictograph in the translator's database. Not all languages are spoken, and some symbols are almost universal." He adjusted some of the settings, put the results on the image display, and began to read. "It has matched seven symbols: tribe, promise, stranger, three, one, death, eternity."

A chill inched over my skin. "Is it some sort of death threat to strangers?"

Reever consulted the hide. "The symbol for death is not connected to the one for the strangers. It's imprinted beside the eternity symbol. They are the only two that appear together."

"Death equals eternity?" I guessed.

He rubbed his chin. "That, or eternity dies."

Reever continued to work on decoding and translating the hide symbols while I prepared a medical report of what little I had observed regarding the health of the tribe. By the time I finished, I was surprised to discover that Reever had made little progress.

"It could be a prayer," he said. "The tribe promises to find or nurture or safeguard strangers, and in return the triad will ensure that time or the world or the universe does not end."

"Jylyj can't read their language, but he can ask what

it means," I suggested. "Why don't we bring it to the gathering?"

"The hide was deliberately concealed," Reever said. "If the tribe sees that we have removed it without asking permission, it may be considered a serious discourtesy." He placed the hide back under the stone platform. "Many of the same symbols are etched into the kiafta hides. I can ask Jylyj to obtain a translation of some of them."

We took a few minutes to change into the thicker, warmer garments the Elphian had given us to wear at night. Reever also brushed out and rebraided my hair, and knotted his own at the back in Jorenian warrior fashion. When we stepped outside into the cold twilight, Qonja and Hawk also emerged.

The Jorenian, accustomed to a much warmer climate, visibly shivered. "I can see why the tribe gathers around a fire at night."

Hawk went to Jylyj's kiafta and called out to him, then looked inside before returning. "He's not there."

I felt a twinge of guilt. Had my conversation with Hawk offended the Skartesh to the point that he would avoid us? "Perhaps he went ahead."

"Why would I do that?" Jylyj appeared out of nowhere, his dark eyes glittering. "Come. They are waiting."

We followed him to the center cooking pit, which had been cleared of pots and piled high with seasoned heartwood. The flames were already climbing up the sides of the stacks and blazing brightly; I felt the heat on my face from twenty paces away.

The tribe had assembled around the point of each spiral in the fire stones, most of the females sitting with their children on hides stretched over the ground while the men stood or moved freely around the fire. I heard only male voices at first, but then caught the quieter murmur of the women as they spoke to the children.

All of the tribespeople fell silent as soon as they spotted us approaching, until the only sound I heard was the crackling of the fire.

Jylyj led us to a place between two spirals where an unadorned hide had been placed, and indicated that I should sit. Reever stood behind me as I sat down, tucking my legs to the side as the tribeswomen did.

A rather noisy procession from the chieftain's kiafta distracted everyone, and I watched as several men in elaborately arranged furs led the chieftain to three large stones used to shape a low platform. Rather than sit on them, Dnoc gestured for the older female following him to sit down, and then strode up to the fire, casting what appeared to be a handful of soil into the flames. It must have been something else, for it caused a wide plume of fragrant purple smoke to billow up toward the sky.

Dnoc began to gesture and speak, and Jylyj again translated his words for us.

"We offer our thanks for another bountiful day, and our hopes for a peaceful night. The people are one with the land, and the land nourishes and protects the people. We ask for blessings on our women and our children, and good weather and luck for our hunters. For the respectful strangers who have come to us, we ask your care and guidance."

Dnoc ended his short speech by tossing another substance onto the flames that this time produced a sizzling burst of golden sparks. This seemed to signal the end of the formalities, for the tribesmen began moving around and speaking among themselves, while the women retreated briefly into the shadows before they returned bearing baskets and platters of food, which they spread out on the hides.

Several of the women brought food over to us, and shyly handed each offering to me. I thanked each female using the words in oKiaf that Jylyj had taught me, which seemed to please them.

After helping themselves to the food their mothers had set out, the tribe's children all left their family groups and gathered around an elderly male, who shook out a hide and attached the carved wooden rings sewn to its upper corners to two of the prong weapons that had been driven into the ground. I watched, fascinated by the firelight that played over the fur, which seemed to shimmer with its own light.

"May we go closer to the old one?" Reever asked Jylyj, who nodded. My husband held out his hand to me, and helped me up from the hide before we followed Jylyj.

We stayed at the edge of the group of children, some of whom gave us curious glances before turning their attention to the elderly male. From here I could see that the symbols rubbed into the hide had been also painted with different colored pigments that contained tiny particles of a reflective material.

"The old male is one of the tribe's storytellers," Jylyj said. "Everything he says is also recorded on the hide. This is how they teach the young ones to understand it."

"What story is he telling tonight?" Reever asked.

"Chetere's loneliness."

The name seemed familiar to me, although I didn't know why. "What does *Chetere* mean?"

Jylyj thought for a moment. "The name is difficult to translate, as it is a person and a thing and a state of being. Outsiders who have heard the story often call him the Star Wolf."

The elderly storyteller waited until all of the children grew still and silent, and then in a deep, dramatic tone began to speak. Jylyj whispered his translation:

"Before the time of living things, there were only stars and emptiness. Nothing moved or grew or breathed. What was then became sad, because the hollow was made to be filled. The lonely stars came together and brought forth the first one, the golden-touched, he who would be the tribe. They called him Star Wolf, and set him upon the world that would be his, and everything he touched moved and grew and breathed. The stars looked down upon the abundance and were glad. They told their son that he would live forever in the abundance, and they would watch over him.

"But Star Wolf alone could not be the tribe, and so he prayed for another to be made and sent down from the skies. The stars did not listen. They only watched from their lonely places, for they did not know what it was to be more than one. When Star Wolf's prayers became too loud, they tired of him and brought down the darkness so they would not have to see his sadness.

"Star Wolf wandered, alone and blind, and still the abundance flowed from him. The small creatures grew larger, and the world richer, but still he longed for the tribe. When he could no longer bear the solitude, he took up his dagger and cut himself in two.

"His blood soaked into the ground, turning it red, and the world that he had made abundant began to wither. The skies wept, and the land shook, until the stars lifted the darkness and saw what had become of their only child. They sent down their healing light, and from one part of Star Wolf fashioned a man, and from the other a woman. To honor Star Wolf, and so that man and woman might never be alone, they gave them the gift of creation. Whenever the two become one, another is made. So the first tribe came to be."

The storyteller made a broad gesture, sweeping his arm to encompass all of the intent young faces.

"Star Wolf's blood still makes the ground under you red. Whenever you see it, remember his sacrifice. He made it so that you could be his sons and daughters, the tribe he never knew."

The children reached out to the elderly male, touching him affectionately on the arms and belly with their small paws. He returned the gestures by placing his paws on their heads and murmuring words too soft for us to hear.

The story probably should have seemed gruesome, but I found it strangely beautiful.

"So this is how the oKiaf believe they were created?" I asked Jylyj.

"It is how they believe the universe was made," he corrected. "The oKiaf believe that Star Wolf was the first humanoid, the father of all people."

A minor commotion on the other side of the fire pit distracted me, and I looked over to see the chieftain and his men had moved away toward a group just entering the encampment. The new arrivals wore heavy cloaks with fur-lined hoods, and along with packs carried two long branches from which the limp body of a big, muscular animal hung.

"Who are they?" I asked Jylyj.

"I don't know. Travelers usually wait until morning to present themselves." He shifted, trying to get a better look. "They've brought a recent kill, which means they have hunting rights in this territory. Only the chieftain can grant them that kind of status."

The game the strangers had brought was taken away by six tribesmen, while Dnoc conferred with the tallest member of the group. He gestured several times in our direction.

"We should go and introduce ourselves," the Skartesh said. "The first to meet travelers are always any other travelers in the encampment."

We walked around the fire, and as soon as Dnoc saw us, he gestured for us to join them. Five of the travelers pulled back their hoods, revealing oKiaf faces, but the sixth and tallest of the group remained cloaked.

"Does the chieftain know what a troublemaker you are, Duncan?" the tall one called out in flawless Terran. "I can tell him, if you like."

My husband's expression softened, and he released my hand to go to the stranger. They curled one arm around each other's neck in a curious embrace before the tall one shrugged out of the cloak.

The traveler was not oKiaf, but a member of some feline species, and had a long, narrow head covered in short black-and-white fur. I guessed her to be Uorwlan, Reever's trader friend, although she wore the native dress of a male, adapted to accommodate an intricate weapons harness that crisscrossed her torso and hips. An astonishing amount of silver ornaments with glittering clear blue gems hung from her neck. Her eyes, much larger and more slanted than the oKiaf's, matched the gems in color and brilliance.

To my eyes she looked rather a starving, dirty jlorra, but Jylyj and every other male around me seemed to be staring at her with great admiration.

"Where is this Jarn you've told me of?" the feline woman asked. "I want to meet the female who convinced you to take her to wife."

I considered that an invitation, and walked over to stand at my husband's side.

"My wife, Jarn," Reever told the female. He looked down at me. "This is my friend, Uorwlan."

"I am happy to know you," I said, and made the Jorenians' polite gesture of welcome. "Do you know you're wearing the garments of a male?"

"She has good eyes." The Takgiba's piercing blue gaze shifted down and then up as Uorwlan inspected me. "But Terrans are usually larger, are they not? Is she a child, or a runt?"

"I am an adult, but I was made in a machine," I told her before Duncan could answer. "Evidently, there wasn't much room in it."

"So it would seem." Uorwlan's thin white lips peeled back from sharp-looking teeth in a faint snarl. "I've tried to learn that Jorenian hand-speak, but it made my wrists sore." Without warning, she bent and slung her arm around my neck. "Good to meet you, little sister."

I returned the embrace, feeling awkward but determined to make Duncan's friend feel welcome.

Uorwlan straightened, cuffed me under my chin, and eyed Jylyj, Qonja, and Hawk. "Are these your other husbands?"

I smothered a laugh and shook my head as I performed the introductions. The Takgiba gave each man the same rough embrace before addressing Reever.

"I thought I'd come down to the planet and see how you were fairing," she said. "I trade with all the tribes in this region; Dnoc and I are old friends. He thinks I'm a male, by the way, so don't wreck my hunting privileges by telling him otherwise. I've no taste for cooking and scraping the ground with my nose."

That explained her choice of garments. "I wish I'd thought of that."

"It helps not to have discernable teats," she told me, rubbing the flat surface of her chest. "Mine pop out only after I breed. Not that I plan to. I've yet to meet a male worthy of siring my offspring." She gave my husband a sly glance. "Well, one, but my kind and Terrans can't crossbreed. Probably for the best. Back when we were slave running, Duncan and I would have whelped an entire colony of kids between us."

My chest felt tight as I realized what she meant. This female and my husband had been lovers.

Dnoc spoke to Jylyj, who said, "The chieftain asks if you want your usual kiafta, Uorwlan."

"Why bunk alone when there are two Terrans to warm me?" the Takgiba said. "I'll sleep with Reever and Jarn."

We took Uorwlan with us back to our kiafta, although I felt a little disgruntled with how quickly Reever had agreed to let her stay with us. I didn't know why it bothered me, either—Iisleg customs gave men the right to have two women, and it wouldn't be the first time I had shared a bed with two other people.

Uorwlan talked a great deal, all the way from the fire to our shelters, and hardly paused for breath. She spoke of her overland trek to reach the camp, killing the game with her escorts, and how paranoid the Elphian had become lately. By the time we bid the others good night, I was almost tempted to ask Qonja and Hawk if I could join them.

As soon as we were alone, the Takgiba began stripping out of her clothing, revealing more black-and-white fur and a long, thin tail that moved as languidly as Uorwlan did.

"Secure the inside of the entry hide, will you, Jarn?" the Takgiba asked. "The natives won't intrude on us, but they've been known to peek."

I saw she intended to remove all of her garments, and turned to Reever. "You never let me sleep naked."

He shook his head at me slightly before addressing the Takgiba. "Uorwlan, my wife and I are exclusive to each other. We will not have sex with you."

"What?" The feline gave him a look almost as astonished as my own.

"She thinks she can *couple* with us?" I said, almost at the same time.

"How else am I to get warm?" Uorwlan gave me a hateful look. "So this is what you've done to him? Turned him into a Jorenian?"

I didn't like that, especially as being exclusive had been Reever's idea from the beginning. "Terrans are usually monogamous," I informed her. "When I agreed to become his wife, I also accepted his ways."

"That Terran"—Uorwlan pointed to Reever—"was never monogamous. Even when he shared my bed. In fact, he went through females almost as quickly as he did blades."

I had forced myself to accept that Reever had given his love to Cherijo before me. Now it would seem a small army of females had had him even before her.

She studied my expression. "He didn't mention that, did he? Ah, well, they never do. All males are seeders, you know, and they're never truly happy unless they can spread it around. Did he ever tell you about the slave harem we liberated from the pleasure colony on Anig-fel? I ended up putting guards on our cabin so he could get a few hours' sleep. You wouldn't believe what I had to do to have him to myself once a week."

"What my husband did with you or anyone else in his past is irrelevant to me." Anger made my voice cold. "All you need to know is that you can't have him now."

"Is that what you think, little sister?" She bared her teeth and tugged a blade out of her belt. "Duncan saved my life, and I'm in his debt. He can ask anything of me, and I will give it to him." She tossed the dagger from one set of claws to the other. "So if he wants a place in my bed, on my ship, or anywhere else, it's his."

I pulled one of my own blades and held it ready. "Not anymore."

"Perhaps I should go and sleep with Qonja and Hawk," Reever said as he stepped between us and with two blurred motions took the blades from our hands. He looked at Uorwlan. "You are my friend, but Jarn is my

wife, and I love her. You will respect that and our bond."
He turned to me. "And you, Wife. You will calm down
and not provoke Uorwlan any further."

"*Provoke* her?" I echoed, outraged. "She drew the
first blade. You wish me to stand by the next time she
loses her temper and let her stab me?"

Reever's eyes darkened. "I wish you to leave her
alone, Jarn."

"If you are finished arguing," Jylyj said from outside
the side entry to the shelter, "we have been summoned
to meet with the master hunter."

Twelve

The frigid air nipped at my hot cheeks and curled around my clenched fists as I stepped outside. The encampment had obviously settled in for the night, for I saw only a few males walking around the outside of the shelters farthest from the fire pit. Like the men on watch who had met us earlier that day, they carried the pronged weapons, but each also held a small torch of flaming heartwood, which they used to illuminate their path.

I wanted one of those torches. I could see myself accidentally dropping it on Uorwlan's twitching tail. Or my husband's thick head.

Reever paced me. "You're angry with me."

"When did you notice?" I didn't look at him. "Before she pulled a blade on me, or after?"

"You don't understand Uorwlan or what she was trying to do. I had to stop you before you did something foolish." He tried to take my hand as if he meant to establish a link.

"So I am ignorant *and* foolish." I avoided his touch and put another foot of space between us. "That is good to know. I might never have come to that conclusion by myself. Thank you for educating me."

He moved closer. "If you will allow me to explain—"

"I need no explanations from you, Duncan," I said flatly. "If you prefer to be with her, all you need do is say so, and I will step aside. But we have a child, and Marel is more important than your desire to . . . how did she put it? Run through females as fast as you do blades?"

He made a frustrated sound. "Uorwlan has a love of the dramatic, and she always exaggerates things. She believes that the relationship she had with me in the past gives her first rights. There is also a more immediate problem with her. She is—"

"*Dævena* take Uorwlan," I snapped, sick of hearing his concern for her. "You can have her if you like. You can have as many females as you wish—create a new harem for yourself, if you desire—but know this: Whatever you do with her, whatever she means to you, when we leave here, you are coming with me."

"I was afraid you would mistake my meaning," he said. "I don't want Uorwlan, Jarn."

Now I looked at him. "I don't care, Duncan."

"The oKiaf consider public quarreling between a male and female extremely distasteful," Jylyj said. "They regard it on the same level as relieving yourself in the open."

I glared at him. "Yes, of course. We wouldn't wish to piss on the ground in front of anyone."

There was no more time for him to say anything, for we had arrived at the master hunter's kiafta. Jylyj called out a soft-voiced greeting, and the entry hide was opened to admit us.

The master hunter's family already occupied their sleeping platforms, and the older male paused to tuck a fur around the smallest child before turning to greet us. He wore few ornaments in his mane, and had heavily scarred arms and paws that bore mute testimony to his experience.

"This is Seno," Jylyj said. "He has hunted this land for many years, and knows of a place that may be of interest to us."

Seno retrieved a piece of hide from a bundle stowed to one side of the table. He spread it out flat and, using a blackened twig, began to sketch what appeared to be a crude map. He pointed to each area as he drew it and spoke to Jylyj, who translated.

"From the encampment, we must walk north approximately five kim, and take the pass between two cliffs for another two." He listened for a moment to the master hunter. "The place beyond the cliffs is the tribe's burial grounds, so we can't go any farther than that. He says there are shining stones lining the gaps in the ground at the base of the east cliff. From his description, the stones are some sort of crystalline mineral."

Reever studied the map and then said something in oKiaf to Seno. The master hunter gave him a confused look in return.

"He doesn't understand what you mean," Jylyj told him. "The oKiaf don't acknowledge things like illness, old age, or dying."

"I used the same words the storyteller did tonight at the fire," my husband said. "You should know; you interpreted them for us."

"The myth of the Star Wolf is just a children's tale,"

the Skartesh said. "What happened to the first one is not what the people believe happen to them."

Now I felt bewildered. "You're saying that the tribe doesn't believe they get sick or die?"

"It's not the words they use," Jylyj insisted. "The cycle of life for the oKiaf is very specific: whelping, weaning, learning, mating, teaching, passing, and flowing. Those are the only states of being that they recognize for themselves."

"What is flowing?" Reever asked.

"I suppose it's the afterlife," Jylyj said. "After life leaves the body, it flows into the bellies of the stars, to nourish them."

"Hunting cultures often have such pragmatic beliefs about an afterlife," Reever said. "I find it interesting, and somewhat bizarre, that the oKiaf mythos is so similar to that of the Jorenians, who believe they are embraced by the stars."

"It is not that unusual to find cultures who share almost identical beliefs," the Skartesh said. "Before the HouseClans were formed, the indigenous beings on Joren were, like the oKiaf, tribal hunter-gatherers."

Seno folded the hide and offered it to Reever, who thanked him in oKiaf for it before we left the kiafta.

As we walked back to our shelter, I noticed that the storyteller's hide had not yet been removed from the frame.

"Could we go and take a closer look?" I asked Jylyj after I pointed it out. "I couldn't get near enough to make out all of the symbols while he was telling the story."

"I can't read it for you," Jylyj said, "and it is very

old. But as long as we don't touch or disturb it, no one should mind."

Up close I saw the hide had been worked even more elaborately than I had imagined, with tiny beads and carvings embedded in the fur around the symbols. It also looked very old, as Jylyj had said; the edges and the underside of the fur had been covered in many places with precisely sewn patches.

I could recall every word of the Star Wolf story, so I tried to follow the columns of symbols and make out which corresponded with the elements of the tale. I could make out almost everything but three symbols rubbed inside a circle of dark stones in the very center of the hide.

Compared to the other symbols, these three seemed much more refined and specific. In the center, glittering silver had been applied to a distinctly humanoid-looking figure. To the right and left of the figure were seven-pointed star shapes, one painted white, and the other black.

"I don't think these three were part of the story," I said to Reever. "The symbols for the Star Wolf and the people of the tribe are painted in brown, gold, and black. The figure can't be one of them."

"They could be symbols representing the name of the tribe, to indicate ownership of the hide," my husband suggested.

"The tribe's name, Parrak, is a word in the old tongue; it means 'a fire that burns from within,' " Jylyj said. "It's getting late. We should go back to our shelters."

The old storyteller came to the frame, nodding to Reever as he took down the hide. The black and white symbols were what interested me. "Jylyj, can you ask him what it means?"

Before the Skartesh could reply, Reever spoke to the storyteller, who regarded him with some surprise before he moved his hand over the center circle and spoke three words.

Reever frowned. "I don't understand what he's saying."

"He says that the symbols represent crystal eternity," Jylyj said at last. "It's probably one of the old terms for the afterlife."

I felt a surge of excitement. "We've never heard them use the word *crystal*, only *rock* or *shining stone*. Could the black star represent the black crystal?"

"No, Healer," the Skartesh said. "The word I translated as crystal only means 'clear' or 'unclouded' to the oKiaf. Another interpretation of what the elder said would be 'to see clearly forever.' "

I recalled the words Dnoc had used when he had spoken to me. "The chieftain used the same word when he called me on who belonged to the great healer."

Jylyj averted his gaze. "Translations are not always exact."

"So what did it mean when Dnoc said it?" I persisted.

"The exact words he used could be interpreted to mean 'crystal healer,' " the Skartesh said reluctantly.

"Such subtle differences in word meanings are often difficult for non-native speakers to learn," Reever said. "You display an admirable grasp of this language."

"I have a small natural talent for interpreting, and even once considered becoming a linguist, like you,"

Jylyj told him. "But the call to healing was too much for me." He moved to help the old storyteller take down the hide. "I will stay and help him carry this back to his kiafta. You should go and sleep now. The guide will be ready to leave the encampment at dawn."

Reever remained very quiet as we walked back to the shelters, so much so that I stopped him just before we entered. The cold air enclosed us in its frigid stillness, and our breaths formed thick white puffs as we looked at each other.

"I am sorry that I lost my temper earlier," I said. "I'll try to get along with your friend."

"It is not that." He touched my arm. "We can't talk out here. Come inside."

We found Uorwlan sitting at the table and cleaning her weapons. She gave me a sideways glance. "Here, little sister." She offered me one of her finest daggers. "I apologize for goading you. I am happy that Reever has taken a wife, even if he had the very bad taste to choose someone other than me."

I accepted her apology and offered my own, along with my finest blade, which seemed to settle matters between us, at least for now. Reever sat down across from the Takgiba and took out the hide map for her to see.

Uorwlan wasn't interested in the map, however. "You have that look in your eyes, the one you used to get whenever a slaver tried to bribe us. What is it?"

"The Skartesh with us is acting as our interpreter," Reever said. "I think he also is deceiving us. I have absorbed enough of the tribe's language to know most of their common concepts. When I asked the Skartesh about a symbol that I believe represents death, he claimed the oKiaf use the word only in their myths, and don't apply the concept in reference to what happens to them at the end of life. Yet tonight when I asked the old storyteller if a symbol on the hide meant death, he wasn't offended. He genuinely didn't know what I meant—as if the end of life, or death itself, had no meaning for him."

"It could be what Jylyj was trying to say," I suggested. "Perhaps he worded his explanation badly. He didn't translate the words Dnoc used to me exactly as he should have."

"I would agree, but there was something else. The storyteller used three specific words to describe the center symbols on his hide. Jylyj only translated two of them to mean 'crystal eternity.'" I know the oKiaf word for eternity: *detorne*. The storyteller did not utter that word."

"What did he say?" Uorwlan asked.

"Naif valen fian."

She shook her head. "I have never heard those words spoken, so I can't translate them for you. But if this Skartesh has lied about the meaning of one word, it's likely that he's lied about others. Tell me more about him."

"He will return soon," I warned. "I will keep watch for him while you talk."

While I stood at the entry hide and acted as lookout, Reever related to Uorwlan everything we knew about Jylyj, including how he had denied being the one I had seen in the water on Joren.

"I know these people," I heard the Takgiba say after my husband had finished. "I've traded with them regularly for the last five years, and spend every summer here hunting with them. I've an ear for languages, you know that, and still I've learned enough of their tongue only to communicate the basics. It would take a lifetime of living with the tribe to understand the things this Skartesh claims he knows."

I saw a tall, lean figure approaching and turned my head. "He's coming."

"Is this the way into his shelter?" Uorwlan asked, pointing to the side entry. When I nodded, she unfastened it.

"What are you doing?" I whispered.

"I mean to see if this Skartesh knows how to properly warm a female," she said, "and if he talks in his sleep." Her tail shivered as she stepped through and vanished.

"She will get herself beaten," I muttered, waiting to hear Jylyj shout at the Takgiba, but hearing nothing at all. Then a faint growling sound came from the direction of the Skartesh's shelter, answered and soothed to a rumble by a higher, more feminine purr.

"It would seem Jylyj found better things to do than beat her," Reever said.

I turned my back toward the side entry, absently blocking out the sounds. On Akkabarr there had been little privacy, so I had learned early on to offer it by ignoring the sights and sounds of things that were not meant to be shared with others. But even as I chose not to hear them, I still didn't like Uorwlan coupling with Jylyj.

"She is reckless," I whispered to my husband.

"No, she is in season," Reever murmured. "That is why she drew a blade on you. The females of her kind fight for mating privileges."

That made her strange behavior seem more logical, and explained why she had wanted to couple with me and Reever the moment we were alone. Still, after what my husband had said about Jylyj and the deceptive translations, I worried. "You are sure she will be all right with him?"

"Uorwlan can take care of herself," he assured me, and tugged on my hand. "Now, come to bed, Wife, and let me warm you."

Sometime later I lay curled up beside Duncan and listened to him breathe. No more sounds came from Jylyj's shelter, and I heard only the occasional footsteps of the men on watch patrolling the encampment as they passed near our kiafta.

In my mind I saw the three symbols enclosed by the dark circle on the storyteller's hide, and thought of what Reever had told me about the triads of different cultures. They didn't seem to fit with the universal God-man-intermediary belief, for the figure of the silver man had stood between the white and black stars. There had also been something odd about the way the symbols had been rendered; they had been simply made, and not intricately adorned like those around them depicting the Star Wolf story.

White like new snow, black like the endless void . . . and a being who stood between them.

It nagged at me, in the same way a half-forgotten word sat on the tongue, waiting to be fully remembered and spoken. Would my former self know what to make of the symbols? Did she know something that I did not?

As I puzzled over the symbols, I finally began to drift off. I swayed between consciousness and sleep, though, neither here nor there, too aware of my surroundings to be completely at ease, but too tired to force myself to keep watch.

A dream came to me, as swift and silent as a raider, and took me from the kiafta and through a labyrinth of shadows until I found myself back on Trellus. I walked through the winding labyrinth of collected objects that Swap had cemented together into his highly unusual art.

Yes. Now show us where.

I retreated from the voice in my head, cringing as I tried to find the passage back to Mercy House. I passed through an airlock, but instead of entering a passage to my friend's dome, I stepped outside.

The surface of Trellus had been transformed. No longer an airless landscape of crumbling, lifeless rock, the planet was now covered with plants and trees. I didn't see the dome colony, but I sensed animals hiding in the brush and watching me. Then I caught a glitter of blue and began to walk toward it.

Where the ore crushers of the abandoned arutanium mine had once stood rusting were now towering columns of blue crystal. Beneath my feet the ground glittered with smaller, paler growths pushing through a mat of fused slivers and shards. All of my senses seemed muted in this place; I could not taste or smell anything, and my hands seemed to drag at my wrists when I tried to touch the crystal.

You were not meant for this.

I turned toward the sound I thought I heard, but saw only my face reflected in one of the columns. The sides of the crystal divided my features in half at first, and then the reflections moved apart and became mirror twins.

"I am here." I turned around and saw myself dupli-
cated, over and over, on the surface of each column. My
faces stared back at me, wide-eyed and pale, narrow-
eyed and scowling.

*What was meant to be can never be, unless the sacrifice
is made.*

I knew what a sacrifice was, but the rest seemed like
gibberish. "What do you mean? What sacrifice do you
demand?"

*It cannot be asked, what must be asked. It cannot be
taken, what was taken.*

I watched my twin faces turn toward each other.
Cracks began to run through the columns as the two
Jarns drew closer. They did not melt back into one reflection, however. They collided and shattered, screams
distorting their mouths.

I ran through the columns, dodging them as I tried to
find my way back to the encampment and Duncan. Only
the sudden appearance of a frowning red-haired female
made me skid to a halt.

"Well, well. If it isn't my favorite, heavily armed doormat." She made a triangular server appear in her hand
and sipped it, sighing with pleasure. "How are you, Jarn?
Want a drink? No one distills a better mind-altering intoxicant than the Terrans."

I watched as a structure built itself around us. It
enclosed us like a dark box, and furnished itself like a
large galley, only not nearly as clean. Terrans of various ages and genders began appearing, some drinking
together and laughing, others silent and alone. In one
corner, a life-sized, rusted drone tried to blow through
a complicated-looking alloy instrument, causing it to

produce squawking sounds that reminded me of a ptar caught in the throat snare.

I recognized nothing. "What is this place?"

"Where it all began," Maggie said, and made a sweeping gesture with her hand. "Welcome to the Slow, Lazy Sax."

I breathed in. It smelled more vile than it looked. "I want to wake up now, please."

"You don't get a vote this time, Akkabarran." The Terran female handed her empty glass to a passing service drone and took my arm. "Over here. We need to talk."

With her usual indifference to my feelings, Maggie dragged me around the tables and Terrans to a dark corner and shoved me into one of the chairs. Before she sat down, she obtained another beverage and put it in front of me.

"Stop looking as if I'm going to hit you," she said, templing her red-nailed fingers. "I came to rescue your submissive little ass."

"Why? I'm on oKia, sleeping next to my husband, who would kill anything that tries to touch me." A pity he couldn't enter my dreams. "I'm not in any danger."

"Clueless as ever." Maggie looked down at her drink and began toying with the plas stick, spearing the two dull green seed pods floating in the liquid.

"Can I interest you ladies in a personal encounter?" A humanoid-sized drone stopped beside us and unfastened the front of the tunic draped over its chassis to display its artificial muscles.

I frowned. "What?"

"I saw you looking at me." The drone grabbed my shoulder and squeezed it. "You know you want it."

"I didn't look at you." I shoved the appendage away.

It braced a hand on the sticky surface of the table. "I am programmed for one- to nine-hour sessions, and can accommodate multiple partners."

I stared up at its lifeless, handsome face. "What does this thing want?"

"It wants to have sex with you." Maggie gave me a sour grin. "Or me. Or both of us. It's a sex drone."

"Get away from us," I told the machine.

"Thank you for your consideration." It moved on.

"I never cared for that model," Maggie said idly as she watched it solicit the interested young male occupying the next table. "Too heavy-handed. Whoever programmed it must have had a taste for rough trade."

"What danger am I in, Maggie?" I demanded. "Will I die of boredom in the next five minutes?"

She laughed. "One reason we're so fond of your species—other than the mesmerizing amount of narcissism you're capable of—is your tenacity. You hold on to life with white-knuckled fists, and you just won't let go. For a bunch of puny, weak primates who still like to kill as often as you breed, that is astounding. No matter what the cosmos throws at you—plagues, famines, climate changes, planetary disasters—you do whatever it takes to survive."

"All species struggle for the right of existence," I said. "Terrans are no different from them."

"Trust me, you are. We should know. We tried to wipe you out a few times." Maggie used her teeth to remove one of the dull green seeds from the stick. "Like the time we diverted a decent-sized asteroid toward prehistoric Terra, and flash-fried North America and everything on it. The few cave dwellers who weren't turned into charcoal endured incredible hardships, relocated, and started breeding again, like nothing happened. Then there was my favorite, the bubonic plague. That came with a personal guarantee from the manufacturer to wipe out all sentient life on the planet. About half of you died, and the other half? Went and developed immunity to it."

"I don't believe you," I told her. "You couldn't have done those things."

"Oh, sweetie, it wasn't malicious," she assured me. "We were simply trying to keep you out of the mix. The grand plan didn't allow for a bunch of clever apes from a hellstar system meddling in things they didn't understand. But despite our best efforts, you evolved into the biggest bunch of troublemakers since the slugs that would one day become the Hsktskt crawled out of the primordial soup."

Her insensitivity made any further discussion pointless. "Can I go now?"

Her green eyes flashed up, bright and narrow. "Your charming doormat qualities make me forget sometimes what lies beneath them. I can't do anything about you or the danger you're in, sweetheart, so a warning would be totally useless."

I didn't say anything. When Maggie spoke of things I didn't understand, silence seemed the best response.

"Such a trooper." Her smile turned vicious. "How did you like the crystal dream?"

"Not at all."

"Can't blame you there. When the universe decides to fuck with your head, it doesn't do it halfheartedly." Now she seemed to be avoiding my gaze. "Despite what we did to your species in the past, we Jxin actually believe in the laws of survival. You fight for life; you earn it. You win; you should get to keep it. It's always been our schtick, and, pains in the ass that Terrans are, eventually we had to accept that you deserved the right to exist. Remember that the next time you dream of crystal."

To be polite, I took a sip of the drink. It tasted vile. "What do they mean? The dreams?"

"Believe it or not, it's kind of an apology." She bared some teeth. "Aka, things have not gone according to plan, we're all very sorry about that, blah, blah, blah."

She was lying. I could do the same. "Then I thank you for your concern."

"Don't even go there." Maggie reached across the sticky surface of the table and seized my arm. "If I could have killed you the moment that stupid skela bitch shot Cherijo in the head, I would have. I knew—we all knew—that you should have never been born. But once you're here, baby, you get your very own bill of rights. No matter who you are or what body you possess. So say the Jxin."

Like her words, her grip was meant to hurt.

"I am sorry that Cherijo died." I leaned forward. "But I live, and I am not giving up my husband, my child, my body, or my life. They belong to *me* now."

"No being undergoing a dimensional transformation preserves its sense of spatial relation," Maggie said flatly in Shon's voice.

Something pushed at the bottom of my footgear, and I glanced down. The seven-pointed apex of a crystal had pierced the pitted surface of the flooring and was thrusting itself up through it. It rose so fast I had to shove back my chair to keep it from impaling me.

Terrans knocked over tables and chairs as they ran to escape a hundred other crystal columns shooting up through the foundation. A crystal silenced the drone making the squawking noise and crushed it between two other columns. The explosion of its power core lit the room with a burst of yellow sparks.

I turned, trying to see an exit, and saw Maggie's image reflected on the surface of the largest and widest of the crystal pikes. Then she pressed her hands against it—from the inside.

I picked up the chair I had been sitting in and smashed it against the surface of the crystal. That failed to leave even a scratch.

"Maggie." I placed my hand on the outside of the crystal, which felt like blue ice. "Can you hear me?"

A web of cracks appeared under my palm and spread out jaggedly in all directions, causing irregular shards to fall from the column. Inside, Maggie underwent her own transformation; her red hair turned black and her features refined themselves into a non-Terran countenance.

"As you have fought for us, child of mind." Her fingertips touched mine through one of the flaws. "So will we fight for you."

Blackness.

I sat up, my body shaking, my skin slick with sweat. The icy air inside the shelter tried to freeze it and my tear-streaked face. I looked over and saw Reever was still sleeping, and slipped out of the blankets, taking care not to let the cold get under them.

I left the shelter and walked out into the frigid night. The sky above the encampment stretched wide and dark blue; the thin atmosphere made the stars seem enormous.

I went to the fire pit, the flames of which had died down to a glowing pile of scarlet embers, and sat on the edge of the still-warm stones to wait for the dawn.

Thirteen

Just before the sun rose, I returned to the kiafta and woke Reever, who prepared a quick meal while I readied what we would need to take on the trek.

"Here." He placed a bowl of cooked grain on the stone table, and then winced. "Can you give me an analgesic? I can't seem to get rid of this headache."

"Of course." I retrieved a syrinpress and, after scanning him to ensure that the pain was not from another cause, administered the drug. "What brought this on?"

"I think the smoke from the cooking fires," he said. "The smell of burning meat does not have pleasant associations for me."

Qonja and Hawk soon joined us, as did Uorwlan, who seemed much more relaxed and happy. Of Jylyj I saw nothing until he arrived with Seno's guide, an experienced scout who said little and seemed impatient to leave.

As she played a male in front of the oKiaf, Uorwlan couldn't show much affection to the Skartesh. Still, she hovered around him and used any excuse to touch him. For the most part Jylyj ignored her, although once or twice I caught him giving her a faintly exasperated look.

With the guide at the front, we left the encampment and traveled north, using another old path through the groves of heartwood. The air began to warm a little as we emerged from the trees into a narrow clearing around the base of the two facing cliffs, both of which were so tall that I nearly had to bend backward to see their snow-covered tops. Beyond them the mountains stood like worn monuments, each forming an uneven procession that never ended but disappeared over the horizon.

The guide halted at the entrance to the cliff pass and spoke in a low voice to Jylyj, who nodded and turned to Reever.

"The scout says that stones sometimes fall from the sides of the cliffs in the summer season," the Skartesh told my husband. "We must move quickly now, but if you hear stone cracking, go to the face of the cliffs and stay there."

The guide increased his pace to a trot, and I held on to the straps of my pack as I tried to keep up. My short legs had to take two strides to match one of the others', and by the time we emerged from the pass my face and longshirt were damp with sweat.

A secluded valley stretched out before us, the red soil completely covered by reedlike amber grass with three-sided seed heads. Here and there I saw the broadleafed blue plants with the white berries, but no trees grew here. All through the heartwood we had heard the rustling of animals in the brush, but here the silence seemed almost eerie.

"This is the tribe's burial ground?" Reever asked. The Skartesh nodded. My husband said something to the guide, who didn't seem to understand him. To Jylyj, Reever said, "Ask him where the graves are, so that we won't walk over them."

"There are no graves," the Skartesh said after conferring with the guide. "I believe they bring the bodies of the dead here and leave them on the ground to decompose naturally."

"Then the place should be littered with bones," I said.

"It feels as if it is." Uorwlan looked about and wrapped her arms around herself. "I don't see any remains. Do you hear that humming?"

Reever listened and then looked down. "No, but I can feel something in the ground." He took out a scanner and used it, turning in a slow circle. "There is something vibrating under the soil."

"We should try to signal the *Sunlace*," Qonja said. "We told the captain we would relay our status every morning."

I glanced at the guide. "We agreed not to use our equipment in front of the natives."

"Seno said the exposed deposit of shining stones was somewhere over there," Jylyj said, pointing to one side of the cliffs. "I will go with the scout and see if we can locate it. While we are gone, send your signal."

The oKiaf and the Skartesh walked off, while Reever set down his pack and took out the small transceiver.

After calibrating it several times, he was able to send off a brief signal. No reply came, however, and after a few moments he switched off the unit.

"Whatever is moving under the ground is also causing relay interference." He handed out scanners to Qonja, Hawk, and Uorwlan. "Walk along the perimeter of the meadow and see what you can detect."

Reever and I walked carefully through the amber reed grass. While I looked for any signs of oKiaf remains, he scanned the surface.

"There are enormous deposits of a crystalline mineral under the soil," my husband said.

I caught my breath. "Black crystal?"

"No. It has far more benign readings—more like a form of quartz. I'm reading tons of it here."

We walked on, but after a few more meters, he stopped me.

"Don't go any farther. There are large subsurface faults filled with liquid all around us. The ground may collapse under us."

He knelt down and placed the end of a sampling probe into the soil, and watched it disappear as it burrowed into the ground. Then we retreated a safe distance.

"Could it be graves?" I asked.

"No. The liquid isn't decompositional. It appeared to be mineral." He watched the scanner display as the probe began transmitting a vid of its progress. The red soil in front of it fell away, and the probe dropped into a void half-filled with a pool of what looked like water.

The probe didn't sink but instead floated on the top of the fluid. All around it the liquid began to bloom with strange, feathery shapes, as if the probe's presence had caused some sort of reaction. As we watched, the feathery shapes solidified into three-sided crystalline shafts.

Memories of being trapped in a pit made of a clear crystal rushed into my mind. "It looks like the Pel." The sentient, shape-changing crystal Cherijo had encountered while forced to work as a slave doctor had been able to communicate telepathically with her, and had even helped her and Reever liberate Catopsa.

"I thought the same thing, but it isn't the Pel," my husband said. "The liquid is some form of protocrystal, but unlike anything in the database."

The crystal growth increased at an alarming rate, until it replaced all of the liquid I could see in the void. "Why is it solidifying so fast?"

"Perhaps coming in contact with the probe's alloy housing caused a chemical reaction." Reever sighed as the vid from the probe grew blurry and then disappeared. "That must be what's causing the transceiver to malfunction. The probe has stopped transmitting, too."

We met with the rest of the team back at the edge of the meadow and compared readings.

"This entire valley is honeycombed with deposits of solid and liquid crystal," Reever said after checking the others' scanners. "In some places the soil barely covers it."

"This place makes my fur stand on end," Uorwlan said. "It's making my head ache, too. We should get out of here."

The guide appeared without Jylyj and began speaking to Reever, gesturing toward the area where he and the Skartesh had gone. I looked over but couldn't see the resident.

"Wait." Reever took hold of the oKiaf's arm and concentrated. After a few moments he released him. "Jylyj slipped away from the guide. He says he went into the forbidden area." He spoke to the oKiaf, who argued with him briefly before gesturing toward the tree line. "He'll track him. He says we have to follow in his footsteps or we could be killed."

"By what?" To me, the meadow appeared completely deserted.

"I don't know," Reever admitted, "but he's terrified, and not just for himself."

We followed the guide in a single-file line as he skirted the meadow and approached the trees. As we passed the cliff face, I saw a section of rock that had fallen away, and the glitter of crystal shining through the jagged dark red stone.

The heartwood trees at the edge of the meadow grew so thick that the trunks proved an effective barrier all on their own. The guide found a gap large enough for us to squeeze through, but held us back and gave Reever a terse set of instructions.

"We have to leave our packs here," he said. Once we had placed everything on the ground, the guide reluctantly led us into the thicket.

We had gone only a short distance before the trees ended and another, smaller clearing appeared, shadowed by an outcropping of red stone that seemed to hang over it like a protective roof. The guide stopped at the edge, scanned the area, and then went still. Backing away, he turned and issued sharp orders to Reever.

"He says we have to go back to the encampment," my husband translated. He then spoke in oKiaf to the guide, who made a violent gesture. "He won't allow us to go any farther."

I heard a faint sound coming from behind the guide's back, and moved to the side to have another look. From this angle I could see a large open pit in the ground. I also heard the sound of a man groaning. "I hear him. Jylyj is in there."

When I tried to go past the guide, he grabbed my arms and pushed me back.

"He must have fallen into the pit," I said, pulling away and turning to Reever. "Tell him we have to get him out of there."

My husband spoke to the guide, who turned and began shouting at him.

I didn't waste any more time, but dodged around the guide and ran into the clearing. Under my feet the ground seemed to shift, collapsing in places the way ice did during the thaw after winter. I moved fast, jumping over the voids that began to form in front of me until I made it to the edge of the pit.

When I looked down, the glitter of crystal hurt my eyes. There, in the center of the pit, lay Jylyj, his body impaled on dozens of crystal shafts.

Later, I would wonder why I did as I did at that moment. I would go over it a thousand times and still not know what made me act. But when I saw Jylyj, his body bleeding from dozens of wounds, I stopped thinking and jumped into the pit.

I landed on my feet after the three-meter drop, but the sharp points of the crystal apexes didn't penetrate my footgear. Instead, they shattered under the impact of my landing as if made of thin ice. Above my head I heard shouts, but only bent over the Skartesh, working my fingers under his mane to check his pulse.

His dark eyes opened. "Leave me and go."

"I'd be happy to, but I don't think I can jump back out," I said. I lifted my head and called out, "He's fallen onto some crystal but he's still alive. I need my pack, something to cut him free, and some ropes so we can lift him out of here."

"You can never free me," Jylyj said. "Leave me here, Jarn. It is the only way for me."

Something was glowing under his shirt, and I ripped it open to see two golden streaks in his fur, both giving off a cool white light. My eyes widened as the crystal shafts that had stabbed through his body turned white with the light from the marks in his fur, and then began shrinking back into the wounds they had inflicted. As Reever appeared above us at the edge of the pit, the shafts disappeared, and Jylyj's body collapsed against the now-flat bottom.

"Jarn." When I looked up, Reever tossed my pack down to me. I caught it neatly. "How badly is he injured?"

I looked at the wounds on the Skartesh's chest, which were also shrinking. "I don't know, but he's lost a lot of blood. Duncan, we have to get him out of here now."

My husband nodded. "Qonja and Hawk are rigging some ropes to the trees. Tie him to you, and we'll pull you both out."

While I waited for the ropes, I took a syrinpress from my pack and administered a painkiller. The Skartesh opened his eyes as soon as he felt the infusion and glared at me.

"You're wasting your drugs." He ducked his head and looked down at the glowing marks on his fur. "Look at this. Look at what you've done."

"What I've done? I only jumped in here." I took his vital signs, which were weak but steady. "You seem to be doing all the healing yourself." When he said nothing, I added, "Is this why your patients recover so quickly? Are you some sort of touch healer?"

He made a disgusted sound and closed his eyes.

By the time Reever lowered the ends of two ropes, Jylyj had fallen unconscious. I turned him on his side and worked the rope under his arms and then lay down and faced him as I wrapped it around me, pulled it tight, and knotted it. I grabbed my pack, wedged it between us, and then rolled onto my back, holding him against me as I called up to my husband.

"Ready."

The ropes bit into my sides as they began hauling us up from the bottom of the pit. On the way up, Jylyj groaned a few times but never regained consciousness, and when Reever reached in to take my outstretched hand, my longshirt and leggings were soaked with Skartesh blood.

Reever cut the ropes, and Qonja and Hawk lifted Jylyj between them.

"Take him," my husband said. "Quickly."

I was about to warn them about the treacherous ground when I saw all the collapsed areas were filled with pools of a white liquid. I turned my head and saw the pit was filling with the same.

"Duncan," Uorwlan called out. She sounded scared. "Move it."

I looked down and saw the liquid crystal erupting through the soil, spreading and covering and solidifying over everything it touched. Reever lifted me off my feet, held me against his chest, and ran for the trees. He jumped over a stream of the liquid crystal, just clearing it before we were in the shelter of the trees. I looked over his shoulder and saw shafts sprouting up like plants.

The guide nearly ripped my husband's sleeve as he pulled us away from the clearing. With a final look, Duncan turned and carried me through the grove.

When we reached the meadow, the guide reluctantly allowed us to stop and catch our breath. Reever put me on my feet, and I opened my pack as I went to where Qonja and Hawk had laid Jylyj on the ground.

I scanned him three times and then pulled back his garments to see the wounds for myself. No longer bleeding or open, they were all now thick scars. As I touched one, I felt it softening and watched it disappear into his flesh. Tiny hairs began to grow, covering the new skin.

I glanced up at my husband. "He heals like I do."

"Maggie once told Cherijo that her people had made others like her," Reever said, his voice tight. "He must be one of them."

Uorwlan loomed over the Skartesh. "He'll be all right, won't he?"

I realized that she and the others hadn't seen Jylyj impaled on the crystals as I had, and debated for a moment on what to tell her. If the Skartesh had been created to be like me, he had probably gone to great lengths to conceal it.

"He has some internal injuries and he's lost a great deal of blood," I said at last. I'd only brought the most basic medical supplies with me; half of my equipment remained in the shelter. "We have to get back to the encampment. If I can't cross-match a donor from the oKiaf, we'll have to evacuate him to the ship."

"That's going to be difficult," Reever said. "When I went after you, I dropped my pack. It fell into one of the holes in the clearing. The crystal engulfed it before I could retrieve it."

"I have one back at camp," Uorwlan said. "You can use it to signal your people."

The guide called to Reever as he dragged several branches from the thicket.

"He says we can make a litter to carry him," my husband said. "Uorwlan, get three of those blue broad-leaf plants. Qonja, Hawk, gather some strong vines." He glanced at me. "What do you need?"

"A hospital." I checked Jylyj's pulse, which remained weak. "He seems to be holding on, but hurry."

The guide and Reever stripped the branches of their leaves while the others gathered the plants from the meadow. I watched as the men built a long, narrow frame by lashing short and long branches together with vines at the cross sections. The guide punched holes with a dagger through the tough edges of the broad-leafed blue plants and lashed them across the frame, creating a supporting surface for Jylyj's body. Uorwlan reinforced it by volunteering her cloak, which Reever draped over the frame before the men brought the makeshift litter over to me.

I showed them how to lift him, and then secured

his body to the frame with pieces of the rope. Qonja and Hawk lifted one end of the frame, and Reever and the guide the other. When I would have moved to the front to lead them toward the pass, Uorwlan shook her head.

"I'll take up the lead," she said, and pointed to the Skartesh. "You stay beside him."

We moved as fast as we could, but carrying Jylyj slowed the men, and the trek back to the encampment took twice as long. Several tribesmen ran out as soon as we were spotted by the watch, and helped carry Jylyj to our kiafta.

"Put him on the platform," I said as I went to retrieve my supplies from the packs. When one of the tribesmen seized my arm, I glared at him. "Let go of me."

He spoke to me in a sharp voice and gestured toward Jylyj, but released me as soon as Reever came over to us.

"They're angry. The guide told them Jylyj entered the forbidden area, and—in his words—woke up the crystal. To them, that is an unforgivable offense." My husband then spoke at length to the tribesman, who seemed to calm a little but spoke sharply again before he strode out.

"What are they going to do?"

"Nothing. You can treat him." Reever rubbed his eyes with his fingers. "We have to leave, though, first thing in the morning."

"We have to leave as soon as Uorwlan can signal the *Sunlace*," I said as I went over to the platform. "I need to move him to the medical bay as soon as possible."

"They won't allow Uorwlan to use her transceiver," my husband said. "They're contacting the Elphian to come and remove all of us from the planet."

My first priority was to examine Jylyj properly, so I drafted Hawk to serve as my assistant as I cut off the Skartesh's garments and began the visual assessment. On the outside of his body I found patches of short, newly grown fur, the only indications of where he had been impaled on the crystal, and counted twenty-eight separate wounds—all of which were healed over as if they had never happened.

I scanned his internal organs, from the top of his head to the pads of his paws, and found only a few traces of cellular disturbance. From the locations, Jylyj had suffered life-threatening penetrating injuries to both lungs, his heart, liver, spleen, and one of his four kidneys, as well as a rupture of his stomach and complete severing of his intestines in five different places.

From the extent of the injuries, he should have died almost instantly after jumping into that pit, and yet he had only a few lingering bruises and a mild inflammation of the abdomen, as if he had just recovered from a minor case of gastric infection instead of what had to have been a terminal-level peritoneal infection.

His remarkable ability to heal had not yet compensated for his blood loss, however, and as I ran the hematology scan, I found the expected drop in his white and red blood cell count. He had lost a little over half of his blood supply; in a normal being that would call for an immediate transfusion. But while the blood loss kept him unconscious and his vital signs weak, his body didn't seem to be suffering any other ill effects from it. Time and plenty of fluids would probably allow his enhanced immune system to regenerate and replace all on its own what he had bled out.

I set up a portable monitor and put the Skartesh on a saline IV, and then tucked a coverlet around him.

"How did he lose so much blood?" Hawk asked. "There are no wounds on him anywhere."

"There were." I trusted Hawk, and he had too much medical knowledge to be fooled by any story I made up. "Jylyj's immune system is like mine. He heals almost spontaneously."

"So that is his secret." The crossbreed gave the unconscious Skartesh a thoughtful look. "Qonja said there was something he wished to hide." He frowned. "Joseph Grey Veil couldn't have made him, could he?"

I shook my head. "Cherijo's creator was not the only one responsible for making her the way she was. The Jxin female who pretended to be her mother also had something to do with it. She claimed there were others made to fight the black crystal. Jylyj has to be one of them."

"That must be the reason he jumped into that pit," Hawk said. "No sane being would do so unless they were suicidal."

The only oKiaf who was permitted to enter the kiafta was Trewa, who kept her head down as she brought in food. I had never had the chance to repay her for the gift of the bracelet, so I stopped her before she could leave.

Now that Reever had absorbed enough oKiaf to speak it, I could have asked him to interpret for me, but instead I removed the moonstone necklace Hawk had given me and offered it without words.

Trewa touched the beads, looked down into my eyes, and inclined her head so I could place the necklace around her neck.

I grasped her paws with my hands and thanked her in oKiaf.

A guard looked in, making both of us jump, and Trewa quickly hurried out. I went back to Jylyj, and Reever met me beside the platform.

"Uorwlan has a short-range backup transceiver in her pack," he said, keeping his voice low. "It's not powerful enough to signal the *Sunlace*, but she can send a relay to her shuttle pilot. He's ferrying supplies from the station and should be in orbit. He'll relay a message to Xonea."

I checked Jylyj's vitals, which had dropped enough to alarm me. "I thought he was stable, but he's getting weaker now. I don't think the oKiaf will volunteer a donor, and the only cross-matched blood I have for him is on the *Sunlace*. I need to get him back to the ship."

"Xonea should be able to convince the Elphian of the urgency of the situation." He traced a half circle under my right eye. "You look exhausted. Let Hawk watch him while you get a few hours of sleep."

"I'm fine." I kissed him. "Go, and don't let the guards catch you. We're in enough trouble already."

Darkness crept up around the kiafta as I watched over Jylyj. If the Jxin had created him with the same immune system I possessed, it had been overloaded or was no longer working. With every passing hour, he grew a little weaker.

Hawk brought me something that I ate without tasting, and kept watch with me until I sent him to rest.

"I will need you fresh in the morning to help me transport him," I said when the crossbreed tried to protest.

"You will wake me if you need help," he insisted, and only after I gave him my word, reluctantly went to join Qonja in their shelter.

When I was alone with the Skartesh, I sat on the ground beside the platform and rested my head back against the edge of the grass-stuffed cushion. I didn't tell Hawk that if Jylyj's condition didn't soon improve he would likely be helping me transport a corpse in the morning. I turned my head to look at the monitors, and saw my patient watching me, his eyelids opened only to slits.

"We're back at the encampment," I told him. "Your wounds have healed."

"Not all," he whispered, his voice a thin thread of pain. "Why save me?"

Had he jumped into that crystal pit in hopes of killing himself? "I never learned how to let someone die. Did they teach you that in medical school?"

"No. Learned it before." He lifted a paw and touched my hair, threading the blunt ends of his claws through the strands. "Never met another like me. Thought I was alone."

Suddenly, I understood many things. "Why didn't you tell me? Of all people, I would have understood."

"Angry. Afraid. The League ... alterforming ..." He drifted off for a moment, and then jerked back awake. "Jarn, after ... destroy my body. Please."

He was afraid of the League, afraid of being

discovered—and terrified of what they would do with his body. I had never considered what would happen if immortal DNA was used to alterform a normal being. Was that to be my fate?

"I will." I pressed my hand over his paw. "I promise."

Fourteen

Reever returned alone, and after refusing the food Trewa had brought, sat with me to watch over Jylyj. I told him about the Skartesh's brief period of consciousness, and what he had asked of me. Reever agreed that if Xonea couldn't get to us in time and we lost Jylyj, that we would at the first opportunity send his body into the oKiaf's sun.

"I don't understand why he's dying," my husband said. "Cherijo explained most of the bioengineering that had been done to her, and from what she said she couldn't bleed to death. Even if she sustained hundreds of wounds, her blood always clotted within a few seconds. If he is like her—like you—he should have done the same."

"Something interfered with Jylyj's immune response," I said. "Perhaps the crystal impaling his body. Now something is preventing his bone marrow from producing replacement cells. I've scanned him a dozen times, but I can't detect anything responsible for it. Here, see for yourself." I handed him the scanner I had been using on the Skartesh.

Reever skimmed through the readings I had taken. "This is calibrated to read the body's cells and other organic substances. Can you adjust it to scan for crystal?"

"I don't have to; it picks up trace minerals, as well," I said, frowning as I took back the device and isolated those readings. Normally, I wouldn't have paid any attention to the minute amounts of minerals that were present in any living being's body, not unless some heavy metal contamination or poisoning was suspected. I scrolled through the list and found a sizeable amount of one mineral had been detected in the bloodstream.

The scanner, which had not recognized it, listed it as unknown.

"I thought his body had forced the crystal out of it as it healed." Cursing myself for making such a stupid assumption, I recalibrated the scanner. "I need to see the readings you took in the meadow today."

My husband retrieved the scanner he had used to detect the underground deposits of protocrystal, and handed it to me. I compared the compositional readings and swore again.

"His body didn't reject the crystal," I said. "It absorbed it."

I ran another complete scan of Jylyj's body and looked at the mineral display. In the hour since I had performed my previous scan, the amount of liquid protocrystal in his bloodstream had increased by two percent.

"It's still circulating through his body." I felt like throwing the scanner across the room. "And that's not all. It's growing."

Reever glanced down at the Skartesh. "Can it be removed?"

"I might be able to filter it out with dialysis, or a complete replacement transfusion." I tried to think, but all I could see was how the liquid crystal had consumed the clearing in a matter of seconds. "Did you hear anything from Uorwlan's pilot? Is Xonea coming for us?"

"The pilot was able to transmit a brief relay. He'll arrive in a few hours and land outside the encampment. If the oKiaf will release us to him, he'll transport us back to the station."

The tribe and the primitive conditions in which they lived no longer charmed me.

"Why do these people live like this?" I said, dragging a hand over my hot face. "They have no doctors, no proper medical facilities. Even on Akkabarr we had healers, and all the medicines and supplies we could salvage from the wrecks."

"He's as strong as you are," Reever said. "He'll keep fighting it."

If he didn't turn into a chunk of crystal before the shuttle arrived. I thought of the heartwood trees, and how the crystal had stopped growing at the tree line. "Do you still have the litter we used to carry Jylyj into the camp?"

My husband gestured toward the entry flap. "It's just outside."

"I need one of the heartwood branches from the frame." If I could discover what substance in the trees repelled the crystal, I might be able to synthesize an agent that would stop it from spreading, or even help flush it out of his bloodstream.

After a brief conversation with the guards, Reever brought back a short branch from the litter. I cut a sliver from the raw end and placed it in the analyzer. The results surprised me.

"It looks like wood on the inside, but it's mostly made of hardened resin." I felt bemused. "This branch is dead, and the resin is almost fossilized. No wonder it takes forever to burn."

The analyzer began listing the elements and compounds it detected in the resin, all of which appeared ordinary: oxygen, nitrogen, carbon, hydrogen, and so forth. Then the display showed a trace of an alloy, Cu^2Au, which apparently accounted for the color of the wood.

"This tree absorbs two metals, copper and gold, from the ground," I said. "They combine into an alloy that is not present in the soil."

"Gold is harmless, but copper in large amounts can be poisonous to many living things." Reever studied the cut end of the branch. "It may bond the gold to the copper to change its properties and keep it from accumulating and killing the tree."

"If that alloy does not occur naturally in the soil, it could be the deterrent we're looking for." I went to the platform and used a probe to draw a few drops of blood from Jylyj, placing them in a vial and scanning them to confirm the presence of the protocrystal. As I did, Jylyj's blood began to crystallize.

Quickly, I extracted a sample of the Cu^2Au alloy from the heartwood resin, and added it to the vial of blood. The crystallized blood instantly liquefied.

I scanned it. "The alloy dissolved the crystal. It's reverted to its liquid phase." I monitored the sample for a few minutes. "The crystal isn't growing. It's gone inert."

"That may explain why the tribe uses so much wood

to adorn themselves," Reever said. "Their luck carvings may be protocrystal repellent." He tapped the bracelet I wore. "That may be what saved your life in the pit."

I paced back and forth as I thought it out. "I can't inject him with a copper alloy. He's not a tree; even a small amount would kill him." I studied my bracelet, and the gleaming slivers of wood between the green beads. "I have an idea."

Convincing the guard to send for Trewa took Reever some time, but eventually he brought the oKiaf woman to our shelter. With Reever as my interpreter, I told her about Jylyj's condition in simple terms, and asked for her help.

She stared at the Skartesh for a long time before she replied.

"She says he is being punished for waking the crystal," my husband translated. "But because we're strangers, and we didn't know what would happen, she doesn't believe he deserves to die. She will go to the other women in the encampment and collect what she can."

Trewa left us, and I began putting together the equipment I needed. I couldn't build a complete dialysis unit from scratch, but with some tubing, an empty IV unit, and parts of an infuser, I was able to put together a crude, portable version of one.

Trewa returned with a basket of the tiny heartwood carvings the women used for their ornaments, and Reever scanned them.

"They all contain traces of the Cu^2Au alloy," he confirmed.

"Bring them here." I could only fit the smallest of the carvings into the empty IV unit, but there were enough to fill it halfway. Once I evacuated the air from the lines, I inserted the needle at one end into the radial artery in Jylyj's right arm, and the needle at the other into the artery in his left. Once I enabled the infuser port, which I had rewired to work in reverse, it began drawing the Skartesh's blood into the line attached to his right arm.

I watched his blood travel up to the IV unit, where it began to drip over the heartwood carvings inside the bag, and then fed down into the line that ran to his left arm.

It seemed to take longer than it did. I kept running a continuous scan on the amount of protocrystal in his blood supply. Gradually, the growth rate slowed, and then finally stabilized.

"It's working." I looked up at Trewa and nodded. "Tell her that she has saved his life."

As my husband translated, Trewa touched the moon-stone necklace I had given her. She replied in a soft voice, gesturing to the Skartesh and then gently cuffing my left shoulder.

"Trewa claims no one has ever survived going into the forbidden places," my husband told me. "She says Jylyj lives because of you."

The oKiaf woman ducked her head and twisted it from side to side, repeating two words several times.

"What is she saying?"

"I think she's given you a proper tribal name." Reever smiled a little. "Among the oKiaf, you will now be known as Crystal Healer."

Auto-infusing Jylyj with blood filtered through the heartwood carvings kept the crystal infection in check, and I felt confident enough to begin preparing him for transport.

The guards came for Reever shortly after midnight to meet with Dnoc and Uorwlan's shuttle pilot, who had arrived and was negotiating with the chieftain for our release.

"Wake everyone and have them prepare to go," my husband told me. "I don't think this is going to take very long."

It didn't. By the time Uorwlan and the rest of the team were dressed and packed, Reever returned with the pilot and an armed escort.

"We have to hightail out of here, Captain," the pilot, a very nervous little humanoid with pale green skin, told Uorwlan. "The Elphian are in total meltdown. They're talking about shutting down all the trades now and keeping everyone out."

"I'll smooth things over with them," she promised.

Uorwlan's pilot had brought a litter from his shuttle, and as we shifted Jylyj from the sleeping platform onto it, he opened his eyes.

"Blood," he said, gazing at his arms and then up into my face. "Whose?"

"It's all yours." I secured the IV to the side of the litter and fastened restraints across his chest, abdomen and hips. "We've stabilized the infection. Once I get you back to the *Sunlace*, we'll start cleaning the crystal out of your system."

Jylyj seized my wrist in a surprisingly strong grip. "You can't remove it from my body. It could infect the rest of the crew."

I exchanged a look with Reever. We knew the protocrystal was dangerous, but we hadn't considered what might happen after I removed it from the Skartesh's body.

Jylyj said my name, and I smiled down at him. "We'll deal with the crystal later," I promised him. "Right now we're going on a little jaunt."

Qonja, Hawk, the pilot, and Reever carried Jylyj through the camp, with Uorwlan in the lead. Every adult in the erchepel came out of their shelters to watch us go. As we passed some of the tribeswomen, they bowed their heads and murmured the tribal name Trewa had given me.

"Crystal Healer," I heard Jylyj murmur. "They think you are the legend."

"You never told me that story," I said, hoping to keep him conscious for the jaunt.

"When the Star Wolf died to create the tribe, the abundance of the world divided itself, too. Time became day and night, summer and winter, birth and death. The stars could not repair the division, so they made a promise to the tribe that one day a healer would be born, one who could make everything right again."

"How?"

"The myth doesn't specify an exact course of treatment," Jylyj said, his tone dry. "After the Crystal Healer is born, he—or she—becomes separated from the tribe and wanders alone through the wilderness for many years. There the healer falls into a long slumber and dreams. When the tribe has made enough sacrifices, the dream becomes time, and the healer travels through it to find the Star Wolf and heal him. As they are joined, so are the night and day, and light and the darkness, and all that has been divided from what it was. The crystal healer brings the Star Wolf back to life, and together they re-create the tribe from the dreams they share with each other."

"It sounds like a lovely romance," I joked.

"It is why the oKiaf have never objected to the *ma-taerel* or *litaerel*," the Skartesh said. "It has always been believed that the Crystal Healer and the Star Wolf were both males."

I chuckled. "Well, I am very flattered, but obviously I am not a male, and I don't think I can suture day and night back together."

"If you try, I want to assist." He coughed and closed his eyes.

Uorwlan's shuttle had landed in the same clearing the station pilot had left us, and while small, the vessel appeared well-armed.

"Are you expecting trouble?" I asked the Takgiba as I nodded toward the oversized pulse emitters mounted on three sides of the hull.

"A girl can't be too careful, especially when she hauls cargo." Uorwlan stopped as the door panels opened and a loading ramp extended. "Linag, did you leave the ship on auto?"

"I couldn't say no, Captain." The pilot's fearful eyes darted toward the shuttle. "They held a rifle to my head. They said they'd kill me if I didn't."

A group of men in battle armor poured out of the shuttle. All of them carried pulse rifles, which they trained on us.

"Who the hell are you?" Uorwlan shouted.

One of the men fired at the ground in front of her,

and then raised his weapon and targeted her face. "Shut up and get on board. All of you. Now."

"Mercenaries?" Uncaring of the threat, the Takgiba turned to her pilot. "You let *mercenaries* hijack my shuttle?"

I felt air sweep over my back as Hawk took off. Some of the men fired at him, but he flew too fast for them to bring him down. A moment later he disappeared around the side of the mountain.

I reached for my blades, but Reever put his hand on my wrist and shook his head.

"Too many to fight," he murmured. "Do as they say."

We were marched onto the shuttle and herded in the back cargo area, where one of the mercenaries confiscated our weapons. Another reached down and yanked the needles out of Jylyj's arms, then pushed him off the litter in order to remove that.

"Stop it." I rushed over to the Skartesh. "He's badly injured. He needs that IV." I tried to grab it back, but the mercenary hit me so hard I fell to the deck. When he drew his foot back to kick me, Reever came at him and knocked him across the hold.

"Back away," the other mercenary said, shoving the end of his rifle into my husband's belly when Reever kept advancing toward the semiconscious merc. "Back away, or I'll cut you in half."

"Duncan, he'll do it." Uorwlan hauled Reever by the arm over to me. "Take care of your wife." She turned to the mercenary, who was helping his dazed companion get to his feet. "What do you want? Cargo? Credits? Let's work this out and no one has to get hurt."

"We have what we want." The mercenary shoved his

companion out of the hold and then backed out himself, closing and securing the door panel as soon as he was on the other side.

Reever helped me up from the deck. "Are you all right?"

"Yes." I went back to Jylyj, who was curled over on his side. "Who are they?" I demanded of the pilot. "How did they get on the shuttle?"

"They intercepted me in orbit," he said. "They used some kind of docking clamp to immobilize me. They were on board before I knew it." He gave Uorwlan a helpless look. "They took out the transceiver and grabbed Pellan and took him on their ship. They said they'd kill him if I warned you."

"Raiders." Uorwlan began to curse softly and paced around the cargo hold.

Qonja took off his cloak and covered Jylyj with it as I checked his vitals. "Can he survive without the IV?"

"Not long." I braced myself against the deck as the shuttle began to lift off. "They must be after the bounty. We have to convince them to leave Jylyj and the others at the station." An unexpected jolt nearly threw me to the deck again. I barely righted myself before the ship rocked violently again. "What's happening?"

Uorwlan ran over to the viewport. "The shuttle's surrounded. They're firing at the stabilizers."

"Who is?" Reever demanded.

She turned and looked at him. "The oKiaf."

Pulse-fire bursts began to hammer on the outside of the hull, and something exploded at the back of the shuttle. It dropped back to the ground and lurched to one side.

"There go my stabilizers." Uorwlan looked around the hold. "Linag, remind me to stow some weapons in with the cargo next time."

"We're all going to die," the pilot muttered, cowering and covering his green head with his four arms.

I heard shouts and the pounding of footsteps as the mercenaries tried to get off the ship. More pulse fire erupted, along with terrible screams. After a long silence, someone opened the door to the cargo hold and ordered us out.

Reever went first, shielding me and Qonja with his body as we supported Jylyj between us. Uorwlan followed. We stumbled down the damaged loading ramp and found the ground outside the ship littered with the bodies of dead mercenaries. A small group of survivors stood to one side, their hands clasped behind their heads.

A ring of oKiaf in League battle armor and carrying pulse rifles completely surrounded the shuttle.

"Thank you," Reever said to the tribesman who stepped up to us.

"Be silent." The oKiaf pointed his rifle at my husband as several light shuttles began descending all around the clearing. "You will come with us now."

The strange oKiaf herded us and the surviving mercenaries onto their shuttles, dividing us up as they did so. I protested as Jylyj was taken from us by two of the tribesmen, but they ignored me.

"Let me go with him," I said to the leader. "He's hurt, and I'm a healer."

"We will care for him," was all he said.

We were directed to sit in the passenger area of the shuttle, where two guards stood watching us. A few minutes later, the oKiaf launched back into the air, flying away from the clearing and into the mountains. Although they didn't try to harm us, they refused to speak to us and made it obvious that they considered us their prisoners.

"It seems not all the tribes abandoned the evils of technology," I said in a low voice to Reever as we inspected the two oKiaf standing guard. "Those rifles are new. So are these vessels."

"They must be the Elphian watchers left behind to guard the tribes on-planet," he murmured. "They probably use surface scanners to monitor landings and launches."

"The attack was none of our doing," Qonja said. "Surely they will be reasonable about this."

"They have the rifles," I pointed out. "They can be as unreasonable as they like." I glanced through the viewport at the launch where they had taken Jylyj. "I have to talk to their healers as soon as we land."

And explain what happened before the crystal infection spread.

The launches didn't land in a clearing or anywhere on the surface, but flew through a series of narrow passes and finally down to a lake at the base of a roaring waterfall cascading down the side of one enormous mountain. I caught my breath as they plunged through the falls and into a wide, long cavern that had been converted into a launch bay.

I saw dozens more launches on the deck of the bay, and hundreds of oKiaf working on them or moving around them. I also spotted well-stocked racks of weapons and other ordnance before I turned to my husband. "Duncan, this is a military base."

He glanced at the guards. "They behave like well-trained soldiers on patrol. Now we have to find out what their orders are."

It didn't take long to do that. As soon as the shuttles landed, we were ordered out of the ship and escorted across the deck to where three oKiaf in strange-looking uniforms waited.

The tallest one in the center spoke first. "We are the Valtas. You are in violation of our laws."

"We were attacked by those men and taken prisoner as we tried to leave the planet," Reever said, and nodded toward the group of mercenaries being herded toward a passage leading away from the bay. "We came to oKia as part of a scientific expedition. We have no interest in committing violence or engaging in any conflict with you."

The Valtas leader didn't seem convinced. "You will be held and questioned."

"I've been trading peacefully with the tribes for years," Uorwlan said. When the leader didn't reply, she added, "You're not putting me in a cell."

"You'll do as you're told. Cooperate, and you will not be harmed." The leader gestured for the guards.

"One of our team members was taken to another shuttle," I said quickly. "He is badly injured. I am a healer, and I can take care of him."

"We have our own healers."

As one of the guards took my arm, I said, "He's infected with the liquid crystal from one of your forbidden areas. I know how to keep it from killing him. If you'll just let me talk to your healers, I can explain the treatment to keep him stabilized."

Now I had his attention. After he studied my face for a few moments, he inclined his head a few degrees. "I will send someone from medical to speak with you."

We were taken from the launch bay through a passage that ran straight through the dark red stone of the mountain and into another, much larger cavern. Here a small city had been built, but in a much different fashion than the abandoned places we had seen on the surface.

Triads of kiafta-shaped permanent shelters made of alloy and stone took up nearly every inch of the cavern floor, interspersed here and there with what appeared to be modified storage buildings. Instead of roads, a complex system of rails hung over the city, on which small glidecars traveled. Everything appeared to be compact, to make the best use of the space available, but it was obvious from the visible activity that thousands of oKiaf inhabited this strange underground settlement.

"They didn't leave their cities," I said to my husband. "They just hid them."

"All these years I've had to bunk down in the dirt with the tribes, when I could have stayed here." Uorwlan looked disgusted.

The guards took us to a glidecar and drove us across the city railings to a structure in the center of the cavern. Unlike the triad dwellings, this building stood alone and had guards posted at every entrance.

From the glidecar we were taken in through a side entrance and down a series of corridors to a row of rooms not unlike the quarters on board the *Sunlace*. The guards then tried to separate us.

"The women stay with us," my husband said.

The guards conferred with each other, and then allowed Uorwlan to go with Qonja, and me to go with Reever.

"Do not try to escape," one of them warned as we entered the room. "If you are found outside this room without a proper escort, you will be shot on sight."

Uorwlan backed away from the room. "No," she said in a strangled voice. "I won't do it."

"They're not slavers," Reever said quickly, trying to go to her. When the guard stepped in his way, he grabbed his arm. "She used to be enslaved. When she disobeyed, her owner would lock her up and starve her, sometimes for weeks. She's remembering that. Let me go to her. I can calm her."

"I'm not afraid." Now Uorwlan sounded furious as she swiped her claws at the guard trying to force her into the room. "I didn't break the law. Let me out of here."

The oKiaf guard slung his weapon over his shoulder and grabbed the Takgiba, who drove her head into his chest and then up, smashing her skull into his jaw. That broke his hold, and she knocked him over onto his back, ripping into him with her claws.

"Uorwlan," Reever called, trying again to get past the guard.

More armed oKiaf flooded into the corridor, and it took four of them to pull the feline off the bleeding guard. They dragged her off her feet and carried her into the room.

Qonja looked over at Reever. "I will try to help her."

"Talk to her. Remind her that this is only temporary," Duncan called back as we were forced into our room. He then spoke to the guard. "I need to see your leader again. I must negotiate for our release."

"Your female attacked without provocation," the guard informed him. "None of you are going to be released now."

Uorwlan began to scream, a sound that was abruptly cut off as the door closed and we were locked in the chamber.

Fifteen

Reever tried to listen at the wall between our chambers, and then to shout through it, but the rooms had been soundproofed. If Uorwlan was still shrieking, we couldn't hear it.

"She will be all right," I told him. "Qonja is an experienced psychologist. He heard what you said; he will know what to do." I recalled Hawk's escape. "Do you think Hawk will be able to find us, or bring help?"

"Not from the oKiaf, and he can't fly Uorwlan's shuttle, not without repairing the stabilizers." He sat down on the sleeping platform and rested his head in his hands. "Even if he does, the bounty hunters have found us. They'll attack any vessel we travel on. We're probably safer here."

I checked the room's storage containers, but found only some nonperishable ration packs that had been left in them. "If you're hungry, there are field rations." I checked the container markings. "These are new, like the shuttles and the weapons. They're not League, either."

"They haven't abandoned their advanced civilization," Reever said. "They've moved it, perhaps redesigned it, but they're definitely protecting it. The tribes who live on the surface must be the camouflage, to fool the League and anyone else who comes here into believing this story about the oKiaf reverting to the old ways."

"I never had the sense that they were acting like primitives for our benefit," I said. "The tribe seemed very natural and happy."

"I'm sure they were, just as I'm convinced the erchepel is only a vacation spot." He saw my expression. "It's when civilized people go into wilderness areas and live as their ancestors did for short periods of time. On Terra, it's called camping out."

I made a rude sound. "On Akkabarr, it's called life."

A guard entered the room with an oKiaf wearing a physician's tunic that had been altered to resemble the other Valtas's military-style uniforms. He was an older male with a lean face and the infinitely weary gaze of someone who had served on many battlefields.

"You are the healer who treated the Skartesh for crystal exposure?" he asked me. When I nodded, he gestured to the guard, who reopened the chamber door to admit Jylyj, who looked thin and shaky but was walking under his own power.

"You will tell me what you did to suspend the crystal's growth," the healer said.

I began to, and then I thought better of it. "I would be happy to share my findings." I paused, looking into those tired old eyes. "As soon as we are released."

"I cannot give the order to release you, not when I

have a guard you wounded in my infirmary." The healer turned to Jylyj. "Things would go better for you if you tell what she did."

"I cannot remember," the Skartesh said. "I was unconscious."

"I can have the men beat it out of you," the healer said, stepping closer to me.

"Signal your staff first," my husband said, also moving in. "In a few moments they will be quite busy."

"It's all right, Duncan. It's interesting to see how an oKiaf physician honors his oath." I regarded the angry oKiaf. "We have a word for men like you." I turned to Jylyj. "How do you say *fool* in their language?"

The Skartesh didn't look at me but bared his teeth at the medical officer. *"Slizac."*

Another guard came in and murmured something to the medical officer, who gestured toward Jylyj. "He is coming with us. I suggest you reconsider, if you wish to ever leave oKia."

"He's not well enough to be questioned," I snapped. "Surely even you can see that."

"I do not make these decisions. Our commander has sent for him; he must go." He hesitated, and then added, "I will escort him and make it clear that he is to be treated carefully."

I abandoned my attempt to bargain for our release. "Let me accompany you to medical, and I'll show you the process I used."

"It will have to be after he is questioned." Without listening to any more of my protests, the medical officer and the guards took Jylyj and left us locked in the chamber.

"Come here," Reever said as soon as we were alone, and took me in his arms as if to comfort me, and established a link. *They are monitoring us; I count five drones embedded in the light emitters and the furnishings.* He slipped one hand between us and passed one of the daggers he kept in his leggings to me. *When they come for us, I'm going to insist we be taken together. Don't try to run, but go along with them. As soon as I see an opportunity to escape, I'll disable the guards.*

Try not to kill them. I quickly tucked the blade into my belt. *What about Qonja and Uorwlan?*

He'll look after her until we can come back for them or find a way to have them released. He smoothed the disheveled hair away from my face. *How long can Jylyj live without the blood treatment?*

I can only guess. I rested my cheek against his shoulder. *Maybe another day or two.*

Reever kissed my brow. *Then we have to take him with us.*

The oKiaf monitoring us saw us only sit together in silence as if comforting each other. Through our link, however, we discussed everything we had seen during the transport from the launch bay to the holding chamber, and what might be the best route out of the underground city.

By the time we had put together a tentative plan of escape, the guards came for us.

Rather than being taken to an interrogation chamber, Reever and I were led outside the building to one of the storage structures surrounding it. There the Valtas's commander stood watching two subordinates and several drones stock shelves with boxes of new rations. He turned as soon as he heard our approach.

"Leave us," he said to the guards. When they withdrew, he turned to Reever and gestured toward a stone path. "Walk with me."

I didn't like being treated like a guest, not when it had been made so obvious that we weren't. "Why?"

"I am taking you to medical," the commander said. "You are needed there. Along the way, I would speak with your mate about matters that concern you both. Is this acceptable, or should I have you returned to your quarters?"

His politeness dumbfounded me, but Reever agreed and followed him away from the food storage area.

"These caverns had existed for millennia," the commander said. "They hold great fascination for the people, and throughout time our tribes have searched for passages into them to explore their secrets. Maps were drawn and handed down for many generations." He stopped at one of the stone markers and looked out at the diminutive city. "When it came time to deal with the League, we knew these places would serve best as the shelters of our future."

Reever seemed puzzled. "So you deceived them into thinking you abandoned technology in order to hide here?"

"It was not a deception. We left all that they had bestowed upon us on the surface." The commander glanced up at the cavern ceiling before regarding my husband. "Everything you see was made or manufactured by the oKiaf."

"That's why the rations in our cell were new," I gestured toward the city. "But why move underground? Why not set up defenses on the surface and in orbit?"

"It has nothing to do with the League, or rather it has everything to do with keeping the League away from oKia." He glanced at me. "No offworlder knows what I am to tell you now."

"We are your prisoners," Reever said. "Why tell us?"

"I have been convinced that you can be trusted." The commander's voice turned hard. "I pray I have not been misled."

The commander began to talk about the destruction of Skart near the end of the war between the Allied League and the Hsktskt Faction.

"The polarization of our orbits around our sun protected oKia from being bombarded by the planetary debris. The remains of Skart were vaporized before they could reach us. We thought we were safe, until the tribes began sending word of hunters falling into pits that opened beneath their feet, and being made into shining stone."

"The crystal," Reever murmured.

The commander nodded. "We have shared our world with the crystal since the Star Wolf created the first tribe. It has always been found in a solid form. But we now believe that the energy released by the destruction of Skart has caused it to change."

Reever's eyes narrowed. "By change you mean it can now convert itself to liquid form."

The commander inclined his head. "The deposits that you and your team found in the mountains are spreading beneath the surface of our planet. Every year they claim more of the land from the trees and the animals that sustain us. "If our scientists do not discover how to stop the growth of the crystal and safely remove it from oKia, in a few decades it will engulf the entire planet."

"Why would you keep such a disaster secret?" Reever asked. "There are scientists on thousands of world who might help you find a solution."

"This is our world and our problem," the commander said.

"You're afraid to tell anyone," I said, seeing once more in my mind the crystal spreading over the clearing. "You think the League will try to take the crystal from oKia and use it as a weapon."

"The crystal has already consumed other worlds." His light eyes met mine. "If the League discovered it here, in its liquid form, nothing would stop them. They would invade oKia to mine it, and kill everyone who got in their way."

The paranoia and isolationism practiced by the oKiaf seemed more rational to me now. "Have you made any progress in finding a solution?"

The commander shook his head. "We have found nothing that destroys the crystal. It kills every living thing it touches. We know that Cu^2Au repels it; large deposits of the alloy left behind by ancient forests are what protect these caverns. But even that will not save us for long.

"When the crystal covers the surface of our world, all of our food sources will die. The oxygen once shed into our atmosphere by the plants will dwindle and disappear, and the surface temperature will drop. Then oKia will die, and take us all into the belly of the stars."

"You have enough ships to evacuate the planet before that happens," my husband pointed out. "You can leave your world, as the Skartesh did, and make a home for your people on a new planet."

The commander shook his head. "Even if we were to send away enough of our people to keep our species alive, the League would learn of it and wish to know what drove them from our world. They would come with their ships and their probes. We could not hold them off for long."

"They will do that after you're gone," I predicted.

"There will be nothing left for them to take," the commander replied. "When the crystal has taken over oKia completely, it will solidify around it and go back to sleep. Nothing can reawaken it once it has eaten a world."

Memories Reever had given me of the year Cherijo had spent on Catopsa flooded into my thoughts. The depot world had been made of the Pel crystal. After he and Cherijo had freed the slaves from the prisons there, the Pel had changed into its liquid form and devoured the slave depot. I opened my mouth to tell the commander this, but felt Reever take my hand in his.

Say nothing yet of Catopsa.

"This is a very dangerous secret," my husband said. "Why are you trusting us with it?"

"Your mate, and the miracle she performed on your interpreter," the commander said. "Before him, no one has ever survived exposure." He turned to me. "Dnoc says you are the Crystal Healer of legend. I do not know if that is true or not, for you are a female, but you did save the life of the Skartesh. Now we would ask that you help us save our world."

*   *   *

The commander escorted us by glidecar to the Valtas's central medical facility, located in one of the largest triad structures in the city. At the entrance the medical officer I had met in our chamber waited, and greeted me with a dour glare.

"Your patient has been a great trial to us," he said as he led us through the assessment area and back into the treatment rooms. "He refuses to let anyone examine him but you. I would have sedated him, but for his condition."

I stopped in front of the isolation chamber, and through the viewer saw Jylyj's shadow behind a modesty curtain. "What *were* you able to do?"

"I managed to take a hematological scan. The level of crystal infecting his bloodstream is rising. I also detected traces of it in his internal organs." He gestured toward a portable dialysis machine. "We have attempted to use the filtering treatment that you described to me. It had almost no effect."

I checked the machine, and in the reservoir saw blackened pieces of heartwood. "You used heartwood charcoal?" The medical officer nodded. "That is where you went wrong. Most of the resin is burned out. Have someone refit the unit with seasoned, unburned wood." I tried to open the door to the treatment room, but it was secured by pass code. "What is the entry code?"

After giving the commander a worried glance, the medical officer told me the code, and I went inside.

"Healer Jarn," Jylyj said from behind the curtain. He sounded relieved, but when I reached for the curtain, he added, "No, leave it closed. Tell the others to leave, and then come around."

I turned to Reever, who nodded and spoke to the commander. "I would like to see the other members of our team and arrange to contact the one who remains on the surface."

After the men had left, I walked around and entered the gap in the curtain. Instantly, I saw why Jylyj had not wanted the others to see him; small spots of crystal glittered in his darkening fur, and the shape of his face had also altered. His once-dark eyes, now a light green, had tiny cataracts of crystal occluding the irises.

"Initiate sterile field," Jylyj said, and a bioelectric curtain formed around us. To me, he said, "This will keep them from overhearing us."

"Just so." I found a container of gloves and pulled on a pair before I went to him. "Either the crystal wishes you to be an oKiaf when it kills you, or you lied to me. Which is it?"

He glanced down at himself. "I told you as much of the truth as I could. Genetically I *am* Skartesh, or at least I was until an hour ago. My body is reverting to my natal form."

"You were born oKiaf, but you were alterformed into a Skartesh." As he nodded, I used a scanner to detect the level of crystal infection, which was indeed rising, before I checked the occlusions in his eyes. "The League scientists didn't do this. Their technology is not this advanced."

"After the initial alterforming, my body did it on its own," Jylyj told me. "My immune system must have responded to the changes made to my DNA. Within a few hours, all of my oKiaf genes were gone, replaced by Skartesh."

"This reversion could be a good sign. Excuse me for a moment. Deactivate sterile field." As the bioelectric field vanished, I went to leave.

"Reinitiate sterile field." Jylyj seized my arm. "You can't tell them. I have already violated tribal law. If they learn of who I was"—he shook his head—"it could be very bad for the rest of you."

"Why?" Now I felt utterly confused. "Who are you?"

"I was a major in the Allied League intelligence forces," Jylyj said. "I was originally alterformed to infiltrate the Skartesh when they fled to K-2," Jylyj said. "My real name is Shon Valtas."

I frowned. "Then these are your people. Your tribe."

"Not since I enlisted," he told me. "My father forbade it, and when I defied him, he cast me out of the tribe. It's the same as being dead to them, and as an outcast, I could never return here."

"But you did." My head hurt. "What laws did you break, and how much trouble are you in?"

"Outcasts are shunned by the tribes and driven from the planet," he said slowly. "If they ever return to oKia and are discovered, they're handed over to Elphian for punishment. As is anyone who helps them."

"What is the punishment?"

"Enslavement, or imprisonment for life." He sighed. "Forgive me."

"Oh, *now* you're sorry." I thought fast. "We can probably keep them from finding out who you are for a little while, but we really have to get you out of here."

"In a few hours, it won't matter," he said. "I regret that I didn't tell you the truth. I only wanted to die on my homeworld."

"You *did* jump in that pit of crystal deliberately." I stared at him. "That's why you kept telling me afterward to let you go. You were trying to kill yourself."

"The League has been hunting me ever since they discovered that I was a touch healer. I changed my appearance, assumed the identity of a dead Skartesh medical resident, and even hid myself on Joren. But I knew they would never stop looking, and I grew tired of running." He lay back on the table and stared into the emitter hanging over it. "My father was like me, although not as strong. He said the crystal was one of the few things that could kill us. After I lost Jadaira . . . I only wanted it to end."

I felt like slapping him. "I don't know who Jadaira is, but you're a healer with a tremendous gift. You could use it to help so many, but instead you decide to commit suicide. That isn't as stupid as it is obscene."

He propped himself up on his arms. "Do you know what the League wanted me to do? What oKiaf touch healers have always done for them? We're used in interrogation centers. Prisoners are beaten and abused to the brink of death, and then we're brought in to heal them, so they can be tortured again. And again. And again."

My stomach clenched. "You could have refused to do it."

"You don't refuse the League. You know what they're capable of." He gave me a weary look. "They murdered my little brother. They drowned him after my father refused to serve as their chief interrogator."

Little wonder the father had made Jylyj—Shon—an outcast for joining them. "But they didn't know about you or your abilities, or they would never have discharged you from the military."

He shook his head. "I concealed what I was from them for years, until one of the aquatic pilots on K-2 fatally injured herself while saving the Skartesh. I found her dying, and because I cared for her, I couldn't let her go. After I used my ability a second time to save the young leader of a neighboring world, word got back to the League, and they came for me. And I wasn't discharged from the military, Jarn. I deserted."

"You did what was necessary." I didn't care if he was a criminal. He had destroyed his life in order to remain true to his oath as a healer and do the work. In my eyes, it had been a noble act. "It must have taken great courage. You have no reason to feel shame."

His voice turned bitter. "I will if the League captures me and forces me to use my ability on their prisoners."

"The League is not here, and you are not giving yourself to the oKiaf, either." I jabbed my finger into his chest. "You are going to fight this infection, and give me time to find a treatment for it. You are going to live, Major Valtas."

"Why should I?"

Anger surged inside me. "In all the years Cherijo Grey Veil was hunted for what she was—for what I am—she never gave up healing. It is why we were made, and to deny it or run away from it or to kill yourself rather than face it is the act of a sniveling coward. I am many things, but I am not that, and whatever happens to me, I will not be remembered that way." I gave him a look of contempt. "Is this how you wish to be remembered?"

"My father is dead. My tribe would have me imprisoned or sold to slavers." He closed his eyes. "There is no one left who cares."

"There is me, and Duncan. There are others like you and me. They are the brothers and sisters of our hearts." I took his paw between my hands. "We will be your tribe now."

He made a rough sound. "You don't even like me."

"Then give me a reason to. Live. Be my brother." I gripped his paw as the tears in my eyes spilled over. "Shon, please. I have never met anyone like me. I can't tell you why, but I know, in here"—I pressed his paw to my heart—"we need you."

Some of the pain left his gaze, and then he looked away. "This is a useless conversation. I will not survive the infection."

"You let me worry about that." I draped him with linens and quickly wrapped most of his face and head with gauze. "I need to put you back on dialysis until we can arrange transport off oKia. I will tell them that the crystal is suppurating through your skin and you have to be kept under quarantine."

He glanced at his arms. "Crystal *is* coming out of my skin."

"You see? I will not even have to lie," I said. "The risk of exposure should keep them out of here." I turned toward the room's control console. "Deactivate sterile field."

I went out of the isolation room and into the corridor. A technician had just finished replacing the charcoal in the filtering reservoir with fresh wood shavings.

"The patient has crystal erupting through his derma," I told the technician, whose eyes bulged. "Anyone who enters this room risks exposure and infection, so I am placing it under strict quarantine. No one enters without first obtaining my permission. Show me how to change the security code on this door panel."

Once I changed the access code, I wheeled the unit into the isolation room, secured the door, and started the treatment.

"What do you think of me now, Healer?" he asked.

"I am glad to know that your name is *not* Jylyj," I mentioned as I monitored the level of crystal in his blood. "I never liked it much. It doesn't suit you at all."

"It was that or Hurkuut."

I grimaced. "That sounds like someone regurgitating."

"So I thought, but the Skartesh language is not known for its lyrical qualities." He watched the scanner with me. "You did see me coming out of the water that morning on Joren. I couldn't risk exposing myself by telling you the truth."

"I knew it." I frowned. "But how did you learn to swim? As a Skartesh, you should have gone into shock from being immersed."

"I did not acquire the Skartesh's biological aversion to water." His voice changed. "Ever since my brother drowned, I'd hated it, and feared it. Then I met Jadaira on K-2, and she was an aquatic. To be with her, I had to learn to swim."

I had no great love of water, and silently gave thanks that Reever had not turned out to be an aquatic. "How did that go?"

"Awkward at first. Dair coaxed me into a little pond, and I thought I'd choke to death on my fear. But she was patient with me, and gradually I learned to tolerate it, and then to relax in it, and finally to love it, as I loved her."

The thought of an oKiaf falling in love with an aquatic should have seemed bizarre, but I found it both charming and sad. "You said you lost her. Did she die in the war?"

"No, I lost her to another male." He grimaced. "She gave her heart to one of her own kind. They are far more happy together than she and I would have been."

"That doesn't make it any easier to accept." I thought of all the jealousy I had felt toward Cherijo for being Reever's first wife. "If you are in love with this aquatic, why have you shown such interest in me?"

"I don't know," he admitted. "It was your scent at first—you may not be beautiful by oKiaf standards, but you smell like the loveliest of females. And then you touched me, and I swear to you, I felt it in my soul. It was as if I recognized you, here." He tapped his chest. "I didn't know how complete your bond was with your mate. I guess on some level I wanted to test it."

"Duncan and I . . ." How did I explain the complexity of our relationship? "We belong to each other. There will never be another for me, or for him."

"I never wished to admit it, but I felt the same for Jadaira. It was never meant to be, however." He looked over at the dialysis unit. "This will stabilize the infection rate, but that is all it will do. We have never found any method of removing the crystal once it has infiltrated a living body."

I was slightly relieved by the change of subject. "It mutates like a virus, spreads like cancer, eats like bacteria. I have never seen any pathogen like it. Yet its composition is mineral—almost identical to that of common quartz."

"Perhaps it is a silica-based life-form." He seemed amused. "If it is, will you name it after me?"

"Shon's planet-eating rock?" I suggested.

"Valtas crystal," he corrected. "It sounds more dignified."

Someone chimed the door panel, and I handed the scanner to Shon before I went to see who it was. Reever and the commander stood waiting in the corridor, and neither looked happy.

"I'll return in a moment," I told him, and stepped outside. To Reever, I said, "I've started Sh—Jylyj back on dialysis. His readings are stabilizing, but the infection has advanced. Were you able to signal Xonea?"

My husband shook his head. "We have been unable to reach the ship at all. The station has been overtaken by mercenaries. They are holding the Elphian hostage and have demanded an exchange. The Valtas have agreed to their terms."

I turned to the commander. "You can't trade my husband and me like we are only commodities. There must be another way to rescue your people."

"The mercenaries did not ask for either of you," the commander said. "They want the Skartesh."

Sixteen

"It is a good trade," the commander insisted. He couldn't quite look me in the eye. "The Skartesh is near death, and nothing can save him."

"Forgive me," I said, "but when did you become a physician? Before or after your military training?"

The oKiaf gave me a sour look. "What I mean to say is, he will not live long enough to be used by them or suffer at their hands."

My astonishment over the fact that the mercenaries had not come for me and Reever became lost in the disgust I felt for this man. "As opposed to be used and made to suffer by you." I nodded. "I thought you were a stupid man. Now I am sure of it."

The commander glanced at my husband. "I cannot sacrifice hundreds to spare one who will not live. We are launching in thirty minutes." He inclined his head toward me before he walked away.

"They're not taking him." I turned around and unlocked the door panel. "I won't permit it."

"We may have no choice in the matter." Reever followed me into the isolation room and watched me secure the panel. "Jarn, you can't barricade yourself in here with Jylyj. The Valtas will simply blast their way in."

"You don't understand," I said very patiently.

"We don't have time to smuggle the Skartesh out of the building, much less the city," my husband said as he examined the room, "but we may be able to hide him. Is there a gurney we can use to move him?"

"You *don't* understand." I dragged him around the curtain. "I don't have a Skartesh in here anymore. Duncan, meet Major Shon Valtas."

"Where is . . . Jylyj?" He took a step closer to the table. "Jarn, what have you done to him?"

"Why does he always assume that I have done it?" I demanded of the ceiling.

"This is my true appearance. I am oKiaf. The crystal has reversed the alterforming that made me Skartesh." Shon sat up. "What has happened?"

Reever told him about the attack on the station, and the commander's stupid decision.

Shon swung his legs over the side of the table. "Disconnect the unit, healer."

"You are not going along with this." I stopped him from removing his IV. "Say you go and you do die on board the mercenaries' ship. What do you think they will do with your body? Eject it into the nearest star?"

"No. My body has to be destroyed. The oKiaf have some powerful ordnance. Most of it is pulse weaponry and too large for our needs, but there will be a selection of thermal fusion grenades stocked for the infantry." He regarded me steadily. "You must implant one in my body."

I backed away from him. "No."

He continued as if I hadn't spoken. "When I am on board and safely away from the station, I will detonate the grenade."

"I am not making you into a bomb," I shouted.

"Then the League will pay the mercenaries for my body, harvest my DNA, and use it to create an army of soldiers with my abilities." He stood, bracing himself for a moment. "I cannot allow them to do that."

An alarm sounded, and Reever went to the panel to check the corridor. Medical staff ran in both directions. An oKiaf began speaking over the com.

"A dozen ships have assumed orbit and are firing on the surface settlements," Shon said, translating for me. "The Valtas are evacuating all of the tribes above into the underground cities."

Outside, the commander appeared with a unit of armed soldiers, and demanded entry.

Shon went to the wall panel, and before I could stop him, spoke to the commander. "You are as impatient as ever, Dagar."

The commander stared at the viewer. "Shon? What are you doing in there? Where is . . ." he stopped as he put it all together. "*You* are the Skartesh? How can this be?"

"Give us a moment, if you would." He lifted his paw to switch off the com, and stared at his crystal-streaked claws. "Reever, can you convince Captain Torin to pursue the ship that takes me?"

"If the mercenaries have not taken over the *Sunlace*, and I explain the circumstances," my husband said, "I believe I can."

"The captain cannot take half measures," Shon said. "The ship I am on must be destroyed."

"No." Everything inside me reacted violently to the thought of Shon sacrificing himself. "We can signal Joren, and hold them off until the HouseClan ships arrive. I was a member of the Ruling Council. They will listen to me."

"There is more to protect here than just Shon's life," Reever told me. "The League cannot be allowed to discover the crystal on oKia."

"To hell with the damned crystal." I saw from their expressions that they had no intentions of listening to me. "I will not be a part of this."

I opened the door panel and strode out into the corridor, nearly walking into the commander. "If you hand Shon over to the mercenaries, they will find out about the crystal. They will tell the League. You cannot do it."

"Now that they know I am on oKia," Shon said from behind me, "they will send every available ship they have in this region, and hire more. I cannot stay. I am a qualified fighter pilot. Give me a strafer, cousin, and I will draw them away before I fly it into the sun."

"There is no guarantee they will believe you are the one for whom they came," Dagar said, and then turned to Reever. "We have made contact with your vessel," he told my husband. "They intend to engage the mercenaries. I am sending our surface patrols up to assist. They should hold them off long enough to get a launch down to the surface."

"One of our team escaped the mercenary attack," Reever said. "An avatar. He is still on the surface."

The commander shook his head. "We found him and

brought him down from the surface. He is with the Jore-nian and the Takgiba."

"We are taking Shon with us," I said. Before the men could respond, I added, "They know he was part of our expedition. Xonea can transition out of this system and take us back to Joren. Then if they want a fight, they can face the HouseClan fleet."

"Why would Joren protect one of us?" Dagar asked.

"Because Dnoc was wrong about me, Commander," I told him. "I am not the crystal healer. Your cousin is."

I expected more arguments, but for once the men listened to me and agreed to the plan. I quickly rigged a portable version of the dialysis unit that Shon could carry on his back, and took as much heartwood pulp as I could fit into my case.

We met Qonja, Hawk, and Uorwlan at the launch bay, where one of the *Sunlace*'s shuttles had just landed. The Takgiba's black and white fur appeared patchy, and there were some deep scratches on Qonja's arms, but she seemed calm now.

"I'm ready to see this place from the display of a remote scanner," she told Reever. "Let's jaunt out of here."

"There is not enough room for all of us," Qonja said. "Hawk and I will fly on one of the oKiaf shuttles."

Shon stayed behind to speak to the commander alone, and when he walked up the boarding ramp, he looked a little dazed.

"Come and sit down." I followed him and checked the lines connected to the unit in his pack before I scanned him. "What is it? Are you feeling weaker?"

"No, I am well." He removed the pack carefully, handing it to me before he sat down. "It seems my father lied to me. According to Dagar, he did not carry out his threat. I was never cast out of the tribe."

"Is that good news," I asked, "or bad?"

"It is confusing," he admitted. "My father made it very clear what my punishment would be if I joined the League. My defiance enraged him. He never responded to any of the signals I sent after I left oKia." He ducked his head. "I don't understand. My father did not make idle threats, and he had every reason to cast me out."

"Perhaps he found a reason to forgive you," I suggested as I fastened the flight harness over him. "It would be fitting for you to do the same."

He met my gaze. "My name has not been rubbed away from the tribe's naming hide. The hunters still call out my name during the winter count. My stories are still told around the fires." This seemed to astound him. "I have never been forgotten."

I smiled. "So now you have two tribes."

The Jorenian pilot said little to us, and took off as soon as the oKiaf gave him clearance. From the viewports we saw oKiaf strafers patrolling the upper atmosphere, and debris from what appeared to have been a ferocious fight, but no mercenary ships appeared or tried to attack us.

"They must have been no match for the *Sunlace*," I said as we entered the blackness of space and approached the Jorenian vessel.

"More likely they retreated to call for reinforcements," my husband said, looking grim.

Once we were back on board, we were summoned to the command center to meet with Xonea.

I needed to take Shon to medical, but I wanted to make sure no more bargains were made in my absence. I also thought Xonea should see for himself what the crystal was doing to Shon's body.

"I have to signal my ship," Uorwlan said. "If I still have one."

Qonja and Hawk offered to escort her to the communications center, and the three went off together.

"We should do this briefing quickly," I told Duncan as we headed for the command center. "Knowing my ClanBrother's temper, I would leave out the part about the oKiaf holding us prisoner."

In one way it was a relief to be back on the ship, and in another it made me feel as if I were back in the locked chamber in the underground city. Already I missed the fresh cold air of the planet, the colors of the trees, and the feel of the ground beneath my feet. Compared to oKia, the *Sunlace* now seemed sterile and lifeless.

"How did you escape the takeover at the station?" Reever asked the shuttle pilot, who was following us to the command center.

The Jorenian checked his wristcom, muttered something, and abruptly changed direction, disappearing down an adjacent corridor.

I had never seen a member of the crew behave so rudely. Then I thought of how vengeful Cherijo's adopted people could be. "Do you think Xonea and the crew are angry with us for keeping them from chasing after the mercenaries who survived the battle?"

"I don't know, but something is wrong," Reever said.

My ClanBrother had assembled all of his department chiefs in the command center for the briefing, and none of the Jorenians looked particularly happy to see us. After offering a terse gesture of greeting, the captain asked Reever to report on what had occurred on-planet.

As my husband related our experiences, I turned my attention to Shon.

"Dagar said that when the crystal completely solidifies over the surface of a planet, it cannot convert back to its liquid phase," I said. "How does he know what it does?"

"Our scientists conducted many tests on the crystal," Shon said. "They found that once the crystal solidifies completely around any living object, it alters the composition so that it cannot change back. Not even Cu^2Au can change it back to its liquid phase."

I could deal with that. "So once crystal has hardened on the outside of your body, it should not be able to turn liquid again and retreat back into your bloodstream and organs."

"In theory, no." He gave me an uncertain look. "What are you thinking of doing?"

"If I can somehow force the crystal to emerge onto your skin and solidify, and I determine how to cut through it, I can surgically remove it." I saw his eyes. "Before you suffocate."

"Is there something you wish to contribute to the discussion, Healer?" Xonea said.

So we were back to calling each other Healer and Captain. "No." I looked at my ClanBrother's impassive features, and felt a little guilty for ignoring the ongoing briefing. "Major Valtas and I were discussing his condition. I will wait until this is over to continue."

"Major, you have considerable knowledge of the oKiaf defense capabilities on the planet, do you not?" Xonea asked abruptly.

"It has been some time since I have lived here," Shon admitted. "All I know is what we saw while underground, but it appears to be considerable. I think the oKiaf will be able to easily repel any future attacks by the mercenaries."

For a moment Xonea almost looked disappointed. "We intercepted a signal from a League vessel that indicated oKia as its destination. Have your people allied themselves with the League again?"

"No, Captain, they have not, and I can assure you, they have no interest in rejoining the League." Shon gestured toward the viewport. "If they come to oKia, they will be treated like any other invader."

"I am glad to hear it. The League has meddled enough in our plans." Xonea turned to Reever. "When you could not raise the ship, did you attempt to contact Joren?"

"Our transceiver was damaged, and then there wasn't time." My husband leaned forward. "I assume you did."

"I saw no reason for it. We were able to defend the ship adequately." Xonea rose to his feet. "Very well, I think we have covered all the pertinent issues for now. We will transition in a few minutes." He turned to gaze at Shon. "Major Valtas, the oKiaf authorities have signaled and expressed a wish to speak with you privately. If you wish to respond, you should do so now."

Shon rose to his feet and headed for the communications center.

"I need you back in medical as soon as you're

through," I called after him. To Xonea, I said, "Are there any wounded?"

"Some of the crew sustained minor injuries, but the medical staff treated them." My ClanBrother didn't seem concerned as he dismissed his officers. "You should go to your quarters and rest while you can, Healer."

"I have to see to Shon and the wounded first." I turned to Reever. "You should check on the crystal in the survey lab." As distracted as we had been with the oKiaf and their killer crystal, I'd given little thought to the specimen we'd left behind on the *Sunlace*.

Reever touched my arm. "Signal me as soon as you get to medical, and let me know about the wounded."

"Why?"

He glanced past me. "Something is not right. I cannot say what it is, but Xonea is not acting like himself. I don't like the way the rest of the Jorenians were looking at us, either. All I sense from them and Xonea is hostility."

"That is usually the mind-set of the warrior fresh from battle." I sighed. "I know what you mean. I feel it, too. Once we're back on Joren and surrounded by the HouseClan fleet, I'm sure everyone's spirits will improve."

I took the nearest lift to medical bay and mentally went over what I would need to continue the filtering treatments to keep Shon alive while I searched for a cure. As I walked into the bay, I expected to see most of the berths filled and the staff busy attending to them. The echo of my footsteps rang against my ears as I surveyed the emptiness.

Every berth had been made up perfectly. Equipment trays stood neatly arranged and waiting to be used. The floor itself glowed, as spotless as if it were brand-new. I knew in my absence Herea would have taken her responsibilities very seriously, but in the wake of the battle, there should have been some disorder.

"Herea? Charge Nurse?" I called out, walking around the unoccupied bay. I found everything in its place, but no one on duty. Frowning, I went to a com panel and signaled Command. "Xonea? No one is here in medical. Did Herea set up a temporary triage in one of the cargo bays?"

The panel must have been malfunctioning, or the captain was ignoring me, for no one responded.

"Fine, ClanBrother. I will go and find it myself." I walked out and down the corridor to the survey lab. The panel was no longer secured, and I opened it to find another empty room—this one stripped of all the special equipment Nalek Kalea had installed. The black crystal was also gone.

"Reever?" I started to cross the threshold, and then stepped back. The door panel closed in my face.

A terrible bleakness washed over me as I hurried to another com panel in the corridor and attempted to signal command. When I received no response, I tried a second panel, and then a third, and sent signals to command, communications, engineering, and the galley. No one on the ship responded to my signals.

That was when I became aware of the emptiness around me. The ship was about to transition; the corridors should have been bustling with crew members preparing for the interdimensional jump. The passages were instead completely deserted. In fact, since leaving command, I had not seen a single member of the crew. It was as if I were the only one left on board.

I ran to our quarters and found them empty. With shaking hands I filled a server with water and drank it to ease my tight throat. Sweat had dampened the native garments I still wore, and I decided to change before I went back to command and demanded some answers from my ClanBrother.

As I went to retrieve fresh garments from the storage units in our bed chamber, I saw Jenner and Juliet sleeping on the end of our berth. I went to scratch Jenner's head as he looked at me with his big blue eyes, and then froze as I remembered.

We had left the cats back on Joren.

"No." I reached down to seize the cat by the throat, and my hand passed through the image of it, causing a brief static disruption of the holographic image.

I ran to the com panel and initiated a ship-wide signal. "Reever, if you can hear me, respond." I waited a few seconds and tried again. "Duncan, this is an emergency, please respond now."

Reever didn't reply to my signal. Neither did anyone else. When I attempted to leave our quarters, the door panel refused to open.

I went to the storage units where I kept my garments and weapons and found them empty. The furnishings turned out to be more holographic images. The only thing the prep unit would produce was water. I searched frantically, but found nothing I could use to defend myself.

Through the viewport I saw the dwindling image of oKia, and rested my brow against the plas.

"Duncan," I whispered. "What have we done?"

"The door panel opened behind me. "Your husband is here, Dr. Grey Veil."

I whirled around to see a short-statured, dark-haired Terran and two mercenaries holding Duncan and Shon, who were bound and gagged. The Terran held a device in his hand, and when he pressed a switch on it the image of our quarters on the *Sunlace* vanished, replaced by another, unfamiliar chamber.

"This is a secured cell," the Terran said to me. "You will be kept here during our sojourn. Follow instructions, and you will be treated fairly."

I knew him now, and the sight of him horrified me.

Reever suddenly broke free of his bonds and shoved one mercenary into the other. As he bent down to grab the rifle the mercenary had dropped, the Terran produced a pulse pistol, turned, and shot my husband in the right arm and both legs. I screamed as Reever went down and blood spurted from the massive wounds in his limbs.

I ran, uncaring of the pistol the Terran pointed at me, and knelt in a pool of Reever's blood.

"Duncan." I tried to staunch the flow with my hands, and then Shon was there, cut free of his bonds. He gently moved my hands aside and rested his paws over my husband's leg wounds.

Light poured out of the edges of Shon's tunic as he closed his eyes and his expression turned to one of great concentration. When he lifted one paw to place it over Reever's arm wound, I saw the terrible gaping hole in my husband's thigh had disappeared.

I looked up at the Terran, who was smiling.

"We had to be sure we had the touch healer," he told me as he tucked the pistol in his belt and walked out.

Shon opened his eyes and sagged back against the wall of the cell. "He will be all right."

"Where are we?" I asked. "Whose ship is this?"

"I don't know." He was breathing heavily now. "But this is not a League ship."

More mercenaries came into the room and dragged me to my feet. When I fought them, one hit me over the back of the head with his weapon, and I lost consciousness.

I came to in a different place, my body sprawled on a deck. Beyond me, a long row of observation panels showed a vast expanse of stars and blackness. The Terran who had shot Duncan stood looking out, but when I propped myself up, he turned around.

"You are awake. Good. It's time we talked."

Joseph Grey Veil began walking toward me.

Seventeen

I knew that he was Joseph Grey Veil. I recognized him from a few pictures that I had found among Cherijo's possessions. His features also told me who he was. Looking upon him was like gazing into a distorted mirror.

I also knew that Joseph Grey was dead, murdered on Terra by Cherijo's brother.

No. Something shriveled inside me, cold and shuddering. *It can't be him.*

"It's been such a long time, my dear." The Terran came to stand over me, and offered a hand to help me up.

Don't let him touch me.

I crawled backward away from it and stood, reaching for the blade I had tucked beneath my belt.

"The guards took the knife," Joseph said. "You should not have fought them. They wouldn't have hurt you if you had obeyed my orders."

Who is he? "Who are you?"

"They said you had experienced memory loss due to a head injury." He studied my face. "I am Joseph Grey

Veil." He waited for me to say something, and took a step toward me. "I am your father, Cherijo."

I have no father. I was made, not born.

I backed away. "Joseph Grey Veil died on Terra years ago." My shoulders hit the wall behind me. "Who are you?"

"You still believe that your brother Jericho killed me. Small wonder, then, that you look so frightened." He smiled at me. "That man who died was a clone, like you. He was, in fact, the oldest of your cloned brothers. In dangerous situations I often used him as a double. I was quite put out when Jericho murdered him."

He's lying. Look into his eyes. I can see it.

My head throbbed and I felt as if I might puke. "I don't believe you."

"Of course you don't. You are in shock," he advised me. "In time, you will come to accept that I am alive, and we will be together from now on."

No. *No.* NO.

Fear crawled all over me, inside and out, and all I could think was that I had to get as far away from this man as I could. "Why did you abduct us? What do you want?"

"You are my daughter, Cherijo. In fact, legally you are still my property. I am simply recovering what belongs to me." He went to a prep unit and dialed up a server of tea. "You haven't stopped drinking chamomile, I hope."

Run.

I ran to the door panel and tried to open it. He had secured it. "I want to go back to my husband."

"Duncan Reever is not your husband. You are not

classified as a sentient being, so you cannot marry." He filled a clear server with a light amber liquid. "You will need it to be sweet for the shock. Do you prefer sugar or honey?"

He'll use it to cover up the taste of the drugs. Don't drink it.

Sweat stung my eyes as it streamed down my face. If I could have crawled up the wall to get away from him, I would have. "Take me back to Duncan."

"I think honey is more soothing." He stirred something into the server and brought it to me. "Here. Drink. It will calm your nerves."

Throw it in his face. Blind him.

I couldn't bring myself to do that, so I slapped the server out of his hand. "Get away from me."

"Why are you so afraid?" Something gleamed in his eyes. "I created you. I raised you. You have known me most of your life. I never harmed you, did I?"

He is not *my father.*

I turned and pounded on the door panel, shouting for someone to help me. When I felt a cold hand settle on the back of my neck, dread made me freeze.

Oh God oh God no please don't—

The voice inside my head abruptly went silent.

"That's better." Still holding my neck, he turned me around to face him. "I am sorry I did not come for you before now. By killing my double, your brother caused a great deal of trouble for me, and then I was blamed for the war between the League and the Hsktskt. Fortunately, I had some colleagues in the research field who knew better and helped me go into hiding. In all the years that we have been kept apart, I never stopped thinking about you, Daughter. I came to find you as soon as I could."

Uorwlan had warned us about the one sending the mercenaries after us ... *a wealthy Terran with friends among the League.*

"You are the one who put the bounty on me and Duncan." I wanted to shout it, but the only thing that would come from my throat was a thin whisper. Sweat now soaked my garments, and I trembled all over.

"I could not personally search the entire galaxy for you," he explained as he steered me over to the observation viewer. "Offering the bounty was the quickest and surest method of finding you."

My father would never trust mercenaries with me. He despised offworlders.

Some of the inexplicable fear drained out of me. "Are you taking me back to Terra?"

He laughed. "No, I'm afraid we wouldn't be very welcome on the homeworld." He released his grip on me. "I can't discuss my plans with you just yet. Later, when you are thinking more rationally, perhaps I will."

I still felt enough terror squeezing my insides to make my voice shake. "Then take me back to my—to Duncan."

"In a little while," he said. "First, I would like you to tell me where Marel is."

God, he knows.

"Marel?" Surely this was the worst of my nightmares. "I don't know that name."

"You should. You and her father picked it out together." He chuckled, as if it were all a jest. "Cherijo, did you really think you could hide her from me? I have been waiting for years for you to make me a grandfather."

I would kill myself before I acknowledged my child's existence. "If you are referring to the one pregnancy I had before you abducted me the last time, I miscarried the fetus. You confirmed that yourself when you examined me on Terra."

"I know your immune system wouldn't allow you to carry a child full-term, as I designed it that way," he agreed. "But recently, the Omorr have made great strides toward the creation of an artificial womb to sustain premature infants delivered in the first trimester. The bulk of the research and design of the chamber was done by an Omorr surgeon. The same one, as it happens, who attended you during your miscarriage."

I said nothing.

"Tell me where she is, Cherijo, and I will see to it that you're reunited with her as soon as she can be retrieved. She belongs with us." He tried to touch my face, but I jerked out of reach. "If you don't tell me, you'll never see her again."

"There is no child," I insisted. "I lost my baby. The Jorenians will give you the medical records to prove it."

"Of course." He sounded thoughtful. "The Jorenians would do anything to protect you, wouldn't they? Part of the problem in finding you was always getting past them. I want to show you something."

When I made no move to follow him, he took me by the arm and hauled me across the deck to a vid panel set into the wall.

"I took great interest in the Hsktskt who was alter-formed into a Jorenian," he said as he switched on the screen. "Jorenians, like the Hsktskt, refuse to live as slaves, and to attempt to abduct one is to sign one's own death warrant. Acquiring samples of their DNA, however, only involves briefly interrupting one of their funerary probes on its flight into their star. I believe that is how the Hsktskt acquired what they used to create PyrsVar."

I saw the image of a young Jorenian male in an empty isolation chamber. He appeared frightened, and moved restlessly around the room.

"I commissioned the alterforming of this slave-born crossbreed to serve as a subject for my viral research," he said, indicating the image. "It took some months, but with my help the geneticists were able to alter his DNA and his body to make him approximately ninety percent pure Jorenian."

A drone arm extended from the ceiling of the chamber and jabbed a syrinpress into the neck of the young male. I flinched exactly as he did in the image.

"Using what I learned from studying this male's physiology, I engineered a virus," Joseph said. "He has just been injected with it." He tapped some of the screen controls. "Now I'll increase the speed of the replay so you can observe the full effects quickly. This will cover twenty-four hours in a few seconds."

The actions of the isolated male began to speed up. He clutched at his belly, began to sweat, vomited, fell several times, and then collapsed. His mouth opened again and again as he apparently called for help. His movements became slower, and he fell, unconscious, and stopped breathing.

The young male's face blurred momentarily, and I blinked the tears from my eyes.

"No need to be upset, my dear. He was bred in a slave

pen. Granted, dying in this manner was quite painful, but really nothing compared to the lifetime of misery he would have experienced as a slave." Joseph switched off the image. "The virus attacks either through the bloodstream or the respiratory system, depending on how it is delivered. But the truth of it is that it only kills Jorenians."

His self-satisfied babbling finally penetrated my wretched sorrow. "You were a doctor once. You took an oath to do no harm to any other sentient being. How could you do such a thing?"

"I had planned to disperse the virus on Joren in order to find you," he admitted, as if it were something of little consequence. "Until now I had thought that would no longer be necessary."

I stared at him. "You are a monster."

"I will have what belongs to me, Cherijo." He used the com panel. "Captain, please set course for Joren."

"You *have* me," I said.

"I want Marel," he told me. "Tell me where she is, and I will destroy the virus as soon as she joins us."

"There is no Marel," I said, desperately clinging to my lie. "You would be murdering millions of people for one child who exists only in your imagination."

"She is as real as you, Daughter," he said. "As for the Jorenians, their fate is in your hands now. You will decide which is more important to you: your daughter or an entire civilization." He turned as two guards entered the room. "Take her back to the cell."

"You can't do this," I shouted as the guards seized my arms. "I will do whatever you want. I will go willingly with you anywhere."

"You are going with me to Joren," Joseph told me. "If you do not tell me what I want to know, you will also watch everyone on the planet die."

I didn't see where the guards took me. The face of the dead alterformed slave seemed imprinted on my eyes. When I blinked, it changed to that of Jorenians I knew: Salo, Darea, Xonal, young Fasala. I told myself over and over that even a sadistic brute like Joseph Grey Veil would not dare exterminate a species merely to get his way. Then I remembered what Reever had told me of him, and what I read in Cherijo's journals. In his efforts to retrieve Cherijo, Joseph Grey Veil had set into motion the war between the League and the Hsktskt. Worlds had been devastated, millions wounded and killed—all because of this one man and what he desired.

I saw myself taking one of the rifles from the guards and firing it into my mouth. The pulse would vaporize my head and most of my upper torso; surely enough to kill me. I would happily die to protect Marel and Joren. But would that even stop him? If he suspected Marel was on Joren, my death would not prevent him from releasing the virus. It removed every obstacle that would otherwise keep him from searching the planet for Marel, and he knew it would not kill my daughter.

The guards stopped outside the room that had been made to look like our quarters on the *Sunlace*, and one of them checked the interior on the outside door panel. It showed Reever and Shon still lying bound, gagged, and unconscious on the deck. Only then did the guard input the entry code and march me inside.

What happened then was fast and violent. Blood splashed over me as a blade whipped across the throat of one guard. Claws blinded the second, who choked on his scream as his head was wrenched too far to one side and his neck snapped.

Reever dragged the dead guard inside and reached with a bloody hand to close the door panel.

"You were on the floor," I said stupidly. "I saw you."

"We made a recycling image of ourselves as we were before we got out of our bonds, and programmed the panel from the inside to display it." He pulled me into his arms. "Did he harm you?"

In ways I could never describe, I thought. "Not yet." I held on to him for a few precious seconds before I pulled away and turned to Shon. Streaks of crystal ran diagonally across his face and encased his right forearm. I knew from the sorrow in his eyes what it had cost him to kill the guard. "Thank you."

"You can thank me, too," Uorwlan said as she came out of the adjoining room. She handed rifles to Shon and Reever, and offered one to me.

I took it and slung it over my shoulder. "How did you free yourself?"

"Remember what I told you about males?" She smiled, showing bloodied teeth. "There's one guard who won't be spreading it around anymore."

Shon began stripping the guard out of his uniform. "Rinse the blood from the other's tunic. It is dark enough that no one will notice it is wet."

As I helped Reever removed the other guard's uniform, I told him about the clone Joseph Grey Veil had used on Terra, how he had gone into hiding to conceal his identity during the war, and why he had offered the bounty for us.

"That man cannot be Joseph," my husband said flatly. "I saw his dead body on Terra. It was not that of a clone."

I wanted to believe him, but I had felt such an instinctive fear of the man that doubt filled me. "If he used a clone, he would look the same."

"Cherijo once stabbed Joseph in the hand. It left a small but distinctive scar. The man Jericho killed had the same scar." He glanced at my face. "Something else happened."

I told him of the Terran's demands and his promise to release the bioengineered virus as soon as we reached Joren if I did not tell him where our daughter was.

Reever stripped out of his garments and dressed in the guard's wet tunic. "If he has this virus on board, then all we have to do is destroy the ship."

"First we have to get off," Uorwlan pointed out. "Which we should do—now."

"We will go directly to launch bay," my husband decided. "As soon as we can find it."

"I am certain this ship has the same number of decks, quarters, and bays in the same places as the real *Sunlace*," I said. "I think it was built to be a duplicate."

"Why use all the holoprojectors, then?" Uorwlan asked. "Why not fit it out like the real thing?"

"They didn't have enough time," Reever said. "One of the guards was complaining about it. From what I overheard, this ship was removed from the construction docks before it was finished. The crew was not supposed to report for duty for another six months."

"The Terran said he had intended to use the virus to find me on Joren," I said. "He must have commissioned the HouseClan ship as part of that plan."

"He would have been able to assume orbit around Joren without arousing suspicions." Shon pulled the guard's headgear down over his face, and to cover the rifle draped my shoulders with the native garment he had removed. "Remember to hold your hands behind your back so they appear to be bound."

To anyone watching us leave the cell, we appeared to be two prisoners being moved by two guards. The ruse worked so well that we passed two crewmen who barely gave us a glance.

We entered the lift that would take us to launch bay, and as soon as it closed us in, I turned to my husband. "We can't return to the station or the planet. Where will we go?"

"My ship," Uorwlan said. "It's not the *Sunlace*, but she's fast, well armed, and can make a jump in under two minutes."

"What is it, all engine?" Shon asked, amused.

The Takgiba gave him a decidedly sultry look. "It's not the size of the weapon, but how much power you put into it."

The lift came to a stop and the doors slid open. I stepped out first with Uorwlan, placing my hands behind my back again to play the prisoner. An alarm screeched as the light emitters began to flash, and something came running down the corridor toward us.

The massive humanoid, easily twice my height, had a body like the front end of a land transport. His hands had been replaced by two weapons somehow welded onto his arms, and he began firing both at us as he charged the lift.

"Drone," Shon shouted.

I had never seen a drone made to look like a living being, but I targeted the center part of the torso and fired. The drone's power core exploded, causing his enormous chassis to break part into three pieces, which fell smoldering to the deck.

"Move your tail," Uorwlan said, pushing at my back.

Reever and Shon took positions in front of us now, and we went around the remains of the drone and ran for the bay. Halfway down the corridor a door panel ahead of us opened and a blue-striped white creature leapt out.

Jlorra.

I stopped, disbelief making me rigid. "It cannot be." No one had ever successfully removed one of the six-legged death cats from Akkabarr. Anyone who had tried had died a messy death.

Beside me, Shon also went still. "It's a torpa," he said, his voice rough. "It's blind but it can feel movements in the air. Don't move, or it will spit its venom at you."

"What are you talking about?" Uorwlan demanded, gesturing toward the jlorra slowly walking toward us. "That's a pralme. It will gut you with its tusks." Under her breath she muttered, "I thought we killed them all."

"It's a jlorra," I insisted, raising the rifle. "You have to shoot it in the space between its eyes. It's the only thing that works."

Reever turned to me. "I see a Hsktskt in full battle armor."

"They must have drugged us," Shon muttered.

"No. We all see it differently." I fought back my fear and raised my rifle. "I know what it is."

The jlorra crouched down and sprang at Reever, and I fired. The pulse round had no effect on the big cat. With a shriek of rage, Uorwlan jumped into the jlorra's path and knocked it to the deck. As she rolled away, Reever somehow adjusted his rifle to produce a stream of fire. The big cat's eyes flashed as orange as the flames and it screamed and fell writhing and burning at my husband's feet.

As he stepped back, the big cat began to shrink into a long, thin humanoid with ghostly silver-white skin and blunted features. It tried to rise, but its burning body fell and went motionless.

"Shifter." Uorwlan walked up to the inert form of the Odnallak. "Think you'd scare me with that? I was part of the Great Purge, you scum." She spat on the body.

Reever looked ahead. "There could be more lying in wait for us. Fire is their only vulnerability." He went around and quickly made the same adjustments to our weapons. "Remember, they can read our fears and assume the shape of them. Don't trust your eyes."

We hurried toward the bay. Although I knew my eyes would deceive me, I still staggered back when Srrok Var came around a corner and threw at us handfuls of the bone dust that had caused the plague of memory on Vtaga. The dust vanished along with the nightmarish image of the reconstructed Hsktskt madman as soon as Reever engulfed him in flames.

We fought our way through a horde of terrifying attackers. I burned a Toskald soldier who had once stabbed me while I'd tried to save his life on the battlefield, the League general who had enslaved Cherijo, and a glowing ring of energy that tried to suck me into its black maw. Each fell as soon as the fire from our weapons touched them, and shifted back into their real bodies.

A pair of Hsktskt prison guards, their mouths dripping with red blood, their teeth foul with ragged strips of flesh, entered the corridor. They stopped at the sight of the burning, fallen bodies, turned, and ran away.

Shon had to blast out the control panel beside the launch bay entrance, which had been locked down, and he and Reever pried the doors apart. Inside a half dozen crewmen scattered, firing at us while trying to take defensive positions behind the launches. Reever and Shon returned fire until there was nothing left but bodies on the deck.

"I'll rig a bypass." Uorwlan, clutching a wounded shoulder, went to the airlock control console. "Prep that small scout over there for launch; it's the fastest thing they've got."

I grabbed a first-aid pack from a storage unit and brought it to the console. "You're bleeding," I told her when she protested. "We need you conscious."

While Reever and Shon boarded the scout and readied it for launch, I applied a coagulant and a field dressing to the wound on the Takgiba's shoulder.

"He told me that you have a daughter," she mentioned as she worked on the console. "What is her name?"

I secured the dressing. "Marel."

"Does she look like you?"

I thought this was a strange conversation to be having under the circumstances. "She is small like me, and likely inherited my nose, my feet, and my temper, but Reever gave her the color of his hair and eyes."

"I wanted to give him a child," Uorwlan said. "My kind can't breed with Terrans, so I knew it was impossible. Still, I thought he would make a wonderful father."

I glanced over at the scout. "He is."

She nodded slowly. "I wanted to tear your throat the moment I saw you, and then I saw the way he looks at you. He told me he couldn't feel love, but I knew different. He only had to find his other half, and it wasn't me." She gazed at me. "That's why I left him, you know. To give him the chance to find you."

I felt relieved and terrible. "What about you and Shon?"

She laughed. "I enjoyed him, but he's too much like me. You'd better get on board now. I'll have this patch finished in a minute."

I felt reluctant to leave her alone at the console, but nodded and went to the launch. Inside Shon sat behind the helm with Reever at copilot; the two of them were finishing the preflight checks.

I surveyed the interior. The scout had not been designed to ferry passengers, but there were two emergency harnesses in the back that the Takgiba and I could use to secure ourselves for launch.

"We're good," Uorwlan said as she boarded and secured the ramp. "That bypass won't hold forever, so get this dink moving."

Shon initiated launch and eased the scout into the airlock. Weapons fire erupted behind us as the massive doors closed and the outer hull doors parted.

"Fasten your harnesses," Shon called back to us. "This won't be a smooth ride."

It wasn't. As soon as the scout departed the ship, the vessel came around and began firing at us. Shon and Reever worked grimly to evade the volleys, but as the scout turned and twisted the hull began to shudder under multiple impacts.

I cringed as I heard the boom of a sonic cannon. "We will never make it out of here."

"Don't be a mewling kit," Uorwlan told me. "We've got friends out there now."

I glanced through the viewport and saw two ships pass the scout—a small, fast trader transport and a massive Jorenian star vessel.

The *Sunlace*'s sonic cannons boomed again, forcing the mercenaries to break off their attack to evade impact.

Shon did something that made the scout turn end over end, and flew after the *Sunlace*.

"We can't risk docking in midflight," I heard Reever say to him. "If the clamps are not perfectly aligned, we'll collide."

"The 'Zangians taught me how to do it," Shon assured him. "They call it poking the shrike."

I held my breath as the scout darted under the hull of the *Sunlace* and into docking position. Clamps extended, reaching for our tiny ship, and somehow the oKiaf managed to catch on to them a moment before we would have smashed into the bigger vessel. Above our heads I heard the rumble of retractors as the scout was lifted into an airlock, and then space disappeared.

"Welcome on board, Major Valtas," Xonea's annoyed voice said over the com. "I assume you did not kill anyone on board your launch with that foolhardy maneuver."

"All present and accounted for, Captain." Shon powered down the engines and glanced back at the Takgiba. "I would have told him myself."

Uorwlan made a casual gesture. "I saved you the trouble." She released her harness, but instead of moving to the docking ramp she went to the pilot's seat. "Let me at the console. I want to see how you did that."

Shon rose and then staggered, putting out a hand to brace himself. Crystal claws cut into the plas seat covering.

I went to the docking ramp, lowered it, and then hurried over to the oKiaf. "Reever, help me."

Between us we supported Shon and walked down the ramp.

"I need a gurney," I said, bracing myself as the oKiaf's knees buckled. One appeared a moment later, and two crewmen helped us lift Shon's unconscious body onto it. "Signal medical. I need an isolation room set up with a dialysis unit, stat."

The deck rocked under my feet as the ship took a massive blast to the starboard hull. I heard alloy groan and emergency alarms going off as a calm Jorenian voice ordered the bay to be evacuated.

The airlock doors began to close behind us, and I turned to see Uorwlan sitting in the pilot's seat. As the scout's engines engaged, she strapped herself in and disengaged the docking clamps.

Reever ran over to a com panel. "Uorwlan, shut down the engines and come out of there."

"Not on your life, lover," she replied.

The outer doors opened and the scout flew off, heading for the Odnallak raider.

I sent Shon ahead to medical and went with Reever to the nearest communication station, where he brought up the scout on the viewer and signaled the Takgiba.

"Turn around and come back to the ship," he ordered. "You can't fight them in a scout. You don't have any weapons. Uorwlan."

"I don't need them," she replied as her image appeared on the screen. She seemed amused. "I'm just going to run a little interference and give you and the Jorenians some time to get out of here."

"We're not leaving without you," I said.

"Hold on." The Takgiba maneuvered the scout around a heavy burst of pulse fire. "I don't know who that shifter has on weapons, but they're good. They've taken out your long-range signal array. A couple more hits and they'll take out the Jorenians' propulsion. I can't see you finding a cure for Shon while you're drifting around the quadrant."

"Shon needs you," I said, seizing on that.

"Shon has everything he needs. So do you." The Takgiba muttered something under her breath as the scout rocked. "I've got to wrap this up; things are getting snarled out here and it'll be a tight fit as it is. Duncan, I love you. Always have, always will."

"No." He reached out and touched the screen. Uorwlan, no."

"Keep your promise." Her image disappeared, and the signal terminated.

Reever tried signaling again, and then put the view of

the scout on the screen. The small ship flew directly into the path of the alien raider, artfully dodging most of the pulse volleys fired at it.

"What is she doing?" I murmured. "She can't destroy the ship by ramming it."

"She isn't trying to collide with the ship," he said, and took my hand in his.

At the last minute Uorwlan cut the scout's engines, and the nose of the small ship drifted into the large emitter of the sonic cannon. The impact breached the scout's hull, which imploded, along with the power cells. A brilliant flare of light engulfed the display. It had barely begun to fade when a second, much more powerful detonation tore the alien raider in half.

I held on to the side of the console and Reever's hand as the shock wave rocked the *Sunlace*.

Eighteen

Xonea transitioned as soon as the ship was secured, and then performed another two jumps to evade the other alien raiders pursuing us. The attack had resulted in several casualties, a few serious, but no deaths. Once reality stopped melting into a transitional swirl, I spent the next twelve hours alternating between surgery and the isolation room where Shon was being treated.

Although I no longer had the supply of heartwood I had collected from the oKiaf—the Odnallak had confiscated it—I was able to glean enough carvings from the remnants of our native garments to keep the crystal infection in check. The oKiaf drifted in and out of consciousness, and I directed the nurses to keep him under close monitor.

Herea efficiently managed triage and supervised the treatment of the ambulatory patients, and to reward her efforts I brought her in to operate on a crew member with a severely fractured pelvis. She didn't hesitate as she gloved and masked and reached for the lascalpel.

"This left hip will need to be replaced as soon as the

pelvis heals," she said as she studied the skeletal scans. She glanced at me. "That is, if you agree, Healer Jarn."

"That's not the standard treatment," I said, and then smiled under my mask. "But you're right. Given her size and weight, performing the usual reinforcement procedure will only delay the deterioration of the joint. I believe she serves as a security officer, which means she spends most of her duty shift on her feet. I agree. A replacement is a better solution for the patient."

She sighed her relief. "For a moment I thought I might have to argue the point." Her tone turned curious. "Can you say what happened to Resident Jylyj? That crystal embedded in his hide—it looks very serious."

As we worked, I related an abbreviated version of what had occurred on the planet, and discussed possible treatment options.

"I can synthesize the resin and continue dialysis until we reach Joren, but we have to purge the protocrystal from his bloodstream." I handed her the retractor she needed and watched her skillful hands as she exposed a jagged break in the right pelvic bone. "The only substance that repels it, Cu^2Au, would also poison him if I introduce it into the bloodstream."

"It's a pity it isn't attracted to his fur, Healer," the nurse monitoring the anesthesia said. "It would exit the body through his hair follicles and give him a very pretty pelt."

I stared blindly at her as I remembered fifteen blobs of mold following Shon around the ship like pets eager for attention. "We've used the Lok-Teel before to remove toxins from patients." I turned to the intern. "Herea, can you—"

She nodded, understanding. "The patient is stable and her vitals are strong. I know what to do, but I will call you if I need any assistance."

I ran out of the surgical suite, stripping out of my mask, gloves, and shroud as I looked for one of the helpful little housekeepers. One crawled up to my feet and sat there as if waiting.

"Hello," I said as I bent to pick up the mold. "I have a job for you."

I took the Lok-Teel into the isolation room, where Shon was presently sleeping. Gently, I placed the mold next to the oKiaf's crystal-covered arm, and thought of Shon's paw as it had been. I couldn't force it to attempt to absorb the protocrystal in Shon's bloodstream, but if it was willing . . .

The Lok-Teel read my thoughts as clearly as ever, for it slowly crawled over the paw and stretched itself out over it. At first it settled down and didn't move, and then it began to undulate and expand.

"What is this?" Shon asked, his voice slurred. "A new type of berth bath?"

"An experiment." I scanned him and checked the level of crystal infection. It had not decreased or increased. "How are you feeling?"

"Heavy-headed." He turned his face toward me, and I saw solid crystal now covered half of it. "It doesn't blind you, you know. I can see through it, although it does make everything look as if it is composed out of colored light."

The Lok-Teel, now bloated and bulging, inched away from Shon's paw. Crystal still covered it, however, and I felt a crushing sense of disappointment.

"That didn't work," I told him. "We'll have to try something else."

"I thank you, Jarn, but you cannot cure this thing." His remaining eye closed. "Not even if you were the Crystal Healer."

"I'm not giving up," I told him, and picked up the Lok-Teel, which had gone stiff and still. "Rest now. I'll be back to check on you shortly."

I took the mold to the biopsy room and placed its inert form on the dissection table. It appeared lifeless, and I worried that I had killed it by exposing it to the crystal, but then it suddenly began bubbling and dividing.

I scanned the mold as it divided into two and then four individual Lok-Teel. Their readings were healthy and, thankfully, free of crystal.

"It was worth a try," I said ruefully as the four little molds moved toward me and caressed my hands with their cool, soft surfaces. "I hope you enjoyed whatever you *did* absorb from Shon."

The Lok-Teel began moving to climb off the table. Doubtless they were hungry, I thought, and removed the lid from the room's waste container before I went out into the ward.

There were no more surgeries to perform, so I made rounds of the patients in post-op, wrote up orders for the nurses, and looked in but didn't interrupt Herea's procedure, which she had almost finished. A yawn almost split my face in two as I watched from the view panel.

"Healer Jarn."

I glanced back at a nurse. "Yes?"

She pointed to the floor, and when I looked down,

I saw that every Lok-Teel in medical now waited in a wide mass around my feet.

"What is this?" I tried to step over them, but the Lok-Teel crawled out from beneath my feet and formed two groups on either side of me. Then I looked down at my tunic, which I had not changed since boarding the *Sunlace*. "Is this your way of telling me that I need to cleanse?" To the nurse I said, "Signal me in my quarters if Major Valtas's condition changes."

"Yes, Healer."

It felt good to strip out of my dirty garments and scrub myself under the cleanser. No one would have noticed my condition on Akkabarr, as we rarely wasted time or water on frequent bathing, but the ensleg had very different standards of personal hygiene. I smiled to myself as I remembered how I had protested when Reever ordered me to bathe daily. How ignorant I had been, and how changed I was.

I had just finished dressing when Reever arrived. I came out of our bedchamber to greet him but came to a halt when I saw him standing by the open door panel. What appeared to be every Lok-Teel on the ship were crawling into our quarters.

"I know I needed a cleansing," I said, giving the horde of mold an uneasy glance, "but surely I didn't smell that bad."

"They were waiting outside in the corridor." My husband made a sweeping gesture. "All of them."

"I used one on Shon a few hours ago in an attempt to remove the crystal infection, but the Lok-Teel couldn't absorb it." I crouched down to pick up one of the Lok-

Teel. It crawled away from me and on top of another, engulfing it. I glanced around as the others began doing the same thing, and I looked up at Reever. "Have they ever joined together like this before?"

He shook his head and closed the door panel. "They may be somehow infected by the exposure to the crystal. Stand back from them." He used the com panel to signal an environmental hazard alert, which automatically locked down our quarters.

The Lok-Teel by this time had melted together into one gigantic mass, which was shrinking in and growing up into a vertical direction.

I went to the storage container and took out a pulse pistol, tossing it to Reever before taking one for myself. "Shoot it."

"Wait." He pressed a hand to his head. "It's not the Lok-Teel. Something else is present."

The merged mold began to stretch into the shape of a humanoid with a head, torso, and four limbs. The bland beige color of the form changed, lightening in some areas and darkening in others. The center of the mold turned green and became filmy, like thin fabric. The top of the shape formed a mass of curly thin red strands.

I knew who it was as soon as I saw the hair. "Maggie."

A half-formed mouth smiled. "Hold your horses, slave girl. Borrowing a corporeal form takes some doing."

I held on to the pistol and took a scanner from my case. The readings showed only Lok-Teel and Reever present in the room. "She's not registering," I told my husband.

"She never does." Reever looked disgusted. "What do you want now, alien?"

"He never calls me Maggie anymore. It's hurting my feelings." Now fully formed, Cherijo's surrogate mother stretched out her arms and studied her red-varnished fingernails. "Interesting. Quite a cooperative bunch, too, unlike some lower life-forms in the room I could mention."

"If we shoot her while she's using the Lok-Teel, will it kill her?" I asked Reever.

"Probably not, but I'd enjoy it, anyway." He aimed for the back of Maggie's head.

"Temper, temper." Maggie flicked the fingers of both hands, and the pistols we were holding went flying across the room. "I can't hold these creepy things together for much longer, so let's get down to business. You have to tell the Jorenian to turn the ship around, go back, and destroy the raiders chasing after you. All of them."

I stared at her for a moment, and then laughed.

"That means *no*," Reever said. "Release the Lok-Teel and get off the ship. Now."

Xonea walked in, his movements stiff and jerky. "Duncan, Jarn," he said, his voice hoarse. "Something has taken control of me."

Maggie waved at him. "That would be me, Captain. Since Grimface and the little woman aren't listening to me, maybe you will. You have to go back and destroy that raider fleet."

"The ship has sustained heavy damages to the weapons array," Xonea told her. "We cannot attack until repairs are made."

"Offer to surrender," she suggested. "When the raiders come close enough, then you can blow your core."

"I am not destroying the *Sunlace* or killing my crew," he told her flatly.

"Why do the raiders all have to be destroyed?" Reever demanded.

"The shifters infiltrated the tribe on the surface," Maggie told him. "While you were going native, they were picking your brains every night while you slept. That's why you always woke up with a headache, Duncan. Even when you were unconscious, you tried to fight them. By the way, you lost, you wimp."

"They made me dream of Trellus?" I stared at her. "Why?"

"They wanted your memories of that happy time. Specifically, of Swap, the friendly neighborhood larval-form omnipotent being. Besides Major Pain-in-the-Ass Valtas, he's the only other being who can accelerate the growth of the black crystal."

I shook my head, trying to make sense of her babble. "Why would they want to do that?"

"You're going to love this: because they believe it will turn them back into what they were before the big breakup." She made a sound of contempt. "We tried to get through to them that messing with the black crystal is a very *bad* thing, but when you're the remnant flotsam of the most powerful civilization of all time, you tend to believe your species' dumb-ass mythology over very wise advice from the people who were actually there when the universe went all to hell."

"If they know about Swap," Reever said slowly, "then they know what he is."

"Right on the money, big guy. And here I always thought that you were the stupid half of the equation." Maggie turned to me. "Because you've prevented the mercenaries from capturing Shon Valtas, they're going to Plan B. In a few hours, they will invade Trellus, capture the worm, and force it to be their alarm clock. When that happens, say bye-bye to everyone and everything that matters, because Swap is going to eat it."

"I don't believe you," I said.

Maggie glowered. "Why else would I send you to a pretty much guaranteed death, kiddo? I mean, you're a nasty bitch with identity issues, but you're still the closest thing I've ever had to offspring."

"You are no mother to me."

"Yeah, well, as a daughter, you stink, too," she snapped back. "And thanks to the little vacations you and Reever have been taking lately, you've totally fucked our timeline. For your information, the space occupied by an object undergoing a transformation does *not* preserve all linear dimensions. There are no other options now."

I shook my head. "You're lying."

"You want proof? My pleasure." Maggie snapped her fingers, and our quarters became the surface of Trellus. "Here we are a little further along the present timeline, at everyone's least favorite vacation spot, the colony from hell."

I knew we couldn't be standing on the surface of the planet, for if we had been we would have frozen and suffocated simultaneously. At the same time, I knew we were there. Somehow Maggie had made that possible.

I glanced over at the domes in which the colonists lived, but they were all dark now. Some had been fired upon and had collapsed atop the ruins of the structures and dwellings they once protected.

Tall, thin beings in envirosuits marched out of Swap's dome in two columns. Between them slid several tons of an enormous pink worm, now harnessed to a device that wrapped its amorphous body with thousands of pastel bands. A probe attached to the end of each band seemed to be feeding some sort of green fluid into the worm's body.

"The Odnallak have forgotten a lot of things, but not how to kill everything that gets in their way," Maggie said, her voice bitter. "Or what controls a baby rogur."

Swap was led up a cargo ramp and into the belly of a massive alien raider. At the last minute he tried to resist, but the shifters' device pumped more green poison into his body, and at last he slithered inside.

Maggie snapped her fingers again, and we were walking across a meadow of orange-gray flowers under a red sky.

"Welcome to Naetriht, home of zip." She kicked aside some of the flowers to reveal the ground, which appeared to be made of black crystal. "A few million years ago, this crap ate everything that might have evolved into something interesting, before it went to sleep." She looked up as shuttles began descending on the meadow. "I swear, you could set a timing device by these guys."

Odnallak, this time dressed in some sort of ceremonial garments, poured out of the shuttles and took up positions around the edge of the clearing. A much bigger shuttle flew overhead, opening its cargo doors and releasing Swap, who fell to the ground in the center of the Odnallak.

The worm tried to crawl away, but the Odnallak took out weapons that sprayed it with the green fluid and drove it back to the center of the meadow.

I turned to Maggie. "Why are they doing this to him? He's harmless."

"Actually, no, he's not," Maggie said. "We evolved the Hsktskt specifically to exterminate his entire species, but somehow he escaped the genocide, and later the attack on the colony. For a worm, he has lives like a cat."

Disgust filled me. "You sent the Hsktskt to Trellus."

"It was a mistake. Occasionally we make them," Maggie admitted. "After that, we saw him taking care of the surviving kids and realized why he hadn't evolved into the adult form. He may be a planet-destroying monster's maggot, but Swap actually has a good soul."

"Is that why he marooned himself on Trellus?" Reever asked. "To keep from evolving?"

"That, and to study the black crystal. Swap has been trying for millennia to find a way to destroy it, same as us." Maggie gave him a grim smile. "Too late now."

The orange-gray flowers withered and turned to dust as the ground beneath them rumbled. Swap curled in on himself as massive shafts of black crystal erupted around him, shifting and crossing each other to form more complex structures. The Odnallak moved in, touching the crystal and calling to Swap, who had become a tight, pulsing ball.

"What are they doing?" Xonea asked Maggie.

"Oh, they think they're going to be transformed now," she said. "The morons."

A burst of red light came out of Swap and swept through the crystal, which dissolved it. I would have thought it destroyed, until I saw one of the Odnallak run into the shadowy air where one crystal structure had stood only a few seconds ago. A delicate black haze surrounded the Odnallak, who went still and began tearing at its robes.

Horror filled me as I saw the haze begin swirling around the shifter, slowly stripping away its skin. The Odnallak screamed over and over as it tried to get away, but the haze followed it, eating away at its muscles and then its organs, until at last all that was left was a skeleton that toppled to the ground. The haze descended, swirling gently, and when it lifted again the skeleton was gone.

All around the meadow the same thing happened again and again to the remaining shifters, until all that was left was the black haze and the tight black ball that had been Swap.

The black haze swirled around the ball now, stripping the dark outer layer away from the worm but not attacking the life-form inside.

Swap had undergone some sort of metamorphosis and emerged from the cocoon as a much larger creature, easily the size of a troop transport, with a lurid yellow-green hide and a hundred spidery limbs. He had no head, only openings on either end of his body. The biggest opened, revealing acres of teeth, and the black haze rushed into that terrible mouth, filling and bloating Swap's new body.

I glanced at Maggie. "Will it kill him now?"

"It should be so lucky." She watched, her eyes full. "He's just packing for the trip."

Once all of the haze had been sucked into his mouth, he closed it and changed shape again, growing armored yellow-black scales. He then crawled across the clearing to the empty shuttles and ate them, one by one, before looking up at the hovering transport that had brought him to the planet.

The ship landed in front of him, and angry Odnallak poured out of it, firing their fluid weapons at Swap. He stabbed his limbs through their bodies and dragged them to his mouth end, into which he flung them.

I turned away as Swap began to chew. "Stop this, Maggie. I've seen enough."

"Oh, come on," she chided. "He's going to N-jui next, and there's nothing like seeing an adult rogur eat a few cities before it gives birth to several thousand versions of itself." She watched Swap crawl into the transport, which lifted off a moment later. "Well, maybe when the little ones have their first meal."

"You've made your point, Maggie," Reever said quietly.

We were back on the *Sunlace*, standing in our quarters. Xonea had vanished, and Maggie looked terrible.

I started to ask her how she knew about Swap, but her form swayed and then suddenly burst into hundreds of Lok-Teel, which fell to the deck and began crawling around in a frantic, frightened manner.

"We promised to protect Swap," my husband said slowly. "And as offensive and ridiculous as Maggie is, I think she was showing us the truth. That is what will happen if the raiders invade Trellus."

"I know. I felt the same thing." I reached down to stroke one of the little housekeepers, which clung to my hand and shivered.

"Duncan," Xonea said over the com panel. "I just had a very long and disturbing hallucination. However, we do not detect a hazard inside your quarters. Are you clear? Is that redheaded female gone?"

"Yes," Reever replied over the com, but the hazard claxon continued to sound. "You can shut that off. It was a false alarm."

"Perhaps here, it was." My ClanBrother disengaged the lock and entered our quarters. "But we have detected another biohazard on the ship. It's in the survey lab."

We accompanied Xonea to the survey lab, the corridor to which had been blocked off at either end with the same type of energy curtains that Nalek Kalea had installed in the containment chamber. One of the ship's engineers had an interior view of the survey lab on monitor, and it showed a dark, cloudy substance had formed around the black crystal inside the chamber.

"Something engaged the failsafe shortly after you sounded the biohazard alarm in your quarters," Xonea said. "But the probe unit never emerged to encase the specimen container. The control circuits appear to have shorted out."

I looked at the monitor. "What is the temperature in there?"

"Seventy-eight degrees Fahrenheit," Xonea said. "The same as the rest of the ship."

"The chamber won't hold it much longer, Captain," one of the engineers said. "The protective field is losing power. I cannot be sure, but the specimen appears to be absorbing it."

"How long until the field is drained?" Reever asked.

"At the rate of power loss, ten minutes," the engineer told him.

"Disengage the corridor seal," my husband said. "I have to go in there and activate the manual override."

"We don't know what type of radiation or energy that crystal is emitting," Xonea told him. "It doesn't register at all on our equipment. Like that female who took over my brain."

"If I don't eject that crystal before the containment chamber fails, the energy will be released into the rest of the deck. It could cause an explosion or worse." My husband gestured toward the curtain blocking off the corridor. "You can reactivate it as soon as I'm on the other side."

"I'm going with you," I said.

"No, beloved." He looked down at me. "We can't both risk the exposure."

"I'll wear an envirosuit," I promised. "I'll stay outside the lab doors. You can't do this alone."

Reever glanced at Xonea and then at me. "It's time to tell your ClanBrother about Trellus." He nodded at the technician, who deactivated the energy curtain.

I tried to follow him, but Xonea grabbed me from behind and held me until the engineer reactivated the seal.

"He will do what he must, Jarn," Xonea said when I turned on him. "Now tell me what I need to know."

As I watched the monitor screen, I told him about Trellus, Swap, and our promise to the Trellusans. I also told him about the alien raider, and the Odnallak who had posed as Cherijo's father.

"Now I understand why she told me to destroy the ship," Xonea said.

"She knew she would be sending us to our death," I said dully as I watched Reever finish donning an enviro-suit before he entered the lab. "But she's right. We can't permit them to invade Trellus, even if it means sacrificing every member of the crew to stop them."

Reever stood inside the lab now, and moved slowly toward the control console. Once there, he used the suit-com to signal us.

"All of the control circuits have been destroyed. I cannot engage the manual override."

Xonea signaled back. "Come out of there, Duncan. We will find a way to seal off this deck."

"There is one more thing." He went over to one of the interior supports by the lab entry, removed a strap from his belt, and began wrapping it around the support and his waist. "Evacuate the deck now, Xonea."

"What are you doing?" I demanded over the com. "Duncan, answer me."

"Go with the captain, Jarn." He turned his helmet so he could look at the monitor. "Please, Wife. Trust me."

I didn't trust him, but my ClanBrother took my arm again, and I went with him to the nearest lift. "Do you know what he intends to do?"

"I have a good idea." He guided me out of the lift and straight to the nearest wall panel, from which he signaled communications. "Put up an interior view of the survey lab on this screen," he ordered. As soon as the image of Reever appeared, he signaled my husband. "The deck is clear. Make sure your tether is secure."

Tether? That meant—

Every thought left my head as I watched my husband raise a pulse rifle to his shoulder and fire across the room at the hull. The ship's emergency buffer should have absorbed the blast, but instead a small hole appeared, and then the wall itself tore open and disappeared into space.

The explosive decompression of the room dragged most of its contents out through the ragged gap. Console panels, storage units, and other equipment slammed into each other and the remains of the hull before disappearing.

Reever fired again, and I looked over at the containment chamber as the plas sides imploded and the fragments along with the dark cloud inside them were also pulled out of the ship.

Reever's body was being tugged away from the post, but the strap he had used held. He fired a final time at the base of the specimen container, loosening and then freeing it from its platform. The cracked sides of the container bulged for a moment, and then it, too, flew out of the ship.

"Engage auxiliary buffer, deck seven," Xonea ordered over the com, and a new curtain of energy formed over the gap in the hull, sealing it off. Reever's body fell to the deck, but before I could blink, he was propping himself up and looking at the monitor again.

"It's gone," he said through chattering teeth. "Would you send my wife down here? I think I need a doctor."

Nineteen

I signaled a medevac team and went with Xonea to level seven, where the engineers were working to override the pass code and gain entry to the survey lab.

"The code is one-six-four-one-seven," I said, pushing past them as soon as the doors opened.

Exposure to space had covered every surface in the now-empty lab with a thin layer of ice, including Reever's envirosuit. I ignored the burn of the cold as I tore apart the strap tethering him to the post and looked into the shield covering his face. Blood stained his mouth, but his eyes were clear and vivid blue.

"That is the last time I trust you," I told him as the orderlies arrived and handed me my case. I scanned him. "Whenever I am on duty, I think I will lock you in our quarters."

My husband stood with some difficulty, and pulled off his protective gloves. "I need to send a drone probe after the container. We have to collect it and fly it into a star."

"You have frostbite, cracked ribs, and hypothermia,

so the only place you need to go is medical." I looked over at Xonea. "The captain will see to cleanup."

My ClanBrother nodded and began issuing orders as the orderlies and I moved Reever onto the gurney and out of the lab.

In medical I treated Reever for exposure, slowly warming his body temperature with thermal packs while performing a more thorough scan of the impact fractures in his ribs. Thankfully, his chameleon cells were already hard at work repairing the bone damage, and by the time I finished my assessment, his ribs were healed.

Reever insisted on signaling Xonea to determine the status of the black crystal. When I threatened to put him in restraints, he said, "If the specimen container was compromised, it may have broken up the crystal. More than one drone probe may be required to collect it."

"One signal," I warned, "and then you must rest."

The captain confirmed that the drone probe had been launched and had successfully tracked down the specimen container. That was the only good news he had for us, however.

"The probe's readings indicate that the specimen container is still intact," Xonea said. "But the black crystal is no longer inside the unit. It reads as empty."

"Considering the effect the black crystal has on our equipment, we can't assume that it is," Reever said. "If you would, Captain, program the probe to fly into the nearest star."

Xonea confirmed that he would, and terminated the signal.

"We must ask Shon to contact oKia," my husband

said, rising from the berth. "They may be able to intercept the mercenaries before they reach Trellus."

"Duncan." I barred his path. "I know you have healed, but the chameleon cells burn a great deal of energy when they repair you. You know you are exhausted."

"So are you." He touched my cheek. "We don't have much time, though, and we must know where the raider fleet is."

Resigned, I followed him out of the treatment room and over to Shon's chamber. The oKiaf was conscious and, after listening to Reever's account of Maggie's warning, agreed to signal Commander Dagar and ask his tribe for help.

The oKiaf responded quickly to Shon's signal. "The raiders returned a few hours ago, but when we attempted to engage them, they transitioned out of the system."

"Were you able to track where they jumped to, Cousin?" Shon asked.

"We did," the commander confirmed. "I'll send you the coordinates."

I glanced at the screen as soon as the position of the raider fleet appeared, and then closed my eyes. "They're orbiting Trellus."

The *Sunlace* had to make four consecutive transitions to reach Trellus, something that nearly caused me to lose consciousness. When my mind cleared and everything finally stopped spinning, Herea reported that the ship was approaching the colony. The jaunt had come with a high price.

"Too many jumps," she said, shaking her head. "The

interdimensional generators have gone offline. We will not be transitioning anywhere for several days."

Reever and I met with Xonea in command, where he reported what we had feared.

"Two raiders have landed on the surface, and the Odnallak have taken over most of the domes." He turned to me. "We have received a signal from one of the domes that is currently under fire. A female Terran asked if you were on board. Thankfully, it was not the red-haired one."

"It must be Mercy." I went to a com unit and sent a relay. A distorted image appeared on the screen and slowly coalesced into an unsmiling face. "Mercy, it's Jarn. We've come to help."

My friend looked grim. "I don't know who these bastards are, but they won't negotiate terms with us. We have two hundred dead, and they're threatening to begin executing more if we don't give them what they want."

I felt miserable. "They've come for Swap."

"Yeah, well, he's not here. He got a signal from some trader friend of his and left the colony a few days ago. I keep telling them this, but they don't believe me." Mercy looked over her shoulder as pulse fire erupted over the audio. "They've breached my grid. Jarn, if you can spare some of your Jorenian pals, we'd—"

The signal and the image abruptly ended.

"The raiders have disabled the colony's transceiver," Xonea said, and his gaze shifted. "Major Valtas."

I turned around to see Shon standing with one arm braced against entry. Crystal streaked over most of his body and had turned his black mane into a hard mass of glittering silver-white.

"You shouldn't have left your berth," I said, going to him.

"I won't be able to talk much longer," he said, his voice rough. "Or breathe. I can feel the crystal in my throat."

That decided things. "I'm taking you back and prepping you for surgery."

"The dialysis is no longer working. The infection has spread to all my organs. I only have an hour left at most." He eyed Xonea. "Give me a launch. I'll send a signal to the raiders and draw them away from the colony." He turned to Reever. "The raiders fly in tight formation. We'll need to rig the core for a five-kim blast radius."

"No. I won't allow you to do this," I told him, furious now. "The *Sunlace* is a powerful ship. Xonea can attack the raiders. We'll send rescue teams down to the surface. *Shon*."

The oKiaf led me outside the room and looked down at me. "You will let me go."

"I have no intentions of—"

Crystal claws touched my mouth, silencing me. "You will let me go because I love you. I love you, more than even Jadaira, and I will never have you. This is the way I choose to die. So that you and Reever and the Torin and the colonists may live."

"I can't." I saw Reever and gave him a beseeching look. "Please, Duncan, don't let him do this."

My husband held out his hand, and Shon put his paw in it. The two stared at each other in silence for a long time.

"Major," Reever said. "I am a telepath. I have seen. You know how it must be."

"I had hoped otherwise." Shon's remaining eye closed, and then opened. "Very well. I will see you in medical, Healer." He limped off.

I stared after him. "How did you do that?"

"Major Valtas has many gifts. One of them is foresight. He knows this is not his time to die." He rubbed a hand over his face. "I can't explain it, Jarn, but I feel it just as you do. He is more important than we know. Whatever the cost, we must do everything necessary to keep him alive."

Xonea joined us. "In the event anyone cares for my opinion," he said, "I am not sending a dying man out on a rigged launch. He is too sick to pilot it."

I glanced at him. "You feel it, too, don't you?"

He made an uneasy gesture. "I know it is wrong. Likely that alien female did something to my brain. However, Shon's idea still has some merit. One pilot flying a launch rigged for core overload might destroy the entire fleet."

"You can't deliberately send one of the crew to their death," I argued. "The raiders have scanners. They will know Shon isn't on the launch."

"I never said I would use a living pilot," Xonea chided. "We have drones for that. Duncan, can you program one of the portable simulator units to project a duplicate of Major Valtas?"

My husband nodded. "I will need some of Shon's DNA. The simulator can duplicate him exactly from it." He glanced at me. "Do you have any hair or tissue samples I can use?"

"I've taken a few blood samples for analysis," I said. "I'll send those down to launch bay. Are you sure this will deceive them?"

"I have used a similar ploy in the past. Once I made a group of attacking slavers believe that my ship was crewed by two hundred Hsktskt," my husband told me. "I can manage a convincing simulation of the major."

Xonea and Reever went to rig the launch while I returned to medical to retrieve the blood samples. Herea met me in the lab and told me that Shon had returned, but his condition was deteriorating rapidly.

"We may have to intubate him soon," she said, showing me the latest scans.

I gave the blood samples to one of the orderlies and sent him to launch bay before I went in to assess Shon. He was unconscious, his breathing labored. My readings showed that the crystal growing in his throat now threatened to obstruct his airway, and I snapped out orders for the nurses to prep him for surgery.

"We'll start by clearing the crystal out of his throat and lungs," I told Herea as we scrubbed. "I also want to take a look at his heart while we have his chest open." I remembered that crystal now covered most of his upper torso and swore. "I have to find a way to cut through that crystal."

"The lascalpel has no effect on it," the intern reminded me, and frowned. "I have a bone saw in my field pack, but the blade is surgical-grade plasteel."

I thought for a moment and summoned a nurse. "Contact engineering and ask them if they have any copper and gold in their stores. If they do, have them bring thirty thousand grams of copper and ten thousand of gold to medical."

The nurse looked mystified, but hurried off to carry out my orders.

"We can heat the copper and gold together in the lab's flash kiln, and then use it to coat the saw blade," I told Herea. "We should plate the other instruments we'll need, as well."

"Won't it take too long for the instruments to cool?" she asked.

"Not if we immerse them in cryofluid immediately after we coat them." I hurried to the lab to prepare the equipment.

A puzzled engineer delivered the metals a short time later. "Healer, we normally do not receive such requests from medical. You do know that copper is poisonous."

"I know." I grabbed the heavy containers from him and placed their contents in the flash kiln, setting it to melt and mix them together. Herea delivered the tray of hand instruments we needed for Shon's surgery, and we went to work.

"Healer," a nurse said behind me. "Did you move Major Valtas?"

"No, he's in isolation room three." I saw her expression. "Was he taken into the surgical suite?"

"I went to finish prepping him, but his berth is empty." She made a nervous gesture. "No one saw him leave, but he is not anywhere on the bay."

"Keep working on the instruments," I told Herea, and went in search of my patient. In his condition, Shon should not have gotten far, but I found no sign of him anywhere on the deck.

My suspicions made me first signal the launch bay. "Major Valtas has gone missing from medical," I told the duty officer. "Watch for him. He may come there and try to take a launch."

Instead of the duty officer, Xonea replied. "Major Valtas signaled a short time ago, just after we launched the drone ship. Duncan has gone to meet him on the observation deck."

I felt like slamming my head into the wall panel. "Xonea, I don't know what Shon is doing, but I have to get him into surgery. Send a security team to meet me there."

I took a lift down to the lowest level of the ship. The plas walls of the observation deck allowed a breathtaking view of the space around the ship, and as I stepped off the deck I wondered why Shon would come here of all places. I found him standing beside Reever as if they had nothing better to do than watch the drone-piloted launch luring the raiders away from Trellus.

"Are you mad?" I demanded.

"He can't hear you," Reever said. "The crystal has deafened him." He touched Shon's shoulder, and the oKiaf turned to look at me. The crystal had nearly covered his mouth, but he was able to wheeze out my name.

"I don't need him to hear or talk to me," I said. "I'm taking him back to medical."

Shon shook his head, and pointed toward the panel. I saw one of the *Sunlace*'s launches slowly flying away from the ship, and all of the raider vessels in a tight cluster pursuing it. As I watched, something emerged from the surface of a nearby moon and flew on an intercept course for the launch.

I heard the low, resonant humming again, only this

time it was coming from Shon's body. The oKiaf sagged but kept himself from falling by clutching the frame of the panel. At the same time Reever's face twisted with pain and he pressed his hands to the sides of his head.

The hum blanked out my thoughts, and I moved toward them like a nightwalker, no longer in control of my body. My husband was not using a link to do this; I felt something else—a warm and gentle presence that wrapped around me and spread through me.

I couldn't free myself, and so I watched with the men as the ship that had launched from the moon picked up speed. As it drew closer, I saw that it wasn't a proper vessel but an enormous transparent bubble filled with an equally gigantic worm.

Swap.

Perhaps it was the distortion of the space between us, but the worm appeared much larger than he had on Trellus. When it drew near the launch and the raiders, the bubble expanded around the worm and came to a stop directly in front of the Odnallak ships. Then it charged the raider fleet.

One by one the ships tried to evade Swap's strange vessel, but the bubble sent out transparent pseudopods and pulled them into itself. As each ship was taken into the bubble, Swap began enveloping them, until he had completely devoured the raiders.

"I have them now, Jarn," Reever said in Swap's voice. "I regret I could not intervene sooner, but I had to acquire enough energy to move into the next stage before I attempted this. You will help Mercy and the others on Trellus? They have many wounded."

Yes. We will go down to the surface as soon as we re-

turn. I couldn't answer with my mouth, so I used my thoughts. *Swap, you can't hold those ships forever.*

"Ah, I see my friend Duncan did not actually put the oKiaf on the launch. Very clever—that even fooled me." One of bubble's pseudopods stretched out impossibly long, caught the launch, and brought it back to join the others. "This will help finish it. I would stay and talk with you, Doctor, but my mind is already fading."

Suddenly I understood what was happening to Swap. *You're evolving.*

"Unfortunately so. I could not hold it off forever, Jarn. The crystal has been calling me for centuries, but now . . . it will no longer wait." Reever came to me and kissed my brow. "You are all very courageous beings. I know you will find the answers that I could not."

The bubble changed direction and began to pick up speed again. I was released from the telepathic control over my body, and rushed to the panel to press my hands against it.

The Odnallak ships fired through the worm as they tried to shoot their way out of his mass. It had no effect on him, and as the bubble disappeared into the star's corona, the launch exploded, destroying everything inside the bubble but the worm. As it began to turn yellow-green, the star's gravitational pull drew it down to the fiery surface, where it vanished into the star.

The second explosion sent a wave of light toward the *Sunlace*, and when it impacted the ship, I lost consciousness.

I woke facedown on the deck, my nose and mouth bleeding. Painfully, I rose and looked over at Reever and Shon. Both of them lay unmoving on the deck.

"Duncan." I crawled over to him and shook him, but he didn't respond. "Duncan, wake up." He didn't move, and when I checked his pulse, I found it dangerously slow. Shon was also barely alive.

I dragged myself over to the com panel and signaled medical.

A dazed nurse replied. "Healer, you are needed here. We have many wounded."

"There are two more on the observation deck," I said, wiping the blood from my mouth on my sleeve. "Send some help down here."

Twenty

I sent the nurses to attend to the rest of the wounded, and stationed myself between Reever's and Shon's berths. For hours I watched their vitals, administered synaptic stimulants at regular intervals, and performed every scan I could think of, but nothing changed. Both men remained locked in a deep, unchanging comatose state, their life signs barely registering.

I even tried to reach Duncan through my mind, holding his hands and opening my thoughts as I always did when he forged a link with me. Whatever kept him comatose also prevented any telepathic connection; I felt as if I were slamming into an endless, immovable blank wall.

Was his mind gone? Was there nothing left to wake up?

Refusing to admit defeat, I began skimming through records of coma cases, looking for any treatment that might prove effective. What little I could glean from the database only made me feel sick. Few deep coma patients ever regained consciousness; most remained in the paralyzed, vegetative state until their organs shut down or life support was removed.

The hours dragged, and time lost meaning. I accepted a server of tea from one of the nurses and held it until it turned cold between my hands. I watched my husband's still face, silently praying to see a single muscle twitch or an eyelash move. He lay motionless but for his chest rising and falling in rhythm with the oxygen being forced into his lungs by the ventilator.

"Jarn."

I looked up to see Xonea looming over me. "There has been no change yet." Was that growl my voice? I cleared my throat. "Forgive me. It's been a long night."

"You have been here for three nights and days." Gently he removed the datapad from my hands. "I will send in a nurse to monitor Duncan and Shon. You must go and sleep now."

"I'm not tired." I stood and adjusted the drip on Duncan's IV. "How long until we reach Joren?"

"Unless engineering can repair the damage to the transitional generators, it will be several weeks." Strong hands turned me around. "I spoke to the nurses. There is nothing more you can do for them."

"They're wrong. That is why they are nurses and I am the doctor." I pushed him out of my way and went around to the other side of Duncan's berth. "As soon as their vital signs improve, I'll be able to administer stronger stimulants. That will rouse them and allow them to breathe on their own, so I can take them off the ventilators. I can't do that if I'm sleeping, now, can I?"

"I can have security remove you," Xonea said.

I picked up a suture laser and enabled it. "Then my

nurses will have more work to do, because I am not leaving."

"Yes, I can see that." Xonea rubbed his eyes and sighed. "Very well. Signal me if there is a change."

Xonea left. There were no changes. I tested each of the monitors to ensure that they were functioning, and then returned to my case studies. I finished reading all the records on humanoid coma cases and went on to read the reports on nonhumanoids. I read so much that my eyes began to itch and then burn.

I switched off the terminal and rested my head against my hand. I needed some saline wash to refresh my eyes, and perhaps something to eat, if I could force my tight throat to swallow. I would get up in a minute and take care of it, I thought. I could rest my eyes for a moment.

"Jarn."

I opened my eyes to see my husband watching me. "Duncan? You're awake." I stumbled to my feet and looked at his monitors, but they were all dark.

"I'm here." He rose from the berth, pulling the infusers and IV port from his arms as he stood and held out his hand. "Come with me."

"I can't leave Shon." I turned and nearly bumped into a dark-furred chest. "Oh, my God. You're awake, too."

The oKiaf steadied me. "No, Jarn. Not yet."

I saw Shon's still body on the berth behind him and turned to Duncan, who stood next to his own. "There can't be two of you. I must be dreaming."

"No." Duncan took my hand and interlaced our fingers as the medical bay vanished, leaving us to stand in an open field surrounded by white mist. "You're awake."

The tall grass around us appeared to be frozen, until

I saw that the delicate blades were covered with frost. "Has the weather changed on Joren?"

"Everything changes." The fur of Shon's paw brushed the back of my hand as he looked at Reever. "Do you understand what has to be done?"

My husband nodded and turned his head. "Better than he did."

My joy faded as I saw another man standing off in the distance. "Why is he here?"

Joseph Grey Veil lifted his hand and then disappeared into the wall of mist surrounding the field.

"He was the first," Duncan said, as if that explained everything. "You don't have to be afraid of him, beloved. Or of me, or Shon."

"I'm not afraid." I was perplexed, however. I knew I was supposed to be somewhere else, doing something else, but all that seemed important was being here. Then I felt something slip from my hair, and reached out my hand. A small purple flower landed on my palm and turned to crystal. "What does it mean?"

"Everything. Nothing." Shon took my hand. "We have a little time left."

Duncan nodded and twined his fingers through mine. "Time enough for a walk."

I felt like laughing and crying, but I was too relieved to be with them to do anything more than walk. The frost-covered grasses parted before us, offering a wide path of amber soil etched with scrolls of salt.

"When the universe was young, so were its people," Shon said. "They thought like children, and so they behaved. The greatest darkness, born in the most innocent of hearts."

I saw the mist wall darkening around the edges of the field, and felt the air grow cold. "We fight the darkness. We have to."

"But we are wrong," Duncan said.

I stopped and pulled my hands free to wrap my arms around my waist. "I'm cold."

"You were born on the ice," Shon reminded me. "Do you remember why?"

"No." Suddenly, deeply afraid, I turned to Reever. "I can't remember. I don't want to. Please don't make me."

"I am with you, *Waenara*." He looked over my head at Shon. "Is there no other way? I love her."

"As do I," the oKiaf said. "But there is only one path." Shon gestured toward the blackened mist. "It is time to take it."

The men walked away from me and I tried to follow, but the icy grass wrapped around my legs, holding me in place. "Duncan. Shon. Don't leave me. Please, I want to go with you."

My husband looked back and almost turned around, but Shon put his arm on his shoulders and urged him along.

"Shon, please, no. I can't lose you both." I screamed that, and Duncan's name, until the cold grass wrapped around my throat and choked off my voice.

You must heal her. Heal her.

I grabbed my head, pressing my hands against my ears to block out the sound of a million voices, all speaking in unison. I pitched over into the grass, shattering the stiff blades.

You must heal her. Heal her. Heal her.

Healer, please wake up.

Healer, please.

Healer.

I tore myself out of the dream and into consciousness. I was back in the medical bay, sitting in the isolation room. I had fallen asleep at the console.

A hum buzzed against my ears, and I turned my head to look at Reever's berth, afraid of what I would see.

A mound of Lok-Teel covered my husband's body; the largest had completely engulfed his head. Each one bulged and flexed as if they were eating him.

The Lok-Teel lived by consuming waste. If Duncan had died while I was asleep—

I wrenched myself upright and lunged at the berth, grabbing and pulling away the mold as I shouted for the nurses.

Jorenians filled the isolation room, and many hands helped me strip the Lok-Teel clinging to my husband's body. Behind me I heard a similar commotion, and I looked back to see three nurses working on Shon, who, like Duncan, was covered with the mold.

"Get them off quickly." I struggled to free the one wrapped around Reever's head, peeling it off his mouth and nose. As soon as I pulled it out of his hair, I flung it across the room and checked the ventilator junction, which had come apart from the tube in Reever's throat. I heard breathing sounds, however, and quickly removed the tube.

"He's breathing on his own." All the monitor leads had been disconnected from his body, so I groped for a scanner and passed it over his chest. His vital signs were strong and stable. Why wasn't he awake?

"Duncan." I put a hand on his cheek and stroked it. "Duncan, can you hear me? Open your eyes."

He did not respond to my voice, and I performed a cerebral scan. My readings made no sense; his brain wave activity had increased three hundred percent. Even using every synaptic connection in his head, Reever couldn't register at these levels.

I tossed aside the scanner and called for another as I checked his pupils, which dilated normally.

I had never seen such levels of brain activity in any being. The only way I could think to disrupt it was to sedate him or subject him to a bioelectric pulse. Both might send him back into a coma.

"Healer Jarn," a nurse working on Shon called. "The oKiaf is conscious."

"Watch his monitors," I told the nurse beside me, and went to the other berth, forcing a smile as I met Shon's dark gaze. "That was some nap you took."

"I feel very rested," he said, and sat up as if nothing were wrong with him. He raised his hands and turned them over. "The crystal is gone."

The scan I performed told me the same thing—not a trace of crystal remained in his blood, tissues, or bone. I glanced down to see the Lok-Teel that had been removed from his body creeping out of the room. They seemed much larger now, and moved sluggishly—as if they had eaten an enormous meal.

Somehow they had done the impossible and removed the crystal that had been killing Shon. But what had they done to Reever?

"You don't have to worry about that funerary ritual anymore," I told the oKiaf, and issued orders to run a comprehensive series of scans on him. Then I turned back to my husband. "Any change?"

"No, Healer." The nurse handed me a new scanner with a fresh set of readings. His brain wave activity remained at unimaginable levels. "Shon, if you feel well enough to get out of that berth—"

He was already standing next to me, and placed one of his paws on Reever's forehead as he closed his eyes. All of the fur on his arm stood up as a faint glow spread out over my husband's face.

I bit my lip as I watched, but after only a few moments the glow faded and Shon took away his paw.

"He is not injured or ill," the oKiaf told me. "I don't know what is causing the synaptic overload, but I can do nothing to stop it." He swayed a little.

"Get back into your berth and stay there."

Desperately, I tried again to forge a link between us, but this time instead of the blank wall, a stream of raw power shoved me back into my own head so hard I nearly blacked out.

When my head cleared, I called for a gurney. "We're moving him to the neurosurgical suite."

We shifted Duncan's body onto the gurney and I pushed it out of the isolation room. If I didn't bring his brain wave activity down to normal levels, and soon, his synapses would overload, become damaged, or even burn out.

As we moved Duncan from the gurney to the treatment table, I mentally ran through the Terran conditions I knew that caused neurotransmitter disorders. One by one I discarded their treatment options, all of which would either have no effect or were too dangerous to try on a comatose patient. I needed a noninvasive method of regulating brain waves that would not cause his higher or lower functions to be impeded or shut down.

Excessive, rapid discharge of the nerve cells . . .

Epilepsy. "Bring the beta-wave generator over here."

The nurse gave me a bewildered look. "But, Healer, your bondmate is not suffering from insomnia."

I felt like ripping her head off, but forced myself to calm down. "Duncan's neurons are in a state of hyperactivity so elevated that he is virtually locked in one long epileptic seizure. We've got to break him out of it, and we might be able to do that by inducing artificial betas."

The nurse frowned. "A presynaptic regulator implant or control medications are the standard treatment for epilepsy."

"If he hadn't spent the last four days in a coma, I'd agree with you. And I'll be happy to debate this treatment later, when my husband isn't dying." I touched her arm. "For now, please, do as I ask."

The nurse wheeled the portable unit over to the treatment table. Together we eased the halo over Reever's skull, attached the wave emitters, and wrapped a cervical collar around his neck. To keep his brain wave activity under close watch, I also attached an EEG lead over his frontal lobe and put the readings on a display monitor above the table. The nurse calibrated the generator's controls while I placed a mouth protector over my husband's lower jaw, which would keep him from choking on or biting through his tongue. When I looked up, I saw Xonea, Shon, and the rest of the medical staff standing outside the viewer and looking in.

"Why is it that every time I tell that oKiaf to stay in his berth, he ignores me?" I asked my husband. "Have you been coaching him on how best to aggravate me?"

"The generator is ready, Healer." The nurse sounded as afraid as she looked.

I bent down and kissed Reever's brow before I stepped back from the table. "Begin with ten cycles. Initiate."

The beta-wave generator made no sound as it sent the first pulses of artificial brain waves through the emitter leads and into my husband's brain. I watched his vitals and for fluctuations in the dense lines of his synaptic activity displayed on the EEG monitor overhead, but saw no change.

"Increase to twenty cycles," I told the nurse.

At some point during the procedure, Shon came into the suite and took up position on the opposite side of the table, watching the readings with me.

"Has there been any indication of atrophy or embolism?" he asked.

I shook my head. "No damage yet. No cause for the hyperactivity, either." I told the nurse to increase the feed again and scanned for any cell loss. "Whatever is doing this isn't destroying his brain tissue. It's just taken it over. . . ." I looked at the oKiaf. "Could it be the Jxin? Are they doing this to him?"

"If they are, we cannot stop them." Shon took my scanner and passed it over Reever's body, pausing at midtorso. "There is something embedded in his sternum, just beneath the skin." He looked up at me. "It is vibrating."

I swore under my breath.

"Shut down the generator," I told the nurse, and grabbed an instrument tray. I didn't waste time with pre-surgical procedures but yanked aside the linens, baring Reever's chest. "I need a specimen container. Shon."

He nodded. "Go ahead."

I used a hand lascalpel to make a shallow incision, and then inserted a probe in the wound, searching until I felt a small, hard mass. The instrument shook in my hand as I seized and tried to extract the shard. It seemed wedged into the bone, and I swore under my breath as I worked to free it. An instant later it came free, and I pulled it out of his chest.

The nurse held the open container under the probe, and I dropped it and the crystal inside. I turned back to watch Shon heal the incision, and then looked up at the EEG monitor.

The number of lines displayed slowly began to diminish, one by one, until Reever's brain wave activity had been reduced to that of a normal sleep pattern.

"Keep him on monitor and prepare to run a chest series." My shoulders slumped as my adrenaline ran out and I felt the weight of exhaustion grinding into my bones. "If his vitals remain stable, we'll move him over to the critical-care room, and then . . . and . . ." I frowned, trying to concentrate. "Do whatever else needs to be done."

"Jarn." Shon brought a linen to me and wiped my husband's blood from my hands. "Let me see to him."

I looked up at him. "You were dying thirty minutes ago. Besides, I have a few hundred tests I have to run on you, too." If I could just remember what they were.

"I think they can wait. Come." He guided me out of

the suite. "There are two berths in critical care. I think Duncan would like yours to be the first face he sees when he wakes."

So would I.

I waited until they brought Duncan to the critical-care room before I occupied the adjoining berth. The moment I did, exhaustion became my dictator and I bowed to its will. I closed my eyes, wondering if I might have another of the crystal dreams, but nothing came but blessed, mindless darkness. Later, one of the nurses told me that I had slept so deeply that I didn't move once in eighteen hours.

I woke, as Shon had promised, still looking at my husband's face. I reached across the narrow space between our berths and touched his hand, my fingers pressing against the pulse point in his wrist.

Slowly, Duncan turned his hand and covered mine. "How long have I been unconscious?"

I glanced at my wristcom. "Almost five days." I sat up, wincing as my unused muscles protested, and made my way over to him. "Do you remember anything?"

"Swap embracing the stars. Pain. Walking with you and Shon through a field of crystal." He frowned. "It must have been a dream. Your father was there."

"You had a piece of crystal lodged in your chest." I touched the place where I had cut it out of him. "When Swap died, you and Shon collapsed and went into deep comas. He did that to you, didn't he? Through the crystal."

Reever sat up and slowly shook his head. "He wasn't trying to hurt us. He was a powerful telepath, on an order I can't even begin to describe. He projected his last thoughts to the crystal, hoping it would relay them to one of us."

"His last thoughts plus the crystal could have killed you." I didn't want to know what they were. "Shon only remembers the suicide, and nothing after that."

"It wasn't Swap's fault," Reever insisted. "We are very primitive compared to him."

"Swap was a larval life-form," I said. "There is very little more primitive than that."

"Rogur live for eons. Swap came to consciousness before the Jxin formed their first tribal settlement. Suppressing his development allowed him to retain his sense of reason and awareness of other life-forms as intelligent entities. Although I could only receive his thoughts, I sensed the knowledge he possessed. He sought to understand everything he encountered, and in the end I think he did." My husband's voice fell to a near whisper. "Jarn, compared to us, Swap was like a god."

Reever might find that wondrous, but I had seen what communicating with Swap had done to his mind. My husband had come very close to having his brain fried by the telepathic powers of the worm-god. "Why would he bother trying to send a message to us, then?"

"He told me that we were wrong about the black crystal," Reever said. "It is not a disease or an enemy. It is beyond that, a part of the fabric of all things that have been or will be. The Odnallak did not create it; they only gave it form. And no matter what we do, it cannot be destroyed."

"I don't understand. Maggie said it was sleeping now, but when it wakes up, it will destroy every living being in the universe."

"Swap knew this. He, too, said it would happen—
unless we can stop it before it awakens."

I threw my hands up. "How are we to stop something
that we can't destroy?"

"I think that part of the message he meant for you."
Reever took my hands in his. "He said you could stop it.
By healing it."

I drew back. "Healing a mineral. Dævena Yepa, Duncan, how am I to do that? Rub it down with silica? Feed
it iron supplements? It's not alive. It doesn't feel pain.
It's barely organic."

"I can't tell you. Even with all his knowledge, Swap
didn't know how it could be done, or I think he would
have done it. That is why he sent the message to me and
Shon; why he risked killing us to do so. He hoped that
one of us would live and remember enough to tell you."

"Tell me what? Riddles with no answers? If he did
not know how to heal the crystal, then how could he expect that of us? We are only . . ." I trailed off and closed
my eyes as I realized the answer to my own question.

"We are immortal," Reever finished. "As he was."

"So if we do not die, we will have the time to acquire
knowledge as he did. Then all we must do is formulate a
cure. For sick rocks." Bitterness soured my voice. "For the
sake of the universe, we must stay forever young and watch
our friends, our allies, our daughter grow old and die."

Xonea came into the room. "It is good to see you
awake, Duncan." He turned to me. "Jarn, there is something wrong with the Lok-Teel. They have gathered in
one spot and have attached themselves to the deck."

"They're probably sleeping," I said. "They prefer to
be stationary when they rest."

"They're in the survey lab, and they're not sleeping," my ClanBrother told me. "They appear to be melting."

Reever felt well enough to accompany me down the corridor to the survey lab, which remained sealed off from the rest of the ship.

"How did they get past the buffer seals?" Reever asked Xonea.

"An alarm went off a few minutes ago, indicating that the buffer had been breached, then reset itself. I came down to investigate." Xonea gestured toward the welded door panels to the lab. "That is what I found."

The door panels appeared as if they had been peeled away to form an uneven opening. In the center of the buffer field, a ring of Lok-Teel hung, tightly constricted. Beyond them lay a pile of more mold on the icy deck of the survey lab. Although the airless chamber was open to space, and should have frozen them solid, they seemed to be turning to liquid—melting, exactly as Xonea had described.

"Have you scanned the lab?" I asked, studying the bizarre scene.

"I attempted to," Xonea said. "Whatever is happening in there, it does not register at all on our equipment. My scanner does not even detect the mass of mold."

"They absorbed all of the crystal infecting Shon's body. It must be the reason they're melting instead of freezing." I turned and saw Reever's expression. "What is it?"

He grabbed my wrist and linked with me. *Go back to medical and wait for me there.*

I'm not leaving you. I squinted as a bright light

erupted from the interior of the wrecked lab, and put up my hand to block it.

The Lok-Teel had disintegrated into a pool of clear liquid, which began to shrink in on itself as a column of light rose from the pool's center. The light intensified, turning all the alloy around it red with heat. Distantly, I heard alarms ringing and the pounding of running footsteps, but I could not move my eyes away from the light.

The column of light turned to semiliquid crystal, which flowed into the form of a humanoid being. As it solidified, the light dimmed, but the crystal remained transparent. The pool vanished under the feet of the crystal being.

It had no features or gender, only four limbs, a torso, and a head. When it moved toward the buffer, I was able to turn my head. Reever looked frozen. Xonea fell to his knees beside me and began murmuring a prayer to the Mother of All Houses.

I moved closer to the buffer, until there were only a few inches between me and the crystal being. I saw the protocrystal form a mouth on the front of the head, which smiled at me before it opened to speak. I heard its voice inside my head.

Were you able to defeat the mercenaries? it asked.

"Yes," I said out loud. "Their ship was destroyed by the larval rogur."

The head nodded. *You and your comrades have done well, child.*

It felt so familiar to me that I almost tried to reach through the buffer to touch it. "Who are you?"

The regular and periodic arrangement of atoms within a structure is a characteristic not only of crystals but of nearly all solid matter. It spoke in Reever's voice, repeating his words to me. *In that sense, every inorganic thing you can touch is crystalline in nature.*

"I don't understand." Frustration welled up inside me. "Are you alive? Are you the crystal?"

It didn't answer me. *Add something that is not—heat, radiation, a soul—and the structure is transformed or destroyed . . . or becomes something that cannot be named.*

It was trying to tell me something important. "You mean that you have no name?"

Before the light was brought from the darkness, they had no name. Before the heavens were lifted above the earth, they had no name. Before the beginning was taken from the end, they had no name. Divided, they chase each other, always apart but forever longing for what was. Needing to be whole. To be healed.

"Are you Maggie?"

Light rayed out from its face, bathing me in a cool blue glow. *You know what you must do, Daughter.*

I cried out as the light filled my eyes, my mind, and my soul. I felt Reever's hands pulling me away from the buffer as the crystal being dissolved into pure light. Only when it vanished did I understand what it had said, and what the crystal dreams had meant.

The time for the sacrifice had arrived.

I left the *Sunlace*, and found myself walking along a shore of amber sand. The waves lapped at my bare feet and drew back, leaving small, perfect *t'vessna* blooms on the shore.

Mama.

Marel came running to me, and I knelt and caught

her in my arms. *My baby.* I held her tightly, burying my face in her hair.

Mama, don't leave me. Take me with you.

I drew back and looked into her tear-filled eyes. *Do you know how much I love you?*

She nodded, sobbing.

Remember that, and I will always be with you.

I picked her up into my arms and carried her across the dunes, where Duncan stood waiting for us.

No. He was shaking his head. *I waited. I believed. Not this. Not this.*

I handed our daughter to him and kissed him. *Xonea was right,* Osepeke. *Nothing that is lost is gone forever. It is my turn to wait now.*

He tried to hold me, but I eased away and turned to face the sea. Light from a figure walking out of the water beckoned to me.

I glanced back at the ones I loved, and then I slowly made my way down the sands.

She was beautiful and kind, and held my hand in hers. *You are ready.*

That she had given me this time with Duncan and Marel made me strong enough to answer her. *Yes.*

Then come, child.

Together we walked into the warm dark sea, and the last thing I heard before the waters closed over my head was Duncan Reever calling my name.

Someone carried me into medical and put me on a berth. I felt the hands of nurses and the cold touch of instruments. I must have sustained a head injury, because it certainly felt as if someone had bludgeoned me repeatedly with a blunt object.

"Her vitals are low but stable," a woman's voice said. "No evident injuries."

"She was exposed to some form of radiation." That voice belonged to Reever. "It had no effect on me or the captain."

I didn't remember any radiation, only pain and cold, and then a terrible explosion of light. I lifted my hand to my face and groaned. "Ouch." I tried to open my eyes and squinted. "Could you turn off that light please?"

"She is conscious and speaking, Linguist Reever," the nurse bending over me said.

I blinked a few times before my eyes focused on Duncan's face. "My head hurts, that's all." I didn't like not knowing why, though. "What happened? Did we transition?"

A furry paw passed a scanner over my head. "No indications of radiation poisoning."

I didn't know the male standing over me, so I pushed the instrument away and propped myself up on my elbows. I was in the medical bay on the *Sunlace*—not where I remembered being. "What am I doing here?"

"You lost consciousness after the crystalline being vanished," Reever said. He brushed some hair back from my eyes. "I think she's all right."

I had no idea what he was talking about, but attributed that to trauma-induced amnesia. "Can I get off this berth? I'm sure someone else can put it to better use."

Reever helped me down and pulled me into his arms, hugging me so tightly I squeaked when I tried to breathe. "Forgive me," he said, setting me at arm's length. "I thought I had lost you."

"I'm right here." I didn't like the way everyone was staring at me. "Are there any wounded?"

"No. None." He kissed me.

I enjoyed the embrace, although I felt a little uncomfortable kissing my husband in front of the entire medical staff. Normally, Reever wasn't this demonstrative; I must have scared him pretty badly this time.

"Hey." I drew back and grinned. "I'm not going anywhere. Tell me about this crystalline being. How did it get on the ship?"

"The Lok-Teel liquefied themselves into a pool of protocrystal. The being formed itself out of their remains. I couldn't hear it, but I think it spoke to you." He cradled my face between his hands. "You don't remember any of it, do you?"

"No, but it seems like I'm a little blurry on a lot of things." I rubbed the sore spot just above my right temple. "You're sure I didn't hit my head on something? It feels like someone took a sledgehammer to it."

Reever's face turned to stone. "You know what a sledgehammer is?"

"A large hand tool used to smash holes in very hard things. Like my skull." I probed one temple and grimaced. "Whatever they did hit me with, it worked."

My husband grabbed my shoulders in an iron grip. "What is your name?"

"You've got to be kidding." I laughed, until I saw he wasn't. "Reever, I'm drawing a whole stack of blanks here, but I do remember my name, and yours, and . . ." I looked around me and didn't see a single familiar face. "Okay. Wait a minute."

Reever released me, and his hands fell to his sides.

The tall, furry resident who had been scanning me on the table put one paw on my shoulder. "Don't be afraid, Healer Jarn."

I didn't know who he was, but he was a little too touchy-feely for my liking. "Keep your paws to yourself, pal." So I turned to the one face I did know—my husband's. "Duncan, what the hell is going on? Who are these people? How did I get here?"

He didn't answer me. "Tell me your name."

"What, did *you* forget?" I laughed, but it made my head hurt. "Reever, it's me. Cherijo. Cherijo Torin Reever. Your wife."

He stared at me for a long time. "Jarn." He strode out of the room.

"Right." Utterly mystified now, I turned to the resident. "Who's Jarn?"

About the Author

S. L. Viehl lives in Florida with her family. A USAF veteran, she has medical experience from both military and civilian trauma centers.

The Stardoc Novels
by
S. L. Viehl

"Continously surprising and
deviously written."
—Anne McCaffrey

STARDOC

BEYOND VARALLAN

ENDURANCE

SHOCKBALL

ETERNITY ROW

REBEL ICE

PLAGUE OF MEMORY

OMEGA GAMES

Available wherever books are sold or at
penguin.com

GET TO KNOW THE DARKYN SIDE OF S. L. VIEHL

(writing as Lynn Viehl)

Discover the *New York Times* bestselling series about an underworld of vampires and the evil Brethren monks who stalk them.

If Angels Burn
Private Demon
Dark Need
Night Lost
Evermore
Twilight Fall

Available wherever books are sold or at
penguin.com

Classic Science Fiction & Fantasy
from
ROC

2001: A SPACE ODYSSEY by Arthur C. Clarke
Based on the screenplay written with Stanley Kubrick, this
novel represents a milestone in the genre.
"The greatest science fiction novel of all time." —*Time*

ROBOT VISIONS by Isaac Asimov
Here are 36 magnificent stories and essays about Asimov's
most beloved creations—Robots. This collection includes
some of his best known and best loved robot stories.

THE FOREST HOUSE by Marion Zimmer Bradley
The stunning prequel to *The Mists of Avalon*, this is
the story of Druidic priestesses who guard their ancient
rites from the encroaching might of Imperial Rome.

BORED OF THE RINGS by The Harvard Lampoon
This hilarious spoof lambastes all the favorite
characters from Tolkien's fantasy trilogy. An instant
cult classic, this is a must read for anyone who has ever
wished to wander the green hills of the shire—and after
almost sixty years in print, it has become a classic itself.

Available wherever books are sold or at
penguin.com

S527

THE ULTIMATE IN
SCIENCE FICTION AND FANTASY!

From magical tales of distant worlds to stories of
technological advances beyond the grasp of man, Penguin has
everything you need to stretch your imagination to its limits.

penguin.com

ACE
Get the latest information on favorites like
William Gibson, T.A. Barron, Brian Jacques,
Ursula K. Le Guin, Sharon Shinn, Charlaine Harris,
Patricia Briggs, and Marjorie M. Liu,
as well as updates on the best new authors.

ROC
Escape with Jim Butcher, Harry Turtledove, Anne Bishop,
S.M. Stirling, Simon R. Green, E.E. Knight, Kat Richardson,
Rachel Caine, and many others—plus news on the
latest and hottest in science fiction and fantasy.

DAW
Patrick Rothfuss, Mercedes Lackey, Kristen Britain,
Tanya Huff, Tad Williams, C.J. Cherryh, and many more—
DAW has something to satisfy the cravings of any
science fiction and fantasy lover.
Also visit dawbooks.com.

Get the best of science fiction and fantasy
at your fingertips!